Mary Medawar lives in Hampstead in London with her husband, where they enjoy long walks over the Heath. She is of Irish/Welsh descent and was born in North Wales and educated there and in the North of England. After leaving school an interest in the visually handicapped led her to teach and work with the blind. Her career changed when the new Royal Free Hospital in Hampstead opened and she became the first Coordinator of Voluntary Services. In the summer of 1985 she gave up her job to write. This is the result.

She is currently at work on her second novel.

MARY MEDAWAR

Under the Tricolor

This edition published 1993 by
Diamond Books
77-85 Fulham Palace Road
Hammersmith, London W6 8JB

Copyright © Mary Medawar 1989

Set in Sabon

Printed and bound in Great Britain by
BPCC Paperbacks Ltd
Member of BPCC Ltd

For Nick, with love

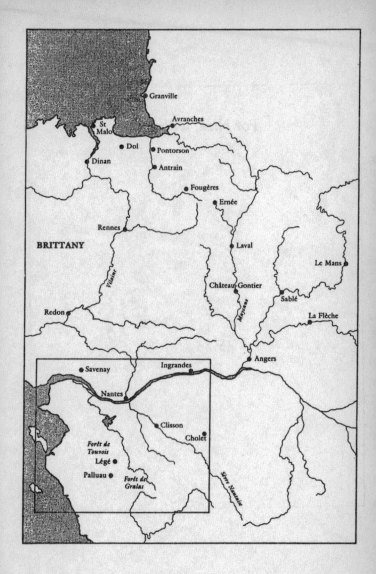

BRITTANY

Granville

Avranches

St Malo

Dol

Pontorson

Dinan

Antrain

Fougères

Ernée

Rennes

Laval

Le Mans

Vilaine

Château-Gontier

Sablé

Redon

Mayenne

La Flèche

Angers

Savenay

Ingrandes

Nantes

Clisson

Cholet

Forêt de Touvois

Légé

Palluau

Forêt de Gralas

Sèvre Nantaise

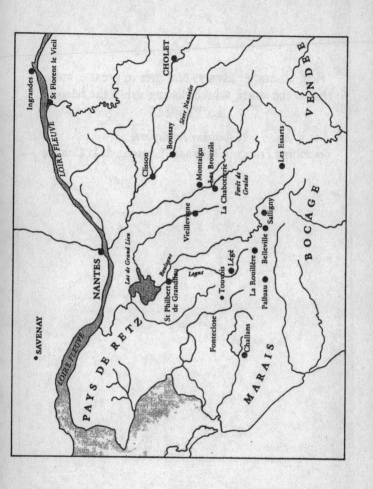

'Real character always emerges in great events: that is the spark which distinguishes the hero of La Vendée.'

Napoléon Bonaparte,
describing François-Athanase Charette de la Contrie

Acknowledgements

I thank for their help and encouragement:

Sue Gale
Douglas Druce
Bruce Allsopp
Lennie Lourie
Kathleen Jarred
Elspeth Sinclair
The Marais family, St-Cyr-sur-Loire
The Mayor of Cholet, La Vendée
Literary Agent, David Grossman
My Editor, Penelope Isaac, for her sensitive handling
of my manuscript

Friends who cheered me on from the start and my
brother Norman Collins and family, Nottingham.

Finally, I thank my stepson for his boundless enthusiasm and unsparing efforts to help me. Thank you
Tony!

PART I

Paris

1782

Chapter One

The whispered name exploded into a roar of triumph as the fireworks surged upwards to the night sky.

'Lafayette! Lafayette is back!'

'Come on, come on,' said the boy. 'Let's get there before everyone else.'

The small girl astride his shoulders tightened her grip, determined not to lose the position which gave her a clear view of the King and Queen; though it was not Louis and Marie-Antoinette who held her attention but a mock temple of Hymen from which the fireworks were being released. Impatiently Pierre Fleury thrust his sister's legs from his shoulders and she fell to the ground. Picking herself up the small girl lashed out at her brother, furious to have lost sight of the golden dolphins gambolling around the temple's base and columns. Just then, the final flight of rockets was released and Madeleine Fleury, her rage forgotten, threw back her head, waiting for another scene of magic to break against the night-blue sky.

'Oh, look!' she cried, clapping her hands with delight as a cascade of golden stars formed around a fleur-de-lys. 'It's a "D"!'

For a moment the golden letter burnt bright and fierce. Then it faded, and the sky was empty. The little girl turned laughing to her brother, but he had

13

gone. Pierre wasn't interested in babies, not even one who was a dauphin, but he was interested in fighting and soldiers, and one soldier above all the rest: the hero of the hour – the Marquis Gilbert Lafayette.

Now the restless Parisians, always avid for new diversion, were also turning their backs on the royal celebrations. Like Madeleine's brother, they were leaving the Hôtel-de-Ville for the Hôtel-Noailles. The succulent smell of meat roasting on a spit suddenly assailed the girl's nostrils, and she wrinkled her nose appreciatively. Just because the famous general had returned from the Americas, there was no need to miss out on the free food and drinks, she thought, running over to the buffet laid out under a gaily striped awning. Gulping down a bottle of lemonade and a pastry, Madeleine then stuffed four hot meat pasties into the pocket of her skirt. Pierre would be hungry later and then, when everything had gone, he would regret his haste. No doubt by now he had arrived at the rue Saint-Honoré: well, she was a fast runner, she would soon be there too. Tucking her skirt up into her waistband, the girl set off in pursuit, enjoying the novelty of the freshly sanded streets and the freedom of flying heedlessly across them, normally not a practice anyone wishing to reach old age would adopt. For every day, less nimble pedestrians than she were maimed or killed, mown down under the wheels of some noble's carriage.

But the young Louis XVI had decreed that the maxim during the thanksgiving for the dauphin should be, 'No deaths because of a birth.' Paris obeyed; chimneys were swept in order to prevent fires, the watermen on the river were alerted and ready to fish unfortunates out of the Seine. Doctors were stationed along the royal routes and there were even midwives: nothing had been left to chance.

Every care had been taken to ensure the safety of the vast hordes of spectators who had flocked into the city.

Madeleine had reached the rue Saint-Honoré, when angry shouts caught her attention. Ahead in the dense crowd people were jerking from side to side, as though they were being pushed. Suddenly she saw a man break through. He was quite young and his face was frantic with fear. Close behind in pursuit were three policemen and she could see they were gaining ground. One of them managed to grab a coat tail, but as the fugitive lurched forward, the thin material parted, and the policeman, with a cry of despair, fell forwards, still clutching the piece of cloth.

Madeleine's merry laughter rang out and was instantly echoed by those who, but a few moments before, had shouted out in anger. Laughing faces and eager hands now pushed and encouraged the fugitive on his way. But Madeleine's laughter had attracted his attention. Panting, he staggered on towards her. She could see he was almost spent. His small dark eyes looked into hers with a desperate appeal. As he passed, he pressed into her hand an envelope. His whisper was barely audible. 'Please . . . destroy.' Then he stumbled past and was gone. Quickly she looked about, but no one was looking at her so, slipping the envelope down the front of her bodice, she ran on.

The news of the return of Washington's friend and France's hero had spread. Already there was a great throng of people outside the Hôtel-Noailles, shouting and laughing, '*Vive Lafayette! Vive Lafayette!*' Madeleine could not see Pierre but she knew he would be at the front, so she pushed and squeezed her way forward until at last she spotted him and fought her way to his side.

15

'Oh, I wish the Queen had a baby every year,' she said, offering Pierre his share of the meat pasties.

'Well she certainly works hard enough at it, even though it's not with the King,' sniggered Pierre, gravy juice running down his chin as he bit into the pie.

'What do you mean?' whispered his sister, nervously looking over her shoulder. For though young, she knew such remarks could land him back on the Place de Grève, not for pasties but a flogging.

'Never mind,' her brother replied mysteriously.

Madeleine bit her lip with annoyance. He always used those words just when he had started to tell her something exciting. Well, now *she* would not tell *him* about the letter.

Instead, she joined in the fun of shouting for Lafayette to show himself. As the hero appeared, Madeleine joined in the ecstatic cheering, though truth to tell she did not think him fine at all. His shock of red hair held no attraction and the small eyes on either side of a long narrow nose reminded her of a bird. But Pierre was almost weeping at the sight of his idol. She nudged her brother's arm.

'He has no jewels, Pierre,' she said disappointedly. The boy turned and stared at her, with an expression of disbelief and disdain.

'Well, I mean, the King's brothers were covered with jewels,' she said stubbornly, meeting the boy's withering stare.

'Jewels don't make a soldier,' he snapped sarcastically. 'Lafayette doesn't need them; he is covered in glory!'

Above, Lafayette had disappeared from the window, and the crowd hooted its disappointment.

'Don't worry, he'll be coming out soon,' said Pierre, with a lofty air of importance. 'Can you hear the heralds' trumpets? They're announcing the arrival of the Queen. She's going to stop right here

16

and acknowledge Lafayette.' Madeleine's eyes brightened with excitement at another opportunity of seeing the beautiful young Queen. 'Oh, Pierre, you are clever! You knew all the time the royal party would stop here.'

Her brother gave a casual shrug and his face turned pink with pleasure under her adoring gaze. He did not confess that he had only just heard the news himself from someone in the crowd.

As the first of the royal household guard came into sight, Lafayette reappeared in his uniform of an American major-general, with the white sash of the Bourbons tied across his chest.

He waited outside the door of the mansion until the golden coach bearing Marie-Antoinette was just a few yards away. Then with a light, quick step he bounded into the street, his hat in his hand; waiting to receive his Queen's recognition.

From her position, Madeleine could not see the Queen's face, but she could see the hand offered to Lafayette. She saw him bow low and raise it to his lips.

'Look,' shouted Pierre excitedly, 'she's honoured him before all Paris! It means she approves of his fight to bring the Americas freedom and independence. Maybe, now, for us . . .' But Madeleine wasn't listening. She was looking at Marie-Antoinette's hands; the elegant slim fingers, the white skin, unblemished, dazzling.

The girl looked down at her own little hands. They were red, the skin cracked and blistered from scrubbing clothes in lime and water. The thought of the laundry cast a shadow over her face and she thrust her hands deep into her pockets so that she should not think of it. And it was easy to forget, for following after the Queen's coach were those of the King's brothers, the second of which drew up right in front of Madeleine. She was able to see, sitting with the ladies who had attended the public banquet at the Hôtel-de-Ville, the Comte d'Artois. His coat, encrusted with diamonds, was made of pale blue satin and on his hand was a sapphire as large as a chestnut which sparkled as he saluted the people. Fascinated, Madeleine examined the beautiful occupants of the carriage. Her heart fluttered as one of the white-wigged equerries sprang down and opened the carriage door. Was the royal party going to dismount? If so, she would be close enough to touch them. But it was only one young lady who was helped out. Almost before her pretty satin slippers had touched the rue Saint-Honoré, Gilbert Lafayette had her clasped in his arms. Tenderly the young husband and wife embraced, oblivious of their cheering audience. Then, with tears of happiness streaming down his face, the young Marquis bore Adrienne Lafayette away. It was the most romantic scene Madeleine had ever seen, and she vowed she too would have a great love. With surprise, she noticed her brother's eyes were shining as he watched the great carved oak door of the Hôtel close on the young couple. He usually made fun of love, but now he had seen how beautiful romance could be, his expression was dreamy and far away as he turned to her and spoke. 'That's where I'm going, Madeleine. To America, where every man is free and every man is equal.'

Each thinking the other silly, brother and sister left the rue Saint-Honoré and its costly boutiques and smart restaurants and headed towards the Faubourg Saint-Antoine. The celebrations would go on well after the wine ran out; but for them the laundry required an early start. Despondency stole over Madeleine once again at the thought of the morrow: a day that would be filled with scalding steam and the equally scalding tongue of Jeanne. Jeanne, the gross, red-faced bully who was in charge, frequently lost her temper, lashing out with her fists or the nearest thing to hand. Once, in one of her drunken furies, Madeleine had seen her snatch up a ladle of boiling water and hurl its contents in the face of her victim. They all tried to stay out of her way — especially after lunch on her return from the wine shop across the street. The rest of the women, though rough, were kind to Madeleine. Especially kind was Simone, who helped her with her work and often brought her little gifts.

Passing now in the shadow of the grim, towering walls of the Bastille, Madeleine shuddered and walked closer to her brother. Sometimes after work she would play with other children, chasing in and out of the alleys and streets around the gloomy fortress. The boys told of the terrible torture chambers within. Though the screams of the prisoners were never heard because of the thickness of the walls, one boy swore that on quiet nights one could hear horrible moans and the clanking sounds of chains. They said no one could escape the Bastille, not even the richest and most powerful in the land. A *lettre de cachet* from the King was enough; you were taken in a closed carriage and never heard of again.

Suddenly she thought of the letter nestling in her blouse and shivered. Was it a *lettre de cachet*? Had the policeman caught the pale-faced young man? Was he now under torture revealing that she had his *lettre de cachet*?

Fearfully she glanced over her shoulder before following her brother under the archway which led into the laundry yard, but the street was empty, the only sign of life coming from the wine shop across the street. Relieved, she helped Pierre swing the large wooden gate across the entrance into the cobbled courtyard. The heavy bolts slid home. Now no one could enter until he opened the gate for the workers in the morning.

Feeling much safer, Madeleine followed her brother to the well in the middle of the large yard. He had drawn up a bucket of water and he offered her a drink. The water was cool and refreshing and she dipped the ladle a second time into the bucket, for the meat pie had been very salty.

Salt! Immediately the thought of salt brought tears to her eyes. Her body started to shake as the familiar unknown terror and blind panic enveloped her. She felt her brother's arm around her and heard his voice anxious and soothing. 'Come on, don't cry. Don't spoil your lovely day . . . think of the Queen . . . her pretty dress . . . all those jewels.'

Madeleine burrowed closer to her brother's body, like a small creature seeking shelter and security. All she could see in her mind's eye was a smiling weather-beaten face. 'It's Father, isn't it?' said the boy, his embrace tightening as his sister's sobs increased. 'Don't worry, Madeleine, I'll always look after you.' Suddenly he released her and, taking hold of her face between his strong brown hands, stared fiercely into her tear-filled eyes. His look was hard and filled with hatred; there was a harshness in his voice she had never heard before. 'One day they will pay for killing our father. We will have our revenge! Now, no more tears, little sister, it's sleep you need.'

Their room was no more than a rough-bricked cubby-hole next to the large laundry room, but in a city where hundreds slept rough in the alleys and under the bridges, Pierre and Madeleine counted themselves privileged to have the luxury of their own room.

Kicking off their sabots they lay down, quickly

covering themselves with an old tattered quilt. In winter, they never removed their outer clothing, for it was much too cold.

Pierre blew out the tallow candle and Madeleine lay back, looking up through the small sky-light. She loved to look at the patch of sky, especially when, like tonight, it was moonlit and starry.

She listened, waiting for her brother's breathing to slow and deepen. Soon he would be asleep and she would be able to open her secret letter. Very gently she pulled it out from its hiding place and in the darkness ran her tiny fingers over its surface. It was sealed with a large blob of wax. Unable to contain her excitement, Madeleine slid off the mattress, hardly daring to breathe lest she should disturb the sleeping boy. She picked up the candle and tinderbox and stole towards the screen in the corner which concealed the chamber pot. The parchment glowed yellow in the candle's light and the blob of wax was a bright orangey-red. Carefully she slid her nail under the seal, slowly easing it from the paper so that it should not break. Inside was another sheet of paper and another envelope bearing an identical seal. This she decided not to break.

Though Madeleine knew one or two of her letters, she could not read. She stared at the fascinating handwriting, and pursed her lips with annoyance. Apart from a large 'C' at the bottom of the parchment, the rest was a tantalising mystery.

Irritated, she vowed that the very next day she would begin to learn all her letters. As for now, she would have to share her secret with Pierre. Dashing across the room she dropped down on to the mattress and seized her brother by his shoulders, shaking him vigorously.

'Wake up, Pierre, I've something very exciting to show you.' Startled, Pierre sat up, his eyes blinking in the light from the candle Madeleine held near to his face. 'What is it, Madeleine?' he asked in bewilderment. 'What's happening?'

'Nothing; but I've something really mysterious to show you. Look!' Thrusting the creamy parchment and envelope into his hands, she sat back, watching his irritation turn to interest and excitement.

When he laid the letter down on the quilt his face was fearful – making her think of the dreaded *lettre de cachet*. 'Where did you get this?' he asked in a whisper, though no one was there to hear. 'Did you break the seal?'

'Yes, I wanted to see what was inside.'

'But where did you get it? Who gave it to you?'

She related the story of the terrified stranger on the rue Saint-Honoré. Pierre, who rarely listened to her, now concentrated on her every word, making her feel very important. He turned the letter over and tapped the seal.

'Now think very carefully. Did anyone see him give this to you?'

Madeleine shook her head. 'No one,' she said firmly and noticed the fear and anxiety slip from her brother's face. 'But tell me, Pierre,' she said impatiently. 'What does it say?'

'Well, it's not so easy,' he said, biting his nails, as he always did when concentrating. 'You see it's in English. But I know who the sender is. So should you. Here, while I decipher the letter, look at the seal. You see it often enough.'

Madeleine picked up the thick parchment envelope and stared at the shiny bright seal. Suddenly, she remembered. 'Why, it's the House of Orléans,' she cried, pleased and excited. 'The shields on the Palais-Royal gates are just the same. I've looked at them often.'

22

'That's right,' said Pierre, his brown eyes sparkling, 'and do you see this large "C" here at the bottom of the letter? It must stand for Chartres; the Duc de Chartres, Orléans's son.'

'And the letter?'

'It instructs someone, your stranger I suppose, to meet the stage from Calais tomorrow evening. The sealed envelope is to be handed to a Monsieur Forth.'

'Then we'll go instead,' cried Madeleine, hugging her knees to her chest in excitement.

'Don't be silly! Whoever heard of a prince of the royal blood sending a girl on a secret mission,' scoffed Pierre.

Madeleine flushed with anger, and with a lightning movement snatched up the sealed envelope and held it near to the candle flame. Brother and sister glared at each other.

'It's my letter,' she said stubbornly; and then in a more wheedling tone, 'besides, I can run very fast.'

Pierre looked at the determined little face and the letter held a fraction away from destruction. 'All right,' he said, 'you can come with me; but you're to stay out of sight all the time. And not a word to anyone, not even Simone.' He took the letter from her and after tucking it under the mattress, blew out the candle.

The next day started at 4.30 a.m. with the usual back-breaking monotony. While Pierre made up the fires under the great coppers, Madeleine filled them up with buckets of water from the well.

It was slow, heavy work and her naked feet, thrust into rough wooden sabots, went numb with cold, whilst her hands, continuously wet, were chapped so badly the icy air striking them made her cry; but she tried to hide her suffering from Pierre. He had done so well to find them a home and work.

He had brought her to Paris from Brittany. She

was so young at the time there was little she could remember about their arrival, or indeed the journey. Neither could she remember their Breton home. Only one image remained: a pile of green apples outside a cottage door and a man sitting beside them, tossing three into the air like a juggler, a man with a smiling face and curly brown hair. She knew it had been her father.

Now they were orphans. God had taken her English mother just a year after her birth, but it was the hated officers of the *gabelle* who had sent their father to his death.

They had lived near to the salt marshes. Though it was illegal, like many poor men Antoine Fleury had gone on to the marshes to collect salt. He had been caught. Suspected of being a member of a salt-smuggling ring, he was arrested and taken to Rennes to be brought before a magistrate. Whilst protesting his innocence of smuggling for profit, he readily confessed that he had taken salt sufficient for his family's needs.

The magistrate, a member of the powerful Tremoïlles family, ordered that he be put to the question to test his evidence. Some days later, through a friend of his father whose brother worked in the prison, Pierre learned that Antoine Fleury had died. His heart had failed when his persecutors poured gallons of water into his body.

Pierre had fled in fear, taking his five-year-old sister with him. One day, hungry and wretched, they had wandered into the laundry.

Luck had been with them, for the owner, a kindly man, had been present. Monsieur Mergault was filled with pity at the sight of the desperate young boy, acting as father to the ragged little creature at his side. Straightaway, he took him on as an errand boy and as help to the elderly caretaker, Jacques.

Within their first year at the laundry, Jacques fell ill. Throughout his absence, Pierre proved his ability and, when the old man died, the bad-tempered Jeanne, who was in charge of the laundry, grudgingly admitted to Monsieur Mergault that Pierre 'would do as well as anyone'.

So they had moved their meagre possessions from a corner in the laundry to the little room that had been Jacques's. Very soon Madeleine too was given small jobs to do and the few sous they were paid each week were enough to buy food. Though life was hard, they ate and had a roof over their heads and counted themselves fortunate.

It was almost quarter to six and Madeleine, as was her custom, took a little of the boiling water from one of the coppers. She made their coffee and then she and Pierre sat and ate a hunk of bread.

'Now remember,' said her brother, 'not a word to anyone about the letter.'

Madeleine nodded obediently and rinsed out their mugs. She heard the clatter of wood on cobbles and opened the door to see who was the first arrival. Her heart lifted when she saw the plump figure of Simone Evrard. She was a plain girl, but very gentle and of a thoughtful disposition. Madeleine waved and shouted, 'Good morning, Simone; you're the first. Come in. You'll soon be warm.'

It was true, she thought, as she helped her friend out of her coat. The laundry might be unbearable in the summer but at least during the winter it was warm.

'Did you see the Queen yesterday?'

'Oh yes,' replied Simone, her gentle eyes glowing with pleasure. 'My sister, Catherine, and I waited at Notre-Dame to see her go in for her churching.' She paused and took a grubby paper bag out of her coat pocket and handed it to Madeleine. 'I thought you might like to have this. Catherine and I made it for you last night. It's supposed to be the Queen's dress,' she said awkwardly, as Madeleine drew out a tiny white dress. The small girl squealed with delight.

'Oh Simone, why it's lovely. I'll put it on straightaway.'

She ran through the laundry to the room which served Pierre and her as bedroom and picked up the little rag doll which Simone had made for her.

The doll's dress had been cut from a piece of sheeting which Simone had probably picked up on the ironing-room floor; and though she knew the Queen's dress was of white satin and covered with pearls and diamonds, Madeleine didn't care in the least.

'See,' she said, twirling the doll, as she approached Simone, 'it fits perfectly. Now she looks like a queen; so I shall call her Marie-Antoinette.'

During the next few minutes the rest of the women arrived, except for the bullying Jeanne.

'I expect it was the free wine yesterday. She's probably still snoring her head off,' said one of the women.

'I'm surprised she touched it,' laughed another. 'Why, she's always calling Marie-Antoinette names and accusing her of ruining the Lyon silk weavers with her passion for muslin and lawn.'

The laughter and clatter continued for a while as the workers discussed the previous day's festivities. Then, in a happy relaxed atmosphere, the women settled down to the steady rhythm of work. By late afternoon Pierre had set out with the delivery cart. When he returned they had cleared away every piece of work for that day.

It had been raining for some hours when Madeleine and Pierre set forth to the coaching station. The dark alleys, deep in mud and slime, had become fast-flowing, slippery streams of filth, making it necessary to hold on to the dripping brickwork.

Strangers navigating these murky corridors of the Faubourg Saint-Antoine were soon lost in a network of cul-de-sacs, menaced by crumbling brickwork and huge potholes and the unseen presence of those intent on taking their wallets and even their lives. But they held no fear for Madeleine; they were her playground, and if her heart now raced it was not through fear, but excitement.

Would the Englishman waiting at the posting station realise that Pierre was not the Duc de Chartres's messenger; and if so, would he then drag Pierre away to the Duc de Chartres for punishment? For the first time the small girl sensed danger. Even she had heard whispered stories of meetings with Satan, on the plains north of Paris, or wild orgies with naked girls. To the Duc de Chartres and his father, Louis-Philippe d'Orléans, Master of the Masons, the destruction of a young boy would be nothing. Suddenly fearful, she hurried forward, intent on delaying her brother; but he was well ahead, deliberately distancing himself from her. As she came out on to the Place des Victoires she saw he had already reached the turning into the posting-house yard. He stopped and looked over his shoulder in her direction and she knew it was meant as a warning to stay well out of sight. Madeleine crept along until she had nearly reached the entrance and then slid into a doorway.

A stage-coach had already arrived, for people were scurrying out of the yard with trunks and boxes to the line of cabs drawn up along the street. One by one the cabbies whipped up their horses and moved off, taking their wet passengers to inns or the warmth of family fires. Shouted instructions and greetings died away. All was quiet, save for the rush and gurgle of water. Her gaze went back to the entrance and she watched the rain bouncing off the shiny cobbles, but the street remained clear; no one else emerged. Impatient for Pierre to return, she was just about to leave her hiding place when a man carrying a small portmanteau hurried out. Though many Frenchmen walked about the smart boulevards in the English style of dress, from his walk and air of hesitation, Madeleine judged him to be a foreigner. Then as he approached the first of the remaining cabs, she heard him speak. He was an Englishman. The driver whipped up the horses, and as the carriage moved forward she noticed a carriage further down the street pull out as well and follow in the same direction.

Moments later Pierre appeared and she saw that he was carrying a large packet. Almost bursting with curiosity she ran to his side. 'What happened? Did he suspect?'

Pierre did not attempt to answer any of her questions, but merely took hold of her hand in a very firm grip, as though to silence her. He led her quickly away from the coach station in the direction of the Palais-Royal, glancing nervously every so often over his shoulder. Suddenly Madeleine heard his sharp intake of breath and felt his grip tighten on her hand. His stride became so fast that she could scarce keep up without breaking into a run. Unexpectedly he pulled her around a street corner.

'Quick, run,' he hissed. She followed his flying figure some ten yards down the street, ducking after him into one of the many alleys leading to gardens behind the row of houses. In the darkness she felt his hand press against her mouth. Bewildered she stood quite still, sensing his fear. Then she understood, as she heard in the silence the hurrying footsteps of a man. Whoever he was he had hesitated at the street corner. Brother and sister shrank back against the rough wall, their ears strained, as the man paused and turned into the street. Madeleine held her breath to try to silence the wild beating of her heart as he approached the entrance of the alley. Then, as though changing his mind, they heard him turn around and break into a run. Gradually, as the footsteps disappeared into the night and rain, Pierre released his hold on Madeleine.

'Phew, that was close,' he said, his voice sounding alarmingly loud in the silence. 'The Englishman warned me I might be followed, but I didn't spot anyone until a little while ago.'

'Who was he?' asked Madeleine.

'I don't know; probably a police agent.'

'I think the Englishman was followed too,' she said, remembering the carriage which had pulled out some moments after his.

'I expect they want to know where he's staying and who his friends are,' commented her brother, his manner, now the moment of danger had passed, confident and knowing.

'I think this is what they're after. He told me to guard it with my life.'

'What is it?' asked Madeleine, reaching out to touch the package.

'I don't know,' said Pierre, 'but I have to deliver it to the Palais-Royal tonight.'

Keeping a watchful eye out for police agents and pursuers, Madeleine hastened after her brother towards Richelieu's old palace; but apart from the occasional carriage, the streets were empty. Even the beggars were sheltering from the deluge.

'How will we get in?' she asked, as the huge ornamental gates of the Palais-Royal came into view.

'Just wait and see,' replied Pierre in the mysterious tone which so irritated her. He led her around to a side entrance of the palace where, inside the railings, was an empty sentry box. Handing the package to Madeleine, Pierre seized hold of the iron bars and rattled the gate vigorously, shouting at the top of his voice. A startled face appeared around the wooden edge of the sentry box.

'Hey, leave that gate alone,' the soldier shouted, making no move to come out into the wet to chase off the ragged urchins.

Pressing his face between the rails, Pierre called across to the man, 'Open the gate. I'm on a very important mission for the Duc de Chartres.'

The soldier, taking no notice, withdrew his head into the shelter of the box. Swearing furiously, Pierre grabbed hold of the gate once more and Madeleine, seized with excitement, screamed at the top of her shrill young voice: 'Let us in, let us in,' whilst Pierre continued to rattle the gates.

This time the soldier, his face red with anger, ran out at them brandishing a huge sword. 'Be off with you, before I lay this across your backsides,' he shouted. '*Egalité*,' hissed Pierre urgently. '*Egalité*.' The effect was magical. The soldier immediately stopped in his tracks. Astonished, he lowered his sword and replaced it in its scabbard. Without saying a word, he marched back into his box and reappeared with a large bunch of keys.

The huge gate swung back, grating along the gravel, and Pierre and Madeleine slipped inside.

Hesitatingly, Pierre turned back to the soldier who was bent over relocking the gate. 'Please, which way do I go?'

The rain cascaded like a small waterfall from the soldier's helmet on to his shoulders as he straightened up and looked at Pierre. His eyes glinted maliciously.

'I would have thought an important agent like you

would know,' he said sarcastically; but he raised his arm and pointed towards a black door set back under an archway. 'Through there.'

The door led directly on to a flight of stone steps, at the bottom of which was a short stone corridor leading to another door. Slowly, almost reluctantly, Pierre walked towards it. Madeleine noticed there was an iron bell pull to the right of the door, set in the wall under the spluttering torch. Before Pierre could stop her she ran towards it and pulled.

'I can't hear it ringing,' she said, pressing her ear against the door and giving another firm tug, 'but there seems to be a lot of hammering.' Pierre hung back, his face white and nervous, but it was too late to withdraw, for heavy bolts were being released and the door was opening.

'You're late, Maillard,' a deep voice growled. The voice belonged to a thick-set man wearing an apron covered with black stains. His sleepy, heavy-lidded eyes opened wide with astonishment at the sight of a little girl smiling up at him and a boy, filthy and ragged, hovering behind her.

'What on earth . . . ? Who let you two into here?' he demanded.

'Egalité,' said Pierre in a low voice, thrusting the package into the man's hands. Again, just as at the gate, the word was magical – the portly man's eyebrows shot up in surprise as he took the heavy package from Pierre.

'You'd better come inside,' he said, opening the door a little wider.

The scene which met their eyes was one of intense activity. The hammering which Madeleine had heard through the door was being made by men who were hitting small metal pieces set into metal frames.

'Why, it's a printing press,' Pierre exclaimed. The man nodded and indicated that they should sit down.

Then, with slow, plodding steps he walked to the middle of the room, where a man in a yellow coat was examining what appeared to be a drawing. Madeleine could see his coat was very grand and at his neck and wrists was an abundance of fine lace. As he listened to the burly man who had let them in, the nobleman raised his lorgnette; curiously, Madeleine returned the cold haughty stare, wondering whether this might be the Duc de Chartres.

Now the package which they had carried to the Palais-Royal was being opened.

'Look,' whispered Pierre, 'they're copper engravings. That one dressed up like a canary looks very pleased. Perhaps they'll give us a reward.'

Both men were indeed looking very pleased as they examined several of the metal sheets.

'Now, my young friends,' said the man in yellow as he walked over, 'tell me how you came by this package and how you obtained the password into the palace tonight?'

Stumbling, red with embarrassment before so fine a gentleman, Pierre related their story.

'Interesting ... Now, tell me the true story,' purred the man and, though he had not raised his voice a fraction, its smooth cultured tone was edged with menace. Surprised, Pierre looked up. 'I don't know what you mean.'

'Don't you?' snapped the man. 'Who sent you?' Like a whiplash, the side of his hand struck across Pierre's face, sending him reeling across the floor. 'And where is Stanislas Maillard?' With a cry of disbelief Madeleine watched the elegant silver-buckled shoe deliver a vicious kick that left her brother sobbing in agony. Something exploded within her and with a shrill scream of fury, she pulled out a small knife from her waistband and hurled herself in front of her brother.

'You monster,' she hissed, ready to plunge the blade into the yellow silk. 'If you touch my brother once more I'll kill you. I wish we'd thrown your beastly packet into the Seine!'

The pale eyes of the chevalier bored into those of the little girl; unflinchingly, she stared back, her body poised like a kitten's ready to spring, to draw blood.

Then suddenly he threw his head back and roared with laughter. 'My goodness, we have quite a wildcat here, Henri.'

Casually he turned to the bench beside him and picked up a long thin ruler. Still smiling, with a movement swift and accurate, he slashed the keen edge of the wood down on the little fingers. Dropping the knife Madeleine cried out with shock and pain.

'Now my dear,' he purred, 'I think you had better put that away. Knives are very dangerous things for small girls to carry. I would not want you to hurt yourself.'

He motioned to the bench. 'There's some wine on there. Give your brother a glass, it will revive him.'

Languidly the Vicomte de Cramoisy inspected the small girl as she wiped her eyes and stalked with dignity over to the wine. How filthy these urchins were, he thought. Did they never wash? He looked at the long tangles of greasy hair which fell to her waist and wondered what colour lay beneath the dirt. Yet she had beautiful eyes – a curious golden-brown, heavily-lashed and slanted like a cat's. He judged her to be about ten years old, maybe younger, but already there was a sensuality about the full curved lips which no amount of dirt could hide. Perhaps he should have the wild little creature dipped into a tub of water to see what lay beneath the grime; the thought amused him.

When Pierre had recovered sufficiently to answer

33

questions, the Vicomte, ignoring the boy's glowering looks, spoke to him once more. 'There is one point which puzzles me. How could you, an ignorant child of the streets, decipher a letter written in English?'

The question hung for a moment in the air and Pierre waited before answering, his brown eyes sparkling triumphantly. 'Because, sir,' he replied in English, 'my mother taught me to read and speak her language.'

Though Madeleine had not understood his reply, she clapped her hands together with a merry peal of laughter, knowing what his answer would be and enjoying the look of surprise on the nobleman's face.

'Then, my boy, you will be extremely valuable to us in our work. Would you like to become an apprentice here?' he asked, his eyes alive with interest as he looked at the boy.

'More than anything,' replied Pierre, his face shining with happiness. Then catching sight of his sister's anxious face, 'but my sister . . .'

'She can stay too; I'm sure you can find her some little jobs to do, Henri,' he said, turning to the man in the stained apron. 'And later . . . I'm sure we will find other things for her.'

They were not allowed to leave the Palais-Royal that night, despite their pleas. Instead a servant was sent to inform Monsieur Mergault that the Fleury brother and sister had been taken into the household of the Palais-Royal. Though no doubt Monsieur Mergault would be cross to lose them at such short notice, he was a kind-hearted man and would not, Madeleine decided, deny them their good fortune. For it really was good fortune that had crossed her path on the rue Saint-Honoré, leading them to the Palais-Royal.

As servants in a royal household, they need never be hungry again. For Pierre, the opportunity to work within a printing shop was like a miracle. Only sons of wealthy families could enter the seven years' apprenticeship and obtain the required membership into the brotherhood of Saint John.

But it did not take Pierre long to realise the Palais-Royal ran no ordinary printing shop. The Palais-Royal was at war and its adversary or victim was a woman.

Left alone to their own devices for a time, curiosity led Madeleine over to the package. 'Come and see, Pierre,' she called, laughing as she lifted up one of the copper sheets. 'It's a drawing of the Queen, though what she is doing I can't make out. Do come and see, it's very funny.'

Joining her, Pierre saw that the package did contain copper engravings and each one indeed depicted a likeness of the Queen. The work was skilful, the artist cruel. Pierre blushed scarlet as he looked at the lewd scene and shuddered at what would have happened to him and his sister had they been caught in possession of them. Hurriedly he replaced them in their wrappings but it was too late. The man in the yellow silk had re-entered the room. They had been seen.

'No doubt you now have a clearer insight into our work,' flashed the Vicomte to Pierre, who blushed crimson to the roots of his hair. 'Now you will understand why I cannot allow you to leave.' Pierre nodded and Madeleine, who did not quite understand, following her brother, nodded her head vigorously. The Vicomte de Cramoisy flicked a speck of dust from the embroidered cuff of his jacket. 'Our work here is to set France free; to rid her of the foreign tyrant. To give the common people their liberty. Will you help us?'

It was as though Pierre had been waiting all the

years of his young life for these words. 'Oh yes,' he cried, his voice filled with passion and fervour.

'Are you both prepared to give your lives for our cause?'

'Yes, yes,' brother and sister answered.

'Good,' smiled the Vicomte. 'But remember one thing; should either of you betray us, or speak to anyone of the work being done in the palace, you will both die . . . Do you understand?'

Silently, Madeleine and Pierre nodded as they gazed into the ice-cold eyes of their new master.

The next morning, when Madeleine awoke and opened her eyes, she was startled not to see the patch of sky which normally greeted her. With a start she sat up, realising she was not in the laundry but in a royal palace. With a nervous giggle she fell back against the pillow, wondering what Simone and the women would think when they heard the news. Were they already scrubbing and mangling, and had she naturally woken at 4.30 a.m.? It was hard to tell, for usually Pierre had to shake her awake.

Sleep had not come easily to her here; she had cried for a long time in this store-room, where a mattress had been thrown down for her. But her tears and terror of sleeping alone without Pierre were now forgotten, and filled with anticipation of an exciting day ahead, she sprang up from her new bed and ran down the corridor towards the men's dormitory and Pierre.

Peeping round the dormitory door, Madeleine saw that some of the apprentices were still asleep, while others in various states of undress were stretching and yawning. With rounded eyes she studied with great interest one, who in a completely naked state, stood singing.

'Hey! Be off with you!' he suddenly cried, breaking

off from his song as he spotted her. Hurriedly, Madeleine closed the door and laughed as she heard the sound of a boot or such hit against the wood.

'Missed!' she called out, and then scampered along in pursuit of the smell of newly baked bread.

Led to an open doorway, her attention was immediately caught by a wicker basket on the end of a long trestle table; here then was the source of tantalising pleasure invading her nostrils, setting mouth and stomach into a frenzy of desire.

'Hello,' she said, flashing her most winning smile at the three men sitting at the table.

'Well, hello to you, young lady. Have you joined the workforce?'

'Yes. My brother and I are going to help set the common people free,' said Madeleine proudly, remembering the words of the man in the yellow coat.

'Are you indeed! Then you'd best come and take some breakfast first, for you've a busy time ahead of you.'

Not at all put out by the men's laughter, she eagerly seized one of the rolls. It was golden brown, warm and delicious, as she bit into it. It was the kind of bread which she and her brother never had; theirs was usually the grey stale of yesterday which was cheaper. How delicious this was, and no one seemed to mind at all that she had taken a second one.

'Here you are, my dear,' said an elderly woman, setting down a bowl of coffee before her. 'Will you take some butter with it?'

Too overwhelmed to speak, the girl nodded as the grey-haired serving-woman slapped a pat of butter into the bowl. Madeleine stared transfixed as it dissolved, spreading a rich creamy film over the dark brown surface; they were indeed in a palace, and she vowed, as she sipped the delicious rich liquid, that she would try very hard to please their new masters.

After breakfast Madeleine went with Pierre and the other apprentices to the print shop. Expectantly, she waited beside her brother, eager to show how hard she could work.

Today, the man who had let them into the palace was not wearing an ink-stained apron, but a brown frock-coat of good material, and a white linen jabot. There was no sign of the Vicomte in the yellow coat, and it was this M. Henri, with the heavy-lidded eyes and growling voice, who was clearly in charge of everyone. He directed Pierre to work alongside the young man she had seen earlier without his clothes. He was called Philippe, and Madeleine was more than relieved not to be sent over to him. Now a little apprehensive, she waited for her orders, but after watching her brother and Philippe for a moment, the man beside her turned and walked away.

'But what am I to do, Monsieur?'

Henri Renolleau halted and looked back at the girl's eager face, its expression tinged with a slight anxiety. He shrugged, thrusting out his lower lip. Hadn't he enough to do keeping the apprentices in order, without playing nursemaid to a girl? Why couldn't she be put to work in the kitchens? But the Vicomte, with his usual lack of regard for others, had decided she should stay here to plague him. Silently he swore and looked around, wondering how to occupy the child. 'You'd best go over there and sit on that sack in the corner,' he said.

'But don't you want me to help?'

'You can help me, girl, by sitting there, keeping quiet, and staying out of èveryone's way!'

Disappointed, Madeleine did his bidding, and set-tled down on the sack which he had pointed to. It was very comfortable, and from the loosely-tied fastening, she could see it was filled with soft wool.

At first it seemed no hardship to sit quietly and watch everyone, for everything was new and exciting. Pierre, she saw, was being shown around, and the dark-haired Philippe was pointing out the various parts of the large black presses. Madeleine bit her lip with vexation, resenting her inactivity; why couldn't she too learn the names of things and how they worked? After all, but for her, they wouldn't be here. She thought of the runaway on the rue Saint-Honoré, and wondered again if he had managed to escape his pursuers. Wherever he was, no doubt he missed the Palais-Royal's breakfast. Remembering the fragrant rolls, and Monsieur Henri's orders, Madeleine immediately stopped her fidgeting, and directed her attention to the man nearest to her, who was operating a press. For some time she watched, absorbed, memorising everything he did, carefully noting how he clipped each printed sheet of paper on to a line which ran between his and the next operator's press, rather like a clothes line. Well there wasn't anything so difficult about that, she thought. It was something she did every day, often with icy fingers, out in the open. Awaiting her chance, Madeleine watched the man repeat the whole process then, just as he was removing his sheet of paper from the press and was turning to walk over to the line, she sprang up.

'I'll do it for you!' she cried, seizing the broadside from the astonished man's hands. Swiftly she turned and, scrambling on to a stool, clipped the paper on to the line, just like a towel, just like the man had done. She spun around triumphantly, hoping that Monsieur Henri had seen how useful she could be. Simultaneously, the stool wobbled, and she felt herself falling backwards. With a squeal of fright,

Madeleine clutched at the line to save herself; it, she and a morning's work fell to the ground.

'I don't believe it!' screamed the man. 'You stupid, wicked child.' Seizing hold of her shoulders, he yanked Madeleine on to her feet, and proceeded to shake her until she thought her head must leave her body. Terrified of what was to come, the girl closed her eyes, barely able to think as her head rattled back and forth, though she could hear all around the loud guffaws of laughter.

The next moment the violent motion ceased, and she felt a firm hand taking hold of her arm. Opening her eyes, she saw it was Monsieur Henri.

'I only wanted to help,' she whispered, trying not to cry.

Henri Renolleau looked at the tears rolling down the young girl's cheeks, and remembered her spirited defence of her brother the previous night, and how bravely she'd taken the Vicomte's blow with the ruler. His heart softened; he nodded, sighing. 'Yes, I'm sure you did. It's all right, Jacques, it can't be helped,' he said to the man who was now on his knees examining the crumpled sheets of paper. 'Now, what can I give you to do?' he asked, turning back to Madeleine. 'Do you know your letters, child?'

'I know C,' replied Madeleine.

'Good, then let us start with C. I'll find you a piece of charcoal, and you shall cover a piece of paper with beautiful Cs, and after that we shall go back to A and move forward through the alphabet. Would you like to do that?'

'Yes, I would very much,' said Madeleine, smiling up into the heavy lugubrious face of her new friend.

It did not take long for brother and sister to settle happily into their new life. There was so much to learn, and while Pierre learnt the difference between *gros-cannon* type and *Saint Augustin*, Madeleine mastered her letters, learning how to put them next to each other to form words. Very soon she could write her name in strong, bold, symmetrical letters which astonished her brother and even drew an approving nod from Henri.

Gradually she was given small tasks, learning how to pound vermilion with a stone for the red ink, to cook varnish in a pot at a small stove. And because she was willing and quick the men soon used her to fetch and carry for them.

It was the most exciting world she had ever known; discovering rooms stacked high with paper, reams of *petit écu* and costly *Grand Raisin* and *Couronne fine* from the Auvergne which, according to Philippe, cost as much as eight livres a ream. There were shelves covered with knives and shears; twine for pages, wool and leather to make ink balls and soft precious Moroccan leathers and fragile gold leaf to beautify the latest volume of poems to a mistress.

Outside in the gardens of the Palais-Royal was even more excitement. An army of workmen rushed about everywhere completing the extensions which the architect Victor Louis had created for the Duc. Often Madeleine saw the royal prince with his secretary, Leray de Chaumont, and the Vicomte de Cramoisy wandering along the arcades inspecting the near completed boutiques and cafés. Madeleine suspected none of the men had counted each arch along the arcading. She had! She had run the entire length of the three sides around the gardens touching the base of every arch and there were 180.

In the new year of 1783, all Paris was in a ferment of anticipation waiting for the opening of the grand enterprise. Beneath the ladders of painters and gild-ers, frantic owners wrung their hands, lamenting that theirs would be the only shop not ready for the grand opening and swearing to face the Bastille rather than part with a single livre of rent.

Finally, the great day arrived. The Palais-Royal arcades and gardens were opened to the public. To mark the occasion, a souvenir pamphlet had been printed and this was to be given out to the guests at the private preview as they walked in the gardens and arcades. Henri had chosen Pierre and Philippe to help distribute the pamphlet and, almost as an afterthought, he had later summoned Madeleine to his side. 'Would you like to help your brother today?'

'Oh yes, I'd love to,' she said, her golden eyes sparkling.

'I thought you might,' Henri said, his serious puffy face creasing into what she took to be a smile. 'Then you'd better wear this. It's from the sewing-room — they cut it down from a discarded court dress for you ... Can't see you going round like that any more,' he said gruffly, placing a pale blue dress into her hands. Madeleine was so overcome by his thought for her that she wanted to kiss and throw her arms around the silent, self-contained man. But she knew him well enough already to know he would be embarrassed. Instead she sped from the room, eager to try on his gift.

It was certainly time for a new dress, for the old which had once touched her ankles reached now only to mid-calf, whilst the bodice was stretched tight across her chest, splitting at the side seams and causing her great embarrassment. Slipping the pretty flowery material over her head, in place of her old grey, Madeleine picked up the accompanying small starched white cap. Not without some difficulty she managed to push her tangled mane of hair up into its crisp folds. Laughing with excitement she immediately returned to the printing room.

'Look Henri,' she cried, holding out her skirt and whirling around. 'Everyone will want their pamphlet from me.' From the expression in his eyes she knew he was delighted, and though to spare him, she had not said the words, she also knew he read in her eyes her gratitude and appreciation.

Philippe proved to be the ideal companion for a high society gathering. He seemed to know everyone: what rank they held, to whom they were married and, more scandalously, which ones were cheating on their wives, and which ones were cheating on their mistresses.

'Look, Madeleine,' he said, touching her arm. 'There goes the gorgeous Aglaé d'Hunolstein. Until recently she was the Duc de Chartres's mistress but it's Lafayette now who is in favour. They are really wildly in love and they say Chartres is furious.'

'But who's that, the man who's standing near the shop of Sèvres porcelain?'

'Do you mean the man wearing the blue fox-fur hat and cape?'

'Yes, he looks very sinister.'

'That, my little Madeleine, is the most famous alchemist in Paris. The Comte de Cagliostro. He claims to have lived 2,000 years. Look at his eyes, Madeleine; they say that he can evoke the dead.'

Madeleine shivered, turning away lest she should fall under the gaze of such a person. Inadvertently she stumbled against a man walking by. 'Forgive me, sir,' she said, discovering it was the Vicomte de Cramoisy.

For a moment he looked startled and slightly puzzled. 'Why of course, it's Madeleine. I did not recognise you in your dress.' The girl saw the pale eyes sweep over her face and body and she felt suddenly uncomfortable under his cool gaze, though she didn't quite know why. 'You look charming my dear. Another year and you'll be quite grown up,' he said with a small smile, then taking the arm of an elderly grey-haired lady at his side, he moved away, leaving Madeleine with a slight feeling of anxiety.

The applause of Paris for the gardens and arcades of the Palais-Royal was rapturous. Ladies flocked to the elegant shops of the arcade, whilst the menfolk took their coffee and talked politics in its smart restaurants and cafés: though restaurants and shops, as Madeleine was soon to discover, were not the only premises Chartres, now Duc d'Orléans, was willing to rent.

Time passed quickly at the Palais-Royal. There was always much to be done, and Madeleine felt contented and happy, living and working alongside her brother and the other men. Early one morning, just as Madeleine was waking up in the tiny store-room which had become her home, Pierre came to her. Still sleepy, Madeleine did not notice at first that he was wearing a thick outdoor coat.

'Wake up, Madeleine,' he said, giving her a shake, 'I've come to say goodbye. I'm going to England!'

His words struck like a handful of cold water, instantly rousing her to a sitting position. 'Am I going too?'

Slowly the boy shook his head, his excitement dissipating a little as he realised the effect his news would have on his sister. Already her face had become quite frightened and tears were appearing in her eyes. 'But we've never been parted before,' she whispered, a sense of dread coming upon her. 'Please, Pierre, don't leave me here alone without you. Please say you'll stay.'

The boy looked away, unable to look at the

pleading brown eyes. 'I have to go, Madeleine; the Vicomte de Cramoisy has ordered it. We have been here two years now, and you are no longer a little girl. It's a wonderful opportunity for me. I'm being sent to the London factory. No one else is going, just me; it's because of my English.'

The girl looked up at her brother's excited face and bit her lips, trying to control her tears and the sense of terror that was beginning to engulf her.

'You'll be all right, Madeleine. Philippe will look after you – and Henri and the others. You'll be all right.'

'But what about the Vicomte?' a sudden voice whispered inside her. Ignoring it she forced a smile, 'Yes, I'll be fine, don't spoil your chances. You'll soon be back.' They flung themselves into each other's arms and kissed goodbye.

Henri and Philippe were especially kind to her throughout the following months and gave her the opportunity to become more and more involved in their daily work. Now she was even trusted to put type away in the cases for the compositors, and when M. Henri discovered the seed of a cartoonist in Madeleine, she was given portraits of the King and Queen to sharpen her artistic claws on. It was astonishing that she, a girl, should be given such a chance, but then this was no ordinary printing house; this was the Palais-Royal, its activities clandestine.

One afternoon there was rushed work for Leray de Chaumont, who administered the huge network of Masonic Lodges for their Grand Master, the Duc d'Orléans. Leray de Chaumont, Philippe told her, as they stacked and packaged the sheets coming off the press, had his fingers on the pulse of France – for the bundles lying along the bench would, the next day, be delivered by despatch riders throughout every province. 'Just think of it,' said Philippe, tossing her the ball of twine. 'Even the King does not have that contact with his people.'

'You mean if these pamphlets ordered men to take their clothes off and run out on the streets at noon, the streets throughout France would be filled with naked men,' giggled Madeleine.

'Well . . . yes. They wouldn't say anything silly like that, but it could be done,' he replied slowly, his intelligent eyes becoming thoughtful.

'Then the King had better stay friends with the masons,' she said lightly.

'And especially the Grand Master,' whispered Philippe under his breath.

Madeleine appreciated that everyone had tried to take her mind off her brother's departure, although recently she sometimes caught a look almost of pity in some of the men's eyes and it puzzled her. Philippe, too, she felt, was a little awkward with her, and she knew he wanted to tell her something. It was later in the evening she learnt the reason. As Henri was passing her she touched his arm. 'Would you like me to work late? Or may I finish my work tomorrow?'

Madeleine saw the moon face turn slightly pink and the puffy, sleepy eyes look away. 'You won't be working here tomorrow . . . I'm afraid we're to lose you,' the deep voice growled. 'You'd better come into my office.'

'But I like it here,' she blurted out, stunned by his words, looking desperately to Philippe to come to her defence, but he looked away, embarrassed and upset.

Henri did not stop at his office, but indicated she should follow him down the long stone corridor past the men's dormitory and the vast kitchens which ran under the palace. Though anxious, she was curious to know where he was taking her, for she and Pierre had explored the long corridor within the first few days of living at the palace. Most of the rooms were locked, the others filled with old furniture and locked trunks. She was sure there was nothing of interest; but this was not so, for Henri, turning into an empty panelled room, was rapping on the wall. Astonished, she saw the whole section sliding back revealing a small wooden staircase.

It was quite dark mounting the stairs, but as Henri, above her, paused and rapped again on wood, a soft light suffused the cavity as part of the wall at the top of the stairs slid slowly to one side. Her fear now forgotten, excitedly she stepped out into a red-carpeted corridor; noting that Henri had pressed on a knot of wood to close the entrance. The carpet and matching silk walls, made bright by huge chandeliers, ran to the right and left like a long red tunnel. Passing under two of these sparkling lamps, Henri stopped before a white and gold door. As he swung it open, Madeleine's swift, indrawn breath was released in a long exclamation of pleasure. 'Ah . . . it's beautiful.'

Impulsively, she ran ahead into the room, across the pretty lilac carpet to a small armchair, covered in green taffeta and with a matching footstool which stood before a white marble fireplace. Carefully she sat down on the edge of the chair and stared about her at the cream panelled walls, decorated with golden leaves and fat cupids with merry faces.

In the far corner was a bed like a cloud of white muslin, its drapes caught back with the same apple-green material as the chairs. She glanced upwards and started with surprise and, rising from the chair, ran forward to the bed.

'Yes, it is, a mirror!' she giggled, pulling faces at her reflection. 'The lady who owns this room must be very vain,' she said turning to Henri, who looked very dour.

'This is to be your room, Madeleine,' he said almost sadly.

'Mine?' she said with astonishment. 'But why?'

'That's not for me to say,' he said stiffly and, sternly ordering her to remain there, with a slight bow of his large round head he left the room.

Madeleine wandered uneasily about the room, examining the paintings and each exquisite object. Henri, she thought, had seemed very disapproving that she should be given such a room. Could he be jealous?

Why was the Vicomte de Cramoisy being so generous? She knew him to be cruel. Had he not nearly crippled Pierre and slashed her fingers that first night at the palace? Why should he suddenly give her something so lovely? She recalled the stories she had heard about the Palais-Royal and began to feel apprehensive.

But she was not allowed to brood for long, for soon after Henri had departed there was a knock on the door. Madeleine stiffened, expecting the Vicomte, but it was a small plump woman who bustled into the room.

Her hair was bright red, almost as light as the skin of an orange. Knowing eyes under arches of black crayon ran expertly over Madeleine.

'Ah, Mademoiselle Madeleine, I am Madame Courbé. I can see you're going to be quite a beauty,' she said, flashing a bright scarlet smile at the girl.

The vivid cerise taffeta of her gown rustled as she walked towards the far corner of the room, where she pushed open a door which was so skilfully set into the wall that Madeleine had not noticed it. As she did so, six maids entered the small boudoir carrying jugs of steaming water which filled the air with a fragrant perfume. She watched them disappear into what she supposed was some sort of washroom. It was growing increasingly obvious someone was about to be washed and that someone was herself. A feeling of resentment swept over her and she went and sat down, her lower lip thrust into an obstinate pout.

'If you please, Mademoiselle.' Madeleine looked up; Madame Courbé, wearing a huge white apron over her cerise dress, stood expectantly at the open door.

'Yes, Madame?' said Madeleine with an enquiring lift of an eyebrow, as though she was totally ignorant of the purpose of the water.

'The bath is ready for you.'

'But I have never bathed. Thank you for your trouble, Madame, but I would prefer not to do so,' and looking away, Madeleine settled further back into the green chair. There was silence as Madame Courbé looked in astonishment at the filthy creature she had been told to de-louse.

'Most girls in your position,' she said cuttingly, 'would be eager and grateful to rid themselves of dirt and vermin!'

Madeleine sprang to her feet; the blood rushing to her face at the humiliating words. 'I am not most girls,' she snapped.

'No, I don't believe you are,' replied Madame Courbé slowly, acknowledging the strength of will in the girl's face. She knew her master's will too, and shivered, sensing the storm ahead. Then she shrugged – that would be a problem for the Comte. For the moment she had her own. Turning, she called out to one of the maids. 'Brigitte, would you call four of the footmen, I require their help.'

With a nod, and a malicious smile directed at Madeleine, the maid moved to the door. Madeleine stood up and, with dignity, walked towards Madame Courbé. 'That won't be necessary,' she said.

The entire bathroom was of black marble, intersected with mirrored panelling, so that everywhere she looked Madeleine saw reflections of her naked body as the blue flowery dress slipped down to the shiny floor.

Later she lay back in the black marble tub, luxuriating in the heady sensation of warm water lapping around her body. The unpleasant part was over; the evil-smelling liquid, which had been left soaking on her hair for a whole hour, had been washed away. The two maids had finished their scrubbing and rubbing and she was free to relax.

She gazed up dreamily into the smiling face of the naked young maiden above her. She was surrounded by cupids and one had released a dart into her heart. Madeleine wondered what it would be like to fall in love.

Reluctantly she rose from the pink scented water and left the playful cupids and their mistress, as Madame Courbé handed her a large towel. As the coating of dirt had floated from her body, so too had her anger; soothed and cleansed, she was totally compliant in the hands of a woman well versed in her trade. Her body was creamed and oiled with sweet-smelling jasmine for her breasts and musk for her belly and thighs. Her hair was dried and brushed until she heard it crackle as though alive.

'Well,' said Madame Courbé, dropping the piece of silk which she had been rubbing along the strands of Madeleine's hair. 'That head of hair will make amends for your feet and hands. Don't worry,' she continued, 'there's nothing wrong with them, but only time will undo what they've been through.' She reached forward and lifted up one of Madeleine's hands. 'You've been working in a laundry . . . yes, I thought so; and those ...' she pointed to Madeleine's sabots, throwing her eyes and hands up to the heavens in a gesture of despair. Despite the gesture, Madeleine could see the woman was pleased. She touched her hair, it felt soft and glossy.

'You don't even know what colour it is,' chuckled Madame Courbé, placing her pots of creams and brushes into a floral bag. 'You'd best go and look. I think you'll be pleased.'

Madeleine, now quite unselfconscious about her nakedness, tripped over to the mirror. She had never seen herself before in a full-length mirror and neither had she ever been completely undressed. Startled and pleased she saw that her hair was a tawny brown, shining with golden lights, thick and wavy, hanging down to her waist. Surprised, she stared at the small, high, pointed breasts and rounded thighs. Seeing now what the Vicomte had realised that day in the Palais-Royal gardens: that she had become a young woman.

The following morning Madeleine had to admit that never had she enjoyed such a delicious sleep. For a long time she lingered in bed, luxuriating in the feel of satin sheets against her skin, delighting in the sight of her glorious hair spread out over the lace pillows. Try as she might, it seemed impossible not to look up into the mirror above her; she was fascinated by her image and the silky perfumed tresses which Madame Courbé had discovered.

Madeleine smiled up at the girl above and decided she liked her very much; what fun it was going to be introducing her to Philippe and Monsieur Henri. A frown appeared on the girl's face as she thought of the Print Master; why had he left her with so little explanation? It was disappointing that he should treat her so.

However, perhaps things were not so bad; supper

had been delicious, and the Vicomte had not troubled her, and though it seemed he was going to make her into a grand lady, there seemed no reason why she should not help out her friends on busy days and continue to improve her drawing.

Feeling once again her merry self, Madeleine swished back the delicate curtains which the maid had drawn around the bed, slid into a blue silk wrapper and thrust her feet into pretty satin slippers which, like the wrapper, were trimmed with ostrich feathers. Whistling, she ran over to the door and dragged away her own barricade, the supper table, which she had put there to ensure an undisturbed sleep.

Though Madame Courbé had left out a dress, one glance showed Madeleine she would not be able to cope with the intricacies of its hooks without assistance. So, fastening the sash of her wrapper securely around her slender waist, she decided to go to the print shop. For a moment she wondered whether the door had been locked, but to her relief the handle turned easily.

Outside in the red corridor, Madeleine hesitated, then remembering, walked under two chandeliers to the left; this must bring her to the secret spring in the panelled wall. For some time she passed her hand over the surface: Henri had opened the door from the inside and she had no way of knowing where the release mechanism was. Then she had it, a slight rise in the wood like a small knot. Giving it a brisk rap she waited, nearly shouting with delight as a section of the wood panelling beneath the red silk wall slid back, revealing a dark cavity. Stepping inside, she explored with her fingers the rough inner wall; it wouldn't do to leave it open. After all, a secret stairway should remain secret. At the bottom of the flight of stairs she was back to groping again in total darkness, seeking the wooden lever to gain admittance to the printing-house level of the palace. Very soon, feeling most pleased with herself, Madeleine was passing the dining room where Pauline was clearing away the breakfast dishes.

'Good morning, Pauline,' she called, unable to resist the temptation of giving her a surprise.

For a moment the elderly woman just stared uncomprehendingly, then she broke into a cackle of laughter. 'Why, is that you, Madeleine? The boys said this morning you'd gone upstairs. You'll be moving up in the world now,' she said, giving a wink and bursting into another high-pitched rattle of laughter.

'Yes, I suppose so,' said Madeleine uncertainly, disturbed by the knowing wink. 'But I'll still be doing work down here,' she added firmly. But Pauline had already turned away, seeming not to hear.

When Henri Renolleau saw the door open he expected it to be the Vicomte. Though his keen eyes, used to detailed examination, recognised Madeleine at once, her transformation nevertheless took his breath away, and he knew now with certainty why his plea and argument to keep her had failed. She was far too valuable an asset elsewhere. Not that he'd argued much – he knew when his master was set on something – and although he had pointed out that the girl was gifted and could in time do valuable work, one icy stare from the Vicomte silenced him. After all, he had his own position to consider.

Madeleine suddenly felt self-conscious. Until now, she had never considered herself different, nor had she been treated as a girl. It was true she slept alone, but other than that she joined in with everything, sharing meals and jokes and holding her own at the rough games with the younger apprentices.

Now, as she walked up to Henri's bench, she

realised from the astonished looks of admiration that to come dressed as she was had been a great mistake. If she was embarrassed, so too were many of the older men who shook their heads and turned away.

'Good morning, Monsieur Henri,' she said softly. 'I was sad you left me so last night, but I wanted you to know that when I have free time, I would like very much to come down here and help. If you approve, perhaps you would tell the Vicomte that you wish it.'

Henri Renolleau thrust out his lower lip, wishing that she had not come: he was uncomfortable with this new Madeleine. He cared little for women and, until now, had been barely conscious of her sex. He stared at the fluffy blue feathers framing the innocent oval face. Soon they'd be daubing paints and powders on it, and in a year or so she'd be like the rest of the women in the basement brothels. Angry at himself, at the Vicomte, at her for the beauty which had singled her out and brought him face to face with his own cowardice, he thumped the bench violently.

'It's not possible!' he thundered. Shocked by the force of this outburst, Madeleine stepped back nervously and glanced towards Philippe for an encouraging smile but, red-faced, he averted his gaze.

Stubbornly she stood her ground, overwhelmed by a sudden feeling of anger.

'But I have a skill. You have said so!'

'Do you think that matters to the Vicomte?' growled Henri. 'I tell you, you are finished here and you must not come to disturb the men in their work. Do you understand?'

'Yes, Monsieur,' said Madeleine, the colour draining from her face and a growing feeling of constraint within. 'Yes, I understand very well — I will not trouble you further,' she added in a tight, cold voice.

Disdainfully she turned, ignoring Henri's helpless, half-apologetic gesture. Blind to the looks of sympathy and anger she departed. Never had she felt so betrayed, robbed; like thieves Henri and the Vicomte had taken away her chance. She hated them, hated them all. She had become more than a skivvy, she had begun to learn a skill and had felt different inside: proud and pleased to see the respect in the older craftsmen's eyes. Now they were taking it from her and she would become just a drudge once more. Broken-hearted, she threw herself against a wall, sobbing and muttering curses against the Vicomte. Finally, when there seemed no more tears to come, she retraced her steps down the corridor, angrily pulling out feathers from the wrapper to leave a trail of blue accusation for Philippe to see.

Upstairs, Madame Courbé was angrily pacing up and down in the boudoir. 'Ah, at last!' she snapped, giving an impatient swish to her cerise gown. 'You have kept me waiting, Mademoiselle – Mon Dieu!' she gasped, throwing her hands up in horror as she caught sight of the bedraggled ostrich collar. 'Whatever has happened? Where have you been?'

'I have been to the print shop, Madame.'

'What, like that?' gasped Madame Courbé again, her black crayon eyebrows nearly touching her wig. 'Now, let us understand each other, Mademoiselle. In future you will go nowhere, absolutely nowhere, without my permission – and never to the print shop. Do you understand?'

'Yes, Madame,' replied Madeleine, calmly helping herself to the breakfast which had been set out on the table.

'Good! You will kindly forgo breakfast today, we are already behind time and there is much to do – one cannot acquire the graces of a lady in a day, you know!'

'But I don't wish to become a lady, Madame,' said Madeleine, hastily stuffing another piece of croissant into her mouth as Madame Courbé signalled for the footmen to clear the table.

During the first few days Madame Courbé was Madeleine's sole companion; like combatants they tested each other out; one bent on resistance, the other attack.

There was little Madeleine cared for in her tutor: the glinting, shrewd eyes never softened to a kind glow and in their hard black depths stirred suspicion, greed and impatience. Madeleine was Madame's assignment and so, when she initially refused to co-operate, meals were withheld and whippings were hinted at. After two days of starvation, it seemed easier to co-operate to some degree.

For Madame Courbé, the Vicomte's orders to polish this rough jewel caused her a little more trouble than usual, but dozens of such girls had passed through her expert hands and she had risen to her present position because of her ability to manipulate men and women: one little gutter-snipe of the Faubourg Saint-Antoine was not going to wreck her career. Brighter than most of the beautiful dummies placed in her care, the girl's one continual cry was to go back to the printing shop. Beatings would leave bruises, so Madame Courbé listened and soon realised that this particular beauty was thirsty for knowledge. Very well, perhaps she would apply herself more readily if her mind was grappling with facts and figures. So, much to the astonishment of the Master of the Duc d'Orléans's wine cellar, his former mistress ordered him to instruct a certain young lady on France's most important product. It worked, and as Madame Courbé held a unique position of power at the palace, various members of the royal household, anxious for future favours to be granted and past favours to be forgotten, visited Madeleine to pass on their learning and expertise on a vast range of subjects.

Gradually as the dry, discoloured skin disappeared from the girl's hands and feet under the daily vigorous toilette, so too did the accent of the slums and the manners of an urchin. Like her beauty, the girl's gracious manner was inbred: the Vicomte de Cramoisy had recognised it and Madame Courbé released it.

Two months and more quickly passed — days filled with activity, leaving Madeleine little pause to think of her previous routine. There were times when she felt lonely for her brother and her fellow workers, but usually she was so exhausted at the end of the day, she would collapse after a light supper into the white canopied bed, her mind reeling with etiquette and architecture and countless other topics, depending on Madame Courbé's current connections.

Madame herself was delighted with the way things progressed and her eyes glittered with avarice at the prospect of additional louis-d'or for this unique approach to the job, though she did sometimes wonder whether it was wise to instil too much knowledge into someone destined to give physical pleasure. Was she creating a boudoir bore? Still, physical prowess was the responsibility of the Vicomte. She had never enquired into his methods, but knew them to be highly successful; for the customers were prepared to pay a fortune for a second taste of one of the household favourites.

Snow had threatened for several weeks and it came in the night when Paris was asleep. Even before Madeleine ran to the window, she knew that, overnight, the city had become winter's bride bedecked and veiled in sparkling white.

Somehow one always could tell, Madeleine thought: there was an intense, heavy, soft silence; the wheels of carts and carriages were muffled; the clip of hooves and the clatter of feet on cobbles were smothered. But it was more than the blocking out of everyday noise: it didn't happen on the second or third day, only the first, as if the hundreds of snowflakes were softly calling, 'We are here, we are here, come and see.'

Laughing with excitement, the girl threw open the window, ignoring the flurry of snowflakes which struck her face and settled on the blue feathers of her wrapper. How magical and bright everything looked, she thought, making a snowball from the deep soft covering on the ledge, her fingers automatically pressing and condensing the snow to get a better flight, just as Pierre had taught her. Was it snowing in London, she wondered, aiming her missile down at the head of a passing guard. With a rueful smile she saw it fall short of its victim. Behind her she heard the door open and was glad, for it would be the servant to attend to the fire and snow-watching would be even more pleasant accompanied by the crackle and heat of logs.

Down below, the palace guard had wheeled and was returning. She smiled, scraping up the remaining snow. Standing on tiptoe, she leant right out over the window sill to get a better angle. Suddenly there was a sharp playful slap across her buttocks, nearly causing her to topple head-first into the garden below. But thankfully the unknown hands gripped around her waist and hauled her back into the room. To her astonishment she saw that her attacker and rescuer was the Vicomte de Cramoisy.

'Forgive me,' he said, looking quite contrite and almost boyish. 'I couldn't resist so pretty a sight.'

Then the look faded and his face became the usual

icy mask of politeness. Slowly his pale eyes examined her. Under the emotionless scrutiny, Madeleine clutched the wrapper closer to her and tried to conceal her panic. She had blissfully put the Vicomte out of her mind, and now here he was, unannounced, catching her off-guard.

For months he had ignored her, apparently not at all eager to view the transformation which the forcible scrubbing at his orders had wrought. Now, it had pleased him to call on her without notice. Remembering Madame Courbé's words on etiquette, Madeleine spoke in the coldest tone she could muster.

'It would have been a kindness, Monsieur, if you had given some warning of this visit. I am not accustomed to receiving visits before my toilette is completed. Nor from gentlemen ...' she left the sentence incomplete, merely dropping her eyes to the carpet, where a pool of water was forming from the melting snow on the Vicomte's cloak and boots. Half expecting an angry rebuke, Madeleine raised her eyes, a shiver of excitement running through her as she saw that the Vicomte's expression as he followed her gesture had again become apologetic.

'You are right to chastise me, but I confess I was impatient to see you straightaway. I've been travelling all night – the roads are fearful. And now,' he said, inclining his head politely, 'I shall disturb you no longer. Tonight over supper you shall tell me how you are enjoying your new life.' Coldly Madeleine watched him leave. 'You'll find a small present in here,' he said, rapping a cardboard box with his riding crop as he passed an occasional table. At the door he paused and looked back, the corners of his sardonic mouth twisting into a small smile: 'Oh, your brother sends his love,' and without waiting for her reaction, he left.

Impatiently Madeleine untied the white satin bow around the gold and white striped box. Could it be a bonnet? she wondered. Now she wished she had been friendlier to the Vicomte; instead of rushing away he might have stayed and given her news of Pierre. She removed the round cardboard lid and immediately gasped with excitement, for the soft tissue was moving. Curiously she lifted up the fine paper, then laughing with relief and joy, she lifted out a small, fluffy, golden kitten wearing an emerald-studded collar.

When the Vicomte de Cramoisy entered the green and cream boudoir that evening, he gave an inward smile of satisfaction. So the kitten had been the right touch: gone was the girl's stiffness and restraint towards him.

Now she rewarded him with a smile full of warmth and gratitude as she held the tawny ball of fur aloft. 'He's adorable,' she crooned. 'Thank you so much.'

'I'm glad you like him . . . I thought he might go with your hair. You see, I was right.'

He moved to the sideboard and poured himself a glass of wine, studying its contents as he twirled the crystal goblet between long slim fingers, appreciatively sniffing its bouquet before taking a delicate sip. How different, thought Madeleine, from the men of the Faubourg Saint-Antoine, who washed wine down their throats like water. The thought made her feel guilty. She knew the people of her district had no time to linger over things; they were too busy trying to earn sufficient to feed their children. The crystal goblet, which the Vicomte now casually toyed with, would keep a family for a year.

'You're sad,' the Vicomte said, noticing the sparkle had left the girl's eyes.

'Yes,' Madeleine replied. 'I was thinking how

unfair it is that people are so poor ... whilst here ...'

The Vicomte shrugged indifferently. 'That is the way of things. There will always be the rich and the rest will be poor.'

'But why can't it change?'

'Because self-interest imposes its natural law. Man is greedy,' he said, moving towards the window. 'It is of course always possible for power and wealth to be taken from those who possess it ...' He paused, looking down at the gardens below, and she moved to his side, noticing the swell of people around the familiar orators. Together they stared down; then he pulled the lilac curtains together, closing off the scene, and led her to the table set with silver and crystal. 'And those who will shortly incite the people to commit the theft,' he continued, 'will abandon them.'

Dining with the Vicomte de Cramoisy was Madeleine's first encounter with a sophisticated man of the world. Like the champagne, his conversation was sparkling and light. He related stories about the court that left her sides aching with laughter. He teased and flirted, and for the first time the handsome, haughty face looked at her with some warmth. When she spoke, he listened attentively in a way which Pierre had never done.

Relaxed and happy, Madeleine judged it a good time to ask about her brother. 'Monsieur, will Pierre soon return to Paris? I miss him very much.'

'I'm afraid not, Madeleine. A great deal of our printing can be more safely produced in London. Pierre is needed to work with the English printers. Are you not happy with your room and your life with us?' he asked in a concerned voice.

'Oh yes,' she flushed, 'you have been very kind to me. It's just that I enjoyed helping Henri. I miss the printing shop and wonder whether I might return to work there each day.'

The Vicomte did not reply, his pale blue eyes became cold and hard. So, Madame Courbé had not exaggerated, and even after all this time the girl was still harping on about her foolish fancy. It made no sense.

'You disappoint me, Madeleine,' he said impatiently. 'I had not thought you so stupid. Why, here you are elegantly gowned, sipping champagne which you are able to distinguish as a Taittinger; in the company of an admiring Vicomte, and you tell me you wish to leave it all behind! Why, even your kitten knows when it is well off,' he said, as the tiny creature purred and rubbed against his legs. 'Would you really prefer to see your pretty hands ingrained with ink and dirt?'

'Yes, I think I would, Sir,' replied Madeleine slowly, meeting the noble's incredulous stare. 'You see, there I was learning a skill. I enjoyed the feel of the place, the noise, the smell, the excitement of seeing a book coming together. One day I could have earned my living.'

'Earned a living!' said the Vicomte, repeating her words derisively. 'Have you taken leave of your senses? Printing houses do not take in girls.'

Madeleine bit her lip, knowing what he said was true. 'Well, you did downstairs,' she said obstinately. 'So why can't I go back? I've been practising my drawing every day – it's much improved. I've made a very good cartoon likeness of Madame Courbé,' she added impishly, rising to get it.

'I'm sure you have captured with great humour our Madame Courbé's salient features, but so could a dozen young men, whereas you possess more interesting virtues. Now, the matter is closed and we will not speak of it again!'

Madeleine thought of the girls who approached the men in the gardens below and blurted out the question that increasingly loomed in her mind. 'Am I to be a prostitute? I will not be one,' she said fiercely, glaring at the Vicomte. 'I would rather return to the laundry.'

The Vicomte pressed the tips of his fingers together and surveyed the angry little face. She was quite the loveliest thing he had seen for a long time. Eagerly he anticipated touching the fine-textured creamy skin, sliding the honey-coloured dress from the round shoulders, kissing nipples that would be rose-bud pink. Mentally he cautioned himself. He must show patience tonight. He must not waste what she had to offer, which was of no interest to him, but for which jaded appetites would pay dear.

He realised the beautiful brown eyes were looking at him, waiting, almost imperiously, for his answer. Already she is beginning to sense her power, he thought with amusement.

'Madeleine, always remember your brother's destiny is linked to yours. England can be a dangerous country for a young Frenchman. I would not wish to withdraw my protection. Come now,' he said, standing up, 'remove that ugly scowl from your pretty face. I have carried from London a letter from your brother.'

Madeleine was overjoyed to receive a letter from Pierre and during the course of the following days read it several times over, for it was crammed with information about his work and life in London. And when she asked the Vicomte whether it was possible for her to write to Pierre, he smiled in his customary cold way and said yes.

Since the Vicomte's return to Paris, Madeleine had taken supper regularly in his company, and it had become his habit when the meal was over to read to her before the fire: she adored it and began to hate the times when he was called away on other matters.

On this particular evening, Madeleine, throughout the exquisite light supper, tried her best to extract the name of the new book the Vicomte had brought. 'Is it about a Frenchman? Or perhaps a pirate, a French pirate!' she declared, rushing to take her place on the footstool before the blazing log fire.

'Patience, patience, you impetuous child,' chuckled the Vicomte, taking his place in the apple-green chair behind her. Playfully the roué placed his hands over the girl's eyes and then, withdrawing them, lowered the translation of *Robinson Crusoe* in front of her face.

'What a strange title,' she said, flashing him a wide grin over her shoulder. 'I hope it's an adventure story!'

'Do I not always choose with care?' remarked the Vicomte with a smile that Madeleine did not see. For a moment he waited while the girl made herself comfortable; settling her kitten on her lap and placing a cushion against his knees to support her back. At such times, she was completely the child, he thought, waiting for her to settle before commencing to read. It was quite touching the sheer enjoyment such sessions gave her: surprisingly he had begun to enjoy them himself; they were a novel experience. Perhaps it was the onset of old age, he thought, as he opened the book at Chapter One.

As Daniel Defoe's tale unfolded, Madeleine listened attentively: she felt happy, secure and loved. She felt loved because, as he read, Armand de Cramoisy often took his hand away from his book and stroked her hair or caressed the nape of her neck. Here, like this, he was different from the cynical, cruel, haughty man she disliked during the day. This side of him had surprised her and instinctively she felt he too was surprised. At first his reading had been languid, almost uninterested, but over the weeks his voice had become animated, adopting different tones for the different characters which made her roar with laughter.

Like the kitten in her lap, basking in the warmth, enjoying the touch of her hands, Madeleine leant back, her head anticipating the Vicomte's caress. The gentle touch of his hands slid from her hair to the lobe of an ear. Soon, as his voice rose and fell, she was transported far beyond the shores of France. Totally relaxed, she felt the soft fingers trace around the neckline of her dress as they so often did, but tonight they did not slide away; instead they dipped low and she felt them skim the tips of her breasts. For an instant Madeleine was shocked by the intimate contact, but it had been so brief that now, as the Vicomte stroked her hair, she wondered if it had been accidental. She decided to say nothing, but on the next evening when the fingers sought to touch, she jerked away.

'Come now,' said the Vicomte, tweaking her ear playfully. 'Can I not love you a little; I try so hard to please you?'

Gently, but firmly, he pulled her back. 'Would you rather I did not bring you books?' he murmured, sliding his hand down the front of Madeleine's bodice. This time her resistance crumbled away as gradually she responded, beginning to enjoy the insistent pressures of his persuasive hand.

The snow, which had once been a deep but penetrable covering over the city streets, was now firm: layer upon layer of impacted, frozen crystals.

'It's so beautiful,' said Madeleine to Philippe, as she walked beside him along the frozen surface of the garden's lawns. 'But cruel for the poor sleeping out.'

'Yes, I fear many will die this winter,' replied Philippe. 'It's bad enough in the palace, so just think what it must be like outside. Though I hear many of the churches have opened their doors to give shelter.'

'Have you heard any news of Pierre being moved back?' asked Madeleine hopefully.

The dark-haired apprentice shook his head. 'No. Haven't you heard anything from London? You wrote to him recently.'

'How do you know that?'

'I have my spies too,' laughed Philippe. 'In fact, I saw the Vicomte give it to Henri to include with the London dispatches. By the way, how are you getting on with him these days?' asked the young man, his eyes gleaming with curiosity and something resembling jealousy.

Madeleine laughed, detecting the latter. 'Very well!' she teased, pleased with the effect of her words on the young man's countenance, for now there could be no mistaking the emotion in his eyes.

Philippe turned away, gritting his teeth, his happiness at being with the girl spoilt by her answer. She was becoming the coquette, he thought, for she never used to look at one from under her long curling lashes, or pout lips that invited kisses. He saw and sensed the change; she was beginning to act like a woman.

It was true, the gradual insidious wooing of the Vicomte was indeed beginning to take effect.

'And of course, he can be very kind,' persisted Madeleine in her teasing. Then she relented. 'After all, was it not he who gave permission for me to meet with my dearest friend and walk with him?'

The Vicomte had indeed suggested the rendezvous; he wanted to please his protégée and ensure her good humour for the evening ahead. For it was time to display her and whet the appetites of certain gentlemen. Also, he had to admit that he could not count on his own restraint much longer. He lusted after her and must have her soon.

From the window of Madeleine's boudoir, Armand de Cramoisy looked down at the dark figures moving across the white ground and pondered about the relationship of the two young people, as their laughter floated up to him. Young, lonely and vulnerable, it had been easy to take advantage. But her will was strong; once the uncertainties of girlhood were passed, she would be much more difficult to handle. Luckily he had found her before she was formed.

Turning from the window, he bade Madame Courbé show him Madeleine's new gown.

'Bring it closer, Madame,' he ordered. Carefully he appraised the white satin covered with tiny silver spangles.

'By candle-light it will sparkle like frost under a moon,' ventured Madame Courbé.

'Yes indeed,' murmured the Vicomte thoughtfully. 'I think just the myrtle leaves around the waist; I don't care for the roses. Have them removed.'

'Yes, Vicomte,' said Madame Courbé with an imperceptible tightening of her mouth.

'Leave all that glorious hair quite natural so that it sets off her shoulders. Apply a little rouge, but don't overdo it; she doesn't need artifice.'

'I think, sir,' remarked the woman, taking out her set of brushes, 'that tonight this girl will turn every wigged head in sight.'

'I am counting on it, Madame,' replied the Vicomte de Cramoisy, with a fierce, exultant light in his eyes.

* * *

A kaleidoscope of colour moved to and fro before the crimson, purple and gold of the salon walls. The air was stifling: a mixture of perfumes and sickly body odours. Around the walls were booths; some with their velvet curtains drawn, others filled with men and women drinking and laughing. Young girls, their naked breasts exposed through unlaced bodices, reclined against old men; impervious to raised skirts and groping, pawing hands, their eyes blank and dull.

Madeleine looked on in fascinated horror at the constant stream of traffic between the salon and a row of galleried rooms. She clung to the Vicomte's arm, terrified that she was going to be deserted; to be handed round like a doll.

Sensing her fear, the Vicomte de Cramoisy patted her hand. 'Don't worry, you're too precious for here,' he said, nodding to where a bevy of pretty girls sat waiting on a plush couch.

Leading off the main salon were many antechambers. In these a deathly silence reigned, broken only by the low call of the dealer, the click of louis-d'or; the noiseless mounting tension as players decided their bid. Through the pall of tobacco smoke, Madeleine studied the players. Some, their linen spotless and freshly starched, had no doubt just arrived. Others, she saw from their desperate eyes and faces, grey with pallor, had clearly been there for days – compulsively courting luck as their stake coins alternately mounted and dwindled.

Madeleine moved quietly amongst the tables, noting the various games under way. A young chevalier in blue silk, no older than her brother, was taking his place at the table. As he sat down he looked up and flashed her a smile. She smiled back, liking him immediately, her girl's heart fluttering as she looked into his beautiful face. She moved forward to watch him play but the Vicomte de Cramoisy, finishing his whispered conversation with a ginger-whiskered man at the next table along, caught hold of her arm and led her away. Her thoughts still filled with the handsome young chevalier, she halted at the entrance into the salon and turned, looking back: 'Who is that young man who is staring after me?'

'Which one?' the Vicomte laughed. 'You have already acquired quite a following.'

Certainly more than one man was looking in her direction, including, she noticed, the man with ginger whiskers pushing out beneath his white powdered wig.

'If you mean the young Marquis in blue, forget him. With his luck in cards, very soon neither he nor his family will be able to buy even your kitten.'

Though the Vicomte had not abandoned her, Madeleine now felt terribly apprehensive, despite the rich surroundings and the beautiful dresses which she had once enviously admired as the grand ladies entered the Opera. She wondered whether their former life in Monsieur Mergault's laundry had been preferable; but if she ran away, what would happen to Pierre? Inside she trembled, not knowing what grown-ups did or what was expected of her.

Upon reaching her pretty boudoir, the Vicomte, raising her hand to his lips, politely bade her goodnight. Then, changing his mind, he asked if she would permit him to take a glass of cognac. Surprised he should ask permission of what was already his, Madeleine invited him in.

He sat in the apple-green chair in front of the fire and motioned for her to sit on the footstool at his feet. It was cosy and warm and she sipped some of his cognac and waited for his caresses. Gradually, slowly, he kissed her ears and neck and then for the first time his lips coolly found hers, applying pressure that began to send unfamiliar feelings of pleasure through her body; feelings which spiralled so quickly that she was lost, bewildered, unresisting to a touch that knew how to bring her body alive. Fearful and yet excited, she felt his lips on her breasts and his hand slide down the flat of her belly, stroking and caressing till she was damp and moaning.

Suddenly she heard him gasp then swear, and roughly he pushed her away from him. 'What is it?' she whispered.

'Nothing, my little witch . . . you're too potent.'

Distracted, she looked at him as he deliberately and unemotionally fastened the front of her gown. The pale blue eyes looked at her, intense and hard.

'I want you, damn it, more than I've wanted anyone for a long time; and I do not want to hand you over. But I have made a contract with someone tonight. I cannot break my word now. I would be dishonoured.' Slowly the full implication of his words struck home and she gazed at him in horror. 'You can't mean . . . ?'

'It will only be tonight, Madeleine, just once, to repay me for future care. Remember also the safety of Pierre,' he added warningly.

At that moment the door opened, and a man she recognised, bull-necked, with prickly red hair, entered the room. Turning so that his back was towards the door and Madeleine was hidden from view, the Vicomte looked down at her. 'Remember, we will have days and nights of fun from tomorrow. But tonight you must work for me.' Then, turning to the door, he called, 'Come in, Charles, and meet Mademoiselle Madeleine.'

Terrified, Madeleine looked at the stranger as the Vicomte de Cramoisy left the room. She bubbled inside with rage and fear, humiliated that her young inexperienced body had been so manipulated and aroused – not even for a man's desire but to complete a business contract. She was filled with a burning hatred and contempt. She bit her lip, recalling her brother and the danger that she might place him in if she did not obey the Vicomte. Obviously unaware of her inner turmoil and distress, the large man had removed his wig and was drinking a large cognac. He noticed her staring at him. 'My dear, you're adorable. Would you like a drink to relax you?'

She shook her head and sat tensely on the edge of the chair. Tossing back the liquid in the goblet, the ginger-haired man smiled and lumbered towards her, his fat hands reaching out to her. 'Come, what about a little kiss for Charles?'

Slowly she walked towards him and raised her face, keeping her eyes shut so that she should not see the anaemic, freckly skin. But the wet mouth sucking and pulling at her lips sickened her and with a cry of disgust she pushed him away. For a moment he was startled, and then he reached out with a deep laugh, catching her to him.

'Oh, you'd escape me, would you?'

'Leave me alone,' she hissed. 'You're disgusting.'

This time his surprise changed to anger. 'You're paid for,' he snarled and, grabbing her by the bodice, tore it apart with a wrench. 'There aren't many virgins in Paris, but I've paid for you and damned heavily too! I intend to have you.'

Screaming, Madeleine clawed at his face and ran towards the door. He lunged forward, catching hold of her billowing petticoat. Whirling her around, he clutched her to him and slapped her face with a stinging blow; then covered her with savage kisses, squeezing her against him until she nearly fainted. She felt him carry her to the snowy bed and felt his fingers ripping the fragile underclothes from her body. Frantic with terror, she lashed out at him and heard him laugh with excitement.

Desperately she looked around and saw the bedside table out of the corner of her eye. With a sudden lunge, her fingers closed around the thin neck of the crystal water decanter. With all her strength she brought it down against the side of her attacker's head. He screamed with pain and clutched at his eye, the blood pouring out between his fingers. Shaking with fright, without even pausing to search for the ruined dress, Madeleine ran from the room.

Outside she hesitated, uncertain where to go. His screams had been heard, for hurrying down the corridor in a state of undress was the Vicomte, followed by a young girl. There was only one way to escape, she thought, and ran towards the panelled wall searching desperately for the hidden spring. She heard the Vicomte shout at her to stop. He was calling for assistance; but the panel slid open – at the bottom she found, despite her shaking, the pressure point. All her life she had been a fast runner and now fear lent wings to her feet as she raced towards the printing shop.

She ran into the storeroom which had been her bedroom. 'Please, God, let it be there,' she prayed. Her hand reached up for her old ragged coat. Relieved, she found it still hanging from the rusty nail. Throwing it around her she dashed on, fastening as she went.

To reach the stairs leading to the garden meant entering the printing shop. With no time for hesitation, Madeleine ran in. The men would either help or stop her.

Only two compositors were at work and neither even lifted their heads, for her naked feet made no noise on the stone floor; but at the far end of the room, nearest the door, stood Henri. He had seen her. Startled, he took in the blood flowing from Madeleine's cut lip, her naked legs and the old ragged coat. As she tried to run past him to the door, he grabbed her arm holding it tight. Her cry of despair was never heard, for his huge hand slipped tightly across her mouth. Then with a gesture to remain silent, he gradually released his hold and beckoned for her to follow him to the door. Glancing over her shoulder he slid back the heavy oiled bolts. Madeleine saw that neither compositor was yet aware of her presence.

Outside in the cold corridor Henri bent over her. 'Quickly,' he whispered. 'What has happened? You can trust me.'

Madeleine looked up into the sleepy, heavy-lidded eyes. They no longer deceived her, for she knew they observed everything, never missing a movement or an error in the printing shop. Now, curiously, they gleamed with an expression of relief and admiration.

'I hit someone; there was a lot of blood . . . now Pierre will be punished.'

'Don't worry, I'll look out for him. Have you anywhere to . . . ?' He broke off as the sound of pursuit drew closer. 'They're in the print shop. Quickly, go.'

She pressed his hand in gratitude and ran down the dimly lit corridor, her feet scarcely touching the large flagstones. She took the stairs two at a time. Behind her the walls and low roof resounded to the heavy crash of boots. Snatching a quick backward look, she saw three guards and with them, his face a mask of fury, was the Vicomte de Cramoisy.

The gardens were still full of people, but no one took any notice of her bare feet. Paris was full of ragged urchins, especially ones escaping from authority. Mustering all her strength, Madeleine turned in the direction of the Louvre. Once there, in the maze of back streets, she would be safe. Even so, she realised the echoing feet behind her were drawing nearer, every moment gaining ground.

Suddenly she heard the sound of hooves, and her heart sank. With all her willpower, she increased her speed, throwing her head back in a final effort to escape this newest peril. As the horse drew alongside, without any slackening of pace, her pursuer, with an amazing feat of horsemanship, leaned low and seized her, whirling her up bodily on to the horse. Oblivious of all but the searing pain in her chest and lungs, Madeleine kept her eyes shut, not wishing to see the exultant look in the cold, blue eyes. She was aware only of the movements of the horse and the sensation of speed.

Then she heard his laugh. A laugh that would stay with her for the rest of her life: reckless and joyful. Astounded, she opened her eyes and found that she was held by a young naval officer.

Unaware of Madeleine's gaze, he leant forward, urging his horse on, his thin lips curved in a smile, his eyes narrowed and concentrated. His was a profile so unusual that she completely forgot her fear, immediately absorbed and fascinated by her rescuer. His nose was quite sharp and upturned and his strong chin was like the toe of a shoe; combined they produced an effect of great bravado and fearlessness. He had started to rein in the horse and Madeleine noticed they were entering the wood of the Champs-Elysées. She felt the horse quivering from its exertions, and the stranger leant forward, patting its neck. Then he glanced down at her. Under the full impact of his gaze her heart lurched, responding to large magnetic black eyes, alive with merriment and tenderness.

'Well, Mademoiselle, I promise we have lost your

pursuers. Tell me, was I right to have plucked you from their grasp?' Full-faced, his large eyes and high cheek-bones dominated his features, giving him the look of a cat. He was like the panther she had seen in the zoo of the Palais-Royal; but there was nothing sinister about his face. His expression was open and boyish, while underneath she sensed a power and grace. Although he bore the mark of an aristocrat, his was not the cold hauteur of the Vicomte de Cramoisy. There was something more in his noble air: a compelling force of energy and hope emanated from him. It enveloped her and, young as she was, she recognised the qualities of a leader. As to his question, she felt at a loss. There seemed no words to explain her plight.

He had started to massage her feet, though they were so cold she scarcely felt his touch. The ragged garments that served as her coat had fallen open, exposing her nakedness. Gently he pulled it together and cradled her in his arms so that her face was hidden buried against his chest. The buttons of his tunic pressed into her cheek, but she didn't care. In these arms she was safe. Female instinct recognised a man who liked women and who would never use them as a commodity to abuse, trade and barter. This young noble was no Vicomte de Cramoisy. Her cheeks flamed red with shame as she remembered the searching caresses and her own bewildering, excited responses. Tears of angry humiliation pricked her eyes as she realised how her yearning for love and affection had made her an easy prey for seduction. Madeleine felt the familiar black terror and despair of loneliness flood over her and she started to cry for the mother she had never known and the father whose face, every day, became harder to recall. She cried for a long time and all the while the young naval officer remained silent, rocking her to and fro in his embrace.

Bemused and somewhat concerned, François-Athanase Charette de la Contrie looked down at the sobbing girl in his arms. He wondered who she was and, more importantly, what he was going to do with her. Already the hour was late and he had to make up the pleasurable hours spent in the bed of his mistress.

He ran his fingers through the girl's hair. The strands were like silk and he could smell the fragrance of roses. Doubtless these tresses had received the attention of a ladies' maid; so, too, had the cheeks and lips, which were rouged and painted. Yet she was dressed like a street urchin. Certainly she ran like one. He smiled with admiration as he pictured the young girl fleeing through the streets.

Though her hunters were three grown men, initially her power of acceleration had kept her well ahead. But she lacked the stamina and strength to maintain her lead. It was then, seeing the three guards of the Palais-Royal closing in on their quarry, that he had decided to even out the odds. He frowned as he thought of the Palais-Royal. Though he had been away at sea for many months, every officer in his majesty's navy knew of its brothels.

The young girl who now clung to him had been blessed with eyes like jewels – the colour of the topaz on his forefinger – and he had glimpsed through the open ragged coat an exquisite, shapely form approaching womanhood. But she was still only a child. He smiled grimly – children were not respected in the dens of the Orléans palace or its rented brothels; those who had savoured every pleasure still paid dear to excite their jaded palates on innocence.

He smoothed away the strands of hair from the young girl's face. Her cheeks glistened with tears,

76

though she was no longer crying. 'What am I going to do with you?' he asked softly.

Madeleine didn't answer, she felt so comfortable and safe pressed against the hard young body. She loved him and had done so from the moment she had looked up into his face. She reached up and touched a cluster of thick black curls and smiled. Her expression startled him for a moment, then laughter filled his eyes and he caught her to him in a brotherly hug.

'Ah, little one, you would have me stay. But a lady awaits me in Brest and one who will brook no delay. Tomorrow I must sail in the *Cléopâtre*. Now, do you have any family and friends?' he asked, his face and voice becoming serious.

'Yes,' she replied, suddenly thinking of Simone. 'I have a friend who is a laundress. I will go to her.'

She roused herself and attempted to jump down but he restrained her. 'Where do I take you?'

'The Cordelier quarter, but I can walk.'

'I'm sure you could,' he said, spurring the horse on to a trot, 'but I am going to take you.'

She guided him to the Cordelier quarter and the entrance to the court where Simone lived. As Madeleine slid down from the young naval officer's mount, he leaned down low and looked anxiously into her face. 'I'm sorry, *chérie*, I cannot stay to look after you; nor am I able to part with any money. But take this as a gift — it should raise enough livres to look after you for quite some time.'

He reached for her hand and pressed something small and hard into her palm. Before he could straighten, she reached up to thank him. The kiss she gave was so full of love and fervour that she almost unseated him, causing his mettlesome stallion to skitter across the slippery cobbles. Once again she heard the joyous roar of laughter. Then, doffing his hat to her, he wheeled the horse around and plunged away, his cloak billowing out behind him. She ran out into the middle of the street, watching him until he was lost from sight.

Her nails pressed deep into her palm as she clenched her fists. It was not possible that he was lost to her. 'I will find him again,' she vowed, 'and when I do, I'll never leave him.'

Chapter Two

Like a caged animal, Madeleine walked up and down before the jeweller's window. The assistant inside, apprehensive at the presence of the ragged sentry, scowled at her through the window, waving a duster in a gesture to move her on.

Her head was splitting with pain and her legs felt weak and shaky. She collapsed down on the pavement and felt through Simone Evrard's dress for the ring. It was still there, secured around her waist by a piece of leather thong which she had found in an upholsterer's yard. Now she was here to sell it. All she had to do was turn the shop's wooden doorknob and within minutes the topaz would provide her with the biggest meal in Paris.

With a desperate little sigh, she rose and wandered on, knowing that she would never sell it. It was ironic: around her waist hung a fortune. Given to her so lightly, in a gesture so generous and impulsive, it could provide her with a home, clothes and food. But she realised now nothing would make her part with it. While she had it she knew she would meet him again.

Wearily she leant against the parapet of the Pont Neuf and stared down into the murky water. Before her she could see his face, eyes that were tender and filled with laughter; a cluster of tight black curls around his temple. She smiled and squatted down against the stonework, remembering her kiss and the startled expression on the young officer's face. Then his laughter . . . no, she would not part with his ring. It would remain with her, and one day she would return it.

Beside her was a puddle of rain water and she scooped a little of it into her mouth to rinse out the vile acid taste that clung to her tongue. She'd lost count of how many days it was since she'd eaten with Simone. The quiet laundress and her sister had taken her in immediately on that terrifying night when she had fled the Palais-Royal. The next day, despite their pleas, she had moved on. She had not wanted to cause them embarrassment, for their resources were so slender. Neither did she want to involve them in her troubles. The Vicomte de Cramoisy would surely search for her amongst her former work mates. If they were found sheltering her, they too might be flung into prison.

Madeleine shuddered as she thought of the grim gaol. Perhaps she would be executed for attacking an aristocrat. Certainly they would torture her on the Place de Grève.

She scrambled to her feet, as though to fly her fear and, like the flotsam on the river, was soon carried along by the swell of people on the bridge. As usual the booth-holders were busy enticing the passers-by to part with their money. No one took any notice of Madeleine; starving urchins didn't book flights in hot-air balloons or need tickets for the theatres. But they did discourage the decent citizens from approaching the pastry booths as they hung around in their droves, waiting patiently for a kind heart or a clumsy hand. For a while Madeleine joined their ranks, the saliva in her mouth running freely as she smelt almonds and ginger biscuits. 'Today I must eat,' she thought desperately, 'or it will not be to prison but to the Hôtel-Dieu that I will be taken.'

There was only one course left to her if she was to avoid a bed in the terrible hospital from which few ever emerged alive. At least, she thought as she sat down, begging is preferable to stealing. Holding out her hand, she looked up and smiled as a wealthy-looking man rode by. 'Have pity on a poor orphan, sir,' she whispered.

The man, without even glancing down, rode on.

'You'll have to do better than that, dearie,' a voice said from behind her. Startled, she whirled round to find a blind beggar prodding her with his stick. The girl flushed red with embarrassment and shame. Here before her was a poor wretched man who never saw sun and birds, imprisoned in a dark world. She made to rise and leave his place, but resting his hand on her shoulder, he lowered himself down beside her. He wore a large battered felt hat, marked with grease and wine stains. As he turned to her he pulled the brim down lower and suddenly she saw the eyes peering at her were no longer blank but bright and curious.

'You're new; never seen you before . . .'course you're on my pitch, you know. But you're pretty, I'll forgive you,' he cackled, leering at her.

Madeleine pulled back to escape the stream of foul breath.

'Tell you what,' he said, thrusting his head further forward. 'I'll teach you the tricks, take you on as a partner. 'Course you're no good as you are, too plump and healthy-looking.' The filthy, bony fingers clutched at her arm. 'We'd need to maim you . . . cut off a hand or something.' The brown fingers grabbed at the girl's naked foot. 'It's even better without a leg. That really touches their hearts.'

With a shriek, Madeleine kicked away the repellent hand and staggered to her feet, her skin crawling at his touch. She shot away into the crowd and heard him calling after her. 'Any time, dearie.'

So anxious was she to escape the cackling laughter, she collided heavily with a girl carrying a wicker basket. The impact knocked the basket from the girl's hands and its contents tumbled out. Quickly Madeleine knelt and helped the girl gather her shopping together.

'I'm terribly sorry,' she apologised. 'I was trying to escape from someone.'

'So I noticed,' laughed the girl in a good-natured way. 'Blind André probably thought you were stealing his spot. He isn't really blind. I live just over there, so I watch him most days; enough to know he can see the difference between a centime and a sou.' She paused, looking at Madeleine's naked feet and ragged dress. 'Were you begging?' she asked curiously.

'No . . . well, yes,' admitted Madeleine, her face crimson with shame. 'I'm desperate for a job.'

Gabrielle Charpentier had never known want, but she recognised it. She took hold of the young girl's hand. 'Come with me. I'm not certain about the job, but I can make sure you eat today.'

Just across the bridge, on the Quai de l'École, was the Café Parnasse. Feeling a little awkward and shy, Madeleine followed the amiable young woman inside. Within minutes she was seated at a corner table, a bowl of chicken soup before her. It smelt and tasted so good she wanted to cry, so great was her gratitude. Between sips of delicate broth, she gazed adoringly at the brunette angel who had taken pity on her. From her intimate manner with the patron and madame behind the cashier's desk, it appeared the young lady was a regular customer; for she nodded and smiled and seemed very much at home. All three now looked across at Madeleine and she realised she was under the scrutiny of Madame's business-like eyes. Her hopes rose a little; perhaps there was work in the restaurant and her days of miserable wandering were over. The patron, a short man with a pleasant round face under a small, round, grey wig, was coming towards her table. She rose to greet him but he gestured for her to sit down. 'My daughter tells me you require a job.'

Surprised, Madeleine looked at her young patroness.

'Yes,' smiled the young woman. 'This is my father, Monsieur Charpentier. I am Gabrielle.'

'Mademoiselle, you've been so kind to me,' said Madeleine with tears in her eyes. 'And I am indeed truly desperate for work, Monsieur Charpentier. I promise you will never regret it if you take me on.'

'I hope I won't,' replied the patron, his bright intelligent eyes twinkling. 'You can help Annette in the kitchen. Free board and lodging for a hard day's work. I daresay Gabrielle can find you something better to wear, then you can meet Annette. You'll soon get used to the routine.'

'Don't believe everything Papa says,' smiled Gabrielle Charpentier, leading Madeleine up to her bedroom. 'No one could possibly get into a routine with Annette.'

'Why is that, Mademoiselle?' enquired Madeleine.

'Oh, don't worry,' replied the patron's daughter, seeing the anxious expression on the beggar-girl's face. 'She is not an ogre, she just doesn't work to a system. Maman always says one should tidy as one goes along, whereas Annette grabs any clean spoon or bowl in sight, until she disappears behind a high muddle of pots and pans, all of which she does not expect to wash up, and which, I'm afraid, will keep you very occupied.'

On reaching the top of the stairs, Gabrielle Charpentier ushered Madeleine into her bedroom, which was situated next to that of her parents. It was a pretty room, low-ceilinged with oak beams. Its walls were papered with a pattern of primroses, which gave a sunny look to the room.

'Now sit down, while I look through my wardrobe for something for you to wear. Here, try this on for size,' she said, tossing on to her bed a heavy wool skirt. As Madeleine slipped it on, she immediately felt the effects of its warm fibres, for Simone Evrard's old dress was but a thin rag. However, it was far too large; its waistband would have spanned twice round her slim waist. Politely she stood holding the skirt to her.

'Oh, that won't do at all,' giggled Gabrielle Charpentier, inspecting her. For a moment she looked perplexed and then her mild brown eyes brightened. 'How silly I am. I have lots of things you could have. I'd quite forgotten Maman packed them away to give to the priest for the needy. I've outgrown them, but they're in good condition.' Quickly she ran from the room and soon reappeared with a large paper parcel. 'Now there are nice warm things in here too,' she smiled, seeing Madeleine still hugging the heavy wool skirt about her. 'This, for instance. Have you ever seen anything smarter? Papa gave it to me as a birthday treat. You could wear it on Sundays or special holidays. Just feel how soft the velvet collar is.'

Madeleine touched the dark brown velvet and smiled, inwardly wondering what this kind young woman would say if she'd seen the blonde silk and the white satin with its spangles and myrtle leaf trimming. She sighed with relief and satisfaction to be amongst decent, ordinary folk, and docilely stood on a stool while the buxom young brunette adjusted the length of a hem. 'There, I think that is straight. Just one more twirl, Mademoiselle.'

Obediently Madeleine turned around slowly to display the hemline of a dark grey wool skirt, which had been decided should be her work-skirt.

'Now you shall start to sew the hem. You can sew?' enquired Gabrielle Charpentier.

'Yes, Mademoiselle Gabrielle.'

'Good. I shall do the dress, and while we sew you shall tell me about yourself. But first I shall give you some wool stockings, for your feet look very cold.' On closer inspection, Gabrielle Charpentier saw the young girl's feet were cut and heavily blistered. Silently she motioned for Madeleine to lift one up. 'I think we should bathe your feet in salt, and put some ointment on those cuts. Are they very painful?'

'Not really. My feet have been so cold, I've hardly felt them.'

'Well that's not good; I shall send for some hot water straight away, and Maman will tell us what ointment to use.'

Rapidly Gabrielle Charpentier's ministrations were carried out and soon, with her feet encased in linen bandages and covered with woollen stockings, Madeleine sat sewing with her new mistress.

'How did your feet come to be in such a state?'

'I suppose they're not used to sabots anymore,' replied Madeleine, without thinking.

'No, I thought not,' said Gabrielle Charpentier. 'For your skin is very soft — softer than mine and I always wear shoes — and your hands and nails are those of a lady. Who are you, Madeleine?'

Madeleine looked into the trusting brown eyes, not wishing to lie, yet afraid and ashamed to tell her about the events leading to her flight from the Palais-Royal. So she told her about Pierre and the laundry and then said: 'A powerful noble took me into his household to be a companion for his friends. But I didn't like it, so I ran away. Please don't ask me where, for if he finds me, he'll take me back and I'm so afraid.'

'You didn't steal or do anything bad?' asked Gabrielle firmly.

'Oh no, Mademoiselle,' replied Madeleine, then flushed a little as she thought of the ginger-haired man. Desperately she looked down at her work, knowing she should mention her attack. But then he had attacked her. If the police were looking for her, though, and they tracked her here, would the Charpentier family be accused of harbouring a criminal? She decided to confess all, even though it might mean her ejection into the frozen streets. But before she could do so, Gabrielle Charpentier spoke: 'Well, I think you did right to run away. You are too young to know what might have become of you, for I do not think this Lord would marry a poor commoner, nor his friends. We will not speak of it again for I see it distresses you. Nor shall I speak of it to Papa or Maman; it would only worry them. I trust you, Madeleine, and I know you won't let me down.'

'I promise I won't do that,' replied Madeleine fervently.

'Good. Now I'll show you your room and you shall meet Annette. You will be sharing a bedroom with her.'

Lulled by the warmth of the Charpentiers' greeting and the care of their daughter, Madeleine was unprepared for the unfriendly greeting from their cook.

'Oh, that's all I need, a novice,' she cried at first sight of Madeleine. 'As if I haven't enough to do, Mademoiselle Gabrielle, without giving me someone with no experience. And for a start you can cut those nails,' she said, catching hold of Madeleine's hand in a whirlwind of action. 'I'll not have them in my kitchen – nasty dirty things!'

'I'll cut them straight away, Madame,' said Madeleine, anxious to please. 'Do you have scissors?'

'Scissors! This is no time for scissors, girl,' gasped the fat woman, flinging eggs around a bowl, her whisk but a blur. 'You can start to grate some nutmeg for me and yes, bring me some sugar and a vanilla pod, and I'll need a clean bowl; and be quick about it, for if there's one thing I can't abide it's a slowcoach.'

Frantically Madeleine ran back and forth, searching for required items in the strange kitchen. If only she would take a few minutes to show me where everything is, I'd be much quicker, thought Madeleine, tugging at a drawer. The next moment another jerk brought the drawer and its entire contents on to the floor. Scarlet with embarrassment she dropped to her knees to gather up the kitchen cutlery.

'Now, Annette,' said Madame Charpentier, entering to see what all the commotion was, for the accident had sent the cook into hysteria. 'Calm down, remember it's the girl's first time; she's only just arrived. You carry on and I will show her where everything is kept. Now my dear,' she said, looking down at Madeleine, 'put the drawer back and then I'll explain things to you. I come into the kitchen every day to do certain dishes myself, so I am always at hand to answer any questions without you disturbing Annette. All we have to do for good food is to try and keep a calm atmosphere!'

The Parnasse restaurant was known for its fine cooking and, because of its position, attracted many lawyers from the Palais de Justice. Two of its dishes were especially loved by its regulars: *pot au feu* and *tarte cerise*.

While Madame Charpentier stood behind her cash desk, graciously accepting homage for her *pot au feu*, Annette, the pastry cook, also received new tributes from Madeleine, who had never tasted such miracles before. Certainly the speed at which Annette worked seemed miraculous. Her deft fingers caught butter and flour together one moment; in the next she was already glazing the fruit, cherries or whirls of apple slices laid out in their light pastry cases.

Annette was a comfortable young woman, made older by the layer of soft fat which covered her body; and which testified to her constant sampling of sauces and creams. Her face, like her body, was round. A small nose and mouth merged unnoticed into her face, and everything but her eyes gave an impression of softness and calm. Madeleine missed those eyes at first and later wondered how that had been possible. For they were not dull and still but gleamed bright, their changing expressions betraying an excitable impatient nature and a lover of gossip.

Gabrielle Charpentier's father had been right; Madeleine soon fitted into the routine of The Parnasse. Every day was always the same. Annette would issue a stream of orders, each one of the first priority. Gradually, like Madame Charpentier, she learnt to work calmly around the excitable cook. Disregarding the mounting tension as the hands of the clock moved nearer to noon, Madame Charpentier would quietly check through that day's menu with Annette, and leave to take her place behind the cash desk as the last stroke of twelve sounded. Gabrielle would station herself behind the counter and Monsieur Charpentier, with a white napkin on his arm, would wait to receive his first customer.

On this day, Wednesday 21 June 1786, The Parnasse was particularly busy. There were many people seeking a hearty lunch and a good bottle of wine after witnessing the flogging and branding of the Comtesse Jeanne de la Motte-Valois.

Annette had happily gone to watch the grim spectacle, and was still bubbling over with excitement about her outing. 'I wish you'd come, Madeleine. You should have seen her kicking and screaming when they dragged her out on the Cour de Justice. She struggled like a devil when they tried to strip her. It took six of them.'

For a moment she paused, eyes closed as she sucked a finger coated in sauce. With a nod of satisfaction she continued, her eyes glinting with excitement. 'Then came the branding . . . what sport! She bit and clawed like a tiger and the creature's struggles made it worse for her, for the second iron missed her other shoulder and landed on her breast – you could hear it sizzling. Then the fun began. She managed to break free . . . what a chase! There's never been such entertainment for a long time. We ached with laughter and all the while she's screaming, "It's the Queen, it's the Queen, I'll tell it all".'

Madeleine did not join in Annette's laughter and felt somewhat sickened by the cook's evident relish at witnessing another woman's suffering. Quietly she concentrated on passing the orders through the hatchway. It was strange, she thought: Annette was a kind, generous woman, yet when it came to public executions and such there was a layer of cruelty, a total disregard for another's misery and agony. Yet she was no different from many others. She handed Gabrielle Charpentier a soup plate, and as she did so the girl gave a wink in Annette's direction, her broad face breaking into a cheery grin. 'Where's your

Christian compassion, Annette?' she laughed, calling through the opening.

'I've none for the likes of her, interfering with a man of God . . . a cardinal . . . the Grand Almoner of France.'

'A handsome one, too,' teased Madeleine, giggling with Gabrielle as the chubby face turned pink. For it was well known that Annette was quite enamoured of the elegant Prince Louis de Rohan. Not that she was alone in her infatuation – for virtually every woman in Paris felt the same.

When news of his arrest – as he was about to celebrate high mass on the Feast of the Assumption – reached Paris from Versailles, the populace was stunned. That he, a member of one of the oldest and most noble French families, had demanded a public trial by Parliament, and that the Queen had also interceded, threw most ladies into a fury of indignation and rage. And even before the astounding story of the Diamond Necklace Affair was unfolded, Paris had chosen its culprit in the person of Marie-Antoinette.

It was an affair which made Madeleine indispensable to Annette. For whilst Monsieur Charpentier each day, after lunch, read to his small household an account of the trial of those involved in the case, it was not the dry account in the *Moniteur* which interested Annette but the juicier stories in the scandal sheets. Unable to read, and knowing that Monsieur Charpentier did not approve of the pamphleteers, Annette was overjoyed when she discovered that Madeleine could. So as soon as they had cleared the morning's work away and were alone, she would eagerly produce the latest news sheet and, child-like, sit docilely before Madeleine, waiting for her to begin.

Indeed, so incredible were the facts that, at times,

Madeleine felt she was reading a fairy story. The cunning and skilful Comtesse Jeanne de la Motte-Valois, using forged letters and an actress resembling the Queen, had managed to dupe Cardinal de Rohan into believing that he had at last found favour with Marie-Antoinette. So overjoyed was the handsome cardinal with the little perfumed notes, a tryst with a cloaked lady in a grotto, the vision of the Queen conjured up by the famous alchemist, Cagliostro, that he became like clay in the hands of Jeanne de la Motte-Valois. Without the least suspicion, he agreed to act on behalf of the Queen in the acquisition of a diamond necklace from the court jewellers, readily believing that Marie-Antoinette wished to keep the matter secret from the King. By pledging his credit, he obtained the necklace and handed over 1,600,000 livres of diamonds to the Comtesse de la Motte-Valois. Expectantly he waited for the favours and honours that would flow to him from the Queen. Nothing happened until the day the distraught court jeweller, Boehmer, approached the Queen, demanding the long overdue payment. And so the scandal broke.

Eventually all concerned were tracked down and arrested. The cardinal was seen to be the innocent victim throughout his trial, genuinely believing that the woman who had encouraged him was indeed the Queen of France. And though it was plainly not she but the actress, Damoiselle d'Oliva, engaged by Jeanne de la Motte-Valois for the part, Paris blamed the Queen. Even now, Annette was echoing what had been on everyone's lips for the last months.

'You see,' Annette continued, her face pink with emotion, 'if the Austrian behaved like a queen this would never have happened. No man would dare to send love letters to his monarch. But a woman who shuts herself up in the Trianon with only men and without her husband; a woman who spends a fortune on her feathers and girl friends, well, is it surprising that the cardinal treated her like any other woman? You agree with me, don't you, Madeleine?'

Madeleine nodded and smiled reassuringly. Their daily ritual of reading had changed their relationship. Now the disparity in their ages and positions had lessened through Annette's respect for Madeleine's education.

'Why, I know which lady should have been receiving the flogging today,' Annette said grimly, looking across in a knowing, secretive way.

'Now, Annette, that is enough,' said Gabrielle firmly. 'You'll get yourself into trouble saying such things; there are many ears out here.' She shut the hatch firmly and Madeleine, feeling a little sorry for the young woman, tried to lift up her spirits.

'At least your lovely cardinal smiled at you, Annette. Do you remember when he was acquitted and we waited for him to drive out of the Bastille? He looked marvellous, he was wearing a cape of violet . . .'

'And a rochet of Melines lace,' continued Annette dreamily. 'He waved at the crowd and smiled straight into my eyes. And now that spiteful woman has banished him from court and Paris,' she said sadly. 'I'll never see him again.'

Madeleine left Annette to her daydreams, feeling a sense of sympathy with the young woman. Would she ever see her young naval officer again? Upstairs she stretched out on her little bed in the attic and held the topaz ring between her fingers. At least she knew his name was François, she thought, tracing the letters engraved on the inside of the gold band. Letting it dangle from the leather thong, she spun the cord round, smiling as it sent circles of bright light flashing around the bare walls of her little room. Despite all, she still had it. She knew they would meet again. It was a thought that filled her whole being with joy.

Whilst Madeleine and Annette enjoyed their day-dreams, Gabrielle enjoyed the attentions of a real, live suitor; though she seemed unaware of the admiring glances sent in her direction as she worked behind the counter or sat beside her mother on her high stool next to the cash desk.

But Madeleine soon noticed. From her vantage point at the kitchen door, where Annette often sent her to see how things were going, her quick eyes were soon drawn to a young barrister who had started to eat regularly at The Parnasse.

Indeed his physical appearance compelled attention. Though ugly – for his face was badly scarred, the skin pitted and marked from smallpox – when he threw his great head backwards into laughter, or his scarred, twisted upper lip drew back into a smile, the vitality and warmth of his personality was like sunlight touching the rough-hewn features of a crag. Madeleine saw that many of these smiles were directed at Gabrielle and, after several weeks, she noticed with amusement that they were acknowledged and returned. So it did not surprise Madeleine when, one day, Gabrielle, with shining brown eyes, shyly approached her.

'Madeleine, I wondered whether you might be free to accompany me this afternoon. Georges has invited me to walk with him and Maman says I may if you are with us.'

'Yes, of course, Gabrielle. I'd be pleased to come.'

'Good. I thought we might take a picnic. Annette is putting some things into a basket for us.'

Pleased and excited to be included as a chaperone, Madeleine ran down to the kitchen to help Annette and found that the basket was ready – the contents covered by a red and white checked napkin.

'I see our young barrister has made his move,' said Annette, pushing the basket towards Madeleine. 'He has a shrewd eye, for a provincial.'

'What do you mean, Annette?'

The small lips pursed and Annette's eyes beamed with a knowing glint.

'Well, our Monsieur Danton is no fool. Young barristers need a great deal of money to buy a law practice. Doubtless he has sniffed out the Charpentier dowry.'

'Oh, I'm sure he loves Gabrielle,' said Madeleine defensively.

'Yes, I think he does,' replied Annette matter-of-factly. 'He has just been ambitious enough to seek love where he has a future.'

It was a sunny, bright, airless afternoon and, though the stench from the Seine was at times nauseating, the blue sky reflected in its waters made it beautiful, like a shimmering length of satin.

Madeleine marched ahead of Gabrielle and Georges Jacques Danton so that they might be free to talk more intimately. With one hand she carried the round wicker basket with its gay covering of red and white; in the other she held the woody green stem of a fern which she used as a parasol, its large lacy leaves casting a shadow over her head. As she walked she sang a Breton song which Pierre had taught her. It seemed a lifetime since she had seen him. Though she had sent her address through Simone to Henri at the Palais-Royal printing shop, she still had not heard from Pierre.

Madeleine frowned as she recalled the Vicomte de Cramoisy's threat when she had objected to becoming a whore. 'So many dangers can threaten a boy in London,' he had whispered. She slashed her fern viciously at a wasp, remembering the cold expression in the pale blue eyes; then bit her lip with shame as she recalled how her body had responded to the experienced hands. She wished it had been his temple she had left pouring with blood from her blow with the decanter. Her dark musing was interrupted by Gabrielle's sweet voice calling to her. 'Madeleine, slow down. We're going to stop here under the trees.'

She turned round, forcing a smile, not wishing to spoil her young mistress's day. Very soon, however, she too was laughing with Gabrielle, for the force of Georges Jacques Danton's teasing and his desire to please swept away all gloomy thoughts.

Annette's basket held a delicious selection of meats and cheese, one of her famous *cerise* tarts and a bottle of burgundy. Whilst they ate, Georges told them about his boyhood in Champagne.

'Ah, it is the most beautiful province,' he sighed, refilling his wine glass. 'The food is fresh, people are polite and the hunting and fishing – why, I've caught fish this big in the Aube,' he said, stretching out his great hands so wide that Madeleine and Gabrielle collapsed with laughter.

'Well it would seem to me, Monsieur Danton, a most dangerous province and its people hot-tempered! For I'll be bound you got that in a fight,' teased Madeleine, pointing to a scar on the startled young man's face.

'I got this,' he said, touching his scarred, twisted upper lip, 'when I was quite small. I'd been put to suckle on a cow's teat, but a bull objected.'

'And this one, Georges?' asked Gabrielle, tenderly touching with the tips of her fingers a long white scar running along the cheek.

'That one . . . ? Well, maybe that belongs to the bull . . . or was it the herd of pigs?' he chuckled, seizing her fingers and kissing her hand. 'But the rest is courtesy of the smallpox.' He stood up, his powerful figure blocking out the sun as he yawned and stretched out his arms. Madeleine looked up, marvelling at his powerful bull-necked physique. Though there was a coarseness about him, she could understand why Gabrielle was attracted to this man. He had an earthy sensuality that was exciting. A life force so powerful, it seemed almost tangible. She had encountered it once before when she had looked up into the face of the young naval officer in the wood of the Champs-Elysées. Though they were different, separated by birth and rank, Madeleine realised both commanded a force that would inspire and lift others well beyond their limitations.

Gradually, feeling drowsy after wine and Annette's tart, Madeleine rolled over on to her back and closed her eyes, feeling the warmth of the sun come and go as the faintest of breezes stirred the overhanging leaves. Sleepily she imagined herself with François on board his ship, the *Cléopâtre*, speeding towards the West Indies or the Americas. Suddenly, beside her, there was a shriek and, simultaneously, a loud splash. Starting up, Madeleine saw with disbelief that Georges Danton, stripped down to his underwear, had dived into the Seine and was swimming out into the centre of the river.

'Come back, Georges,' cried Gabrielle anxiously. 'Just see, Madeleine, he thinks he is in the Aube at Arcis . . . Come back, Georges, it's filthy!'

Though Madeleine nodded in agreement with Gabrielle, she watched Georges Danton's progress with admiration. He surged through the water with power and speed. Curiosity overcame caution and she ran down the bank to where he had left his outer clothing. Cupping both hands to her mouth she called to him across the water. 'Georges, will you teach me?'

He waved to her and shook his head, indicating that he would not. But having made up her mind, nothing was going to stop her; running behind the shelter of a bush, Madeleine kicked off her shoes and pulled off her skirt and blouse. Making sure that the leather thong with its precious ward was secure, she ran back to the edge of the river, clad only in her shift. Ignoring Gabrielle's cry of protest, she slid down the edge of the bank into the cool water, holding on to a branch of willow to keep herself afloat. There was a booming roar of laughter and she heard Georges swimming towards her. Nervous and excited she looked up into the anxious face of Gabrielle.

'Oh do come in, Gabrielle, it's lovely, it's so cool.'

'And so dirty. Besides which, it is not usual for young ladies to undress in public.'

'Well, I'm not a young lady,' giggled Madeleine, as Georges slid his great hands under her chin. 'I'm just an urchin,' she spluttered.

For a whole hour Madeleine, under Georges's tutelage, learnt to keep herself afloat and, by using her arms and legs, to move through the water. She was a natural athlete and his prowess in the water inspired total belief, so that when he first removed his supporting hands from her body Madeleine moved forward calmly and with confidence. It was the most exciting experience she had ever had; a unique feeling of freedom – an accomplishment which years later, in the most grisly and nightmarish situation, would save her life. But as she splashed and frolicked with Georges in the sparkling water of the Seine, neither pupil nor master knew of the fate which destiny had planned for them.

More immediate was the deception of a summer's

day, when water glitters and gleams. For, as Gabrielle had warned, the Seine was not the clean, fast-flowing Aube of Georges's boyhood days. It was a turgid sewer which, hours later, would try to reclaim both swimmers.

Gabrielle promised to say nothing about the picnic bathing, for Madeleine knew that Annette would scold her for days for such foolishness. Therefore, although she was beginning to feel very unwell as Annette knelt and said her prayers, she said nothing. But long after the candle had been blown out she tossed restlessly, unable to sleep. Her head ached and though the night was very warm, she felt one moment ice cold, the next burning hot. Waves of nausea swept over her and she felt peculiar, ill. A powerful urge to be sick made her struggle out of bed to use the bucket in the corner of the room. Unable to reach it in time, she collapsed to her knees, retching, her body shaking as she tried to support herself on all fours. Eventually through the dizziness she was aware of Annette bending over her. Suddenly it seemed the whole Charpentier family was present and the room was unbearably hot and bright from additional candles. Then the room was empty, and she could hear Annette's voice wailing and sobbing. 'I'll not go back in there, Madame. I'll not!' More crying and then: 'She should go to hospital. What if it's the pox?'

Then gradually the lowered voices outside the door drifted away. Vaguely Madeleine became aware of cool hands touching her forehead, then sponging her burning face and body. She opened her eyes and saw the grave, anxious face of Gabrielle.

'It's all right, Madeleine, you've caught a chill, that's all. Papa is sending for a doctor, and I'm going to nurse you well again.'

The chill was, as Gabrielle learnt two days later, a fever — typhoid. Despite her parents' objections, she had insisted she be isolated with Madeleine, pointing out that she was the only one who could be spared from her work. No one thought to suggest removing Madeleine to the Hôtel-Dieu. They had become too fond of her. Indeed, when the doctor had confirmed typhoid, Monsieur Charpentier himself, to oblige the worried Gabrielle, had called upon Georges Danton. He found him alone in his bachelor lodgings and very sick. Straightaway, the kind-hearted man went back to The Parnasse for the horse and cart, and within the hour Gabrielle had a second patient to care for.

Both of her charges were young and strong, and fought for recovery. Gradually, as their fevers broke, and the pinkish weal across their stomachs disappeared, so too did the vomiting and diarrhoea.

At the end of three weeks, presented with a bowl of Annette's soup, Madeleine felt her appetite return for the first time. It was chicken broth and it reminded her of the first time she had eaten at The Parnasse. She had been so hungry then. Suddenly she felt hungry again and glad to be alive. She took a spoonful of the fragrant golden liquid and turned with a smile as Gabrielle entered the room.

'I'm glad to see my second patient is eating too,' Gabrielle said, drawing up a chair and sitting beside Madeleine. Despite the dark shadows of exhaustion, Madeleine saw that Gabrielle's eyes were filled with happiness. Even before she said the words, Madeleine knew what they would be. She dropped her soup spoon and flung her arms about her friend – for that was how she thought of her now. Once she had been her mistress taking pity on a ragged beggar, now she was the sister who for three weeks, impervious of her own danger, had fought to keep her alive. For a moment Madeleine could not speak and both girls clung to each other, crying with happiness. Through her tears Madeleine laughed. 'You'll make the perfect wife for a barrister, although it's a pity Georges isn't a doctor – no one could make a better nurse!' she said, tenderly squeezing the dark girl's hand.

'Well, as your nurse, Mademoiselle, I hope you are going to finish Annette's soup. I will receive a scolding if I take a single drop back to the kitchen. Fuss over her when she comes up to see you, Madeleine. She's terribly embarrassed and upset that she didn't nurse you herself. She wanted to, you know, but I insisted on doing so myself! So instead she has spent hours boiling up bones for marrow to strengthen you.'

Madeleine smiled at her friend, knowing that she was covering up for Annette's words that distant night. 'Tell her I'm longing to see her, and if she brings some gossip, I shall read it to her.'

Gabrielle Charpentier nodded appreciatively. 'I'll go and see if Georges has finished his soup, and then I will come back and brush your tangled mane.'

Madeleine needed no urging to finish the soup, and while awaiting Gabrielle's return, sat by the window and watched a tight-rope walker cautiously progress along his wire in front of an admiring audience down below on the Pont-Neuf. With a smile she saw that the beggar André too was there.

'See, Gabrielle,' she said as her friend returned. 'Down below – André. He looks very convincing.'

'Just wait until he counts his day's takings later. He won't be at all convincing then,' laughed Gabrielle, picking up a brush and drawing it in long gentle strokes through Madeleine's golden hair. It was very soothing and Madeleine sat back, feeling cosseted and cared for as Gabrielle chatted to her.

'You know, Madeleine, I was tempted to cut all these curls off when you were ill, but I couldn't bring myself to do so. It's glorious; yet always you push it under an old woollen cap. Why do you hide it?'

Madeleine did not reply. How could she possibly explain that since one terrible night she had done everything possible to hide her femininity. She didn't want men to notice her. At fifteen her figure was already curvaceous. Even Georges had started with surprise when he had supported her body in the Seine, for she deliberately wore loose, shapeless garments that would deceive the predator's eye.

'Is it something to do with the ring?'

The question, asked so gently, made Madeleine start. Her hand flew to her waist; she hadn't even noticed it was gone.

'I'm sorry,' murmured Gabrielle. 'I didn't mean to startle you, but I had to remove it . . . It's here, quite safe.'

She moved away to a small set of drawers on top of a heavy oak chest and returned carrying the topaz, still on its leather thong. 'Forgive me if it's your secret,' she continued, handing the ring to Madeleine, 'but I had to wash you quite often and it was easier to do it without the ring. It's quite lovely . . . just like your eyes.'

She had picked up the hair brush once again and resumed her work. For a while there was silence between the two friends and Madeleine knew the quiet, gentle girl would ask no further questions. Her steadfast, loyal nature made her a most precious friend. Madeleine decided to tell Gabrielle her secret.

Though she did not reveal all about the Palais-Royal, she told Gabrielle about the young naval officer; how he had rescued her and pressed his ring into her hand. She told of his reckless smile and laughter, of his large black eyes and curly hair. The curious tilt to his nose . . . and all the while Gabrielle brushed and listened until at last she started to chuckle.

'Enough, enough. You've convinced me, you crazy girl. You are in love with a god! When I think you were half-dead with hunger on the Pont-Neuf, yet around your waist you carried something that all the beggars in Paris would have killed for. I can only conclude you are a silly goose. Or,' she added more seriously, 'a woman who will love grandly. I am sure, Madeleine, you will meet your chevalier again; but remember, to love grandly one will suffer grandly.'

The romance between Gabrielle Charpentier and Georges Jacques Danton was to change all their lives. On 14 June 1787, the Café Parnasse was closed all day. Yet inside all was merriment as family and friends raised their glasses to the happy couple.

At the end of October the café was closed once more, but this time there was no laughter, only tears, as Madeleine and Annette waved goodbye to their former employer and his wife. 'It'll never be the same again,' wailed Annette, staring after the departing gig. 'They were like a family to me.'

'Then why didn't you go with them? You know how much they're going to miss you,' said Madeleine.

'Why, what would I be doing in Fontenay-sous-Bois? Besides, they've become a bit too grand since acquiring a Counsel to the King's Bench as a son-in-law. If Gabrielle had married an ordinary fellow in trade, do you think old Charpentier would have sold up and run out on his customers?'

'I don't know, Annette. Perhaps they just want time to enjoy their grandchildren.'

'Grandchildren?' exclaimed Annette in astonishment.

'Why, yes. Do you mean to say your sharp eyes haven't noticed?' teased Madeleine. 'Our King's counsel is to be a father in April.'

Madeleine was always a welcome visitor at the Dantons' new home in the Cordelier quarter of the Left Bank, an area populated by writers, printers and theatre people. Their comfortable apartment in the Cour du Commerce became a focal meeting place for ambitious, articulate and inspired people. Madeleine revelled in the whole new world that had opened up for her, but, like Gabrielle, she sat silent through discussions on Rousseau and Corneille, unable to contribute, content to absorb and learn from others' excitement and anger.

It was after such an evening, when walking home, that Madeleine became aware of a shadowy figure lurking outside The Parnasse. Immediately she stiffened with anxiety, for although the Vicomte de Cramoisy, after questioning everyone at the laundry to no effect, had apparently abandoned his search for her, she had not lost her fear of him. Slowly she moved forward, instinct telling her she was being watched. Suddenly a figure detached itself from the shadows and ran forward towards her. Before she could scream or run, the man's arms were around her.

With a cry of joy, she realised that the stranger hugging and kissing her was not an assassin of the Palais-Royal but a delighted brother.

'Pierre, is it really you? You've grown so tall,' she laughed, pushing him away from her. 'Come inside where I can see you properly.'

The restaurant had long since closed and from the soft glow from the window above, Madeleine knew that Monsieur and Madame Maulu, the new owners, and Annette had retired for the night. Just as she was about to lead Pierre around to the side entrance another figure came out of the shadows.

'It's a friend,' said Pierre, laying a reassuring hand on her arm. 'I'd be grateful, Madeleine, if you could give us both something to eat, we're both starving.'

Disappointed that she was not to be with her brother alone after so long a time, she led both men into the kitchen and lit the big oil lamp. As she turned with a polite smile towards her brother's companion, it took all her restraint not to scream. For his appearance was truly terrifying. His hair was unkempt and hung around his neck in greasy strands, whilst his yellowish eyes continually moved, rolling wildly in their sockets. Madeleine found it hard to meet the man's gaze — not only because of their perpetual movement, but because of their wild expression of hatred.

Collecting herself, she calmly bade both men sit down and gave them a bottle of wine. Then she cut some slices of beef from a left-over joint and warmed up the remains of some vegetable soup.

Both men ate like famished animals. As she watched them she hoped that Monsieur Maulu would not mind. Certainly, for Pierre, he would not begrudge one bit; for he would be delighted the brother she had talked about so frequently was at last returned to France.

'I'm sorry there isn't any bread,' she said. 'There hasn't been any in Paris for days.'

The mad, yellowish eyes stared up at her. A piece of bloodied beef hung between the loose, slack lips as her brother's companion paused in mid-bite at her words. 'Is there ever any bread for the people of France?' he snarled. 'Soon I will tell the starving they have the right to cut another man's throat and devour his palpitating flesh.'

Sickened and horrified at his words, Madeleine

turned to Pierre. But he was looking at the gesticulating man, his face filled with admiration. 'You see, Madeleine,' he said, 'Paul is going to produce a paper and I am going to help him print it.'

Dumbfounded Madeleine just stared at her brother. Had he taken leave of his senses to consort with a man so clearly deranged? But he had changed. He had lost his boyish softness and merriment. Gone was the Pierre of her childhood who cheerfully delivered Monsieur Mergault's laundry, whistling as he pulled his cart through the streets of the Faubourg Saint-Antoine. Gone too the eager apprentice of the Palais-Royal who joked and laughed with Philippe and the other boys. He talked now of compassion for the poor, yet his eyes were cruel, mean. For one instant, she disliked him. Then, ashamed, she swiftly changed the topic of conversation. 'Tell me about England.'

Just for a moment the old teasing Pierre appeared. 'Well, it's full of English ... it's green and the food is quite dreadful. And the wine, unspeakable! However, I have to confess the girls ... well, they're much prettier.'

With a laughing shriek of protest, Madeleine clipped her brother across the ears and they laughed just as they used to, forgetting the presence of the other man until his rasping voice cut through. 'Tell your sister about your work, Pierre.'

At once the young man's eyes lit up with the fervour that Madeleine had seen before when he had looked at Lafayette on the rue Saint-Honoré. 'Oh yes, Madeleine, you should see the work the London factory is producing. It's all smuggled back into France, either through Bordeaux or through Holland.'

'But why London, Pierre? With the printing

presses at the Palais-Royal, I've never understood why you went to London.'

'Because there are no police agents of the King of France there,' he said, shrugging his shoulders impatiently, 'and when the Duc d'Orléans takes over the throne, the pamphlets which are flooding the new political clubs and the Masonic Lodges will not be so easily traced to him. The English don't care; they turn a blind eye to our presence.'

'But surely the Duc d'Orléans will never topple Louis?'

'Well, he's spending a lot of money . . .'

'Let him,' snarled Paul Marat, thumping the table with his fist. 'We, the people, can wait!'

Madeleine picked up the two dirty plates. As she did so, Pierre touched her arm. 'Can we stay the night?'

She looked at his thin, strained face, and then at Paul Marat, and thought of the kindly patron upstairs asleep who had kept her on so readily. 'You may stay, Pierre, just for tonight. But I am afraid, Monsieur, I cannot offer you hospitality which is not mine to give. Pierre is my brother and you are a stranger to me.'

The short, thin man nodded in understanding, but Pierre flushed with anger. 'Then I'll go too,' he said abruptly. As he reached the door he paused and looked at her, his eyebrow raised scornfully. 'One day, Madeleine, you and the people of France will find your liberty through men like Paul Marat.'

Wearily she locked the door and went upstairs to bed. For a long time she lay awake thinking of Pierre and the disturbing Paul Marat. Their conversation, their aspirations seemed more brutal than at the supper table in the Cour de Commerce. Yet the men had one thing in common: the belief that they would change the order of things. Like Gabrielle, she sensed that she was caught up with people who would affect her life and those around her. She touched the ring on its leather thong, now smooth from its constant contact with her body. What would happen to the officer of Louis XVI's fleet in the approaching winds of change? One thing she was certain of: he would not be at Paul Marat's side.

' "Go and tell your master that we are here by the will of the people and that we shall not stir from our seats unless forced to do so by bayonets." '

'The will of the people,' repeated Annette, her eyes wide with wonder as Monsieur Charpentier, with his glasses perched on the end of his nose, read from his paper the Comte de Mirabeau's words at Versailles. Monsieur Charpentier cleared his throat and silence fell around Gabrielle's table. 'Then,' he continued, 'Bailly rose and said: "The assembled nation cannot be given orders." '

'What does it mean?' asked Madame Charpentier, anxiously turning to her son-in-law.

'What does it mean, Maman . . . ? Why, it means we, the people, have given our King his first order.' Georges laughed, smashing his fist down on the crisp white linen cloth so that the knives and forks jumped into the air.

'It means,' said Monsieur Charpentier, laying down his paper and removing his glasses, 'that the Third Estate will give us a Constitution. But I fear,' he said, shaking his head, 'that though Louis is anxious for reform, he will be persuaded by his ministers to crush the new National Assembly with force.'

'Then we must fight,' declared Madeleine.

Georges's swift, shrewd eyes for a moment rested on the girl with interest. Then he picked up his knife and proceeded to carve slices from a plump, juicy

107

capon. 'Yes, it is inevitable,' he replied, handing a plate of meat to Madame Charpentier. 'The Queen and her party will bring pressure to bear on him and our well-meaning monarch will give way and scurry back into his workshop.'

'Georges, dear, Papa and Maman haven't come to visit us to hear politics,' admonished Gabrielle, looking adoringly at her husband. 'And I'm sure Annette and Madeleine don't want to listen either, for it's all the lawyers can talk about at The Parnasse. Tell me, dears, how are things going for you both?'

'Very well indeed,' replied Annette, somehow managing to speak whilst her cheeks bulged with food. 'Of course it's not as successful as when you were there, Madame Charpentier, and we miss taking lunch with you and Monsieur. That is why it's such a treat to be invited here today,' she said, sending an ingratiating smile across the table to Gabrielle.

'And what about you, Madeleine?' asked Monsieur Charpentier, adjusting the angle of his little grey wig. Madeleine smiled at the familiar nervous gesture.

'Yes, I find Monsieur Maulu a kind employer.'

'There are no suitors yet?' he enquired, his round face breaking into a kindly beam.

'She sends them all packing,' snorted Annette, as Madeleine blushed, finding herself the centre of attention. 'Well that's not quite right,' said Annette, correcting herself. 'She either ignores them or hides away, like the other day, when a young man from the Palais-Royal came looking for her. A nice-looking boy too, with hair as black as a raven's wing,' she said wistfully.

'It sounds as though you're the one looking for suitors, Annette!' interjected Georges Danton with a roar of laughter.

'Georges dear, hush!' murmured Gabrielle, seeing the fat young woman's face quiver with emotion. 'Now let me hurry you all along,' she said firmly. 'I want you all to see Georges's study which I've had decorated in the most daring shade of red.'

For her part, Madeleine was glad the subject of suitors had been dropped. She had known very well who her caller from the Palais-Royal had been: it was Philippe. But she had not wanted to see him. Not because of mistrust: she liked him. No, somehow she felt he would remind her of things she wished to forget. Pierre, she knew, would make his own way to her.

Later, as Madeleine and Annette walked back to The Parnasse arm in arm, they felt once more part of that loving family circle.

On Sunday 12 July 1789, Madeleine had promised that Annette could go with her to see the fountains at Saint-Cloud. Monsieur Maulu kindly offered them the loan of the horse and cart which she and Annette usually drove to market. So, armed with some refreshments, they set off early in the day.

The fountains were beautiful; their upward surging plumes of white quite breathtaking and hypnotic.

'I can see why the Queen wanted the Château so much,' sighed Madeleine as she and Annette walked back to their cart.

'Yes. It was rumoured the Duc d'Orléans wanted ten million for it!'

'And no doubt that was reported in one of your scandal sheets,' laughed Madeleine, amused at Annette's authoritative air.

'Well, whatever she paid, it's just another example of the woman's extravagance ... what about over there?' Annette said, pointing to a sunny spot beneath some trees, away from the road.

While Annette fussed, laying out their picnic, Madeleine gathered foliage which she threaded under the old horse's bridle to keep off the flies. Then she sat down beside Annette, glad to have left behind the city, its smells and tensions.

'Mm, this is delicious, Annette,' she said, biting into a piece of pâté. 'You really are a marvellous cook. You should be working for some great lord. What would you really like, Annette? Would you like to work in the royal kitchens at Saint-Cloud, or at Versailles?'

'Oh no, nothing like that,' replied Annette, her round face glowing with pleasure. 'I'd like to own a café, not as big as The Parnasse. But I've no head for figures . . . I'd need someone to help me,' she added a little awkwardly.

Madeleine sensed the longing and loneliness in the young woman's voice and looked at her with surprise. 'You mean a husband?' she asked gently.

Annette blushed scarlet; her plump white hand picked some crumbs from her skirt. 'I know I'm not much to look at,' she said, smoothing back the thin layer of mousy hair, 'and I shouldn't eat so much . . .'

'But many men like curvaceous women, Annette. Perhaps if you could just eat fewer pastries and walk more. I'll walk with you. You'll soon see, someone will notice your sparkling eyes.'

'Do you think so? Well, at least,' laughed Annette, 'I won't have to give up pastries. The way things are going, there'll be no food coming into Paris, with all those Swiss and German troops in tents on the Champs de Mars, and the regiments camped around Paris. The Queen intends to starve us all to death.'

'It does seem very threatening,' sighed Madeleine. 'There is no grain to be had anywhere. But I don't think it's the court, I think it's businessmen holding back supplies to raise prices. Anyway,' she said, rolling over on to her back, 'let's just enjoy the countryside.'

Silently Annette considered Madeleine as she lay stretched out on the daisy-strewn grass. Grudgingly she had to admit that Madeleine had a very good figure, the kind that she yearned for; but for once the cook was not filled with the deep resentment, sometimes verging on bitter hatred, which she usually felt against those blessed with beauty. Madeleine was different: she never flaunted herself; indeed it was as if she deliberately went out of her way to make herself unattractive. Though this pleased Annette, it also puzzled her. Thoughtfully she bit into a piece of cheese, and for some moments concentrated on its full creamy texture.

'If you smartened yourself up,' she said, a sudden generosity possessing her, 'I bet you could catch a rich husband.'

Half-dozing, the unexpectedness of the observation shocked Madeleine into opening her eyes wide, to see Annette gaping at her with avid curiosity. Somehow, it struck her as funny and she was seized with helpless laughter. Then, realising that her merriment was making Annette uncomfortable, she made an effort to compose herself, acknowledging that for the first time, Annette had said something nice. Earlier on in their relationship, Madeleine had realised that when, on Sundays, she put on Gabrielle's brown velvet dress and brushed her hair into coils, Annette's behaviour towards her changed, and not for the better. So it became no hardship to neglect her appearance: it suited her own purpose and it made Annette happier.

'A rich husband you say,' repeated Madeleine, still with a faint smile on her lips. 'Do you mean an old, rich husband, or a young, rich husband?' she teased.

'Well, I suppose as you're only a kitchen-girl, it

would have to be an old one,' replied Annette, her small lips pursing as she considered. 'A fair exchange you see: you would enjoy his money, and he would enjoy your youth and the envy of younger men.'

'No, I don't like the sound of that,' said Madeleine, spinning a daisy between her fingers.

'Well, what would you like?' asked Annette impatiently.

'I would like,' said Madeleine, slitting with her fingernail into the thin green stalk of the daisy, 'first of all to be an officer in the navy and be stationed at Brest ... or ...' she said, slipping another daisy through the moist slit, 'I would like to own a printing press.'

Annette puffed out her cheeks with astonishment. The typhoid had obviously left its mark on Madeleine's brain, for the girl was clearly half-mad.

It was late in the afternoon when they returned to Paris. They noticed with pleasure as they drove into the city that another hated customs barrier had been burnt. At once they were aware of confusion and excitement. A man rushed up to them, a bunch of chestnut leaves sticking up from his hatband.

'I see you've got your cockade,' he laughed, looking up at the chestnut leaves hanging over the horse's forelock. All around Madeleine saw people carrying branches of horse chestnut. Everywhere the long green leaves fluttered from hats and lapels.

'What's happening?' she asked.

'Don't you know?' asked the man in surprise. 'Why, Necker has been dismissed and Camille Desmoulins, the lawyer, has called upon the people to take up arms. The dragoons fired upon a peaceful demonstration on Place de Louis XV, but,' he cried, tossing his hat in the air, 'the French guards from the Chausée d'Antin barracks declared for the Third

Estate and put the murderers to flight.' He ran on and Madeleine whipped on the horse.

The next day the restaurant buzzed with just one topic. Would the king order the troops to attack the city? Madeleine guessed that her brother Pierre was deeply involved in the rioting and the burning of the customs posts, but he had not been to see her very often and was silent about his activities.

So when he called upon her on the Tuesday to accompany him to the Café de la Monnaie on the rue de Roule, she was very surprised and, fearing that the frightening Paul Marat would be there, she hesitated, reluctant to go.

'I'm not sure, Pierre. Monsieur Maulu may need me.'

'Never mind about the patron. France needs you; or have you forgotten what an empty belly is like, Madeleine?' he glared down at her fiercely. 'You've had an easy life compared to those sleeping out under the bridges. Dying in their hundreds in the winter frosts. But then you've had me to look after you, and now you've charmed your way into getting two good meals a day. No, you've forgotten Father and Tremoïlles and the way they made him suffer for some grains of salt. Do you think they've ever wanted for salt or bread?' he shouted, shaking his fists after a gilded coach.

'It's not true; I haven't forgotten,' she cried.

'Yes you have,' he snapped. 'Your old friends are forgotten. Philippe told me you wouldn't see him; and when was the last time you called on poor Simone Evrard. No, you only think of yourself, Madeleine, and mixing with the Dantons.' He turned on his heel.

Tears of shame filled Madeleine's eyes. His words had wounded deeply; how could she explain her feelings about Philippe and the Palais-Royal? But it

113

was true about Simone. The woman's lack of education and the filthy state in which she lived had led Madeleine to abandon her. Filled with guilt she ran after him. 'Pierre, wait, I'm coming. I'll help.'

The Café de la Monnaie was crowded when they arrived; the air was thick and hazy with tobacco smoke. Evidently Pierre was well known, for a shout went up when he entered, and many men stood up to embrace him as he led Madeleine to the centre of the room. With amazement, she saw that the dark-haired man rising to greet them was no stranger. She had seen the sallow consumptive face, the narrow eyes before. Here was the fugitive of the rue Saint-Honoré. The man who had handed her that letter so long ago, and whom she knew to be Stanislas Maillard. He embraced Pierre, and the suspicious eyes briefly inspected Madeleine, but he gave no sign of recognition. After the waiter had served them drinks, he spoke; his voice was low, intense. 'We need more weapons, and quickly, before they can dissolve the National Assembly. We must meet force with force. Tonight arms must be obtained; and tomorrow from the Invalides.'

'The troops on the Champs-de-Mars have pledged their allegiance to the Third Estate. They promised me not to fire on the people,' said Pierre.

'Good man,' said Stanislas Maillard, 'you've done your work well. The sections must be alerted to build barricades tonight. Tomorrow we assemble before the Invalides. I leave you to pass the word,' he said, rising to leave.

Madeleine was relieved that he had departed. Though subdued, this Stanislas Maillard was as sinister as Paul Marat, she thought. There seemed little to choose between either of them.

That night there was to be no sleep. With a group of young men and Pierre, Madeleine raced through the city, alerting all the sections, giving instructions for the following day, leaving them to build their barricades. They then broke into the gunsmiths' shops, taking anything that would fire.

By dawn, sixty thousand people bound in common purpose stood calling for arms outside the Invalides. No one seemed tired. Indeed many, like Madeleine, had never felt more alive. Her spine tingled with excitement. Breaking into the shops had been thrilling and for the first time she understood there might be more to robbery than acquisition.

Curiously Madeleine looked at the people surrounding her before the Invalides. There were fishwives, respectable matrons, priests, butchers and wealthy nobles. It seemed that all Paris had come to defend the city; and the right of the Third Estate to have its Assembly.

Impatiently Madeleine stood on tiptoe trying to see over the shoulders of the man before her. 'Has the Governor opened the gate yet?' she asked her brother.

'No, you'd soon tell if he had,' replied Pierre. 'We'd be pushed forward. He's as bad as that lily-livered Jacques Flesselles at the Hôtel-de-Ville. They'll both pay for their reluctance,' he said darkly.

Suddenly there was a movement and a great cheer went up. 'I think they're through,' yelled Pierre, grabbing her hand. 'Start moving forward or you'll be pushed over.'

Holding tightly on to him, Madeleine moved on. They were some distance from the front, nearer to the edge of the throng. Suddenly from the ranks at the front, a new cry was taken up. 'No powder . . . to the Bastille . . . to the Bastille!'

'Come on!' cried Pierre, jerking her sideways, pulling her through after him till they broke free.

'They're right, there's powder there, barrels of it were taken there yesterday.'

Because Pierre had acted so quickly, they were ahead of the crowd, enabling them to run through the city towards the Place de la Bastille.

Approaching the great fortress down the rue Saint-Antoine, Madeleine looked up at the eight towers rising twenty-five metres high against a grey and threatening sky. 'We must be crazy,' she whispered.

But Pierre was not listening; he was pushing his way forward through those who had come direct from the Hôtel-de-Ville.

Fearing that they would be separated, Madeleine pushed forward and grabbed hold of his coat tail. He turned, giving her one of his old cheery grins, and she was glad she was with him, sharing his danger.

Already the other approach roads were filling up as people poured into the rues des Tournelles and Jean Beaussire so that, bit by bit, they were pushed into the Cour de Passage of the Bastille.

Astonishingly, surrounded by so many people, they found themselves next to Philippe and some of the apprentices of the Palais-Royal. He was the last person she wished to be near but, to her relief, he acted as if nothing had happened.

The slim, dark-haired young man kissed Madeleine warmly on both cheeks. 'Why, Mademoiselle, how you've grown! But for Pierre, I would not have known you,' he grinned impishly. 'Life has been very dull since you left ... My, what a bad temper you left the Vicomte in; I believe you quite put a certain Marquis off young ladies for ever. Perhaps,' he added in a lower tone, 'he has put a certain young lady off men for ever?'

Madeleine blushed and laughed nervously.

'Don't worry,' he continued, 'your Vicomte isn't here. In fact he's not even in Paris.'

'Is Henri here?' asked Madeleine, feeling more at ease.

'Naturally,' replied Philippe, thrusting back his straight black hair from his forehead. 'He's behind us somewhere: we got separated.'

Madeleine turned round but she could not see the printer. She saw that Pierre was looking up at the cannon at the tip of the tower. 'Do you think they'll fire on us, Philippe?'

'Well, they've trained those eight-pounders to fire down along the approach roads, so they must be considering it. But let us hope it won't come to that. The lawyer, Thuriot de la Rozère, has just gone in with a second delegation to persuade the Governor to allow a citizens' militia to take over . . .'

His last words were drowned by terrified screams. 'Dear God, save us, they're pulling back the cannon!'

True enough, as Madeleine and her companions looked up, the guns were being withdrawn for firing. There would be carnage, no escape for any of them. What cowards, she thought contemptuously. Blinded with anger, her fear forgotten, she shouted with all those around her. 'Down with the Bastille . . . we want the Bastille . . . down with the Bastille!'

'Look!' cried Pierre, 'over there.'

Madeleine followed his pointing finger and saw a group of men had climbed on top of one of the shop roofs which lined the north side of the Cour de Passage. From it, they had reached the walk along the rampart wall. Nimbly keeping their balance, they were now running along it. A silence fell as everyone followed their progress. Then, as they dropped down into the Cour du Gouvernement, a loud, long cheer like the crash of thunder erupted as the heavy drawbridge and footbridge, cut free from their cables, crashed down across the moat.

There was no turning back, nor did any think to try as they hurled themselves forward across the moat into the Cour du Gouvernement. Filled with a fierce elation, Madeleine ran through under the archway and then halted, uncertain where to go. On her left across another wide deep moat was the entrance into the Bastille itself.

'Down with the drawbridge,' someone shouted defiantly.

From across the yawning gap behind the firmly shut drawbridge, a voice cried: 'Withdraw or we will open fire.'

'Down with the drawbridge . . .! Down with the Bastille!' responded the crowd. At once the crack of musketry fire broke out.

'Over here, Madeleine,' yelled Pierre, as a hail of balls fell into the courtyard. Without hesitation she ran after him, seeking cover in a small passage that ran between the guard house and the Governor's quarters.

Several of the men, she saw, were bleeding, though no one had been killed.

'It's impossible to launch an attack in the open,' said one of the men. 'We'll be cut to pieces.'

'What we need,' said an old soldier, 'is a smoke screen.'

'Yes, burning hay,' said Pierre excitedly. 'Madeleine, run to the brewer Santerre, tell him we need two wagons filled with hay.'

'I'll go,' said Philippe, frowning. 'It's not right to endanger Madeleine.'

'Can you spring like her?' asked Pierre crossly. 'Besides, they'll not fire on a girl,' he said, pulling Madeleine's cap off so that her hair fell about her shoulders.

'I wouldn't count on that,' replied the apprentice tersely.

'It's all right, Philippe. Listen, they've stopped firing. Pierre's right.' Without waiting, Madeleine took three deep breaths and launched forward across the open clearing towards the drawbridge. Her feet barely touched the planking and whether they had fired she knew not, so great was her concentration.

On the other side the press was as great as ever. 'Let me through,' she shouted, 'we need two fire wagons from Santerre's brewery.'

The men around her took up her cry and eager volunteers ran off to the brewery. They returned shortly and Madeleine, sheltering behind the piled-up hay, went back across to the Cour with Santerre and the men.

The flaming hay sparked and shot sheets of orange flame into the air. Behind a pall of smoke the attackers fired at the soldiers of the Salis Samade regiment, safe and secure behind the five-metre walls. Madeleine, crouching on the ground, loaded the men's guns as quickly as her inexperienced fingers allowed. Their attack, she could see, was pitiful. Already three of their number were dead and several were badly wounded. She imagined the fine officers within laughing at their attempts, and bit her lip in fury as she rammed the rod down the barrel of a gun.

From the Cour de Passage, a tremendous roar went up and then came a rumbling as though something heavy was being dragged across the bridge. She looked around, wiping the sweat and soot from her face. Despair replaced delight as an officer appeared, leading the Gardes-Françaises and a cannon. Quickly they lined up before the drawbridge into the Bastille.

As the lieutenant opened fire, a tall officer who

had placed four more cannon at a different angle, also roared his command.

From the battlements a white flag was waved, but everyone kept on firing, too many lay dead.

'Total capitulation,' shouted Pierre, holding his hand out to her for a new gun.

'Look,' she said, 'they're pushing a note out through a slit in the door. We'll need a plank to reach it . . .'

Without bothering to take the gun from her, the boy ran across the drawbridge leading back to the Cour de Passage. 'Send for a long plank,' he yelled.

Just as quickly as the carts had arrived, so did two carpenters with a plank. One of them ran along it to grab the note, but as he reached sideways to seize it Madeleine, with horror, saw him sway and overbalance into the moat below. Immediately another man ran forward: it was Stanislas Maillard. Successful, holding the note high in the air, he ran back along the narrow plank and handed it over to the officer behind the cannon. The tall, bearded giant glanced once at it then roared like a lion. 'De Launay states that he is prepared to blow up the Bastille and the whole district with it. What do you say to that, my friends?'

'No capitulation! Down with the bridges!' responded Madeleine with her friends. 'Down with the Bastille!'

Chapter Three

For a *vainqueur de la Bastille* there was to be no anonymity, as Madeleine soon found. Hundreds of citizens were curious to explore the silent gloomy corridors and remote towers of the grim fortress. For hundreds of years it had been shrouded in mystery and now it was open for all to see. Children, wide-eyed with self-induced terror, asked to be led down to the torture chambers. And though isolation was, in truth, the only form of torture practised at the Bastille, still the visitors chose to believe otherwise.

Chosen as a guide with many of those who had flung themselves across the final drawbridge on that momentous day, Madeleine felt embarrassed by the admiring regard of those who queued for hours to gain admittance. She, like many, had simply been carried along by the momentum of the occasion. Now they had become national heroes, on display as much as the Bastille. Like a vanguard, they had led the realisation of the Comte de Mirabeau's words, 'the will of the people'. It now existed! Its power had been witnessed!

As Madeleine guided groups of visitors, anxious for a glimpse of the prison before it was demolished, she was seized with an idea. Though not a stone of the prison was to be left standing, it was evident that for years Frenchmen and foreigners would make their pilgrimage to the site. Upon learning that a Monsieur Palloy had been awarded the demolition contract, Madeleine went to see him. 'Monsieur Palloy,' she said, rushing into his office, 'I understand tomorrow you are sending 1,000 workmen to tear down the Bastille?'

'That is correct, Mademoiselle,' replied the builder.

'Then I would like to buy a quantity of the stone.'

'That's not a problem,' shrugged the man. 'Some of it is earmarked for a bridge and works – you can buy all that's left. But what do you intend to do with it?'

'That, Monsieur, is my secret.'

The thick-set contractor rubbed his chin thoughtfully. He knew the girl had been amongst the first into the great fortress. She had also been a guide during the summer months at the Bastille. Suddenly his eyes cleared with comprehension. 'Well done, Mademoiselle. You're more far-sighted than I. You have seen what I have not. Every Frenchman is going to want his souvenir of tyranny. It's a splendid idea!' he cried excitedly. Madeleine bit her lip in annoyance. Now he had discovered her purpose the price of the stone would escalate.

'Come now, Mademoiselle, this is no time for sulking,' said Palloy, seeing her downcast face. 'You're the first to approach me, but be assured that by tomorrow there will be others who could take the whole quantity of stone off my hands. Can you do that?' he asked, keenly observing her.

'Well, no, not all of it,' replied Madeleine, conscious that unless she raised a loan she could not buy more than a few pebbles.

'And do you have a yard for storage?'

'I thought perhaps, Monsieur Palloy, you might be

prepared to keep it for me until I have acquired suitable premises,' she said hopefully.

The builder looked at the young girl's earnest expression and her tightly clenched fists. He sighed, remembering his own youth. She was trying to make something of herself, taking that first unnerving step into business. That, too, required courage. 'Don't worry about storage,' he said kindly, his shrewd eyes relaxing. 'You've seized an opportunity and you have shown me the way. Now, where do you intend to sell your souvenirs?'

'From a booth on the Pont-Neuf and perhaps from a basket in the streets.'

'Yes, you'll do a fair trade there, but you'll not use a great quantity. Nor, I suspect, have you the resources to set stone in gold and silver for the luxury trade?'

Madeleine shook her head. 'No, Monsieur. I was thinking of simple things, like door-jams and paper-weights . . . perhaps simple pendants on ribbons and such.'

'Exactly,' he said. 'Your trade would not threaten mine. Yes, Mademoiselle, I am going to steal your idea, but in return I will let you use my yard whenever you wish, taking stone sufficient for your immediate needs. Should your business greatly increase, then we'll come to an arrangement for a low fixed price for the stone. Agreed?' he asked, stretching out his hand.

'Agreed,' laughed Madeleine, taking the rough hand, her eyes sparkling with excitement at the prospect of becoming a woman of business.

The money to launch her small enterprise had come from an unexpected source. Since 14 July, Madeleine had been spending time with many of the companions who had fought around her on that glorious day. In particular, a tall student who had loaded one of the four cannon regularly sought her companionship. He was an American, tall and very strong, but of a gentle and quiet disposition. Not thinking for one moment that Thomas Adams was different from any of the impoverished circle of friends who had begun to meet in the Cordelier quarter, Madeleine told him of her problem. The next day he called at The Parnasse and shyly pressed on her a loan.

It was, of course, a great disappointment to the Maulus when she announced her intention of leaving The Parnasse. But, filled with admiration and enthusiasm for her enterprise, they gave her their blessing. Whereas Annette, right up to the day of her departure, could hardly bring herself to speak, sulking like a child, avoiding Madeleine's eyes, and all the while muttering under her breath about ingratitude.

But on the last day, when Madeleine carried down her small box of belongings, she appeared at the kitchen door holding the corner of her white apron to her eyes, then disappeared and returned with a cardboard box. 'It's just a tart,' she sniffed. 'Thought you might be hungry tonight.'

'Oh Annette,' said Madeleine, taking the gift, 'thank you. It will probably make me feel very homesick for you all.' She leant forward and kissed the round, tear-stained face. 'But I shall see you every day. My stall will be just outside on the bridge and my room is very near to Gabrielle's, so I'll still see you often for Sunday dinner. And when I've made my fortune, I shall buy somewhere just like The Parnasse and you shall come and run it.'

At once the lively eyes gleamed with interest and the small mouth, for the first time in days, smiled. 'See that you do then,' she said fiercely to Madeleine, 'and no getting into trouble with that brother of yours.'

With Thomas Adams' help, Madeleine had found a two-roomed apartment on the rue Crébillon. Though small, it was perfect for her needs, as it led out into a tiny yard, allowing her to keep a working stock of stones, whilst inside the apartment she made the larger of the two rooms into a store and a workroom.

During the winter months she worked into the early hours of the morning building up her stock in readiness for the hundreds of deputies who would be converging on Paris the following summer for the first Fête de la Fédération. There was no time to sit with Pierre and his friends in the cafés, dreaming of a better world. She had a loan to repay and a living to earn. Nonetheless, like every other woman in the district, she had answered the bell of Sainte Marguerite in the Faubourg Saint-Antoine, leaving her work to march with the fishwives on Versailles. In their hundreds they had marched, driven on through the October rain by anger and hunger, to demand bread from their King.

Now, three months later, the situation was little improved. Bread was still scarce and expensive, costing more than half of a labourer's daily wage. But at least they had the King in Paris, thought Madeleine, working late in her apartment on the rue Crébillon.

She started to hum softly as she patiently lined small presentation boxes with tricolor ribbon. Whenever she thought of their muddy day of triumph in October, two women's faces appeared in her mind: one in a yellow and white striped dressing-gown – a queen who stood alone on her balcony, unbending before a sea of hate, her courage diluting it, turning for a moment the tide; the other, a marquise, showing a face of fear – bewildered as she peeped out

125

through her carriage window surrounded by a dancing forest of bread rolls on pikes.

At the time Madeleine was part of that jubilant escort, perched astride one of the cannon, singing with those around her that they were bringing the baker and his family back to Paris. Impishly seizing a young hussar's hat, she had placed it over her own cap and with mock gravity waved a dramatic salute at him. Immediately he had closed up on one of the royal carriages. It was then that she saw the pretty blue eyes staring at her through the carriage window. Their expression held and upset her, for they were not only filled with horror, but a kind of contempt. She had wanted to run up to the fair-haired young woman, reassure her that they were not going to harm anyone, but the contempt had held her away.

Lining the last presentation box, Madeleine sighed with anger and frustration. Perhaps she was glad, after all, that they had frightened the ladies in their silks and laces. What had they cared for the starving and the poor? She hoped that one day the young aristocrat would know the feel of an empty, clawing belly.

She rose, dismissing her angry thoughts and started to fill each box with a small piece of Bastille stone. Suddenly a low insistent knocking on her street door broke the silence of the night.

Seizing the candle, she ran through into the tiny hallway. 'Who's there?' she whispered.

'Pierre . . . Let me in . . . hurry!'

Hastily, Madeleine unlocked and flung the door wide and her brother, followed by Jean-Paul Marat, pushed past her. Sensing danger from their manner, she thrust the bolts of the worm-eaten door home, top and bottom, and followed both men through to her small living room. Already Marat was at the window overlooking the street.

126

'I think we've lost them,' he said. 'No, wait, they've just come out of the alley opposite. Is there a back way out?' he asked Madeleine, drawing the curtain back into place. She shook her head, feeling the sides of her throat contract and her stomach heave as she looked at his face. It was a mass of oozing pus-filled sores. 'It's from hiding out in the sewers,' he replied to her unasked question. He walked towards her with his customary jerky movement. 'Is there somewhere we can hide? They'll be here soon.'

Sickened, Madeleine recoiled from the stench of him and turned to find that Pierre, too, was covered in a filthy greenish slime. Thankfully his skin was clear of sores but it was of ghastly pallor and his eyes were filled with fear. Before she had time to speak to him there was a heavy knocking on the door. 'Quick, both of you. Under the bed,' she whispered, pointing towards the small bed in the corner of the room.

Hurriedly she tore off her dress and put on her nightgown. Again, the heavy knocking, and this time a man's insistent voice. 'Open!'

With one swift movement, Madeleine pulled back the bed covers and rumpled them. Then, checking that both men were concealed by the hanging covers, she ran outside into the hallway. 'All right, all right, I'm coming,' she muttered in a sleepy cross voice. 'Who are you, what do you want?'

'We are police agents. Open your door at once!'

Grumbling and without hurrying, Madeleine unlocked the door. 'Come through, gentlemen,' she said, at once taking the initiative. 'I'm sorry to have kept you waiting but, as you see, I was in bed.'

The taller of the two men, silver haired with hawk-like features, glanced at the rumpled bed linen and the girl's sleepy face. 'Two dangerous criminals were seen entering this apartment,' he said, wrinkling his nose in obvious disgust at the foul smell pervading the room. 'Where are they?'

Madeleine shrugged, smiling inwardly; knowing that she now had the advantage, for Marat had seen them searching the house opposite . . . 'Monsieur,' she sighed, 'if you think you will find dangerous criminals here, please search. But I think you will find there is no one here . . . apart, that is, from two dead rats under the floorboards.'

With relief, the girl saw her casual, relaxed manner had struck the right note. Although the silver-haired man gestured for his younger companion to go through into the other room, it was evident that he believed her and was anxious to depart the evil-smelling room.

'Go back to bed, Mademoiselle. If you should hear or see anything, ask for the Inspector at police headquarters. We'll make it worth your while.'

Madeleine opened the door leading out onto the street and, as the Inspector passed her, he paused. 'I'd do something about those rats if I were you.'

'Thank you, Monsieur, I will indeed.'

Quickly she shut the door before the man could see her laughter and waited until she could no longer hear their footsteps. Then, unable to restrain her merriment any longer, she ran back into her living room. 'You rats can come out now. They've gone away, near fainting for fresh air.'

Despite the winter night, the girl flung open the window, shivering as a draught of icy cold air blew into the room. 'I'm not sure whether I care for your reference to rats,' laughed her brother. 'You soon get used to the smell; after two days you don't even notice it.'

'I'd never get used to it,' retorted Madeleine, breathing in great gulps of air. 'But tell me, why do the police agents want you? Have you printed more attacks on our Mayor Bailly and Lafayette?'

Her brother nodded and looked to where Marat was sitting on a stool. 'He's got another of his headaches,' he said. 'We've been on the run for over a week without sleep. Can we stay just for tonight?'

Madeleine looked at Pierre's pleading eyes and across at the man crouched, holding his head between his hands. Like some wild creature in agony, he rocked back and forth, moaning and gnashing his teeth. No matter how vile she thought him, she was moved to pity at such a sight.

'Yes, I'll boil some water for you to wash. I'm sorry I have no clean linen for you. I will get some tomorrow.'

'Don't bother,' snapped the dry, croaky voice of Marat. 'If we're driven like rats into the sewers by Lafayette's agents, then we'll smell like rats.' He looked up at Madeleine, his wild, tormented eyes filled with hatred. He groaned, clutching his greasy hair as though gripped in mortal agony. 'At least,' he snarled through clenched teeth, 'it's not the smell of the aristos; the vile smell of wealth, produced on the rotting corpses of the people.' He cried out as another pain ripped through his head.

Disregarding his ravings, Madeleine tore up a narrow length of linen and, dipping it in vinegar, wound it tightly around the man's head. 'This may relieve the pain a little,' she said. 'It's all I have . . . I'm not quite sure what to do for your skin.'

'Don't waste your time; nothing will help. I'm a doctor, I know it's useless. Just let me sleep.'

Pierre watched his sister as she tentatively dabbed at the running crust of sores on his companion's face. With a sense of surprise and sadness, he realised she was a young woman, no longer a child. Her thin cotton nightdress clung about her body revealing high, full breasts and rounded buttocks; legs that were long. Pierre smiled. They'd been long since she was a tiny girl, giving her an enormous burst of speed when she ran. How often they had raced through the alleys in the Faubourg Saint-Antoine, played at tag around the wall in the laundry yard.

Now he saw that his sister was beautiful and wondered why he had never noticed before. The Vicomte de Cramoisy had not been so slow to realise his sister's potential earning power, he thought grimly. He would have hired her out like a beast of burden. The thought fuelled his hatred. For the moment they would use the creatures of the Palais-Royal ... Later all of them would pay! Every damned aristo in France would pay!

Madeleine rose early the next day and stole quietly from her apartment, afraid of disturbing the exhausted men. Never had she seen Pierre look so tired and wretched. But his fatigue was more than physical; it was as though he was absorbing Marat's violence and anger and this, like rust, was beginning to eat into his being, corroding his spirit.

She walked to the bakery feeling lonely and isolated. Too young to remember either her father or mother, Pierre was all to her. Yet the longer he worked with Marat, the more she felt the gulf between them widen.

Already at the bakery there was a queue of a dozen women patiently waiting, shivering in their black woollen shawls. 'Good morning, Madeleine,' one of them called. 'How is the souvenir trade ... People tiring of bits of the Bastille?'

'Not yet,' smiled the young girl, 'the English especially seem to like taking it back across the Channel.'

'If they pulled down their Tower, they wouldn't need to,' rejoined Michel, a young artist. Then, turning to Madeleine, he lowered his voice. 'I'm glad I've seen you. My cousin is in the National Guard and he told me yesterday they have been ordered into the Cordelier quarter today. Bailly and Lafayette are sending in 3,000 troops to search for Marat. I know your brother helps him print his paper; I thought you might be able to warn them.'

'Thanks, Michel,' smiled Madeleine, pressing the fresh-faced student's hand in gratitude. 'If I see them, I'll warn them.'

The artist flushed with pleasure at her touch. 'If there's anything I can do, just let me know,' he said.

'Thanks, I'll remember,' said Madeleine, but decided not to involve him further. There was only one man who was powerful enough to deal with the situation and that was Georges Jacques Danton.

Leaving the bread queue, Madeleine hurriedly made her way to the apartment in the Cour de Commerce. She found Georges Danton working on a text for a new pamphlet.

'Good morning, Madeleine. You're an early visitor,' he said. 'Go through to the bedroom, Gabrielle is still in bed.'

'No, I won't disturb her. It's you I've come to see, Georges. I need your help. Lafayette is sending 3,000 troops into the Cordeliers today to arrest Marat and Pierre.'

'I'm not surprised,' commented Georges with one of his crooked smiles. 'Marat's attacks on our Commander of the National Guard and Bailly have been vigorous, to say the least. Where are they now?'

'With me.'

'Then you must move them quickly. Someone's bound to tell them you're Pierre's sister sooner or later.'

'Yes, two men from the Châtelet came to my

rooms last night. Fortunately they did not ask me my name.'

'Then it is only a matter of time before they correct their error. As for Bailly and Lafayette,' he roared, throwing back his great head, 'neither they nor their troops shall enter our quarter. I, Georges Jacques Danton, President of our district, will prevent it.'

'Georges, dear, what is it? What has happened?' cried his wife, rushing into the salon in her nightgown.

'Nothing for you to alarm yourself about, my love,' he said tenderly, stroking her long braided dark hair. 'Foreign troops are about to invade us and I, Georges Jacques Danton, will . . .'

'Foreign troops?' repeated Gabrielle, her face turning pale with alarm.

'Well, the National Guard,' admitted Danton, allaying her alarm; 'but Parisians or no, they still count as foreigners in our kingdom.'

'Oh, do be careful, Georges,' said Gabrielle, dropping her gaze down to her swollen body.

'I'm in no danger, my dear,' he replied reassuringly. 'But I intend to show that we are masters here. When the dauphin of the Cordeliers is born,' he said, playfully patting her belly, 'there will be none of Lafayette's tin soldiers in sight. Now, Madeleine, run to the curé and tell him to ring the tocsin, while I go to the District Assembly to arouse our patriots at the Tribune.'

Kissing Gabrielle goodbye, Madeleine did as she was bid. Soon the great bell of the Cordeliers and of Saint-Sulpice rang out their alarm. Within moments, people responding to the summons poured out on to the streets. Actors from the Théâtre Français, typesetters, journalists and students all rushed about excitedly, asking why the tocsin was ringing: so many prepared to fight to defend two fellow Cordeliers.

She left to search for Thomas Adams. By good fortune he found her, catching her by the shoulders as she dashed through the streets. 'Madeleine, I've been looking for you. Everyone says that the National Guard are coming to search for Pierre and Jean-Paul Marat.'

'It's true,' gasped Madeleine, regaining her breath. 'What do you want me to do?'

'Please don't let them take my brother!'

From the look in the American's grey eyes, Madeleine knew that the quiet giant of a man would shed the last drop of his blood in the attempt. Her heart filled with gratitude. Impulsively, she reached forward, cupping the golden-bearded chin between her hands and kissed him. At once she realised her mistake, for his usual expression of quiet reserve lifted, revealing such deep longing and passion that she looked away in panic. What a fool she had been not to guess why he had visited her so frequently, and helped her to set up her stall. Yet not once had he made a gesture or a sign. He had been content to wait until she made the move. Her heart tore with guilt and sorrow, knowing that she could never love this kind, gentle man in the way he loved her. Oh why had Thomas spoilt their friendship with such a look? And why did the thin cord around her waist with its ring biting into her flesh make it impossible for her to look at another man? To freeze at the thought of anyone but him.

'Thomas,' she said, avoiding his eyes, 'I can't let you endanger yourself for my brother.'

At once, from her voice and manner — usually so open; by the flush on the beautiful face, Thomas, a sensitive man, knew that he had misinterpreted her action. He controlled the disappointment in his voice; he could wait. She was sexually immature, shying away like a young colt whenever anyone tried to come close to her in a relationship. He had watched her in the cafés, rebuffing all advances. Deliberately dressing like a boy, avoiding everything that would expose her vulnerability. Something, someone had frightened her and she had withdrawn into her own world. But he had had enough women to recognise the passion and fire within her. Soon that sensuous body would make its own demands, forcing her to put aside her childlike fantasies and fears. When the moment came, he, Thomas Adams, would be there. Casually, in a brotherly manner, to set her at ease, he slapped her across the shoulder. 'Pierre is a good mate of mine. I'll not leave him to finish in some rat-infested cell. We *vainqueurs de la Bastille* must stick together, don't you think?'

'Yes,' replied Madeleine, relaxing; hoping that she had perhaps been mistaken. That the expression in his eyes had really only been affection for a friend.

'Then leave it to me,' said the big man, suddenly chuckling. 'I think I know how to get them out of Paris. Out of France if they think it necessary. And it will be the Americans who will help me!'

There had been no time to question Thomas on his intriguing rescue plan. The approaching drums of the National Guard had sped Madeleine and Thomas on their separate ways.

Now, however, at the Dantons' flat, Madeleine was, like the other friends present, filled with admiration for the audacity of Thomas's ruse.

'Ladies and Gentlemen,' boomed Georges Danton, holding up a bottle of wine, 'this is an occasion for celebration. We are about to drink the grapes of '84 in honour of our friend Thomas Adams' daring rescue of Marat, France's most gifted writer.'

'Ah no, I cannot drink to that,' stuttered Camille Desmoulins. 'The toast must be to a discerning American ambassador who had the good taste to ship French wine to a fellow countryman marooned in a wine-starved country! To Jefferson and Château-d'Yquem!'

'To Jefferson!' everyone cried, standing and raising their glasses.

'What a brilliant ruse that was,' said Madeleine as Tom helped her back into her seat.

'Not really,' he smiled, 'it was just luck. I'd heard that Jefferson was shipping a large consignment of wine to the London ambassador. It seemed an opportune way to smuggle Marat and your brother out of Paris.'

'I hope they weren't drunk when they arrived in Calais,' laughed Georges, raising a glass to his thick, sensuous lips. 'Mm, it really is an excellent year.'

'I hear, Gabrielle, that our little Danton is to play a leading role in celebrations for 20 June,' said Lucille Duplessis, her lively black eyes sparkling with interest.

'Yes,' laughed Gabrielle, 'but I'm not allowed to tell you anything. The Society of the Tennis Court Oath have planned the fête. Only Madeleine knows.'

'Well whatever it is, it should be something befitting a dauphin,' giggled Camille Desmoulin's pretty friend.

'Yes, I can't think why the neighbourhood have christened him so,' smiled Gabrielle.

'It's because he has big lungs like his father, Gabrielle. Don't you realise it took only one roar from the King of the Cordeliers to disperse the National Guard?' said Stanislas Fréron, an actor.

At Madeleine's side, Camille Desmoulins touched her arm. 'I have a new pamphlet with me, Madeleine. Is there any chance you could sell them for me tonight? I don't like to ask you really, because if you were caught . . .'

'Don't worry, Camille,' interjected Madeleine. 'I'm always very careful. They go under my souvenirs, and I can spot a police agent at a glance, even if he's disguised as a rustic with straw in his ears and a cowpat for a hat.'

'Thanks, Madeleine. I can always do with the money,' he said, pressing her hand warmly.

'Yes I know,' said Madeleine, looking at the lawyer's frayed cuffs. 'I suppose Lucille's parents haven't given permission yet for your engagement?'

The young man shook his head despondently, then tossed back his wavy hair in a defiant movement. 'They'll soon change their minds when I'm a famous writer.'

'But you're famous now, Camille!' boomed Georges, overhearing the end of their conversation. 'Why, everyone knows it was you who plucked the chestnut leaves and called Paris to arms.'

'And you, Madeleine,' asked Lucille Duplessis. 'As a *vainqueur de la Bastille*, what will you wear for the fête?'

'Ah,' said Madeleine, 'that is a closely guarded secret until the day.'

'Well, I hope for once they'll persuade you to look like a woman instead of an errand-boy,' boomed Danton across the table.

'I think, Georges,' replied Madeleine, not in the least embarrassed by his teasing, 'that even you will approve of my costume! And when you see what your son is going to do, why you will be put quite in the shade!'

On 20 June the sun shone and a canopy of young green summer leaves fluttered over the heads of excited young nymphs and shepherdesses as they gravely led guests to their places at the long tables set out in the Bois de Boulogne. For many days their mothers had sewn their costumes, proud that their own daughter had been chosen to represent their district.

Misty-eyed, Madeleine, standing at her assembly point, watched two small children, bedecked in tricolor ribbons, give out small posies of flowers to the ladies. Of all the children in Paris they had been singled out because their fathers had given their lives in the taking of the Bastille. For everyone it had been a day charged with emotion. All along the route to Versailles, old men, young mothers, merchants and soldiers had cheered and wept. Children had run alongside them, strewing flowers in their path. Madeleine, as the only woman *vainqueur de la Bastille*, led the procession, with six of the men. She and Thomas and Lieutenant Elie held stones of the Bastille. Behind, the other four men carried a tablet of bronze, bearing the inscription of the Tennis Court Oath. Following them were the deputies of the Third Estate who were going to renew their oath – never to disband until they had given France a constitution. Listening to the renewal of the sacred oath every heart blossomed with hope that the evils of the past were over. At last the people had a voice! Now the young children held aloft in their fathers' arms would know a fairer world. A world without hunger. Like the Americans they would be free and equal. We must make it happen; not let it slip through our fingers, thought Madeleine, watching the guests of honour take their place at the top table.

The detachment of the National Guard commenced a roll on their drums.

'Now, Antoine,' whispered Madeleine under her breath, 'your moment of stardom has come.' Praying that he would not wake and spoil the surprise,

Madeleine glided forward from the concealed position among the trees.

A gasp of admiration left everyone's lips as they saw a tall young goddess emerge through the dappled foliage. Her hair, twisted into a coil, hung heavy over one bare shoulder. The burnished gold curls at her temple were encircled by green laurel. As she moved, her simple white robe clung and flowed against her body. Yet, though each ripe curve was clearly visible, the grace and majesty of her walk, the noble expression on the lovely open face, suppressed all sexuality. Slowly she walked towards an elevated altar, followed by the four bearers who laid down before it a large model of the Bastille. In a dramatic gesture, the beautiful goddess drew out from the tricolor sash about her waist a Phrygian cap. As she held it aloft, with one swift stroke four swords sliced through the cardboard walling of the Bastille.

A loud frightened bellow, followed by another of rage and fury greeted the incredulous audience as Madeleine lifted Antoine Danton from his ruins.

Then, taking the Phrygian cap, she placed it on his head and lifted high the symbol of newborn liberty.

The Fête de la Fédération was long over and it had been good to her. Thousands had flocked into Paris to see the King swear his oath to the nation; thousands had bought their souvenirs from her stall. It was the beginning of autumn and the bulk of the tourists had left the city. Looking up and down the Pont-Neuf, Madeleine decided to close her booth and try her luck at the gardens of the Palais-Royal.

'Going off early?' asked the next stall-holder.

'Yes, it seems a little quiet. I thought I'd give the gardens a turn,' said Madeleine, starting to fill her large wicker basket. Along with some souvenir pendants of Bastille stone, she packed some small statuettes of Lafayette on his great white horse, and several small busts of the Friends of Humanity: Mirabeau, Rousseau and Franklin. They were cheap things, but her gamble to extend her stock had paid off: she had sold hundreds of them.

Financially, her situation was secure: the loan from Thomas was repaid and she had even a little money put on one side. She had also been able to provide Annette and the Evrard girls with a little extra money. All three had been glad to put their needles at her service; turning out hundreds of the popular blue, white and red cockades.

It was a pity she had not had the wherewithal to employ skilled craftsmen to encase the remains of the grim fortress into works of art as Palloy had done. He'd earned a fortune by employing jewellers to set precious gems into the Bastille stone. Every lady of fashion wanted a brooch just like the Duc d'Orléans's mistress, Madame de Genlis, with the date in July set in emeralds and diamonds. Nevertheless, she'd sold a large quantity of stone herself, and even Palloy had been astonished. She sighed contentedly: she had been right to move away from The Parnasse.

She glanced in the direction of the Quai de l'École and, to her surprise, saw the plump figure of Annette running towards her. Alarmed, for the young woman never ran, and by the sight of her cap all askew and the fine covering of flour still clinging to the fleshy arms, Madeleine ran forward to greet her

'What is it, Annette? What has happened?' Relief flooded over her as she saw the small button eyes were shining with excitement. 'Well, at least I know it's good news,' she declared as Annette tried to speak.

'Madeleine, I think I've found your restaurant!'

Thunderstruck, Madeleine stared at the panting woman. 'But I can't afford a restaurant,' she said slowly, trying to suppress the excitement rising within her.

'Well it's going very cheap I hear . . . Look, I must go back; I'm in the middle of baking. I'm coming to visit you tonight so I'll give you all the details then! Look out, here's that wretched brother of yours.'

Unlike Annette's, Pierre's expression forewarned of trouble, and Madeleine felt irritated. He'd only returned two weeks ago and yet here he was, obviously in trouble again. Well, this time she would not ask her friends to risk their lives on his behalf.

Her brother looked furtively over his shoulder as he approached her booth. 'Keep a look out for the police,' he said wearily. 'They smashed Marat's press last night, but we managed to get away.'

Madeleine refrained from commenting and beckoned to a passing lemonade vendor.

'Have you eaten?' she asked, paying for the drink.

''Fraid not,' he said, tossing back the lemonade in one swallow.

'Here, take this. It was my lunch, but I didn't feel like it. Pierre, my dear brother,' she said, suddenly wanting to cry as she watched him devour the bread and cheese, 'how long can you go on like this? You're beginning to look like an old man! Please leave him,' she entreated softly.

'I can't, Madeleine; I believe in him and what he is trying to do for France. My life is unimportant compared to his.'

Sadly, Madeleine saw there was no persuading him and so she put her arms around her brother and held him close. For a moment, they stood thus, both moved by the emotion which would always bind them together. Then roughly Pierre pushed her away and tweaked her ear in a brotherly way.

'I feel better already with something in my stomach,' he grinned. 'Little sister, are you going to help us? Without a press we can't operate. Look, these are a few of the last edition of *L'Ami du Peuple*,' he said, removing a bundle of newspapers from his ragged sack. 'I thought you might sell them for us,' he said. 'But I have come to secure a loan from you so that we can buy a new press.'

Inside Madeleine froze and she stared at him speechless with dismay.

'Come on, Madeleine, I know you've got the money. You must earn plenty selling trash like this,' he said, picking up one of the statuettes of Lafayette and throwing it down contemptuously.

'You once called him the hero of France,' Madeleine said with an ironic smile.

'I knew no better then – all aristos stick together in the end. Now are you going to help?'

'No Pierre, I'm not,' replied the girl firmly, and looked him straight in the eye. 'Any money I have is for future business plans.'

'I can't believe what you're saying,' he gasped. 'We are trying to persuade the nation to shake off their shackles and you talk of such petty matters. *Merde!* Why, if you had the money here I'd take it from you, for you've the limited thoughts of the bourgeoisie.'

'Say what you like,' retorted Madeleine, her eyes blazing. 'I'll not help relaunch a paper filled with wild ravings and obscenities. But I'll not see you starve,' she said, reaching for her cash box.

'Keep your damned money!' replied Pierre, walking away.

Shaking with temper and unhappiness, Madeleine looked down at the sack which her brother had left behind. She picked it up, wondering what to do, then walked over to the parapet and dropped it in the river below.

There was much to occupy Madeleine's thoughts

as she walked towards the gardens of the Palais-Royal. She felt deeply upset by the angry scene with Pierre. She had no regrets about her decision; he and Marat would have to find money elsewhere. Certainly she had not strained her eyes sewing for hours throughout the night to see her money frittered away on vile printed invective. Pierre seemed incapable of understanding why she would risk her life for some political writers and refuse others like Hébert and Marat. Well he would have to think it out alone; she had other things to consider, such as Annette's startling news.

Smiling, Madeleine proceeded to move slowly along the crowded arcades of the Palais-Royal. She was no longer afraid of coming here; she knew too many people who would spring to her defence immediately if a Vicomte threatened her. Times had changed, and police agents and nobility did not make trouble in such places.

Though it was September, the evening was very warm, and many people were sitting outside the cafés with their drinks. For a moment Madeleine stopped, cautiously looking around before digging deep into her basket to sell one of her regulars a pamphlet. She moved quickly away from the incriminating sheet of paper and proceeded to show her pendants to a group of people sitting at a table. Suddenly, from behind, hands encircled her waist and she was pulled down on to the lap of a young man. It was Philippe.

'You monster,' she gasped. 'Why, you frightened me out of my wits, and lost me a sale,' she scolded.

'Sales, sales, do you never think of anything else, Madeleine? When are you going to start being a girl and let me take you out?'

'Soon, Philippe, but I'm very busy right now.'

'That's what you always say,' grumbled the dark-haired apprentice, his slim, vivacious face assuming a doleful expression. 'Look, I'll sell these for you, then you can sit with us – get your souvenirs here, ladies!' he suddenly shouted, grabbing one of the statuettes and holding it up in the air. 'Come and buy: Lafayette, Rousseau, Franklin – the latest in political thought!' he cried, digging deeper and snatching up a pamphlet.

'Philippe, stop it, please. You'll get me into trouble,' she said, snatching back the pamphlet. 'And now will you let me go,' she said crossly.

'You'd be better staying here to help us consider how we can topple the King.'

Madeleine surveyed the table of young men grinning at her. 'Gentlemen, who brought you your King from Versailles to Paris?'

'The . . . er fishwives?' ventured a young man.

'Yes. And where are they today?' asked Madeleine, raising an eyebrow.

'Selling fish?' queried Philippe in a quizzical tone.

'Precisely, and here are you men drinking wine and still making the decisions.' And with a saucy smile, Madeleine went on her way.

For the rest of the evening, Madeleine was extremely cautious about selling pamphlets, for Philippe had made a great fuss and had attracted attention to her. So that when she was leaving to cross back over the river and go home, she sensed danger straightaway when a man hurried after her.

'Mademoiselle, my friend bought a pamphlet from you a little while ago. Have you any left? I'd like to buy one too.'

'I should read your friend's copy, Monsieur, for I only sell souvenirs,' replied Madeleine, walking on.

'But I saw you with my own eyes,' protested the

man. 'You need not fear, I'm a Jacobin,' he said, keeping pace with her.

'You are mistaken, Monsieur,' replied Madeleine, wondering whether she should turn around and run back to the Palais-Royal.

'Then let me show you where you keep them!' said the stranger, seizing hold of Madeleine's arm. He expected her to pull away; instead, she went with his action and at the same time kicked her wooden sabot hard against his leg. She felt it connect with his ankle bone and he screamed, releasing his hold. Without waiting, she was off, flying across the Pont-Neuf at breakneck speed. Nor did she stop until she had reached the rue Crébillon. Whether her victim had managed to hobble after her, Madeleine knew not. Certainly, no one was in sight when she entered the house where she lived.

'Why, what on earth has happened to you? Has the Châtelet run so short of customers that they're chasing them across Paris?' asked Annette, looking up from her sewing.

'Yes,' replied Madeleine, leaning against the door, as she regained her breath.

'It's those pamphlets. Why don't you let the brave writers sell them themselves,' grumbled Annette. 'We started supper without you. Yours is on the hob. It's some stew I brought with me; it was left over from lunch.'

'Thanks, Annette, I am hungry,' said Madeleine, sitting down after greeting the Evrard sisters.

'And what did that brother of yours want?' asked Annette, her needle flashing.

'Money,' said Madeleine, hungrily spooning up the stew in the saucepan. Annette looked up, her small eyes suddenly fearful. 'You didn't give him any, did you?'

'No,' replied Madeleine, knowing what she was

thinking. 'I only offered him money to buy food, but he wouldn't take it. He was angry because I wouldn't loan him any for a new press for Marat.'

'Filthy creature,' snorted Annette disapprovingly.

'Well, so would you be if you had to hide down sewers. The poor man's skin is in a terrible state. He needs someone to look after him,' Simone Evrard said wistfully.

Madeleine studied the emotion on her face. 'Why Simone, are you falling in love with our rabble-rousing friend?' she asked as she joined the girls at the work table. Simone blushed and her sister Catherine giggled.

'Well, he need not ask anyone else for money for a press. He is welcome to have my savings.'

'You must be mad,' said Annette, who, like Madeleine, was astonished that the unkempt girl should have savings. 'You keep hold of your money yourself, Simone. Who knows what times are ahead of us.'

Simone Evrard did not answer and Madeleine sensed Annette's words would go unregarded.

That evening Madeleine brought work to a halt earlier than usual. 'I want to catch the Dantons before they retire for the night,' she explained. 'I need some advice and help on a business matter.'

'Then I'll walk you as far as their door,' said Annette, beaming with approval. 'Gabrielle has got plenty of money,' she whispered later, after they'd waved goodnight to the Evrard sisters. 'I'm sure she'll lend you enough for the restaurant. Best of luck!' she said, leaving Madeleine at the entrance into the Cour de Commerce.

The street door, Madeleine saw with surprise, was ajar. So, without pausing to ring the bell, Madeleine went straight in. Although not expected, she was always a welcome visitor and knew Gabrielle would not mind her calling in. Approaching down the carpeted corridor to the apartment door, Madeleine smiled: there was no mistaking the rich boom of Georges's voice; but suddenly she realised that his discourse was not in French.

She paused, her hand in mid-air, about to knock, when a second voice changed her mind; made her blood run cold, as its cultured icy tone filtered through the heavy door. It was a voice she would remember always; a voice she had last heard at the Palais-Royal! Curious and frustrated she listened, unable to interpret the English words. Then suddenly, the Vicomte de Cramoisy lapsed into French. 'You see, Monsieur Danton, you would have much to gain from a regency. The Duc d'Orléans would be generous to all who have displayed their interest in his cause.' A third voice cut across the Vicomte and the conversation resumed in English. Despite the fact that her curiosity had been aroused by this scrap of conversation, Madeleine decided to leave. Her horror of meeting the Vicomte again and the danger she would be in if caught listening convinced her that immediate escape was advisable.

Turning quickly, she crept forward on her toes. Behind her there was a sudden movement from within the room and she heard the word 'Calais'. There was no time to reach the stairs; Danton's visitors were about to leave. Desperately she wondered whether to make a run for it, but already footsteps were approaching the door. There was no time. In seconds it would open and she would be discovered. Her only refuge was behind the heavy velvet drape. Usually in winter evenings it was drawn fully across the corridor, but tonight the curtain was draped back, secured to the wall with a brocade sash. It was not much protection, but in a moment she was behind it, thankful for its thick folds. She

146

crouched low in the shadows, her body pressed hard against the wall, praying that no one would look down as they passed.

As the door opened and the men made their farewells, Madeleine's heart seemed to beat so loudly that she expected any moment to be dragged out of her hiding place. Then, just as the visitors reached the curtain, something metallic struck the floor, followed by a muttered oath. Whatever it was had rolled to a stop the other side of the curtain. Madeleine held her breath as one of the men stooped down to grasp the object. He was so close that she could touch him; take his fingers in her hand. Surely he would sense her fear.

But, softly cursing, he drew away. 'I have it,' she heard him say. Then he gave a short rueful laugh: 'But I've lost most of my snuff.'

As both men moved past, Madeleine peered up at them and saw she had been right. Despite a large-brimmed hat which cast a shadow over the man's face, she recognised at once the haughty profile of the Vicomte de Cramoisy. His companion was the Englishman who had given Pierre the copper engravings of Marie-Antoinette to take to the Palais-Royal!

Long after their footsteps had receded down the stairs, Madeleine sat and thought about what she had overheard. Had Danton dealings with England? Was he in the pay of the Duc d'Orléans? Certainly of late there seemed to be no shortage of money. There was the estate Georges had bought outside Paris and, not so long ago, another large estate outside his home town of Arcis. Until tonight Madeleine had thought little of it. There had been some gossip in the quarter about his apparent new-found wealth. People had hinted that it wasn't from his law practice, but she had refused to listen; fiercely brushing aside conjecture.

Now, as she let the brass knocker fall against the door, she wondered – was he being paid to bring about the fall of a king?

'Ah, Madeleine, what a pleasant surprise,' said Georges, opening the door with a smile. 'How unfortunate, you have just missed two very good friends of mine . . . Perhaps they let you in?' he enquired, his shrewd eyes narrowing ever so slightly.

'No, I didn't see anyone leave, though I thought it strange the street door was not closed.'

'Ah, they must have left it open on their way out . . . Can I offer you a glass of wine?'

Madeleine nodded, noting his manner visibly ease. Obviously he was relieved that she had not encountered his evening visitors.

'Come, sit and talk to me while I sign these.' He gestured towards documents spread out on a table and smiled apologetically. 'My work for the Cordelier club, it occupies more and more of my time. Now, tell me, what are you doing with yourself these days? How is business on the Pont-Neuf?'

'It's a bit slow at the moment, but in winter it's to be expected . . . Is Gabrielle not home, Georges?'

'No, she decided to take the baby into the country for a few days. She's bored; Paris is too quiet for her.' His twisted lip drew back into a grin that exposed large, strong teeth.

'Georges, I don't believe you for one moment. It's your political activity she's escaping from. If you're not careful she'll probably meet a nice quiet farmer,' teased Madeleine, a peal of laughter escaping her lips.

The big man looked up from his papers and stared at Madeleine. Her white throat was slightly arched, her head tilted backwards, the soft full lips parted provocatively in a gurgle of laughter. Suddenly he wanted to kiss her. He stood up and walked towards her, placing one thick strong finger under her chin, raising her face to look up into his. Immediately the laughter left the topaz eyes and she made to draw back, but he prevented it. 'No,' he murmured, pulling off her woollen cap with his free hand. 'I want to see the goddess who set every heart on fire in the Bois de Boulogne.'

The released mane of tawny, tangled curls tumbled down about Madeleine's shoulders. For a moment the girl stared back, hypnotically held by his will. Then the lynx-like eyes narrowed until only black pupils gleamed through her curly lashes, and angrily she pushed him from her.

His response was a delighted chuckle and he caught her roughly to him. Holding her head so that she could not move, his eyes were alive with expectation as slowly, deliberately, he lowered his scarred lips to take possession, stopping her cry of protest with a brutal, demanding kiss. She struggled, unable to breathe, but his strength was astounding. This was not the sensuous, insinuating approach of Vicomte de Cramoisy – it was a volcanic explosion of male desire. Her lips were bruised and battered by the consuming violence of his kiss. Gradually she weakened, drawn deeper and deeper into the abyss of desire. Helpless, hungry, she parted her lips, responding. She heard his gasp of excitement, felt his body harden as he crushed her to him. They clung together, possessed, driven on by inner urgent forces. Then she was in his arms and he was carrying her towards the bedroom – Gabrielle's room. The thought was like an icy shower drenching her scalding brain.

'No, Georges . . . Gabrielle, please!'

As though not hearing, he pushed open the boudoir door with his foot. 'I said No,' she snapped, pushing hard against his chest. 'Think of your wife!'

With a look of surprise he shrugged. 'What has this to do with Gabrielle? I want you,' he laughed, the scarred and pock-marked face filled with an expression of earthy sensual delight, 'and you, my love, want me! It has nothing to do with marriage.'

Filled with anger, more against herself than him, Madeleine lashed out and clawed at his face. But he was quicker than she and caught hold of her wrist in a steely grip. '*Mon Dieu*, you're more wildcat than goddess. I see, Madeleine, I will have to teach you some manners,' he laughed, slinging her over his shoulder just as though he were carrying a trouble-some animal across his farm at Arcis. Desperately she punched her fists against his back but he only laughed the more. Then she suddenly knew what would stop him and save her betrayal of the girl who had fed her and given her a home, her chance in life.

'I know about the Vicomte de Cramoisy . . . and the Duc d'Orléans!'

Immediately Danton stopped. He stood quite still. Apprehensive of his reaction to her words, Madeleine remained motionless, hanging against his back. Then he pulled her up and released her. All laughter had left his face and it was suffused with rage. Trembling, he drew his hand back to hit her. She felt his anger and his need for her and braced herself for the blow; welcoming it, to expiate the guilt she felt, but it did not come. Dropping his hand to his side, he turned and walked back into the salon.

'Here, drink this . . .' he rasped sarcastically, offer-ing her a measure of brandy. 'It's a fire that always satisfies.' Gratefully she took it from him; they both needed the drink while their bodies calmed, their pulses ceased to race. 'So . . . how much did you hear?' he asked, casually refilling his glass.

'Sufficient to know you're in the pay of Orléans,'

replied Madeleine boldly, then started back, regretting her words, for an angry flush darkened his face, exposing his scars, white and terrible.

'You make a poor spy,' he said, his lip twisting back contemptuously. 'Perhaps you should learn English from your brother before sneaking behind keyholes and condemning a friend.'

Now it was Madeleine's turn to flush crimson.

'However,' he continued, 'if I convinced you of my allegiance to the Duc d'Orléans, then perhaps I convinced our two friends also.' He laughed harshly. 'I am not ready to move the pieces on the board yet, Madeleine, and it will not be the rook that threatens the king and queen, but the pawns. Now tell me why you were listening at my door?'

'I'm sorry, I didn't think you might have visitors . . . I was about to knock when I recognised the voice of the Vicomte de Cramoisy.'

'Ah yes, the Vicomte,' said Georges thoughtfully, detecting the hostility in the girl's voice. 'You move in high circles, Madeleine. I had no idea that the Vicomte de Cramoisy was a friend of yours?'

'He's no friend of mine,' replied Madeleine softly, her eyes gleaming with hatred.

So, thought Georges to himself, it seems we have here a protégée of the Palais-Royal who somehow escaped the final sacrifice. For he felt certain Madeleine was still a virgin. He was about to put more questions to her but, seeing her unhappy, downcast face, he moved forward and took her hand in a brotherly manner.

'Now let us put from our minds what has passed between us. You are a beautiful, desirable young woman. It is only natural that I and other men will want you. You responded because you are passionate; needing to love and be loved!' His words, he saw, had brought tears into the lovely brown eyes.

'Come,' he said, understanding the source of her unhappiness, 'you have not threatened Gabrielle in any way. Our love is different, deep and strong. In her arms, I do not look for the passion that you would give. I find a peaceful haven. Gabrielle is one of those blessed women who create harmony. When I come in through that door at night, Madeleine, and sit here before the fire-side, I can forget chaos and even, for a time, my own ambition. Are you selfless enough to love a man in such way?'

She did not answer and he lifted up, once more, the beautiful face and stared at her. 'No . . . I think not,' he chuckled. 'There are other urges driving you – Gabrielle's shiny kitchen is not enough for you, and,' he sighed wistfully, 'it would seem a pity to waste all this beauty on one man.'

Chapter Four

Annette's great find was, in reality, little more than a wine shop. Even so it was a large undertaking for Madeleine, requiring greater capital than a small booth. Because of her brief entanglement with Georges, asking Gabrielle for help seemed out of the question. Neither was she willing to approach Thomas Adams. Desperate, and determined not to lose the little restaurant whose owners were anxious to emigrate, Madeleine instead thought to seek assistance from the contractor, Palloy.

On the appointed day she dressed with the greatest care. Everything she wore was new, bought especially for their meeting. Usually she cared little for her appearance, but on this day Madeleine was determined to use all her feminine wiles.

The dress she chose was of the latest fashion, having a high tight bodice of blue and a narrow tubular skirt of tricolor stripes. Around her shoulders she draped a delicate white fichu, caught together with a small nosegay of cornflowers, poppies and daisies. A high bonnet and shoes of matching blue completed the picture. Its effect was not lost on Palloy when, later, she entered his office. Immediately he rose with a smile full of charm; then he looked puzzled as though trying to place her. Madeleine introduced herself stiffly and formally, then burst out laughing as the contractor's puzzled air changed to delighted surprise. 'Why, Mademoiselle, I hardly knew you ... Why you're quite ...' he spread his hands apart in a gesture of delight.

'Pretty?' teased Madeleine, fluttering her curly lashes.

'No ... you're beautiful, and I hope you'll allow me to take you out for lunch. I'd like to show off my old business associate to my friends.'

'Well, before I accept, perhaps I should tell you why I'm here.' Madeleine leant forward in her seat and told him about the restaurant, what she intended to do with it, her present resources and the money she needed to borrow.

All the while Palloy sat watching her, a small smile playing about his lips. When she had finished he sat silent, drumming his fingers on the desk. Anxiously, she examined his weatherbeaten face, the trade mark of former days that no amount of wealth would ever hide.

'So, Mademoiselle,' he said, looking up with a twinkle in his round, grey eyes. 'The Pont-Neuf is no longer enough for you! You are becoming more ambitious?'

'No, Monsieur,' retorted Madeleine, with a cheeky little grin, 'that I've always been.'

Palloy leant back in his chair and his thick, stubby fingers resumed their movement on the desk top. Madeleine noticed, with interest, the black springy hairs on the backs of his hands and a large diamond ring on his little finger. The Bastille had indeed been good to him; to them both. 'Very well.' He pulled his thick-set frame up out of his chair. 'You have your loan, at five per cent per annum. Agreed?'

'Agreed,' said Madeleine, taking, for the second time in her young life, the strong, rough hand to seal their contract.

Annette, of course, overjoyed by Madeleine's news, wanted to leave The Parnasse immediately, but Madeleine firmly dissuaded her. It would be some time before she would be able to pay her a wage. Further, it would be unfair to Monsieur and Madame Maulu, who should be given longer notice.

Madeleine was sad to leave her plot on the Pont-Neuf. She had made friends with many of the other booth-holders. Even blind André now shouted a cheery greeting as he tapped his way past. She would miss the lively chatter, the hurly-burly, the visitors from all corners of the world; for everyone who came to Paris walked across the Pont-Neuf. One day, too, her naval officer would return and doubtless pass along, but Madeleine did not mind, for it was not as a booth-holder she wished to be reunited. First, she would make something of herself. She was leaving the beating heart of Paris to become a property owner, and the prospect made her throb with energy and excitement.

On the day she took possession of her new restaurant, Madeleine arrived with her few belongings on a handcart, pushed by Thomas Adams.

'Well, this is it!' she said with pride as she unlocked and flung open the green entrance door. 'You'd best stay there Tom, I'll go inside and open the shutters. It will give us more light.'

Thomas watched the eager girl enter the dark premises and, leaning back against the cart, felt for his pipe. Thoughtfully he looked around: certainly there need be no shortage of customers, for on either side of the long street were cabinet-making factories. Their craftsmen and apprentices would all want a midday meal and a bottle of wine, though he very much doubted they had ever eaten or drunk at this grimy hovel. For a few more moments he puffed on his pipe and surveyed the drab façade; then the slatted inner shutters were opening and, through the filthy grey glass, he could see the misty figure of Madeleine.

'Come inside,' she called, flinging wide the window. 'I'll show you around. I thought we would start at the top and work down.'

'Well, Madeleine, you've chosen a good spot for trade,' he said, trying to forget the appalling café area as he followed her up two flights of stairs.

'Yes, that was my first thought when I came with Annette to see it. I can't fail with all the factories in the area!'

Despondently Thomas searched for other words of encouragement; but words, even in his native language, never sprang easily to his lips and, embarrassed, he stared at the floor.

'I know there's a lot of hard work to be done,' she said, following his gaze to the mouse droppings on the dusty floor. 'But compared to taking the Bastille . . . why, a few little mice are no challenge at all.'

Before him, Madeleine Fleury positively glowed with enthusiasm. She is like a flame, he thought, and has already begun to illuminate these drab surroundings. How he loved to be with her, to feel his spirits soar as they responded to her optimism.

'Madeleine,' he smiled, 'you're incorrigible. Come, show me what you want me to do. To begin with, you must have that worm-eaten counter downstairs torn out and replaced. Just remember, I'm the son of a wine importer.'

Carpentry was not Tom's trade; indeed, he had no trade. Born to parents with money and social aspirations, he had been sent to France to improve his French and study the wine trade.

Now stripped to the waist and wielding a heavy hammer to split apart the unwanted counter, he laughed as he pictured the expression his mother's face would wear if she could glimpse him at this moment. And she would be right, too, he thought, pausing to wipe the sweat from his hands, for he had money enough to hire others to do this. But he knew Madeleine would not accept that kind of help. Above him he could hear her singing and the sounds of frenzied scrubbing; he smiled thinking what a splendid frontier-woman she would make. Then he sighed, acknowledging that the prim Protestant town he longed to take her to as his bride would stifle her like a cage. Nor could he see himself returning: the French, their women, their politics were too rich a mixture to leave yet. France, like Madeleine, was under the quiet man's skin.

It took many pails of water and several coats of paint before the greasy, nicotine-stained walls gleamed a spotless white. Beneath Tom's sturdy counter, rows of white earthenware plates waited on shelves in neat stacks for their inaugural trip to the yellow-clothed tables. These bright, buttercup-yellow tablecloths, which gave a sunny appearance to the room, were a gift from Gabrielle Charpentier. Indeed, everyone had been very kind, thought Madeleine as she balanced high up on a ladder outside her restaurant. There had been many hands to help and, today, on her first day of opening, even her brother had just appeared bearing a large potted fern.

With a flourish, Madeleine added the final 'R' to the new name of her restaurant.

'I think you could make more money as a sign-writer,' her brother called up to her as, emerging from the restaurant, he walked out into the street to survey the golden letters she had painted over the entrance.

'So it's all right?' she called down.

157

'Yes, it's a good name. Perhaps it will remind you to come more regularly to the debates. I left the plant on top of your counter,' Pierre Fleury added, making to leave as his sister climbed down to the pavement.

'Thanks for coming, Pierre,' she said, kissing his cheek. 'You know there will always be a meal and a home if you want it.'

With a smile and a casual wave Pierre Fleury sauntered down the street, leaving Madeleine to admire the large golden letters which proclaimed the Faubourg's newest and smartest eating house: The Cordelier. Just as Danton and Desmoulins had formed the Cordelier Club when the district had been absorbed into that of the Théâtre Français, so now Madeleine, back once again in the poorer Faubourg Saint-Antoine, sentimentally brought the former district name with her. Nor did the old Cordeliers forget Madeleine: a whole group of them trouped across from left bank to right to ensure she had customers on her first day.

By Madeleine's third night, The Cordelier had had a good many customers, all curious to see the new owner. It was well past midnight and wearily she had thrown herself across her bed, too exhausted to undress. Suddenly she heard something small hitting the window pane, like a stone. Thinking it was some of her rough young customers come back to tease her, Madeleine grabbed hold of the water jug and flung open the window.

Looking down to see who the culprits were, she paused and set the jug down on the flat sill. For in the darkness there was only one small figure. 'Who are you? What do you want?' she asked the boy.

'Are you Madeleine . . .?'

'Yes, what do you want?' the girl asked impatiently.

'Please come down, I have a message for you.'

158

Madeleine closed the window and ran down the stairs. The boy was about twelve years old, white-faced with dark shadows under his eyes. She saw that under the flimsy covering of rags he was painfully thin. 'You're to follow me, Mademoiselle,' he said in a rough country accent. 'Your brother, Pierre, needs you. He says you must come tonight!'

Madeleine nodded, taking in the boy's bluish, naked feet; she well remembered her own desperate days. 'All right, but before we go you'll sit down and eat something. What's your name?'

'Paul.'

'Well, Paul, could you manage a bowl of soup?'

A desperate expression filled the large dark eyes, but his answer was quite restrained and polite. 'Yes, Mademoiselle, I'd like that very much.'

Raking up the still-warm embers of the fire to heat the pan of soup, Madeleine felt the boy's gaze following her every move. The poor wretch was obviously starving and his polite restraint near to breaking point as he looked up at the hams and sausages hanging from the ceiling. But she knew it was dangerous to overload a hungry stomach. The soup would be lighter and more sustaining. The moment she set the bowl down before him, he started to lap it up like a hungry dog, his eyes darting quickly about as though any moment someone might snatch the bowl from his hands.

Then suddenly he stopped, laid the bowl down on the table and pushed it away. 'Don't you want any more?' Madeleine asked in surprise.

'I'd like to take it with me if you wouldn't mind, Mademoiselle. I promise I'll bring the bowl back to you tomorrow.'

'Of course,' replied Madeleine, looking at the boy's anxious face, wondering why he had made such a request; for it was clear that he could have drunk the entire contents. 'Is there someone at home you wish to give it to?' she asked, slowly beginning to understand.

'Yes,' he replied, his eyes filling with tears. 'I'd like to take it to my mother.'

The girl turned away from the weary little face, robbed of its childhood, lest he should see the tears filling her own eyes. 'Finish your soup, *chéri*,' she said gently. 'We'll take your mother all she needs.'

Paul led the way through the meanest streets of the quarter; dark labyrinths of foul smells. Carrying a basket heavy with provisions, Madeleine questioned him as they walked, learning that his father was a weaver from western France. A slump in the industry had driven him to seek work in Paris but he had found nothing.

Though Madeleine had grown up in the Faubourg Saint-Antoine, this part of the quarter was unfamiliar to her. They were in a series of steep narrow alleys, made slippery by unseen, dripping water. Suddenly the boy stopped and turned into a narrow niche that Madeleine or a stranger would have passed by, so small was the gap. But pushing through and feeling with her foot, she discovered she was at the bottom of a flight of damp steps. In the darkness, the boy grabbed hold of her hand and placed it on to a thick greasy rope. 'Be careful,' he warned, 'it's easy to lose your footing. Here, give me your basket. I'm used to it.'

Madeleine did not argue. With both hands holding the unseen life-line, slowly she hauled herself up what seemed to be a sheer ascent, sometimes hanging on to the fraying fibres as the steps crumbled and fell away, clattering to the alley below.

At last they were at the top and, as they emerged out into pale moonlight, she saw an old house, the windows of which were planked over. The door which swung open to the boy's touch was held only at its top by hinges.

'You'd best hold on to my hand till we reach the stairs. Your brother's on the floor above us.'

Madeleine noted the eagerness in his voice. He is excited, she thought, to be taking food to his family.

The stench which had hit her the moment they entered the dark building became overpowering as they mounted the stairs. Unable to prevent it, she started to retch as her nostrils received smells of excrement and rotting food left outside the doors. Against her foot she felt the touch of fur as a rat scurried by. Horrified, she screamed. 'Nearly there,' the boy said cheerfully. 'Just wait until they see the basket.' His jubilation reached out to her, overcoming her claustrophobia and rising panic. 'This is it,' he said, stopping presumably outside a door; though it was so dark she could not see. His knock was soon answered and a dim light fell on to the landing as a door creaked open.

It was a wretched sight which met Madeleine's eyes. Straight ahead in a small squalid room was a bed on which lay two little girls wrapped in an old quilt. Despite the hour, both were awake and sat up as Madeleine entered.

'Father, this is Pierre's sister,' said the boy, taking hold of Madeleine's hand. 'She has brought us some food for Mother.' The man did not speak, and hung back at the door viewing Madeleine with distrust. His clothes were shabby, patched over several times in differing materials, though the colours were faded under a covering of dirt.

Madeleine smiled over at the careworn face. 'It was kind of your son to bring my brother's message. I was bringing him some food, and I thought perhaps your wife might also like some of my gruel. For Paul told me she is not well.'

161

'It's kind of you,' replied the man, awkwardly twisting his hands together. His accent, Madeleine noticed, was broader than Paul's, and she found it quite difficult to understand. But she was aware of his pride, and strove to set him at ease.

'It's not so easy in Paris when you're a stranger looking for work. I hope you didn't mind my calling in ... but, well, I remember when we first came down from Brittany, things were very difficult.'

'You're from Brittany? I know it well,' the man exclaimed, his embarrassment falling away, the dull, hopeless look replaced by one of interest. 'Why, we're from the Vendée – near neighbours!'

'Well, you'll have to speak more with Pierre, Monsieur,' laughed Madeleine, unpacking her basket, 'for I can only remember cider apples.'

At the sight of food, the two little girls had leapt up and now Madeleine saw a woman in the shadows at the other end of the bed. She was lying back, supported by two pillows, quite motionless. From the yellow, waxy appearance of her skin and her heavy, slow breathing, Madeleine could see she was in a very bad way. The man followed the direction of her gaze and the look of hopeless despair filled his eyes once more.

'Have you had a doctor?' asked Madeleine quietly.

He did not answer, and she cursed her stupidity for even asking. When children were starving there was usually no money for medical care. 'Monsieur, as a Breton, would you allow me to send you a doctor?'

The weaver took the girl's hands and pressed them in gratitude. 'Bless you, my friend. But I fear it's too late. My Jeanne hasn't long now.' He suddenly started to shake, shedding silent tears. 'I should never have made her leave her home and come to this wretched city. But what was I to do?'

162

'You did your best,' whispered Madeleine. 'That is all any of us can do.'

With a heavy heart she left the tragic little family and went up to the floor where Pierre was living. She knocked, as the boy had directed her, and after some moments her brother opened the door. He was supporting himself on a stick and limped badly as he showed her to a stool. 'They nearly caught me this time,' he said, lightly tapping the stick against his injured ankle. 'But for that little chap downstairs who dragged me into an alley, I'd be on my way to the galleys.'

'Do you want me to ask a doctor to come and look at your ankle?' Madeleine asked.

'No, it's too risky. No one must know I'm here. Besides it's only a strain. I'll rest here a while; when things quieten down Marat and I can get back to work. Tonight I want your help. Read this while I eat – I'm ravenous.' He handed her a piece of paper covered with his writing. 'It's a translation I've done of the Manifesto by the English radical, Thomas Paine,' he said, taking a piece of cheese from the wicker basket.

Madeleine glanced casually at her brother's bold letters, and the words of Thomas Paine leapt up at her from the white page, immediately seizing her attention. 'The nation,' she read, 'can never give back its confidence to a man who, false to his trust, perjures his oath, conspires a clandestine flight, obtains a fraudulent passport, conceals a king of France under the disguise of valet, directs his course towards a frontier covered with traitors and deserters, and evidently meditates a return to our country with a force capable of imposing his own despotic laws.' Madeleine paused, recalling the royal family's bid to escape, the silent day Paris had watched the dusty green Berliner crawl down the Champs-Elysées to the Tuileries. Not a sound or a whisper was heard, all heeded the notices promising hangings for insults; floggings for cheers. But though silence was the order of the day, it had seemed as natural as reverse arms for the National Guard. For they were at a funeral, that of a king. He had renounced them, and Madeleine and her friends felt only pity for the humiliated man. Paine was right, a king should not sneak out of his country.

Madeleine read on, struck by Paine's thoughts: 'What kind of office must that be in a government which requires for its execution neither experience, nor ability, that may be abandoned to the desperate chance of birth, that may be filled by an idiot, a mad man, a tyrant, with equal effect as by the good, the virtuous and the wise?'

She finished reading, stunned by the implication of these words. 'What do you intend to do with this?' she whispered, nervously.

'I want you to take it to Henri at the Palais-Royal. He is waiting to print it. And then when you return with a copy I am going to take it and hang it on the door of the National Assembly. Even if I have to crawl there to do so!'

'That you will not have to do,' stated Madeleine, her eyes burning with a fierce light. 'I will hang it on the door for you!'

The gardens of the Palais-Royal were dark and deserted when Madeleine reached the palace. Though she had tried to dissuade him, the young boy, Paul, had insisted he escort her home, to protect her – as had his father.

Now, as she made her way to the door which led down to the printing shop, Madeleine was grateful for his company. As arranged, the side door had been left open for Pierre. And if Henri was surprised to find her there with a strange young boy, he did not show it. Merely a flicker of the eye and a warm embrace. 'It's good to see you. You have the copy?' Madeleine nodded and handed him Pierre's translation.

Leaving Henri to set up the print, she wandered idly through the room, breathing in the familiar smell of ink. Already the young boy was examining the presses, just as Pierre had done on his arrival. Her skirt brushed against a stack of paper, causing the top sheets to flutter to the ground. She smiled, recalling the many accidents she'd had in the early days. The upset red ink over Henri's pamphlets; her flight in terror down the long stone corridor to the kitchens, where later kind Philippe had found her.

She wondered how he was, and whether he might be awake. Impulsively she slipped out of the room and walked towards the men's dormitory. Quietly she opened the door and peered in. All was peaceful, the room filled with the regular breathing of sleepers. Philippe, she saw, was in the third bed along. She could see his straight black hair spread out on the pillow. But he was asleep too and it seemed wrong to wake him.

Very gently she closed the door and walked across the corridor to the little store room which had served as her bedroom. To her surprise she saw it was just as she had left it, with the old mattress and bedding still in position.

Would the pretty green room still be the same as well? she wondered. Or would there be a new occupant installed? She turned back towards the print room, but stopped, filled with an urge, a curiosity to see the room once again.

Quite easily she found the hidden springs in the panelling and left the secret doorways open, intending to stay for one brief moment; for even though the gamblers would be sleeping by now, the thought of the Vicomte de Cramoisy made her highly nervous and it would not be wise to stay too long.

The splendour of the long corridor quite took her breath away. She had forgotten its magnificence, and the contrast between this and the hovel where a woman lay dying in the Faubourg Saint-Antoine made her want to scream out loud at the injustice of it. But now was no time to think of such things.

Stealthily she turned the handle of the boudoir door, and found that it was not locked. With a thrill of excitement she moved forward in the darkness. There was no sound and, from the chill atmosphere, she felt certain it was empty and had not been used for some time.

Lighting the candle she had brought with her, Madeleine lit also the large candelabra on a rose-wood table. Gradually the room came to life – the golden cupids on the mother-of-pearl panelling glowed, their fat faces laughing down at her, eyes mischievous and knowing.

Then, to her amazement and fright, she saw the room was just as it had been on that terrible night. The shattered decanter was still on the floor by the bed and, across the bed's delicate white counterpane, a stain, large and brown. Horrified, she walked towards it, knowing it was dried blood. The man she had hit had obviously bled like a pig.

'Quite a mess, you'll agree.'

Madeleine whirled around as the icy, suave voice cut the silence of the room. You fool, to return, a voice screamed in her head, as she gazed at the pale blue eyes of the Vicomte.

'You were surprised to find the room so?' he enquired, taking a pinch of snuff in an elegant movement. The girl nodded. 'It was a fancy of mine, a dream if you like, that one day I would enter and find you here. And here you are,' he said, removing his richly embroidered coat. Dumbly she watched him lay it neatly across a chair and then begin to unbutton his velvet waistcoat. 'As you see,' he said politely, 'if you want something hard enough you can make it happen.'

At least they had that in common, thought Madeleine, turning away from him, though now it seemed unlikely that she would make her own dream a reality.

Her mind was suddenly wrenched back from the warmth of a stranger's arms to the presence of the Vicomte behind her. The nerves along her spine tingled with fear as he drew near. She felt his hot breath on her cheek as he whispered in her ear. 'And now, you bitch! I am going to turn you into a whore! You'll beg to pleasure me.'

Madeleine turned to push him away and gasped, seeing his nakedness; desperately she looked to the door behind him. Then lost all power of thought as he caught her arm and twisted it up behind her back. She gasped with pain and tried to struggle free, but his grip only tightened.

'I should come quietly, Madeleine,' he purred, dragging her towards the bed, 'or you'll find you have a broken arm.'

Slowly they moved towards the bed, she co-operating, thinking that the moment he released his hold would be the time to thrust him away.

But as he drew alongside the white muslin hangings he violently jerked her arm higher, causing a shooting, flaming pain to run through her upper arm. She was flung across the mattress, felt him wrenching at her wrist and securing it with what felt like thonging. Shocked, she opened her eyes and saw in disbelief that he had tied her injured arm to one of the bedposts. She launched forward to release herself but he had moved around the bed and had caught hold of one of her ankles. Within minutes she was restrained, spread-eagled and helpless. Then he spoke and she shivered in fear at his words.

'Before I take you, Madeleine, as a member of the lower orders you are going to learn your true station in life.'

Then his hands were at the back of her neck and she felt the cold tip of a knife. It lingered for one moment then, thrusting downward, it slashed through her clothing, exposing the whole length of her thighs and back. The cold air struck her flesh and she shivered.

'You'll soon feel warm,' he laughed, sliding his fingers under the thong around her waist. Her emotions shattered as she felt the leather part under the knife's blade. Now it was lost, the ring was lost to her, it would be all over. From the sudden silence, she knew he was studying the coat of arms on the ring, and she hated him for touching it.

'Well,' he said, 'there is no doubt that you are beautiful, but I must confess that to find the ring of François-Athanase Charette de la Contrie around your lovely waist astounds me. However, we will talk of that later.'

The first lash of the whip caught Madeleine unprepared and she cried out in pain. But her heart was singing; her joy bore her up above the pain. She clenched her teeth together. Let him beat me all night: I have the name, I have the name!

Over and over she repeated to herself the name of the naval officer, François-Athanase Charette de la Contrie, as the lash fell across her body. Then it was over, and the tension slackened in her arms and legs as he released her.

The girl looked up at him through half-closed eyes, her lips curling in a contemptuous smile. 'I'd rather take another beating than have you pollute my body.'

A yellow flame of madness flickered in the pale eyes, and with a snarl of fury the Vicomte sprang forward, flinging her over on her back so that she cried out as her lacerated buttocks and back made contact with the sheets. He dealt her several stinging blows across the face until she felt a warm trickle of blood run from her nose. Then he grasped a breast, viciously twisting the nipple until she screamed. Brutally he forced her legs apart and she shuddered, seeing him fully erect. Revulsion, anger, lent her new strength, and she brought her knee up sharp. The Vicomte howled in anger, then slumped, the full weight of his body falling upon her.

There was no movement; he lay absolutely still. Astonished, Madeleine tried to lift him from her. She slid her hand around his naked body to get more leverage and as she did so, she gasped with horror. For the sticky trail her fingers encountered led to the hilt of a knife.

Bewildered, she looked up at the mirrored ceiling and stared transfixed at the terrible scene. Like a painting; motionless except for the dark red blood flowing steadily down the man's back. At the edge of the frame stood a ragged boy, staring at the knife, buried hilt-deep in the naked back.

With a small cry of revulsion, Madeleine somehow struggled free of the inert body. Immediately the small boy ran to her, his eyes wild with terror.

'He was hurting you . . . I heard you scream,' he sobbed. Numb with fright, Madeleine held him tightly.

'It's all right,' she whispered, stroking his hair. 'Hush now, it'll be all right.'

Her mind reeled as she considered their position. To confess would cost Paul his young life. To take the blame herself would cost her her life, and she wasn't ready to die yet. The only person who knew they had entered the palace was Henri. She knew he would not betray them.

'Paul, *chéri*, is the knife yours?'

'No, Mademoiselle, I found it on the table.'

'Good, now run and bring Henri. Be careful not to let anyone see you.'

The boy left and Madeleine sprang from the bed, securing her ripped clothes around her with a ribbon from the bed drapes. On the bedside table lay her topaz and the cut thonging. She snatched it up and tied it round her neck; all the while averting her gaze from the dead man on the bed.

After what seemed like hours, the door opened and Paul, together with Henri, appeared. Except for the merest flicker of the heavy eyelids, the printer's face remained impassive as he walked over to the bed. 'He's dead all right,' he said, tonelessly, withdrawing the knife from the Vicomte's back. 'Leave this to me. The manuscript is ready, you'll find it on my bench. Now go quickly. You have not been here!'

Madeleine ran across the room and gazed up anxiously into the calm heavy face.

'I'll be in no danger,' he reassured her. 'But speed must be with us. Go!'

She embraced him and then, without delay, fled with the boy down the secret stairway, back to Henri's workbench and out of the Palais-Royal.

Dawn had already lifted the curtain of night as Madeleine and Paul ran through the streets towards the Manège. Once it had been the royal riding school, now it housed France's National Assembly. Glad to be free of the suffocating atmosphere of the palace, Madeleine breathed in the cool, damp air of early morning, hiding with Paul behind the shelter of a tree as a patrol of the National Guard went by.

The birds were serenading the city with their first chorus, and already there were many workmen going about their business.

Despite the murder of the Vicomte de Cramoisy, the physical pain she still bore from his beating, Madeleine was filled with a joyous exuberance. Her chevalier really existed; she had his name, and soon she would find him.

Now she was making her contribution to the cause of equality for all the people of France. Paine's words would stir the hearts of the people. They didn't need a king, least of all one married to an Austrian.

With the heel of her sabot, Madeleine hammered the nails into the radical's address, standing back for a moment to admire her work.

'Please God,' she prayed, 'when we meet, let him be wearing the tricolor!'

Somehow Madeleine struggled through the day, though her nerves and emotions were in a fearful state. But it was vital not to lose a day's takings, and she was determined not to disappoint her customers.

The Vicomte de Cramoisy's beating she could not conceal. Her face had swollen, and dark, purplish bruises had risen to the surface of her skin. Despite all, somehow she managed a smile for the first customers. But her forced gaiety could not deceive; her appearance made them angry and concerned. She shrugged their questioning aside, pretending it had happened in an unlit alley. Muttering threats against her unknown assailant, the men accepted her explanation. Annette did not.

In response to a message delivered by Paul, she came to Madeleine in the late evening. Using warm water she soaked the girl's dress and shift, which had stuck to the lacerations.

'Alley thieves my foot,' she snorted. 'Since when

do thieves wield a flail. You're protecting someone, Madeleine, and if Thomas finds him, he'll snap him like a twig.'

'Then there's no need to tell him, Annette. The man is dead and that's all I'll tell you.'

'It's enough,' said Annette in a satisfied voice.

After the evening at the Palais-Royal, Paul became a daily visitor at The Cordelier, helping to lay tables, run errands and wash dishes. In short, he became Madeleine's devoted assistant. And when his mother died a few days later, Madeleine insisted the little family came to live at The Cordelier. For, as well as two spare rooms, she also had a troubled conscience. Troubled, because she held a gem whose sale would easily alleviate their hunger and misery.

But the topaz had been hoarded and protected too long to part with now. Madeleine was ashamed of her selfishness, but there it was. Nothing and no one but the giver himself would take it from her. At least she would give Jacques Metalier and his little children a home. Most of all, she would provide the means whereby the weaver regained his pride. She would give him work. It proved a very satisfactory arrangement from everyone's point of view. The two little girls – Marie, aged ten, and Suzanne, nine – were both of a sweet disposition and helped Madeleine in the kitchen; whilst Paul helped his father lift up wine barrels and heavy provisions from the cellar.

Very soon Madeleine wondered how she could have managed without them. It was comforting to have a man on the spot. It discouraged familiarities from the customers and, when tempers became too hot, a word and a nod from the weaver was enough to subdue the dispute. For, though short in stature, Jacques was well made and muscular. Only one person, she feared, might resent the arrangement.

Annette, she thought, might see her place at The Cordelier disappearing. Perhaps that would have happened were it not for the widower. He, of course, was still bowed in grief from the loss of his dear Jeanne, but Madeleine saw that he and Annette liked each other and she hoped that, with time, the relationship might blossom for the romantic and neglected cook.

There was so much to do, so many improvements she wanted to make. But they would cost money. For the moment she must concentrate on providing good, hot, nourishing lunches at competitive prices.

Every morning Madeleine woke excited by the day ahead. It was like the theatre, she thought: each day was like a new opening, hoping the customers would enjoy the performance and return for the next. The Metalier family shared her enthusiasm, for if she thrived, so too did they. And though, as Madeleine readily acknowledged to her friends, the clientele were somewhat rougher than at The Parnasse, they were certainly lively, and also interested in politics. She felt in touch with what the ordinary man was thinking. At her souvenir-booth her customers had been transient visitors to Paris; buying once, never returning. Her other contacts had been pamphleteers whose writings she sold. Mostly they were extremists.

But seated at her yellow-topped tables were workers – fathers with children and responsibilities. One thing she recognised: they were angry! They had been angry since the massacre of the Champ-de-Mars and the introduction of martial law. Nor was the unrest confined to the Faubourg Saint-Antoine. The whole city was in ferment, aggravated by soaring prices and unemployment.

* * *

It was late February of the new year of 1792, and Madeleine was just coming out of Monsieur Bodin's cutlery shop in the shopping arcade of the Palais-Royal, when she heard Gabrielle Danton's voice hailing her. 'Madeleine, wait!' cried her friend, running up and embracing her.

Madeleine saw her face was flushed and excited. 'Oh, I'm so glad I caught you,' Gabrielle cried, adjusting a pretty bonnet of burgundy with matching feathers. 'It has saved me sending a messenger to you. Will you come to supper tonight? There'll just be the three of us. I've something wonderful to tell you.'

'Why of course,' laughed Madeleine. 'But won't you give me a hint now? It's cruel to leave me in suspense all day.'

But Gabrielle merely put her fingers to her lips in a most secretive manner. 'Until tonight, Madeleine,' she whispered and, with a merry wave of her hand, she left.

Throughout the day Madeleine puzzled as to what Gabrielle's good news could be. It must be important, Madeleine decided as Gabrielle, later that evening, led her into her salon. For her face, usually so modest, was ablaze with pride.

'Tell me your news,' begged Madeleine. 'Why are your eyes sparkling so?'

Gabrielle giggled, looking more like the girl who had teased Annette through the hatchway at The Parnasse than the serious matron of a member of the commune. 'Well, I shouldn't really say anything because it's not official. But the King has asked Lieutenant General Dumouriez to form a new ministry. It's rumoured that Georges will be given the Ministry of the Interior.'

'Why that's wonderful news, Gabrielle. It will

make up for his disappointment in not gaining a seat on the Legislative Assembly.'

'Quite,' smiled Gabrielle. 'It might also mean he'll give up the Cordelier Club. I'd like that. There seem to be some terrible men who belong to it.'

'Oh, many of them appear worse than they are. They're all trying to do their best for the people,' replied Madeleine, defensively. She didn't want to argue with her friend, but they saw things differently. Gabrielle, though kind, had never been poor. She lived only for Georges: if he was happy, so was Gabrielle. Though if she were to have her true wish, judged Madeleine, it would not be as the wife of the Minister of the Interior, but as the respected matron of an obscure country landowner.

But there could be no obscurity for Georges Danton, mused Madeleine, as the man strode into the room. It would be like trying to silence a trumpeting elephant, a bull at the height of the season.

Responding to her hostess's gesture for silence, Madeleine made no comment on his good fortune as she accepted a glass of champagne. 'Mmm ... delicious,' she said, sniffing the golden bubbles. 'Tell me, Georges, do you think war with Austria will come? Robespierre speaks against it at the Jacobin Club.'

'And the Brissotin party urge it at the Legislative Assembly,' replied Danton, throwing himself into an armchair. 'Well, as for me, within these walls, I say a country going to war must go from a position of strength. We have neither equipment nor men. If we are defeated we may lose the Constitution.'

'And the King, will he use his veto against war?' asked Madeleine.

'I do not think he wishes for war, but the Queen urges it: she sees it as her salvation, and a means of snatching back power.' Danton sighed and kicked off his shoes, warming his feet on the fender. 'What our poor vacillating monarch needs is a Minister of Strength. A man who fears no one.' He tossed back his champagne and turned, eyes gleaming with ambition, on Madeleine. 'What he needs is a man like me. Together Louis and I could save France!'

But the champagne had been drunk too soon! On 10 March Madeleine flicked through the *Moniteur* twice.

'Well it says nothing here about Georges,' sighed Madeleine to Jacques Metalier, who was standing beside her, behind the service counter. 'It says a Jean-Marie Roland has been made Minister of the Interior. I've never heard of him, have you, Jacques?'

'No, I can't say that I have. Ask Philippe, he knows everything, don't you, Philippe?'

Madeleine pushed her newspaper across the counter to the apprentice who had just arrived. Without even glancing at it, he spoke. 'I know what you're asking,' he grinned. 'It's what all Paris wants to know: who is Roland? Well, my friends, I can tell you. He is a nobody, some correspondence clerk from the Jacobin Club, pushed forward by the Girondist deputy Brissot. I can also tell you that, like our poor unwanted monarch, he too has a domineering wife, by the name of Manon, who no doubt will also start to meddle in politics. Really, all women should be kept in the kitchen, better still in the bedroom,' he added swiftly, leaning over the counter and kissing Madeleine full on the lips. 'Now don't just stand there gaping, Jacques,' the young man laughed as he dodged the blow of Madeleine's newspaper. 'A decent bottle of wine, if you please, to the corner over there, where I am going to teach our American friend how to lose at chess.'

Jacques Metalier laughed softly as he pulled the cork from a bottle of wine. 'He's a devil that one.

He just loves to stir things up, and he knows he has only to look at you and Thomas will respond.'

'Well Tom shouldn't,' replied Madeleine. 'After all, I don't belong to him.'

'Well, he thinks you do.'

Irritably Madeleine's eyes settled on the two men playing chess at Tom's usual table. Most days he sat there playing dominoes or chess, his face screened by a haze of pipe smoke; yet she knew his grey eyes watched her every movement. If she was having difficulty in lifting something, or if an attractive man spoke too long to her, he came over. She knew it was because he cared for her, but his constant presence and attention was beginning to stifle her, and though she had been grateful for his help in the refurbishment of The Cordelier, her indebtedness to him now only added to her feeling of suffocation. Sometimes she was tempted to respond openly to Philippe's advances, to deliberately hurt Tom, but she didn't, and such thoughts left her miserable with guilt.

'What do you think will happen to us, Jacques, if war does come?' asked Madeleine, purposely changing her train of thought.

'Well, it won't be good, Madeleine. Whenever there's a crisis, prices go up. They've started already, and those with capital are stockpiling now. You'll see, the moment war is declared, the grain depots will be empty. To be fair, it won't be the Court's fault. I'm from the country and I've seen it happen before: the farmers and peasants will hang on to grain for themselves. Though judging from the weather last year, there should be enough for the whole country.'

'I hope you're wrong,' said Madeleine, anxiety clouding her brow. 'If this business is to survive we can't afford to lose our customers through an empty larder.'

But Jacques Metalier's forebodings were borne out: the moment war was declared on Austria, the spiral of scarcity and soaring prices began. And as the French offensives turned into defeats, leaving the Austrians poised to enter France, panic, hysteria and hatred against the Court enveloped the city.

Chapter Five

'*La patrie en danger*,' yelled a newsboy, his thin voice intercepting each boom of the cannon on the Pont-Neuf.

'The Assembly have declared a state of emergency,' announced Tom, looking up from his newssheet. 'All able-bodied men are to enlist for the front. That means me, Madeleine. It's my fight too,' he said, meeting her startled look. 'You French helped us gain our independence; I'll fight to save yours!'

Madeleine looked up into the earnest grey eyes, knowing what he was thinking – that he might never return – for France was reeling back from the Austro-Prussian forces. She tried to speak, but the cannon from the Arsenal, now lending its voice to that of the Pont-Neuf, drowned out her words. She took his arm and they hurried on. Everywhere on the streets, people were rushing about as though the enemy were at the city walls.

'We'll get a drink at the Café du Foy,' yelled Tom at the top of his voice. Madeleine nodded in agreement and they pushed on through the excited crowds to the gardens of the Palais-Royal. The gardens and arcades were packed, dense throngs of people surrounding the orators.

'Why do you think our brave lads are losing?'

shouted a voice above the hubbub. 'Shall I tell you why?'

'Yes . . . yes,' roared the crowd.

'We're losing,' yelled the young man, flinging out his arm in the direction of the Tuileries, 'because that is the Austrian headquarters! And their commander in chief is no other than our popular Madame Veto!'

Eventually they found seats in the Café du Foy, where Tom ordered two mochas at an exorbitant price. Madeleine sipped her coffee. She wondered how Henri was. He had visited her at The Cordelier, but they had not spoken of that terrible night; nor had she ever spoken to Paul of it. For the safety of all of them, it was best forgotten. Laying down her cup she looked, with interest, at the tray a waiter was carrying to a table. I wonder where they are getting their sugar from, she thought, staring at the two large pastries. Perhaps they're using honey, she decided. At that moment Tom pulled his chair closer to hers and took hold of her hand. 'Madeleine,' he said gruffly, 'I have to speak. You know what's on my mind?'

Miserably she nodded, wanting to turn away yet not wishing to insult him as he stumbled on.

'You're so brave and beautiful . . . everything I've ever wanted in a woman. I've loved you so long and I've never dared to speak in case I lost you. But now I must . . . If I go to the front I may never return.' In a swift, passionate movement he raised her hand to his lips, and held it tight to his mouth.

'I want to marry you,' he said gruffly.

Stricken and silent, Madeleine looked down at the bowed red head. With all her heart she wished she could love him. 'It's an honour you do me, Thomas,' she said, withdrawing her hand. 'May I think about it?' It was as if she had said yes, for the curly head lifted and the grey eyes shone with such happiness that she felt sick with anxiety, regretting her cowardice, knowing she had given false hope.

Awkwardly making her excuses to leave, Madeleine hastened home, and was just entering the gateway which led through to the back of the restaurant, when she heard a great clucking and squawking. She ran forward immediately, ready to snatch her precious hens from the jaws of death. But it was only Paul, scattering grain to the half-starved creatures.

'I thought you'd be pleased,' said the boy, his serious face glowing with pride, as Madeleine clapped her hands in delight at the sight of grain.

'I found it in an abandoned house of some aristos – there was a whole sack of it in a garden shed.'

'Well done!' said Madeleine, patting the small boy on his shoulder. 'I thought we might end up boiling them, the way things were going,' she said, too happy to care where Paul had made his find.

'And Papa has got tripe for you, and onions too.'

'It gets better and better,' laughed Madeleine. 'When you've finished that, *chéri*, see if you can find a nice brown egg for Monsieur Artaud.'

'But he's an aristo!'

'No he isn't, Paul. He is a poor unfortunate man who used to make lovely fans, and now, as most of his noble customers have run away, the poor man is destitute, like so many of the craftsmen,' she sighed as she entered the back door of the café.

'Girls, you are my good fairies!' said Madeleine interrupting Marie and Suzanne's onion chopping with a kiss. 'But, do fairies always cry when they slice onions?' she teased, making the girls laugh amidst their onion fumes.

Smiling, Jacques Metalier's head appeared through the open hatch leading down into the cellar. 'Don't worry about this,' he said, pointing to a swelling over his right eye. 'Tempers got a bit frayed this morning, but as I was first in the queue I wasn't going to be cheated of what was clearly mine. I think you'll be pleased,' he said, motioning for her to descend. At that moment, however, Madeleine heard the door of the restaurant crash open and a large number of people enter. Surprised, for it was too early for customers taking lunch, she hurried through to serve.

'At last! – Friends, this is my sister, a patriot, who took the Bastille single-handed and who has lived on its proceeds ever since,' sniggered Pierre Fleury, supporting himself against the counter. Appalled, Madeleine surveyed the room, filled with rough, violent-looking men.

'What do you want, Pierre?' she asked in a low voice.

'What do men usually want in a wine shop – wine! Patriots,' he spluttered, lurching from Madeleine to the laughing men, 'give my sister your song – you shall all sing for your wine!'

It was the strangest choir Madeleine had ever seen, but just as they'd sung when entering Paris, so these dark-skinned men from the south, named the Marseillais, now sang Roguet de Lisle's song in Madeleine's café. It was a glorious, thrilling moment which caught her up in its fervour.

'You are welcome, *fédérés*! Drinks on the house, Jacques,' she cried.

'I don't think that was the wisest thing to do, Madeleine,' Jacques said, running an anxious hand through his thinning brown hair as the smiling girl returned. 'Give men like these free drinks and they'll never go. See, you're losing all your regulars who counted on your meal today.'

Madeleine looked towards the retreating backs

and bit her lip in annoyance, knowing what he said was true. She shrugged and smiled. 'Oh well, it's only for an hour or so, they'll be gone soon. We had to give them a welcome. After all, they're here to defend the city!'

'And their place is in their camp at Soissons. The King didn't give them permission to stay in the city. There are enough mouths to feed with the hundreds of unemployed flocking in every day.'

'Well, after this round of drinks I shall tell them they must pay,' said the girl with more confidence than she felt.

'You're not to do that Madeleine, they wouldn't think twice before slitting your throat. They've settled in for the night, my dear, and you'll just have to accept your loss.'

'But I can't, Jacques,' gasped the girl. 'A carafe or two is one thing, but solid drinking for hours will ruin me. I'll speak to Pierre.'

Within a moment she had returned and Metalier knew from the tight expression on Madeleine's face that Pierre was either too drunk, or just did not want to oblige.

'As I should have guessed,' she said, her low voice bitter with disappointment. 'I will have to speak to them myself.'

'*Citoyenne!* A man could starve here! Where is my food?'

Madeleine coldly examined the man. Above the waist, but for a sleeveless leather waistcoat, he was naked, with black hair on his chest as thick as an animal's. He was quite short, but his arms were rounded with bulging muscles.

'First your money, patriot!' she said firmly, retaining her hold on the dish.

'Go to hell! Everything in Paris is free for us!'

laughed the man, his cunning dark eyes examining Madeleine's body.

'If you wish to eat here, you must pay.'

'Then I won't eat, I'll have you instead!' cried the man, jumping up. Before she could stop herself, compelled by fear, Madeleine dealt him a hard blow. The tiny man before her blinked and shook his greasy black head in surprise. Then, joining in with the laughter of the men around him, he put up his fists and started to dance around her. As he passed behind her, his hairy arms flew around her, pulling her back against his body. Desperately Madeleine fought to break free, but like some small bear he squeezed her tighter. Gasping for breath, from behind she felt him start to butt against her in an obscene fashion, and a rhythmical clapping started in the room.

'Jacques,' she screamed, 'Pierre!' Through the blur of grinning faces, she saw her brother, his face scarlet with anger, speed towards her and violently thrust her aside. Numbly she stared at the chaos of flailing arms, trying to make sense of what was happening to The Cordelier: before her horrified eyes it was being broken apart.

To her right, the entrance door crashed open and Jacques Metalier, leading some thirty carpenters, ran to her brother's defence. Gradually the pandemonium ceased as the lads of the Faubourg evicted the city's protectors.

Madeleine surveyed the shattered room: the ripped yellow cloths hanging in shreds from upturned tables, lying soiled and discoloured amidst broken carafes and splintered chairs.

A hopeless feeling came over her and she covered her face with her hands and cried, just as she had done outside the basement print shop of the Palais-Royal.

A hand touched her shoulder and she heard the voice of her brother uttering words of comfort.

'Go away,' she sobbed. 'You've pulled me down, now leave me alone.'

When Thomas arrived the next day his broad face under the red curly hair was white and tense and a murderous light flickered in his eyes as he surveyed the damage. 'By God, I'd like to get my hands on the man who did this! I should never have left you alone, with all the strangers that are roaming the neighbourhood.'

'You can't stay here all the time, Tom. You have your own life to lead,' said Madeleine quietly.

'I should be at your side. Surely now you see you need a husband?' said the tall American, then added as Madeleine looked away, 'Well, anyway, I'll not take "no" on money. I'll have this place put in order and you'll not deny me that, Madeleine.'

'Tom, I . . .' faltered Madeleine, as new tears sprang to her eyes at this gentle man's generosity. Suddenly she saw the anger return to his face as her brother, Pierre, entered from the street. To her amazement, accompanying him was the small, fierce-looking man who had brought on her troubles.

'Please, Tom, let me handle this my way,' she said, placing a restraining hand on the big man's arm. 'He is my brother, and he did try to stop it.'

Swiftly Madeleine moved forward to greet the two men, her expression as cold as ice. 'I am surprised you had the courage to return,' she said to the small Corsican.

'I caused you harm and your house, and I am ashamed. It is not good to treat the sister of a friend so,' the man said, nodding towards Pierre.

'Yes, Madeleine, all the men are sorry,' said Pierre, setting a leather bag down on a table. 'They meant no harm; it just got out of hand, we'd been drinking all day. I hope that will cover everything,' he said, gesturing towards the bag. 'Everyone made a contribution.' Suddenly he stepped closer and, to her surprise, Madeleine saw tears in her brother's eyes as he embraced her.

'I love you,' he muttered gruffly, and then before she could speak, he and his fearsome friend sped away in embarrassment.

August blazed into the city like a sun god, burning up the trees and the leaves, changing their colours, causing them to drop to an early death. It was no weather to build barricades and the sweat ran down Madeleine's forehead in large beads. Her hands were cut and bleeding from the jagged edges of paving stones. Slowly she staggered forward with Annette and together they heaved the heavy boulder up on to the barricade.

'There,' snorted Annette with satisfaction, 'if this Duke of Brunswick thinks his troops will walk down our streets he's in for a big shock!'

Madeleine laughed, feeling quite light-headed from hunger and weariness. Looking around her she saw that she was no different from anyone else. Everyone was staggering: old ladies, children; all exhausted yet driven on by fear and anger. A window above them was thrust open.

'Look out!' she cried, pulling Annette out of the path of a descending mattress. With a soft thud it hit the ground, the cover splitting on impact, disgorging its feathers in a great white cloud. Helpless with laughter, Madeleine collapsed amidst a flurry of down, and stared up at the cross red face thrust out from the window.

'That's not for your pleasure, *citoyenne*,' bawled the owner, which only made her laugh the more. 'There's no time for resting when Prussian boots are outside our walls . . . If there were, I'd be lying on it up here, not you down there! Now be off with you to the barricade!'

'I think he's exaggerating a little,' Annette spluttered, hauling Madeleine to her feet. 'Why, I'll be the first under my bed if Prussian boots are kicking on our walls.'

'Come on, lovely ladies, it's no time for talking,' said a strapping coal merchant, heaving one of his sacks on to the barricade. 'Still gabbing?' he enquired as he returned empty-handed.

'You watch yer lip,' retorted Annette, perking up at his raillery. 'We're deciding whether to cut off this Duke of Brunswick's balls or ears.'

'I'm for balls on toast!' shrieked an elderly hag with blackened gums.

'But citizens, he is going to raze Paris to the ground if we touch our Queen!' cried a man in mock gravity. 'What shall we do?'

'We'll send him her gizzard!'

The young owner of The Cordelier turned away, sickened by the increasing obscenities, a dark foreboding filling her at the outcome of the morrow. But then she brushed the feeling aside; tomorrow the decent citizens would not let the rabble take over. The world would be watching their protest against a King and Queen who were betraying their soldiers and people to the enemy. No bloodshed, only abdication.

It was between midnight and one o'clock when the great bell of the Cordeliers summoned the people of the district to take up positions outside their doors. The sky was clear and bright with the stars, the night sultry; the heat of the day still with them. Despite their growing apart, Madeleine felt close to her brother once more; just as they had felt as children talking to each other in the darkness of their little

187

room at the laundry. Standing in the shadows of the old monastery, Madeleine could not see his face or that of Thomas. But she felt secure, flanked by the two men. After half an hour, two shadowy figures approached. Madeleine thought she recognised the voice of Stanislas Maillard, though she couldn't be sure. Yet it seemed more than likely, he always seemed to be present at such times. Had she not recognised him on the women's march to Versailles, masquerading in bonnet and shawl, urging them on to violence?

'What is it?' she whispered to her brother, when the men had slipped away into the dark.

'We have control of Paris now,' he said, his voice expressing his excitement. 'We've replaced the Committee of the Municipality! Santerre has taken over from Mandat de Grancy as Commander of the National Guard! We control the army!'

It became difficult to speak as one by one the church bells of Paris answered the summons of the Cordeliers. Soon the air was filled with the jangled reverberating clarion on the tocsin, a sound that set the dogs barking, imbuing each heart with thrill or threat.

Abruptly the bells stopped and there was silence. Such a silence! Madeleine felt she should not breathe lest she break it. All about her shadowy figures stood motionless, listening, waiting. Waiting for what? It was they who were the attackers.

> *'Allons, enfants de la patrie,*
> *Le jour de gloire est arrivé*
> *Contre nous de la tyrannie . . .'*

The strong husky voice broke the tension. Madeleine heard herself singing the opening of the 'Marseillaise', and within moments the men and women in the long column took up the chant. The drums at their head started their beat. And as the blood-red sun started its fiery ascent, they moved forward together.

In the upstairs window of the palace, Madeleine could see men of the royalist battalion of the Filles Saint-Thomas alongside many nobles and *chevaliers de poignard*. Despite Pierre's earlier boast, the situation looked very threatening. Most people only carried pikes and staves, little use against artillery.

Almost immediately an outburst of boos and cat-calls attracted their attention.

'What is it?'

'It's the King,' yelled an excited voice. 'Monsieur and Madame Veto are making a run for it to the Assembly!'

'*Vive la Nation* . . . Down with the fat pig and the Austrian!' shrieked a prostitute, whom Madeleine recognised from the gardens of the Palais-Royal.

'The day is ours! *Vive la Nation!*' shouted the crowd, surging forward through the gates leading into the outer courtyard.

'Thank God it's over with no bloodshed,' said Madeleine, smiling at a young soldier who had just thrown down his gun.

'Looks like it, *citoyenne*.' But he'd hardly spoken when firing broke out near to the steps of the palace. Immediately all was panic and confusion.

'Help! Help! The Swiss are killing us,' a voice cried. 'To arms, citizens!'

Blindly, Madeleine ran forward, not knowing what to do or where to go, terrified by the cannon fire and the heavy fusillade pouring down from the palace windows. But then Thomas grabbed her by the hand.

'Come on, over here where there's cover,' he shouted, dragging her towards a marble statue.

'Who started it?' she asked, as they crouched behind the shelter of the stone.

'I don't know. We got what we came for. It was either a misunderstanding or someone wants to fight.'

She saw a courtier lean out from a window and point his gun at a man fighting below with a Swiss guard. He held his fire, waiting for the two combatants to break apart. Suddenly, with a savage thrust, the man ran the guard through with a pike. Now the courtier will fire, Madeleine thought, then screamed as the *sans-culotte* turned. It was her brother!

'Pierre . . . look out!' she shouted, running forward. He heard her cry, and looked towards her as the shot rang out. The ball sent him reeling and he staggered towards her, blood gushing from his neck. Before she could reach him he had dropped.

'Pierre!'

Impervious to all, the girl crouched, cradling the lifeless body in her arms. Pressing him closely to her, rocking him as though he were asleep. His warm blood spurted out over her breast until her shirt and hands were running red. Gradually she became aware that someone was pulling at her arm. She looked up to see the concerned face of Tom.

Her isolation invaded, the full force of her loss struck home. 'No . . . no. Leave me alone!' she cried, pushing him away. A wild fury erupted inside her and pulling out her gun she ran towards the palace.

Inside, the marble corridors resounded to screams of pain and terror. Propelled by anger, desiring revenge, Madeleine ran unseeing past scenes of carnage, her sabots crunching on shattered mirrors, slipping on pools of blood.

Behind followed a howling mob, like a pack of hounds on her heels, as though she were leading them to a kill. Though she might never find the man who had taken her brother's life, no matter. For they were all guilty!

Still running, she swung around a corner and saw ahead a gilded door. Cocking her pistol, she flung it open, but stumbled across the dead body of a *sans-culotte* stretched across the entrance.

Inside two young men of the court were reloading their guns. They looked up in surprise at her sudden entrance. Immediately one of them withdrew his sword. A third man, dark-haired, was kneeling, stripping the carmagnole off a *sans-culotte*. Without looking around he withdrew his pistol, and then with the agility of a cat he sprang to his feet and turned to face her. His large black eyes narrowed as he took aim. They were the eyes of François-Athanase Charette.

Chapter Six

François-Athanase Charette de la Contrie, son of an old and noble family, responded like other young noblemen responded to the desperate plight of the royal family. Two hundred such chevaliers sped to Paris to lay down their lives. To shed their last drop of blood in defence of their king and queen.

Many of them were seasoned officers, confident that they could hold the palace against a poorly armed mob. The Swiss regiment of 900 men summoned from Courbevoie were crack troops, as was the royalist battalion of Filles Saint-Thomas.

Less certain were the 2,000 soldiers of the National Guard. Though with firm leadership, decided the twenty-nine-year-old Charette, the majority would remain loyal.

In the past, serving as a First Lieutenant in Louis XVI's navy, he had fought his way out of far tighter situations. They had arms and ammunition enough to withstand the siege easily. All that was needed was a boost to morale.

Charette did not, however, reckon with the loss of the Commander of the National Guard, nor with the review of the troops by his Most Christian Majesty. In dismay he watched, along with his companions — the Marquis Henri de La Rochejaquelein and Charles d'Autichamp — as the purple-suited king waddled dispiritedly along the ranks of the National Guard. Every line of his tired, sagging face suggesting defeat.

'It would have been better done by the Queen!' snapped Charette, compressing his thin lips in irritation.

'Look!' cried La Rochejaquelein, who was leaning out of the window to obtain a better view. 'The battalion on the Pont Tournant is marching to join the Marseillais on the Place du Carrousel.' Immediately this action received a huge cheer from the crowd, then another, as a second battalion followed suit. Pathetically, Louis XVI gazed about him, hesitant, uncertain what to do, as the insults and obscenities grew louder.

'Mon Dieu! A parade ground is no place for you,' muttered François-Athanase Charette under his breath. Then, with a dismissive shrug, he turned to the two other young nobles. 'Let them go!' he cried, carelessly waving his hand in a flurry of lace towards the retreating soldiers. 'What, after all, is a rabble of 20,000, compared to 200 chevaliers!'

La Rochejaquelein and d'Autichamp returned Charette's reckless grin, and all three burst out laughing, excited by the scent of danger. All were deadly with gun or sword. None feared death; only dishonour.

Since dawn there had been frantic activity and din within the palace, but as the 84-year-old Maréchal de Mailly entered the room, they heard a new clamour. The black eyes of Charette widened in disbelief.

'Yes, Messieurs,' said the old man, inclining his head in the direction of the great staircase. 'The royal family are leaving with the attorney-general, Roederer, to seek the protection of the Assembly.'

No one spoke. Each man keeping back his private thoughts.

'As you are aware, Messieurs, the King ordered we should only fire if fired upon. He has not instructed us to lay down our arms. Therefore, I, as the most senior officer present, intend to take command.' He paused, endeavouring to straighten his bent, aged frame; his eyes no longer dull, but shining with memories of other campaigns, the glory of yesterdays. 'I intend to defend the Tuileries! Be so kind as to stay at your posts.'

The three young noblemen bowed and took up their positions for the struggle to come. But as they looked down on a mass of people now streaming into the courtyard below, they were surprised and relieved to see the atmosphere had changed. A few of the Swiss officers had moved forward from their men and were standing talking in a friendly manner to a group of the insurgents. With the King's departure, the crisis seemed to be over. Then, one of the Swiss fell backwards, clutching his arm; immediately his companions rallied, dragged him through the swirling throng, up the steps and behind the troops, still arrayed in battle order. At once the Switzers discharged a round of ammunition into the crowd. Amid screams of fright and anger, the fragile peace was broken. Shots were returned – but not for long. The deadly fusillade pouring from the palace windows and the Switzers' disciplined fire soon put all to flight, leaving only the dead, and an abandoned cannon.

'You see, *mes amis*, how quickly they fly,' laughed Charette, reloading his smoking gun.

'Even so, it seems somewhat premature for the Switzers to march back to barracks,' murmured La Rochejaquelein.

Startled, Charette strode back to his side at the window. Sure enough, the Swiss had shouldered arms and were marching away. Dumbfounded, the young men watched them go; saw a wave of people overtake them and tear them to pieces with knives and hands.

'Obedient to death; unresisting, not one shot fired,' said Charette bitterly. 'Only one man could have given them that order. It would seem our vacillating monarch has sent the command to lay down arms!'

'Not the best of timing!' commented Charles d'Autichamp with a wry little smile. 'I think, Messieurs, we are lost,' he said, pointing, as the same angry wave surged towards the palace door.

Brave though they were, the three nobles paled as those to be first engulfed cried out in terror. Their shouts of agony mingled with savage whoops of joy. Every moment the spine-chilling sounds grew closer as the mob sought for fresh victims. Soon, the breaker carrying death and destruction would crash on their strand. They waited – eyes, nerves, tense for the onslaught. It began very soon, as a dozen ragged fiends rushed into the pale blue salon. Instantly six dropped as, gun in each hand, the chevaliers discharged both barrels. In unison they unsheathed their swords. Seeing their comrades so, and faced with three men who would sell their lives dear, the hyenas fled in search of easier pickings.

But there was no respite. A second attack was followed by a third, leaving the polished salon floor bloody and strewn with bodies.

'I think, Messieurs,' said Charette, crouching beside the dead body of a Marseillais, 'that, as I have only one shot left, a bottle of Burgundy in a quieter quarter of town would have its attractions!'

Too late! As he spoke, once again there was the unmistakable sound of sabots on a polished floor. Aware that La Rochejaquelein and d'Autichamp were unprepared, with lightning reflexes, Charette spun around, taking aim. In that split second, as finger pulled back trigger, the blood-drenched attacker smiled and uttered his name. So the flight of the bullet went high, plunging into the shoulder instead of the heart.

The youth staggered from the force of the ball, a look of bewilderment and hurt appearing on his face as he stared at Charette. Then, at the sound of clattering feet racing towards the room, the wounded boy flung himself at the door, pushing it closed. Amazed, Charette watched him slither down to his knees and turn the key in the lock. A pointless precaution, he thought, as the new assailants rattled the door-handle and then the blow of an axe caused the timber to shiver. But before the second blow came, the boy, supporting himself on the door-handle and obviously making a supreme effort, cried out, 'You cannot get in this way! It's me, Madeleine, Pierre Fleury's sister. You must go round the other side, the door is open.'

There was a muttering of voices and then a man shouted out: 'Many thanks, *citoyenne*. We'll join you in a moment!' and the group could be heard moving away.

With his mind whirling, bewildered by the use of his name, Charette rushed forward to help what was apparently a girl. Supporting her with one arm, he gazed down, for once in his life quite at a loss. Her face, tear-stained and smeared with blood, was strong and beautifully boned. And the eyes that gazed up at him, adoring and full of love, were exquisite, stirring memories of he knew not whom.

'Tell them you're my friend,' she murmured with a voice so husky he'd taken it for a boy's. 'The clothes . . . take the clothes,' she urged. Charette laid her back gently on the floor as she gradually lost consciousness; then joined La Rochejaquelein and

196

d'Autichamp who were already pulling rough trousers over their breeches.

'It seems, François, that one of your mistresses has come, like an angel of mercy to deliver us,' laughed Charles d'Autichamp.

'What is more serious,' replied Charette, pulling on a carmagnola, 'is that I cannot even remember who she is. For I declare I have never seen her before ... Quickly; they are almost upon us. Smear some blood on your faces and you'd best sever that leg!' Both men looked in horror as Charette pointed at one of the dead bodies. He smiled at them grimly. 'It's either the leg or his head. The Red Indians take scalps; and our liberators, I believe, take heads! So unless either of you want to grace a pike end ...' There was no need to continue. La Rochejaquelein, following his meaning, seized an abandoned meat cleaver and with one blow, severed the dead man's leg at the thigh.

'What about the girl?' he asked. 'She's losing a good deal of blood.'

'She comes with us,' replied Charette. 'She is our passport to freedom ... Besides,' he added with a roguish grin, 'I'm consumed with an overwhelming curiosity.' He stooped and picked up Madeleine as the door burst open.

'Too late, citizens,' he cried in a rough, coarse voice, striding to the open door before any of the horde could study closely the bodies on the floor. 'Make way, *citoyen*. Madeleine took a ball earlier from one of these cursed aristos. We have his leg in return,' he laughed.

'*Vive la Nation ... Les aristocrates à la lanterne*,' cackled an old hag viewing the leg dripping blood on Rochejaquelein's shoulder. Then, howling with glee, she led her party on for livelier sport.

'We must make for the river,' whispered Charette. 'It's our best chance.'

Appalling carnage met their eyes as they sped through the palace, every doorway framing slaughter. Yet they dared not stop, no matter how piteous the cries. To render assistance meant certain death!

At last they reached the doorway into the garden; welcoming the sun and air, and found another hell. Maids, courtiers, footmen, lay mutilated in pools of blood; whilst others, like crazed chickens in a coop beating their wings in useless flight, sought to escape the bloodstained knives.

Unhesitating, the three chevaliers plunged towards the terrace, passing a man perched high on a statue, sobbing with fear as his persecutors, shrieking with laughter, sought to dislodge him. For a moment Charette paused, adjusting his hold on the girl. The movement caused her to cry out, and he saw her eyes, now clear and comprehending, were flooding with pain.

'Hang on, little one,' he murmured, smiling down at her. Despite her suffering she returned the smile. 'Ah, François . . . at last,' she breathed.

'Yes, *chérie*,' he replied, humouring her. 'Forgive me if I hurt you, but we must make speed.'

Everywhere were groups of *sans-culottes*, but the small hurrying group aroused no suspicion. Indeed the grim trophy now hanging over d'Autichamp's shoulder, and a wounded youth in a Phrygian cap inspired only tributes. So that when they ran down the river bank towards a small boat, no move was made to stop them.

'I can't believe our luck,' remarked Charette grimly, pointing to several corpses near to the craft. 'They might even have escaped had they changed their white wigs for a liberty cap of red.'

Cautiously he lowered the girl into the bottom of

the boat. Suddenly a party of ragged women standing nearby ran towards them, but already Charette and La Rochejaquelein had the oars and were moving upstream.

'Why don't you throw them a bone, Charles?' asked Charette, looking with distaste at the leg which d'Autichamp still carried.

'Gladly,' said the blue-eyed young man with a merry laugh. 'Here my pretty hags,' he cried to the women who stood looking after them. 'With my compliments.' At the sound of the chevalier's voice which he had not striven to disguise, their expression of curiosity changed to mistrust; but then their attention was transferred to the falling leg. Like a pack of dogs they jumped and snapped to take possession.

'*Vive la Nation!*' shouted the victor, waving her prize at d'Autichamp.

But no one in the boat noticed; instead they looked with horror at a corpse floating downstream. A corpse wearing the uniform of Commander of the National Guard.

'So that's why he didn't return from the Hôtel de Ville,' commented Charette, revealing the gaping gun-shot hole in the Marquis de Mandat's back. He pushed the body away with his oar in disgust, his expression darkening with anger. 'They speak of liberty, when they know only treachery and murder.'

'And arson,' said La Rochejaquelein, pointing back towards a spiral of smoke ascending from the palace. In gloomy silence they disembarked and made their farewells, each seeking the succour of a friend.

In the undisturbed peace of the Marais, where his family's old retainer lived, it seemed to Charette the events across the river were a terrible dream. But his aching arms, supporting the wounded stranger, were a constant reminder of the tragic events. And though it was quiet, he noticed that all windows were firmly shuttered and no one was abroad.

At least, he thought, raising the heavy, lion-head knocker, there are fewer prying eyes. For he feared to endanger Étienne Gaspard and his wife, Thérèse. But the situation was desperate. The girl needed urgent medical help and he needed shelter whilst he devised a plan of escape from Paris.

The elderly retainer stared back in fear at the sight of the ragged man, but Charette spoke quickly. 'It's me, Étienne – François.'

'Oh, Master François, what in heaven's name . . . Come in, come in,' the elderly man said, nervously glancing out into the street before shutting the door. Straightaway the frail old man went ahead, leading Charette through to the back of the house and downstairs to a small kitchen. As the two men entered the room, Thérèse Gaspard, a short, stout woman, flung down her vegetable knife and, wiping her hands on her apron, rushed forward.

'Why, merciful heavens, what is it? Whatever has happened, Master François?' She ran back to the table gathering her utensils so that the men could lay down their burden.

'At least you recognised me, Thérèse, my dear,' grinned the young chevalier. 'It's more than Étienne did. He thought I'd come to slit his throat.'

'Pooh,' snorted Thérèse Gaspard, 'I've washed the mud off that face of yours too many times when you were a boy for a little blood and rags to fool me. Is this a lady of the court?' she whispered, gesturing towards Madeleine. For though the girl lay still, the eyes in the deathly white face were open and she was conscious.

'No,' replied Charette likewise in a low voice. 'I don't know who she is. But I do know she saved my life and if she loses hers I will be to blame. Try to staunch her wound until I return . . . I must fetch Davide des Naurois – you remember, my old school friend at the College of Anjou? He's studying medicine in Paris, he'll know what to do.'

'Let me go, Master François,' pleaded the old man, but Charette was already striding from the room.

Within the hour he had returned with the medical student, who gently took away the pad of cloth Madame Gaspard had been holding against the girl's shoulder. For a moment he looked at the wound and then he walked over to Charette.

'She's lost a lot of blood, that's why she's so weak, but the ball will have to come out . . . First I must find it. I'm afraid it will be very painful. You and Étienne will have to hold her down. Will you tell her or shall I?'

Charette shook his head. 'No, leave it to me.'

He walked back to the kitchen table and sat on the edge, taking the girl's cold hand between his own. 'Madeleine,' he murmured, recalling the name she had called to the *sans-culottes*. 'Madeleine, listen to me.' The thick curly lashes fluttered and the girl stared up at him. 'You have my bullet in your shoulder. It must come out. My friend, Davide, is a medical student. He will try not to hurt you, but it will be painful. We will have to hold you still. Do you understand? Will you be brave for me?' The girl nodded, and he gave her hand a reassuring squeeze as he felt its slight tremor.

Leaving Davide des Naurois to prepare, Charette stationed Étienne and Thérèse at the young girl's legs whilst he positioned himself so that he was looking down into her face. He talked to ease her embarrassment as the medical student, cutting away the blood-stained shirt, exposed a firm young breast.

Then, after a nod from Davide, he placed his

hands firmly against her shoulder and upper chest. As soon as the student inserted the probing rod, the girl released a cry of pain, then bit her lower lip in an effort to stop her cries. Used as he was to the horrors of naval surgery, Charette felt beads of sweat forming on his brow as the agonised amber eyes fixed on to his. He gritted his teeth, trying not to show his own distress, for he hated to see women cry. It was worse to see one struggling not to, but the pain was more than she could bear as the rod moved within the wound, searching for the ball. Tears rolled down her cheeks and she tried to raise herself and twist away from the agony. Relentlessly, he and the old couple pressed down, containing her efforts.

'Hold on, *chérie*; be brave just a little longer,' gasped Charette, leaning forward still closer to her face. With an intake of breath she remained still, held by the compelling black eyes.

'I have it,' muttered the student, the rod to his ear. 'Thank God it is not near the bone. One more big effort,' he said, nodding towards the girl as he picked up fine long tweezers. Once again the girl fought and cried out in an attempt to throw off the merciless hand. And then it was all over and, with a grunt of satisfaction, Davide des Naurois stood up, holding a lead ball between the fine points of the tweezers.

'Thank you,' said Charette, wiping his brow. 'I believe that belongs to me!' The medical student raised an eyebrow.

'I've never known you to catch your lady with a gun before, François.'

'It wasn't evident at the time she was a lady,' remarked Charette, taking the bullet to show the girl. 'There, young lady,' he said. Then he stopped, for her eyes were closed.

'I think she has fainted!' he said, pocketing the ball.

'More than likely, poor, brave thing,' clucked Madame Gaspard, handing Davide des Naurois a bowl of steaming water.

'Well, for those who have not fainted, I think a glass of cognac is called for, Étienne,' said Charette. 'I would not like to go through such an ordeal again!'

'Nor I, Master François, though she showed a lot of pluck.'

As the old man shuffled away for the brandy, Charette sat and watched his friend apply a dressing and bandage to the girl's shoulder. During her struggles, the red Phrygian cap had fallen off and her hair hung over the end of the table, like the drop of a waterfall, its golden glints sparkling in the firelight. Thérèse had removed the tattered shirt and, in the detached way of a connoisseur, his eyes slid over the half-naked girl. Her creamy skin was fine and like satin, would be smooth and possibly cool to the touch. In her supine position, the curve and fullness of her breasts were lessened, but he could see they would be full and luscious.

He tore his eyes away as his emotions stirred, and looked at her slim waist. With interest, he saw knotted around it a leather cord. Around her neck they had found the medal of a *vainqueur de la Bastille*. What now? he wondered. Picking up Thérèse Gaspard's abandoned knife, he slit through the leather. Then he withdrew the greasy cord, his large eyes widening with shock as, dumbfounded, he gazed at his own ring. Given so long ago to a terrified urchin. Involuntarily he turned towards the girl and found she was watching him through half-closed lids. Despite her pain, she smiled — a slow, warm smile that suffused her whole face with a glow.

Charette looked at her in wonder, saw the pride shining in her eyes, and suddenly felt a tenderness towards her almost painful in its intensity. Moving forward, he took her hand and raised it to his lips, acknowledging the sacrifice she had made. They did not speak, could not, for there were no words. It was a brief touching of two souls, beyond physical and mental attraction; a mutual recognition of noble aspirations that, for common men, are merely worthless dreams.

The night, like the day, was hot and stifling; for Madeleine, sleep was impossible. Even though the old lady made her drink a sleeping draught, its effects were useless. For the deep throbbing pain in her shoulder dominated her mind and entire body. She tried to distract herself by listening to the conversation in the room below. She could only hear the occasional word, though she guessed they were discussing the day's events.

Nor would the day leave her. With the brilliance of lightning, jumbled pictures flashed into her mind. One appeared more than most: over and over again she saw her brother turn, the blood spurting from his neck as he stumbled towards her. Then would come a relief of sorts, as her physical pain blotted out her mental anguish, causing her to weep, to find the relief of tears. Sometime, hours later, she heard movement from the room below and, moments after, the door of her chamber creaked open. Then, very quietly, someone approached and she felt the lightest touch of fingertips on her forehead. A feeling of relief, of safety, drifted over her and she knew it was him. She smelt the faint perfume of lavender as, very gently, he placed a damp cloth on her forehead. Then he sat down in the chair beside the bed. Gradually, fitfully, she fell asleep.

When Madeleine awoke, it was daylight. Charette

was still there, but freshly shaven, dressed in an exquisite jacket of honey-coloured silk. At his throat and wrist was a froth of delicate lace. He was reading and she noticed he was wearing the topaz and diamond ring. How well it sat, she thought, on his finger; fascinated, she stared at his hands. They were beautiful in their elegance, the tips of the long fingers lightly holding the small leather-bound volume as though it were crystal.

As if aware of her gaze, he turned and smiled, raising an eyebrow of enquiry. 'So, my little friend of the Palais-Royal, we meet again.'

Madeleine gazed back into the black, magnetic eyes, her heart pounding with excitement. The moment she had so longed for, so many times dreamed of, was here.

Suddenly the young man threw back his head and roared with laughter and she saw his eyes, no longer curious, were knowing and mischievous. 'Ah, *ma petite*,' he said, moving to sit on the edge of the bed. 'So it is true, and you kept the ring.' And once again he chuckled with delighted laughter.

Madeleine turned away, feeling foolish and angry that she had betrayed her emotions. She gasped as the movement set off waves of pain. But Charette, quick and sensitive to women's moods, took her hand and pressed its palm to his lips. Sensuously his lips lingered and caressed, while with his other hand he turned her face back to look into his. She saw the mockery and laughter were no longer there, only tenderness.

'Forgive me,' he murmured, planting a kiss on the tip of her nose. 'It was only my joy and delight in finding you. You're so free of artifice.'

His face, looking down at her, was so close that she could feel the warmth of his breath on her lips. Impulsively she reached up with her lips, seeking his mouth. A shiver of excitement running through her at the contact.

But he jerked away from her, spoiling the moment, an expression of delighted surprise on his handsome face. 'So, my patient wishes to be kissed,' he murmured, his eyes dancing with laughter. In a swift movement he slid his hand under the pillow, raised her from the bed, and brought down his mouth on hers. His lips were warm and firm, their caresses unhurried as they savoured and explored. Each parting and each renewal escalating pleasure, filling her with wild excitement and joy. As the urgency and passion of his kisses increased, so she was filled with an overwhelming desire to be his, to become as one.

Suddenly she felt his sharp intake of breath, his hesitation. Then he was all control: gradually lessening the intensity of his mouth on hers; ending with a kiss, gentle and full of sweetness.

He laid her back against the mattress, though fierce points of desire still gleamed in his dark eyes. Silently, he stared down at her, running a coil of her hair between his fingers. His expression becoming dark and brooding, as though thinking of other things. Then suddenly his mood changed and he stood up. 'I think, Mademoiselle,' he said, giving her a boyish smile, 'I'd best summon Madame Gaspard; for you are indeed a very dangerous young lady.' He chuckled, seeing her lips pout. 'I seem to recall the first kiss you stole nearly unseated me from my horse, whilst today I nearly forgot you are my patient!'

He walked across to the bell pull, almost relieved to put distance between himself and the girl; for the current was so strong between them that he wanted to touch her all the time. He knew that she, too, was affected. He'd taken and enjoyed many women, but

206

the passionate response of this girl had almost over-whelmed him. Only his experience had enabled him to draw back, to stop desire ripping away the thin dividing sheet and making love to her.

'Ah, Thérèse,' he said, turning as the stout little lady entered the room, 'I rely on you to see that Mademoiselle Madeleine does not attempt to get up, and rests.'

'You can rely on that, Master François. As soon as I have looked at that nasty wound, it's a bowl of something nice, and sleep!'

'Good,' smiled Charette. 'I leave you in the hands of a fine nurse, Madeleine.'

'Well, you of all people should know,' remarked the little lady, setting down her tray, a look of pride on her jolly face.

Madeleine watched the tall athletic figure of François-Athanase Charette move towards the door. 'François,' she said, suddenly fearful, 'you will be back later?'

His large black eyes laughed back at her, filled with excitement. 'Nothing, Mademoiselle, would keep me away!' And with an elegant flourish of lace he saluted her, and was gone.

Thérèse Gaspard's fingers were knotted and twisted with age and rheumatics, but their touch was swift and sure. 'There, does that feel better?' she asked after applying a new dressing to Madeleine's shoulder.

'Yes, thank you, Madame, it feels less painful and cooler.'

'Good. There's nothing to worry about: you've got good healing flesh, my dear. It will soon mend. It will be stiff, mark you, and you should keep it in a sling to rest it. And rest is what you need today. Tomorrow you can get up, but not before, or Master François will be furious with you and me.'

'How long have you known François?' asked Madeleine shyly.

The old lady straightened from tucking in the bed covers. 'Why, I've known him from the day he thrust his curly black hair into the world.' A fond, faraway look came into her eyes. 'Oh what a noise he made. I remember it was spring, 21 April.'

Handing Madeleine the tray, on which there was a small bowl of gruel, she sat down in the chair occupied by Charette the previous night. 'Yes,' she sighed, 'I've tended more than one cut and bruise. He was always into mischief as a boy. Étienne, my husband, taught him to ride, you know; he rides like the devil! There's no one can catch him at the hunt.'

'Does he have brothers and sisters?' asked Madeleine, eager to know everything about her naval officer.

'Oh, yes, his mother Marie-Anne had seven. But the four boys born before Master François died. So there is only another brother, Louis-Martin, and a sister, Marie-Anne.' She paused and nodded. 'He was a good scholar though, despite his wildness, brilliant at mathematics, you know ... but lazy, always one for pleasure, hunting and dancing.'

'And now he serves in the navy?'

'Oh, no,' replied Thérèse Gaspard in surprise. 'No, he resigned his commission about two years ago. You must get him to tell you about his adventures. Why the stories he has told Étienne about his life at sea ... and in the Americas. Ah, but I miss the old life and his father; what a romantic day when the Sieur de la Contrie brought home his bride.' She laughed, clapping her hands together in remembrance. 'Do you know how Master François's father met his wife? It was when Louis-Michel was in the army; he was out walking with two friends in a town in the Ardèche. Marie-Anne was standing at a window with two friends and straightaway he told his friends he would marry her. It ended up they were all married, all three on the same day! Have you ever heard anything like it!'

Madeleine shook her head, smiling – beginning to feel a part of the young chevalier's life. 'Oh do tell me more!' she urged as Madame Gaspard, looking at the empty bowl on the tray, rose to go.

'I could talk to you all day,' the old lady replied, patting her hand, 'but you must rest now. Is there anything else you need?'

'Only to send a note to my friends. They will be anxious for me . . . Of course, I won't put where I'm staying,' she added quickly, seeing the sudden frightened look on Madame Gaspard's face. The old lady nodded in understanding and disappeared to return moments later with pen and ink. Madeleine scribbled just a few words to Jacques Metalier. 'Am safe with friends. Will return soon, Madeleine.' Then to reassure her kindly hostess she handed back the note unfolded, together with the envelope.

Immediately, the old lady relaxed. It's not surprising she's nervous, thought Madeleine, as she watched her leave the room. After all, they must all wonder what role I was playing at the Tuileries.

For the rest of the day she slept, exhausted by her ordeal and weakened by her loss of blood. Sometimes she would wake when the deep throbbing pain reached through to her unconscious. Then she lay listening to the sounds of the house and the street below. In the evening, when dark shadows gradually filled the room, Thérèse Gaspard brought her another sleeping draught, and this time it masked the dull ache of her pain and she slept throughout the night.

The next morning she awoke feeling more vital

and, after Thérèse had renewed her dressing, she insisted on taking breakfast before the open window.

It was there that Charette found her, dressed in a frilly cotton nightgown with a shawl of cream wool around her shoulders. 'Good morning, *ma petite*. I see your cheeks have acquired a little colour since yesterday. Have you missed me?' he teased, kissing the nape of her neck. 'Mmm, most becoming,' he said, touching her hair piled up on top of her head.

'Thérèse thought it would be cooler for me,' she explained.

Gracefully, as with all his movements, François poured himself a small cup of chocolate and sat down opposite her, stretching out his long legs. Like the day before, she saw he wore tight white breeches and riding boots of a soft supple leather.

As he sipped his chocolate, she was aware of his gaze over the rim of the cup, but it was not possible to guess his thoughts. Yet it was easy to feel his restlessness. Again, the moment they were together, the thrilling tension between them grew.

'What is the news?' she asked, slightly flustered, for she felt he divined her thought.

'It's not good. The King and Queen are being taken to the Temple and many people are being arrested. I must leave Paris; every day I stay endangers Étienne and Thérèse. They've started searching houses. It's only a matter of time before they come here, *ma petite*. Now that Paris is back in the hands of men like Marat and Danton . . .'

'Danton?' queried Madeleine.

'Yes, he has been made Minister of Justice and has virtual control of Paris.'

'Oh, I'm so pleased,' blurted out Madeleine, not picking up the note of revulsion in Charette's voice. He stared at her in amazement.

'Pleased! . . . You're pleased . . . that a man who has caused the overthrow of our monarchy . . .'

The large black eyes narrowed to slits. 'Of course . . .' he said slowly, in a voice that was cold and full of contempt, '. . . that is why you were at the Tuileries. I've been so blinded by your noble rescue that I forgot you were also with your friends on a mission of murder.' He stood up and turned away with a gesture of anger and disgust.

Helplessly, Madeleine looked at his retreating back. How could she explain the uncontrollable emotions that had driven her from her dead brother into the palace; that they had only wanted abdication not blood.

'The people were fired on first by the Swiss,' she said dully. 'We marched on the palace only to force the King to abdicate.'

'Then, my dear,' he said, turning about with a face of stone, 'you succeeded. And who, pray, will you replace him with? No doubt, from your obvious admiration, Georges Jacques Danton.' He flung the name out with heavy irony, his noble head tilted back with the arrogance of birth.

'Danton has many fine qualities,' Madeleine snapped back, her eyes blazing with anger. 'Perhaps it's time for the people to guide the destiny of France. You nobles have suppressed the people for years. We have fought to free them, so that all will be equal!'

'Equal!' he laughed. His face was cruel and mocking. 'Equal! You call that scum, who murder and terrorise decent folk like Étienne and Thérèse, equal. You would let the half-witted, the irresponsible, the malleable, have an equal voice in the running of France. Bah, they will never be equal. Merely manipulated; tools to be used by the clever rascals at the Jacobin club who know nothing of *noblesse oblige*! But enough of this matter,' he said impatiently, his manner becoming cold and formal. 'I leave Paris soon. So I thank you once more for saving my life, and that of my companions. I would beg of you not to betray to your friends Étienne and Thérèse's former employment; it would be a kindness in return for their help to you.'

Madeleine shrank back from the insult and cruelty of his words. Looking straight through her, he saluted stiffly and turned on his heel.

'One moment, *citoyen*,' she hissed savagely, enjoying the revolutionary term of address, 'I think you have forgotten your manners!'

Startled, Charette stopped and turned, imperiously lifting a black brow.

'As I am condemned to bear the mark of your poor markmanship for the rest of my life,' Madeleine said in a cutting tone, 'I had hoped that a gentleman might have shown some remorse!' The black eyes sparked and his countenance, she saw, paled at her rebuke.

'Mademoiselle, for the scar you have my profound apologies,' he replied in a tight voice, 'and my assurance that, should we meet in similar circumstances, I shall not miss my mark a second time!'

Then with another bow he went, quietly closing the door behind him and leaving Madeleine alone.

'So, Gabrielle, how does it feel to be one of the most important ladies in France, wife of the all powerful Minister of Justice?'

'I'm not sure,' responded Gabrielle, anxiously inspecting Madeleine's gun-shot wound. 'But Georges is ecstatic. Oh, what he is going to do for France!' She laughed, shaking her head. 'Why, he hardly allows himself any sleep. Did you know he has appointed Camille Desmoulins as Secretary-General and Fabre d'Eglantine as Secretary of the Seals?'

'All the old Cordeliers,' mused Madeleine, wincing sharply as Gabrielle applied a clean dressing.

'Oh, I'm sorry, was I a little rough?' asked Gabrielle pausing in her work.

'No, it's kind of you to do it. I didn't think Jacques at The Cordelier would know what to do and Annette, well . . . she would ask too many questions. Besides I haven't forgotten what excellent nursing pulled Georges and me through the typhoid.'

'Nor have I forgotten what difficult patients you both were,' laughed Gabrielle, disappearing into the bedroom.

When she returned she was carrying a large red handkerchief. 'I thought this would make an ideal sling,' she said, placing it into position. 'You know, *chérie*, we were very worried about you. Thomas told us when Pierre was killed you rushed into the palace. He followed, searching for you, then spotted you being carried away to the river by three men. Until Jacques received your note we were nearly out of our minds wondering who the men were . . . so many terrible things happened that day.'

Madeleine sat silently. She had no wish to discuss the nightmare she had witnessed.

'Oh well, it's all over now,' sighed Gabrielle, patting Madeleine's hand. 'But bring those brave fellows around to take a glass of wine. I'd like to thank them for taking care of you.'

'He'll leave today,' replied Madeleine mechanically, oblivious of her friend; suddenly feeling a black emptiness welling up within her, a sense of loss verging on despair.

Gabrielle looked sharply at her friend, surprised by her dispirited voice and look of sadness. Obviously the death of her brother had affected her deeply, but there was more to it than that. Who was this man she spoke of?

213

'Then I can meet your friend,' she said watching closely Madeleine's reaction, 'for unless he is on very important business for the government, he will have to stay. No internal passports are being issued. It's the only way to stop the spies and the aristocrats joining forces with the émigrés and the Prussian troops. Anyone trying to leave will be arrested. But I'm sure they'll be released later if they're innocent,' she added hastily, seeing Madeleine's lassitude change to alarm.

'What is it Madeleine . . .? Is this friend of yours in some kind of trouble . . .?' Gabrielle searched desperately in her mind as to who this man could be. There seemed to be no one, for though she had tried to foster the relationship with Thomas, Madeleine had shown little interest in him or, indeed, any other suitor. Yet by the fear in her eyes and the pallor of her face, it was someone she cared for deeply and who was in danger from the emergency laws. Suddenly she thought of the ring she had found tied around the girl's waist, and her confession of love that day. 'It's your naval officer, Madeleine, isn't it?'

The question took the wounded girl completely by surprise, and her reaction was immediate, confirming Gabrielle's intuition. 'Trust me, Madeleine,' she urged. 'You know I will not betray you. What you tell me is only between you and me. But if your friend is of noble birth, he must remain in hiding. You must warn him if you wish to save him!'

'That he will never do,' said Madeleine, recalling Charette's concern for the Gaspards. 'I know he will try and leave.'

'Then you must think of a way to smuggle this man out of the city. Oh, if only I could ask Georges to help.'

'No, you mustn't, Gabrielle. It's enough that I can confide in you. Don't worry, I'll think of a way.'

Madeleine rose to go and at the door Gabrielle took her hand. 'Take care, my friend,' she whispered. 'You love him very much!'

Madeleine nodded miserably. 'Yes, but I fear he hates me.'

'Yet, you will try to save him?'

Madeleine nodded.

'Then it cannot be that he can hate you; rather, I suspect you'll find he loves you too.'

Outside in the hot sunshine Madeleine lingered, wondering what to do. She had not yet been back to The Cordelier, having come direct from the Marais quarter to the Cour du Commerce. It was almost noon, for she had left the Gaspards immediately after the scene with Charette. Despite Thérèse Gaspard's questions and concern, she had said nothing of their quarrel, merely saying her friends would be worried for her.

For a while she sat on a low wall near the Théâtre Français, wondering how best to get Charette out of Paris. Of one thing she was certain, nothing would persuade him to go into hiding.

Slowly a plan evolved, and with it her earlier lassitude disappeared. Purposefully she strode towards the Place Vendôme and the Chancellerie, her will to succeed filling her with energy.

Carried forward on this energy she entered the beautiful, intimidating building confidently, impervious to its overwhelming embodiment of power. The marble corridors were awash with people, the atmosphere tense with anxiety.

Finding an usher who was not besieged with questioners, Madeleine flashed him a winning smile. 'I wish to see the Minister of Justice,' she said.

'Join them,' he growled, jerking his thumb in the direction of a crowd of people slumped against walls

215

and crowded together on a long bench, their weary faces telling of their long wait.

'But I am a friend,' protested Madeleine.

'So are they . . . all of them, his friend, brother, sister . . .'

'Look,' said Madeleine, reaching inside her bodice and pulling out a chain. 'Do you see what that is?'

'Well, it's the medal of a *vainqueur de la Bastille*,' he said respectfully.

· 'Precisely . . . and as a *vainqueur de la Bastille*, I tell you I am Danton's friend. I would like you to go now and tell the Minister that Madeleine wishes to see him urgently. If you do not, it will be more than your job you lose . . . you understand my meaning?'

'Oh yes, *citoyenne* . . . immediately!' responded the usher under the girl's fierce stare. 'Perhaps you would like to wait in the ante-chamber.'

Within half an hour Pare, Danton's secretary, came to her and led her through into the Minister of Justice's office. For the first time, Madeleine saw Georges as others might, who entered this room in fear of their lives. Wearing the large ostrich-plumed hat of office he looked larger than life, dominating and fearsome. How coarse and vulgar he looked compared with Charette, she thought, as he walked forward to greet her.

'Madeleine, my dear, how good to see you. Never let it be said I don't have time for old friends, even in these busy first days of office,' he said, gesturing towards a stack of documents covering the desk.

'I promise not to take up your time; it's more than good of you to see me. Forgive me for disturbing you here but I need your help urgently! I want an internal passport.'

'For yourself?' queried Danton, his eyes narrowing slightly.

Madeleine thought rapidly, dare she ask for two. 'Yes, and for a friend.'

'I see, and when do you and your friend wish to leave Paris, Madeleine?'

'Tonight. We wish to visit friends in Nantes and bring back provisions in my cart from the country.'

'Tonight! You seem to be in rather a hurry. Wouldn't it be better to wait? For I see you are wounded, no doubt at the Tuileries. Would you leave Paris so soon after Pierre has died? And your friend? Do I know him . . . her?'

Under his powerful gaze Madeleine felt some of her calm desert her. 'Please Georges, it's very important to me.'

Danton sat for a moment on the edge of the massive desk, studying the girl's anxious face and the excited gleam in the slanted eyes. He began to understand what was involved.

'Very well, Madeleine, I will give you all the necessary documents to leave Paris in order to bring back provisions . . . However,' he said, holding up his head at the happiness flooding her face, 'your, er, friend will have to fend for himself. I cannot allow you to compromise me in this rather urgent venture of yours.'

He moved towards her and held her face between his great hands, staring down into the liquid bronze of her eyes and smiled, seeing them flash with irritation at his lack of compliance. 'But of course,' he said softly, forcing a small kiss on the sultry lips, 'what you take out of Paris and what you return with is a matter for you. Only remember, as lovely as you are, I will not save you!'

'Thank God you're safe, Madeleine,' said Jacques Metalier, as she slipped quietly into the kitchen of The Cordelier. 'Why, you're wounded . . . What happened? Why didn't you come back here? Tom Adams is nearly out of his mind, poor chap.'

'I know, Jacques. There's no time to explain. I'm leaving Paris today. I need the horse and cart. Put in some fodder for the horse and some food and a couple of bottles of wine. Enough for three days for two people. And then cover it over with some sacking.'

'But where . . . .?'

'Jacques, I am leaving Paris on Danton's authority. It's better that none of you know more. But I'll be back within a week, I hope with grain and vegetables.'

'You can rely on me, Madeleine,' the short stocky man said, grasping her hand. 'You saved my life, I'll not forget that. Annette won't talk either – I'll see to that. We've become a bit closer of late,' he said shyly.

'I am so pleased, Jacques,' she smiled, touching his arm affectionately. 'Now, while you get the things together, I'll change – an old lady's dress of twice my size looks rather odd, even for these strange days. Where's Paul?'

'He's gone out on one of his foraging trips. He says you called him a magician who can conjure up everything we need.'

She raced upstairs, a feeling of exhilaration at the dangerous adventure opening up before her. She folded Thérèse Gaspard's dress neatly and, tucking it under her arm, slipped downstairs into the back yard.

'Jacques, you've done splendidly,' said Madeleine, clambering up into the driver's seat of the cart. 'Thanks for taking care of everything. You know I wouldn't leave it all to you if it wasn't something urgent.'

'Don't you worry,' he said, pulling back the high gate leading into the street. 'I'll look after things for as long as you need me to. Are you sure you can manage?' he asked, looking with concern as she clumsily gathered the reins up with one hand.

'I'll be fine. Give my love to Paul, the girls and Annette.'

He waved cheerily and she turned the old mare, Rouge, out into the street. Just as she passed the door into The Cordelier, out of the corner of her eye she saw Tom's tall figure emerge. She flapped the reins smartly against Rouge, hoping that he had not seen her. But the sound of running feet told her she was discovered.

'Madeleine, wait ...' Groaning inwardly, she slowed Rouge down to walking pace as Tom ran alongside.

'You're back,' he said, his face full of hurt. 'Didn't Jacques tell you I was in?'

'No, Tom. I saw you myself but I am in rather a hurry. I have no time to stop and talk.'

'No time!' he said incredulously, his usual mild manner threatening an explosion. 'You've no time; when I've searched Paris for you, lying awake sick with worry, wondering if you were dead or alive. You owe me an explanation, Madeleine,' he shouted, his face crimson with emotion. 'Where have you been, and who have you been with?'

'I owe you no explanation,' replied Madeleine, more sharply than she had intended, but the heat of the day and the pain in her shoulder had robbed her of all patience. 'You're a dear friend ... but ...'

'But ...' he barked, his eyes red-rimmed from lack of sleep and tortured with jealousy, 'but you don't love me, is that what you're trying to say?'

Madeleine flicked the reins to move Rouge forward, but in one bound the desperate man leapt up on to the seat beside her. 'Perhaps you're incapable of love,' he said harshly, seizing her and thrusting his mouth on hers. The stench of brandy assailed her nostrils and she realised he had been drinking heavily. 'You're not going anywhere until you tell me you love me,' he said, almost weeping like a child.

Filled with disgust and embarrassed to see him like this, Madeleine pushed him away. 'Leave me alone, Tom.'

Again he lunged for her and she cried out as his body hit her shoulder. Consumed with pain and anger she turned and caught him under the chin, catching him off balance so that he fell backwards from the seat.

'You're right,' she cried, glaring down at him. 'I'll never love you . . . How could I love you or anyone like you! You're not even French.'

Then, sobbing with pain, with a fierce lash of the reins, she set the horse in motion, averting her eyes from the humiliated man sprawled on the pavement.

The city, as she drove to the Faubourg de Temple, seemed like a fortress. Everywhere there were the barricades which she and others had built. Before them armed men prowled like jealous watchdogs, guarding entry into their section. Yet Madeleine did not fear them. She spoke their language, carried their scent. Progress through the hot dusty streets was tedious, made slow by long columns of soldiers on the move, the tramp of their feet giving new fervour to the bands playing before the tricolor-draped recruitment posts. There were other soldiers too. They, unlike their comrades, were not marching to the front, but to the prisons. And each of the escorted tumbrils she passed confirmed Gabrielle's warning of widespread arrests. The sight of these grief-laden carts filled her with dread and she scanned each face, terrified that he might be amongst them. Madeleine felt no sense of triumph in seeing the proud brought low, only a wondering unease that small children and old ladies could be seen as a threat to the city.

Further on, she passed the old grim fortress of the Temple but she could feel no pity for the incarcerated Queen. Too many times as a child in winter she had watched the gay cavalcades of royal sleighs hurtle along the icy boulevards, the night air filled with the jingle of bells and careless laughter, as Marie-Antoinette and her friends glided along in cocoons of warmth and ease. The lights of the torches, falling short of the shadows where children crouched, blue with cold, some never to see the wintry dawn. Let her now feel cold and want, thought Madeleine savagely, hitting the lion-head knocker against the Gaspards's door.

It was a nervous Étienne Gaspard who, moments later, opened it. 'Why, Mademoiselle, we did not expect to see you again. Please come in,' he said, blinking in the bright sunshine.

'It's Master François I've come to see, Monsieur. It's very urgent!' she added, worried that Charette might have left instructions that he did not wish to receive her.

'Why, he's gone,' replied the old man, ushering her into the salon.

At the window, Thérèse Gaspard sat, holding an embroidery ring. She dropped her work into her lap at the appearance of Madeleine. 'Why, Mademoiselle Madeleine, is anything wrong?'

'No, Thérèse, calm yourself,' said the old man, gesturing for his wife to remain in her seat. 'Mademoiselle wishes to see Master François and I have told her he has already left.'

'Étienne,' said Madeleine urgently, 'do you know if he had a passport? Otherwise he will be arrested and sent to prison. You must tell me where he went.'

221

The elderly couple nervously exchanged glances and Madeleine realised they did not completely trust her. Little wonder, she thought wryly, for she had dressed for the barrier with exceptional care.

'Please, Madame, Monsieur, trust me! What can I say ... other than that I care for him ... I would give my life for him!'

Étienne Gaspard looked at the girl without surprise. Since childhood his young master had captured women's hearts by the score. Even so, this was a young lioness staking claim. Her word he did not doubt, for the strong passionate face was free of all duplicity.

'He will leave by the Porte de Versailles tonight at 6.00 p.m.,' he answered promptly.

'How will he be dressed?'

'Oh, he looks magnificent!' replied Thérèse Gaspard, quickly volunteering the information now that her husband had demonstrated his trust. 'Why he was wearing sky-blue, just as he did on the day he married Marie-Angélique.'

The pretty name, deadly as a knife thrust into the girl, caused her to start and pale to a deathly white. A terrible, awkward silence fell upon the room and Gaspard cursed Thérèse's loquacious tongue; now was not the time to disclose a wife. But it was done. What their chevalier had omitted to tell the beautiful girl, his wife had. And from the worried glance Thérèse shot at him, he knew that she too realised the possible consequences of her casual remark. For already a dark angry flush was sweeping upward over the girl's face and the eyes, which but a second before had expressed shock and disbelief, now flashed cold with anger. Like a caged animal she glanced towards the door and then, muttering something in a voice so low that his old ears failed to hear, she ran from the salon, dropping Thérèse's old dress as she went.

Blinded with scalding tears, Madeleine saw not where she was driving. All she wanted was to distance herself from the sympathy she had seen in Étienne Gaspard's eyes. What a fool she had been! A romantic, childish fool; to have based her life on a dream, an obsession. Let him perish! Let the *sans-culottes* at the barrier fall upon the sky-blue coat. He loved another woman. It was not for her to care.

The pain of disappointment twisted inside her and the words of Gabrielle, 'If you wish to save him', kept ringing in her ears. Miserably she slackened her hold on the reins, barely noticing when Rouge seized the opportunity to halt.

For a long time she sat, staring ahead, the sense of loss like a weight within her. She remembered their first meeting; the sound of his joyous laughter as, at full gallop, he had snatched her up and away from her pursuers of the Palais-Royal.

And later, the thrill of his lips as she had reached up in the darkness to steal a kiss. Nor had the childhood memory she had cherished in her heart proven false. Still his lips excited her, even more so. For now she had the desire of a woman and her instincts told her that he too desired her and wanted her.

No, it was not possible to abandon him; it never really had been, she thought, with a wry smile. With the back of her hand she wiped her eyes and looked about. Already there were shadows and the rays of the sun were weakening. It must soon be 6.00 p.m.; even now he might be approaching the barrier. There was no time to lose.

Despite the withdrawal of internal passports,

within sight of the city gate Madeleine saw there was a queue of people hoping to leave. Some were being turned back, but many were being marched to the guard house. A jeering, yelling mob had taken it upon itself to encourage soldiers in their work, and yells for death and worse soon emptied the street of other would-be travellers. Even with papers, thought Madeleine, it was risky to pass, but without them it would be sheer madness. The mere sight of a lace ruffle led to arrest; whilst from Thérèse Gaspard's description, Charette would be torn to pieces on sight. Surely he was not such a fool to appear as a chevalier of the court. Hopefully not, for it was striking the hour and there was no sign of a sky-blue coat anywhere. Hastily Madeleine put the thought of his allegiances and the woman named Marie-Angélique from her mind, before the desire to hurt and cause him pain could consume her once again. She had made her resolve; he was not to be taken. He now scorned and despised her, but at least she would not let Marat's thugs at the gate debase the revolution in his eyes.

Now that the approach to the gate was empty, the rowdies – having no other distractions – had spotted her. Madeleine began to feel a little uneasy as their hoots and whistles increased. Their attention had aroused the curiosity of the National Guard and, out of the corner of her eye, she glimpsed the approach of a uniform. It was a captain of the National Guard, she saw, as he drew alongside. But he did not stop and, relieved, Madeleine watched him progress towards the gate. She wondered who he was, for there was something familiar about his walk, an elegance to the purposeful stride.

Her heart lurched and missed a beat, and she brought the whip down so suddenly that Rouge reared from shock and plunged forward in terror.

For it was François, and whether he had a pass or not, Madeleine could not sit and watch.

At the sound of the horse's hooves clattering over the cobbles, the captain turned, as did the soldiers at the barrier.

'*Citoyen*, Captain, I have been waiting for you,' Madeleine cried. She alone saw Charette's surprise and the thin bow of his mouth tighten in annoyance. Clearly he thought she had ruined his opening. 'Come, Captain, up beside me,' she called gaily, giving a wink to the crowd as she patted the seat beside her. As yet the audience were uncertain how to react, but as she planted a kiss on Charette's cheek, and winked again, the laughter and the obscenities began. Madeleine tried not to look at the man beside her, for she felt his anger. Instead she addressed herself to the ragged women and leering men, many of them dark-skinned from the south; strangers, not Parisians.

'You see how our Minister of Justice takes good care of us women,' she called, waving Danton's letter in the air. 'Even I did not expect a Parisian captain to escort me for my cabbages. Perhaps,' said Madeleine, pouting her lips and leaning down low so that her blouse fell away from her shoulder, treating the onlookers to a generous glimpse of curving breasts, 'perhaps you should all come and protect me from these terrible aristos. What do you say . . . care for a whiff of country air with the good captain and me?' She smiled provocatively at the lusting men and, as one of them ran forward to grab at her, playfully she brought the whip down on his outstretched hand, though smartly enough to make him cry out in pain. His companions roared with laughter and the soldiers, barely glancing at Danton's letter, waved her through.

'You be careful it's not more than cabbages you

bring back, *citoyenne*,' shrieked an old hag, laughing up at Madeleine.

'Yes, have one for me, Captain,' roared a man, making to open his breeches as they rolled past.

Thankfully, Madeleine stirred Rouge into a fast trot, relieved to be rid of the city's foul-mouthed sentinels.

'Congratulations, *citoyenne*,' said Charette, a small mocking smile playing on his lips. 'It seems you have friends in high places.' He leant across and relieved her of the reins and she was grateful, for it was tiring and not easy controlling Rouge with one hand. He turned to her, his black eyes quizzical, an eyebrow raised in polite, icy enquiry. 'Pray, does the protection afforded to you by the powerful Danton extend to me also?'

'No,' smiled Madeleine.

'You mean I am completely reliant on your good will and . . . er, acting ability?'

'Completely.'

'And should I decline your offer of assistance?'

'Then, Captain,' responded Madeleine playfully, 'regretfully I shall be forced to reveal your identity to the authorities.'

She did not flinch as Charette's black eyes stared into hers, and when he finally spoke his voice was as cold as his manner.

'It seems, Mademoiselle, that you are determined to save me.'

Before Madeleine could reply, the measured beat of a drum forewarned of the approach of soldiers. Then, around the bend in the road appeared the drummer, a boy no more than twelve years old or so. Behind him, mounted on a white horse, was a captain of the National Guard in command of a small troop escorting prisoners. Madeleine's heart raced as the officer, holding up his gloved hand, halted his men and rode over to the wagon. Beside her Charette brought Rouge to a halt and nodded towards the laden tumbrils.

'I see you've had good hunting, Captain. I envy you. I don't know how I've displeased our new Minister of Justice, but for some reason I'm destined to play nursemaid to the *citoyenne* here.'

Straightaway the curiosity left the young officer's face and he smiled down sympathetically at Charette. 'Yes, we've had some good sport and some big names in the bag too. Got that one at Louveciennes, the Du Barry's lair,' he chuckled, pointing at a dark-haired young man in the first of the carts. 'As you'd expect, we found him in a bedroom. Not between the sheets, mark you; hidden under them. Times have changed, haven't they?' he said with another chuckle, then he wheeled his horse around and signalled his column to advance.

'Poor Maussabre,' said Charette quietly, watching the wretched cortège pass.

'You know him?' asked Madeleine.

'Yes,' replied Charette, 'he was at the defence of the Tuileries.'

They drove on, speaking no more; only when challenged by passing patrols or at a barrier. Soldiers were everywhere, hunting down the survivors of the Tuileries. The danger for the chevalier was great, but a combination of Danton's letter and his adopted uniform allowed them to proceed without hindrance. Not once were passports requested.

Soon it became too dark to journey further, so they stopped within the shelter of a little wood, thinking it safer than a village inn where curiosity would lead to questions.

While Charette fastened the nosebag on Rouge, Madeleine opened a bottle of wine and set out some of the food packed by Jacques. Silently Charette took his portion and walked to a fallen tree trunk some distance away. Madeleine was relieved to be left on her own. After the demands of the day she felt exhausted; her wound ached and the atmosphere between them was tense and strained.

Barely eating anything herself, Madeleine roughly divided the sacks in the cart into two heaps, then gratefully threw herself down on one of the rough mattresses.

It was a soft, warm, balmy night. Overhead, above the dark tree tops, was a dazzling canopy of bright, clear stars. The same stars, thought Madeleine gazing up, that would be above the sailors at sea, and the Red Indians on the plains of the Americas. She wondered which was the north star, the star which guided the ships at sea, which she knew he would be able to point out immediately. Drowsily she listened to the chirp of crickets and the rustlings of small creatures scurrying through the long rough undergrowth. Pale moths fluttered back and forth over the side of the wagon and every so often came the chilling shriek of a hunting owl. Even here there was fear, thought Madeleine; tiny hearts beating fast, muscles straining for the safety of a hidden nest. As sleep drifted over her, she was aware that Charette had climbed up into the wagon. And with his back towards her, had stretched out on the other mattress.

Like clarion bells, the birds at dawn awoke Madeleine with their vigorous, joyful songs. Surprisingly, the rough bed had proved quite comfortable and she snuggled down deeper under the sacking cover, waiting for the first rays of sun to gather strength.

Gradually, after the birds fell silent, the warmth increased and Madeleine stretched out, luxuriating in the sensation and the sense of freedom amidst the trees. She smiled and opened her eyes and found that she was looking into the shining jet of François-Athanase Charette de la Contrie's eyes. How long he had been lying watching her she did not know. She returned his smile, content to remain still and lazily absorb every detail of his face.

Already a vigorous stubble marked his jawline and the curious rounded, upturned chin, a chin denoting strength and stubbornness. In fact, every feature of his face, she decided, betrayed this characteristic. But there was more than courage and fixity of purpose; the sharp, uptilted nose, the thin inverted bow of his mouth bespoke impetuosity and a mercurial temper. Black, tiny curls framed his high forehead and playfully Madeleine seized one, pulling it straight, then watching it spring back into its tight coil.

Finally, with beating heart, almost shyly, she brought her gaze down to his waiting eyes. Finding no mockery or laughter in their depths; only a naked, fierce desire.

Languidly he traced with a fingertip the outline of her lips, touching their pouting fullness as though he were touching a petal. Slowly he followed the line of her throat until he met the cotton neckline of her blouse. Imperiously his fingers untied its cord and she felt air and the warmth of the sun strike down on her skin as the thin cotton fell away. The intense black eyes gleamed and widened as he stared down at her, but he did not touch her, and Madeleine trembled as the tension mounted between them.

Then the curly head lowered and she felt his lips caressing her breasts, covering her with urgent, passionate kisses; awakening each fibre of her body until the whole sang with joy. Their breath mingled as they kissed; a kiss so long that she thought he would draw the life out of her. He paused, raising his eyebrow to question, yet the expression in his eyes was compelling and impatient. Madeleine responded with a smile, trembling as she felt him open his breeches, and then the thrill of his warm flesh was pressing against hers.

For a while he lay still against her, his kisses long and languorous, until she thought she would faint, for she wanted him so. Impatiently she pushed up against him, but he laughed and shook his head.

'Ah no, *chérie*, this moment is not to be hurried. It is to be savoured, remembered, always.'

He lifted away, and the tip of velvet phallus touched gently into delicate tissue; the feeling was delicious and they smiled at each other, delighting in the moment which made them one. Slowly he began to explore deeper, setting off ripple after ripple of pleasure which, mounting in intensity, filled her with a desperate, urgent need.

'You are making it very difficult for me,' he chided as she covered him with passionate little bites and kisses. But she took no notice, and he lost control, filled like her by a fierce, wild joy, as hand sought hand and fingers twined together, as lips, tongues, touched and parted, then again caressed, finally finding relief in the explosion which launched them simultaneously into a timeless rapture.

For a while they dozed, luxuriating in the peace which lay between them. Regretfully Charette roused himself and sat up and looked around. In the strong sunlight the wood was a blaze of colour; a mixture of greens and reddish golds. 'The leaves and bracken change their colour early this year,' he murmured, turning back to look down at the girl. His heart bounded with pleasure. 'Why, you are like autumn itself, a beautiful daughter of Ceres,' he laughed, running his fingers through the skeins of Madeleine's hair. 'And your eyes, my little revolutionary, are the colour of my topaz.' Seizing the ring from his finger, he leant forward and held it against Madeleine's eyes. 'You see, the perfect match,' he laughed, his face excited and boyish, planting a swift kiss on her lips. Suddenly he sent the ring spinning up into the air. 'My mother will be glad to meet the young lady who saved her ring,' he chuckled, reaching up and snatching it in flight.

'You gave me your mother's gift?' asked Madeleine in amazement.

'I had nothing else to give, *chérie*.'

'But you were an officer, a noble.'

'Even nobles can be poor, you know, and I can assure you that a First Lieutenant's pay in His Majesty's Navy did not go far ... but all that's changed now,' he added grimly. Like a cloud passing over the sun, the happiness left his face and he scowled, as though recalling something unpleasant. For a while they sat in silence; she wondering what had angered him. But as suddenly as his good humour had left, so it returned. With a decisive, wilful gleam in his dark eyes he reached forward and took her hand and slipped the heavy ring on to her finger.

'Come away with me, Madeleine,' he urged. 'Come to my manor of Fonteclose. Like you, it is beautiful and natural, set amidst oak trees and the forest. There we can forget Paris and let these times pass us by.'

'But can we forget your wife?' There at last it was out, the question which had tortured her so.

With a look of surprise Charette stared at her, but he did not flinch. 'I have, and you must, for as a Catholic I am not free to divorce.'

'But you are free to take a mistress? A convenient faith, Catholicism. Does the good priest give a heavy penance each time you err?' snapped Madeleine ironically, an irrational jealousy making her want to hurt him.

231

He sprang to his feet, white with rage, the black eyes blazing. 'Madam, you go too far.' For an instant she thought he would hit her, but with one bound he jumped from the wagon and his tall athletic figure disappeared amongst the trees.

With a cry of despair Madeleine realised what she had done, but it was too late. She had driven him away.

Chapter Seven

Though devastated by Charette's departure, Madeleine continued south, determined at least to return to The Cordelier with a full cart.

Scarcity of rain during the summer months had made for a poor harvest. Even so, she found no difficulty in filling her sacks with vegetables and flour. No one showed reluctance to help a city wench who carried the authorisation of Georges Jacques Danton. Her only mishap, which caused delay, was a broken axle on the old wagon. And this, together with Rouge's slow pace, meant it was early September when she returned to Paris.

At least there will be no queuing at the market for a while, she thought as she approached The Cordelier. To her surprise, she saw that her café was firmly shuttered and outside, sitting on the step, sharing a bottle of wine between them, were three rough-looking men. As she passed, one of them looked up and proffered her the bottle. 'Care for a celebration drink, *citoyenne*?' he leered.

'Celebration ... Why, have our troops won a battle?' asked Madeleine curiously.

'You can say that again, sweetheart — and we're the brave boys who have won it ... here ... right here,' he said, staggering to his feet and staring up at her through drunken, glazed eyes, the grey whiskers of his face glistening red from dribbled wine. 'We've killed the lot, every stinking aristo in Paris!'

Madeleine stared at the filthy wretch in a mixture of disbelief and horror as he tottered back to the doorway of The Cordelier. With a sudden sense of foreboding she turned Rouge under the stone archway into the cobbled courtyard.

At once her misgivings were confirmed by the frightened face of Annette which peered at her through the parted curtains. 'Oh Madeleine, thank God you're back,' whispered the stout young woman, throwing her arms about her and breaking out into loud sobs. 'It's been terrible, terrible, Paul's been arrested for stealing.'

'Stealing! Paul wouldn't!' exclaimed Madeleine.

'He was caught red-handed, Madeleine, stealing a sack of sugar.'

'So that's how Paul always met our shortages,' sighed Madeleine, sadly.

'But it's far worse,' continued Annette in a strange hollow voice. 'They've been killing all the prisoners.'

'Annette, what are you trying to say?' asked Madeleine gently. 'Paul isn't in danger, even in a prison. He is just a small boy and a poor one.'

'That's what Jacques said,' replied Annette, wiping her eyes with her apron. 'He went to Bicêtre early today but he said the mob were only after aristos and priests.'

'Yes, I'm sure he's right, Annette. Why don't you start a meal for us all? I'll go and see what's happening.'

With the thought of something practical to do, Annette brightened and started to bustle around the kitchen.

Madeleine set off immediately, pausing only to take her pistol from under the seat of the wagon. She could scarcely believe what Annette had told her. It did not seem possible that prisoners who had not come to trial could be murdered. No doubt Annette had been mistaken, the victim of an exaggerated rumour.

Entering the rue de la Roquette, Madeleine could see no sign of Jacques, but what she did see caused her to halt in alarm. Ahead were the grim dismal walls of Bicêtre and emerging through its gates was a wagon: a wagon piled high with bodies, their naked limbs hanging over the sides, swaying and swinging to its jolting motion.

Madeleine's heart began to pound with fear as it drew closer. Horrified, her eyes inspected the bloody, battered corpses. They were boys, some no more than ten years of age.

Nauseated, she recoiled and turned away, retching, her limbs trembling with fright and disgust, unable to accept the outrage. A red anger exploded within her and she ran forward, gaining the prison gate as a lethargic turnkey was still fumbling with the lock.

'You've missed the party, *citoyenne*,' he slurred, 'but I can still offer a pretty wench a drink.'

'That won't be necessary,' snapped Madeleine, pushing past him through the narrow gap. 'I am here to enquire about Paul Metalier. Is he amongst your prisoners?'

'Well, now, that would be a state secret,' replied the man, somewhat huffily, turning the key in the lock. 'You'll have to come inside and persuade me to tell you,' he said with a leer of a smile as he walked into a small office.

Ignoring him and putting some distance between them — for he reeked of vomit and brandy — Madeleine thought quickly.

'I am told, *citoyen*, that last week, Paul Metalier,

a twelve-year-old boy, was brought here for stealing sugar.'

'So?' replied the turnkey somewhat peevishly, irritated by the girl's aloof manner.

'I have come for him; you are to release him immediately.'

'On whose authority?' growled the turnkey, becoming immediately surly and suspicious.

'On the authority of the Minister of Justice, Georges Jacques Danton,' cried Madeleine, slamming her letter on the counter and gambling that the man could not read. Withdrawing her pistol from the tricolor sash around her waist, she pointed it at his signature. 'And if the signature of Danton is not enough, then perhaps this will convince you,' she said, lifting the muzzle until it was level with the man's eyes. 'Do you understand, or do we have to summon the rest of the guards to point out to you your duty to the nation!'

The man, bewildered and fearful, stared at the tall, imperious young woman. Clearly from her style of dress she was a patriot, but it was her manner which unsettled him, especially the cold lynx-like eyes.

'But it's too late, *citoyenne*,' he mumbled.

'Too late?' queried Madeleine icily.

The drunken, red-rimmed eyes looked even more bewildered and the man shrugged helplessly. 'If you will come with me,' he said, picking up a large bunch of keys.

The sight which met her eyes in an inner courtyard of the prison would haunt her for the rest of her life. It was littered with corpses, many of them children, their upturned faces stamped with terror and pain. The filthy rags on their emaciated little bodies were stained with blood. Nearby six men were loading carts, throwing the bodies in like sacks of corn.

'As you see, *citoyenne*, we worked hard to rid

Paris of the vermin,' the turnkey said proudly. 'It's unfortunate you wished to see the young thief!' he sighed.

Whirling on him, a murderous rage ripping through her body, laying low her grief, Madeleine lashed out with the butt of her gun. With a shriek of pain the man beside her staggered back, clutching his face, the blood spurting between his fingers.

His cries of pain caused the men at the carts to pause in the work, but seeing only a girl they burst out laughing, one of them calling across, 'Gone a bit too far with one of your whores, Antoine?' Then they carried on with their grim work, still weary and half-drunk from their nocturnal exertions.

Impervious to her perilous situation, Madeleine cocked her pistol at the man before her who, recovering from the shock and pain, was about to call for assistance. 'Do not disturb your comrades in their work, *citoyen*,' she said quietly. 'The nation does not want to drink the blood of babies. Who gave you orders for this carnage?'

'Our orders came from Stanislas Maillard,' replied the man sullenly, prompted to answer immediately by the menace of Madeleine's gun and her tone of voice.

'And your name?'

'Antoine Frechet.'

'Well, Antoine Frechet, you will now escort me to the door and I will try to forget your name for, believe me, this monstrous crime will not go unpunished!'

Back outside the prison, alone on the street, Madeleine collapsed. Not from her encounter with the turnkey; subjecting him had been astonishingly easy. Her blind anger and disregard for death had done that. It was an overwhelming sense of grief which sapped the last of her strength. On her knees she crouched, her head buried in her hands as she thought of Paul amongst the pitiful, broken bodies.

In her distraction she had not seen the man running towards her; faltering as he saw her sink down on her knees. Only after some time did she become aware of his presence. Jacques Metalier was pulling her up within the ambit of his arms.

'It's too late,' she choked, 'too late, my friend.'

Stricken father and friend clung, their bodies racked with sobs. Using the circle of their arms like a bulwark to shut out cruel reality; but the grind of wheel on cobble cut through as another cart passed, bearing its grim load to the Montrouge Quarries.

'Why, Georges, why?'

Georges Jacques Danton looked at the beautiful face ablaze with anger and wished heartily that Pare, his secretary, was present to remove her. Facing the interminable accusations across the floor of the National Assembly was one thing, but here in the salon from one of his wife's friends it was irksome. As irksome as the conceited bitch at the Ministry of the Interior, Manon Roland, who, through her husband, would not let the matter drop. Damn women, could they never see the larger issue? Right now Prussian troops were marching on French soil. He flashed the trembling girl a placatory smile.

'Madeleine, I can only repeat what I have said before. When a ship is wrecked the crew throws overboard everything that endangers it. In the same way, everything that might endanger the Nation must be expelled.'

'But were my young errand boy, old priests, women and children a threat to France?' cried Madeleine.

'I, too, am a father, Madeleine,' thundered Danton impatiently. 'Things happen in a revolution that no one would wish. But in my hands lies the survival of that revolution. I will not let its enemies destroy it. My sole concern must be for the destiny of France.'

Looking at him standing with his great head thrown back, as though he were standing at the tribune in the Manège, Madeleine sighed. In her heart, she knew it wasn't Georges whose hands had guided the prison massacres. Perhaps he had lacked the will or means to stop them, immersed as he was with the defence of France. The sadistic maniacs who sat on the Comité de Surveillance had taken full advantage of his preoccupation.

'Is France in great peril, Georges?'

'Yes, Madeleine. Our troops under General Dumouriez and Kellerman are drawn up on the hills around Valmy. If they fail, nothing will stop the Prussians from entering Paris. All that we have fought for will be lost.'

'Then, Georges,' smiled Madeleine, 'we must dare, and dare again, and dare forever, and France will thus be saved!' she said, repeating word for word the thrilling challenge which, on the floor of the Assembly, he had flung out to all Frenchmen. 'Through your inspiration, Georges, you will see our soldiers will not let them take the tricolor.'

Nor did they. On 20 September General Dumouriez became the hero of France and her church bells rang out the glad tidings of victory.

The sense of relief throughout the city was enormous. Though within The Cordelier no one felt like joining in the rejoicings; too deep was the hurt at little Paul's death. And when Annette stayed on and did not return to her job at The Parnasse, it seemed only natural, for the tragedy had bound them together like a family.

At first, Madeleine had thirsted for revenge, wishing only to shoot Stanislas Maillard and any of the thugs who had instigated the massacres. But Jacques had restrained her, pointing out it would not only be her own death warrant she would sign but all under the roof of The Cordelier. But when her anger abated, she was seized with a dark depression. She had lost her brother Pierre and Paul, whilst all that remained of a broken dream was a ring. Once more the topaz hung from her waist where she had automatically tied it; like tying back on a part of herself. Two men she had driven away with angry words: Thomas Adams to the army, and Charette perhaps to his death. There seemed nothing else to life but work and sleep.

Even when she received a stiff white envelope containing a gilt-edged card informing her that the Minister of Justice requested her presence at a reception at the Chancellerie, she was not moved to excitement. Though she was touched by the kind thought that lay behind it, for undoubtedly it was Gabrielle who had placed her name on the invitation list.

Not wishing to go, but anxious not to seem ungrateful, Madeleine went to see Gabrielle at the Chancellerie. How different Gabrielle's life had become, Madeleine thought, as the footman opened the door of her small private salon, far away from its state apartments, and she glimpsed her surrounded by a froth of dresses. Usually at this time of the day she would be found singing in her kitchen, happily stringing a fat chicken or making pâté.

At the sound of her entrance, Gabrielle dropped the dress she was holding before her and turned. 'Why, Madeleine, the very person,' she exclaimed, relief sweeping over the red, harassed face. 'You can advise me what I should wear for this reception.

Georges has made me spend a fortune . . . I'm just hopeless at this sort of thing. At least you'll be there, so I won't feel quite so nervous.'

'Yes, it was very kind of you to invite me, Gabrielle,' said Madeleine, deciding to wait a little before admitting that she would not be accepting.

'Oh it was all Georges's idea . . . well partly mine too,' she giggled, seeing Madeleine's quizzical look. 'I've just got to have some familiar faces around me, Madeleine, or I'll swoon away with fright. Have you anything to wear?'

'Well . . . I hadn't really given it much thought,' confessed Madeleine, not having the heart to disappoint her friend — realising how much she was counting on her support.

'Then take one of these. We're quite different shapes and you're taller, but the dressmaker will soon put that right. She's coming soon . . . What about the buff, or the green?'

'All right, Madame Minister,' said Madeleine, laughing and picking up an armful of silk and satin, 'lead me to a mirror.'

It seemed a long time since Madeleine had felt soft, luxurious fabrics next to her skin and she had to admit the feeling was pleasant. Though the polish she had acquired under the Vicomte de Cramoisy's tutelage at the Palais-Royal had been hidden through choice and necessity, it remained a part of her being, needing only occasion for it to re-emerge, adding dazzle and focus to her natural attributes.

As naturally as if she had moved in diplomatic circles all her life, Madeleine, poised and relaxed, drifted amongst the guests at the Chancellerie reception. Gold braid and the blue, white and red of the army was everywhere. For the guest of honour was General Dumouriez, on leave in Paris before his next offensive.

Amused, she watched the various guests jockeying for a position near the General. How small he seemed beside Danton, yet he had presence and the same decisive self-seeking qualities as his host. Brushing aside outstretched hands, they moved together to greet the Commander of the National Guard, Antoine Santerre.

'Our new Minister is most judicious,' an amused voice beside her murmured. 'With an introduction to the brewer he hopes to provide our general with arms and the support of the *sans-culottes*.'

Whirling around, Madeleine found a young man had stationed himself behind her. Immediately she recognised him. It was Charles Barbaroux, a deputy from the Gironde. Like many of the Girondists, as they were known, he wore the enormous white muslin cravat which was tied in a large bow, whilst his dark hair, falling straight to his shoulders, was cropped at the front, Roman-like, into a short fringe. It was a style which suited him, emphasising the beautiful classical lines of his handsome face, framing fine eyes of dark brown which were watching her with more than casual interest.

'It's a privilege to meet you, Charles Barbaroux. I have heard you speak often – you are a fine orator.'

The young deputy inclined his head, accepting her compliment. 'But I am sad to think I did not know someone so lovely was watching me,' he said.

'Oh I don't think you would recognise me there,' laughed Madeleine, thinking of her usual rough clothes. 'I live and work in the Faubourg Saint-Antoine and this wouldn't please my customers at all,' she said, touching the cream and brown silk dress.

'Customers?' Again the brown eyes swept over her face and the flesh-coloured silk draped over the rounder curve of her shoulders and breasts.

'Yes, I own a restaurant ... well, really it's no more than a café.'

'Then I must come and dine with you.'

'But it would not suit you at all,' laughed Madeleine, viewing the crisp starched cravat, 'though our food is very good.'

'Come, its name,' pleaded the young deputy, his expression persuasive, 'or will you force me to indigestion, exploring the culinary offerings of the Faubourg until I find you?'

'Ah, that would be too cruel,' laughed Madeleine, beginning to enjoy herself. It was an exhilarating feeling, seeing the glow of desire in the young man's eyes – the same look she had seen directed towards her from many of the men present. It was not new to her. But here, amongst men of power, cultured and sensitive to a woman's disposition, it was exciting. More, there was now a sense of power which Charette had liberated in her when he had shown her how to love.

Suddenly, the young man with her exclaimed in irritation. Madeleine saw a short figure in uniform bearing down on them. Then, General Dumouriez and Danton were beside them.

'Madeleine,' said Georges Danton, smiling at her like a proud father, 'our general is most anxious to meet you.'

'Indeed! I did not come to Paris to spend my time talking to Ministers when I see a pretty woman across the room.'

'Then, General, why do you intend to march into Belgium? I believe the women are far from pretty,' teased Madeleine, offering her hand for the small man to kiss.

'Is that so?' laughed the hero of Valmy, eagerly accepting another glass of champagne from a passing waiter. 'Well, in that case I shall order you to join me in Brussels; but for tonight you will take my arm. A man needs a lovely face to look at after seeing only Prussian backsides!'

Without more ado, he whisked her away, and soon they were immersed in an admiring throng. Smiling, Madeleine watched Dumouriez bask in the euphoria, becoming more and more talkative and flirtatious with every additional glass of champagne. Nor would he be parted from her, much to the annoyance of the young deputy from the Gironde, whom she saw in the mirror of the salon watching them with jealous and possessive eyes. For the present, the spoils of victory belonged to the general, though only until the end of the reception; for she had no desire to become embroiled with the lascivious little man, whose hands had begun to stray.

The very next day Charles Barbaroux came to The Cordelier. He looked like a member of the Roman senate, his cloak flung casually around his shoulders in the manner of a toga. At the time Madeleine was adding up the lunch receipts. She looked forward to this quiet time after the noisy hubbub of the customers so, hearing the door open, her immediate reaction was a small rueful smile; she would not be able to enjoy a quiet glass of wine after all. Looking up, her smile broadened as she saw Charles Barbaroux and his reaction on seeing her.

'I see now what you meant last night,' he chuckled, taking in her appearance. 'But for those wondrous eyes and pretty lips, I should wonder if you were a figment of my imagination.' Madeleine slammed shut the till and gestured for him to take a seat; but he remained standing.

'Gabrielle Danton told me where I might find you. I thought perhaps if you were free we might take a ride to the Bois de Boulogne ... that is ...' he gestured helplessly, causing Madeleine to break out

244

into a merry peal of laughter before he finished off his sentence.

'That is if I should care to change. Come now, deputy, it would endear you more to the men of the Mountain if you were seen giving a poor *sans-culotte* a spin in your carriage.'

'I'm sure you're right. Marat and his like would be happy to escort you as you are, but I do not seek the approval of the Montagnards and I do like to see the jewel in a good setting. But ... I'm a desperate man,' he grinned, seeing the girl's defiant look, 'So all I ask is the removal of your red cap and a glimpse of your hair.'

'What, would you ask a patriot to remove her Phrygian cap?' teased Madeleine in mock horror, leaving the room to change.

She put on her one smart day dress. It was not very worn, for she kept it for special occasions. Finally, to complete her hasty toilette, she brushed out her hair and arranged it into three heavy coils. Then, without even pausing to look in the mirror, she tied on the matching blue bonnet as she ran down the stairs.

The effect her appearance seemed to have on others always came as a surprise to her. She rarely studied her reflection, and inside she felt quite ordinary. Yet, as she twirled around so that the tricolor-striped skirt billowed out, she laughed, seeing the proud, pleased expression on Charles Barbaroux's face. 'There, am I now respectable enough for a deputy of the Convention?'

His embarrassed flush set her off into another fit of laughter, causing Jacques and Annette to peer with curious faces around the kitchen door. 'Don't worry, I'm not losing my mind,' she reassured them. 'Or perhaps you think leaving my work and going for a drive in the pouring rain to the Bois de Boulogne is crazy?'

'No, I think it's the most sensible thing you've done for a long time,' said Jacques, his eyes twinkling with pleasure as he looked towards Madeleine's visitor.

'And see that you don't rush back,' said Annette fiercely. 'Jacques and I can manage quite well without you!'

Despite the heavy rain which forced them to stay within the carriage, Madeleine found the afternoon drive a refreshing change. As a companion, Charles Barbaroux lacked nothing. He was witty and charming. Of a warm southern disposition, it was not long before he had caught her hand in his and declared that he was in love as never before. But there was still only one face she could see. Teasing, she kept their meeting light, declaring that she and all Paris knew of his amorous liaisons. Though none of the ardour died from the brown eyes, she had established an unspoken boundary. He recognised her heart was not free and, though he did not cease to flirt and steal small kisses when subsequently they met, for the rest his behaviour was restrained.

Certainly meeting Charles Barbaroux opened up Madeleine's life. Starved of fun and wishing to dispel her sadness, she threw herself into the new social whirl with an energy that was almost desperate.

Within days of her début at the Chancellerie reception, the brown and cream silk dress hung between a dozen new companions. Where the money was going to come from to pay for this froth of hemlines over matching little slippers, Madeleine neither knew nor cared. Nor, apparently, did the dressmaker, who seemed part relieved and part ecstatic that Paris's new masters were ready to ape the old. On Charles Barbaroux's arm, passing through hotel doors which, as children, she and her brother had gaped at with wistful curiosity, Madeleine relished every moment; enjoying the impact of her entry into the salons; seeing heads turn quickly again to inspect with open admiration Charles Barbaroux's new friend. The flattery was as heady as the golden bubbles of the champagne and Madeleine enjoyed both.

Almost as intoxicating was the conversation under the dazzling chandeliers. Politics, art, music, and theatre — all were equally discussed with intensity and fervour. Often after such receptions they would make up a party with some of the other guests, and either go to the theatre or on to dine. Involved with food all day, Madeleine ate very sparingly — content just to sit and watch her companion enjoy himself. For never had she seen a man eat with more relish.

'Why, Charles,' she said one evening as they sat in the Café du Foy, 'you make the artisans who eat with me seem like sparrows.'

Pausing between forkfuls, the young deputy flashed her a smile, displaying his strong white teeth. 'But that is what life is for; to eat with a full heart . . . and to love with a full heart . . .' He paused and took her hand. 'And I have to eat! For you have turned me into a sparrow where love is concerned. Ah!' he said wistfully, 'I could give you such pleasure, Madeleine. You are made for love and I could take you to Paradise . . . won't you let me . . .? Bah! It's this dark stranger you have tucked away somewhere,' he said as she started to pull back her hand from his lips. 'Yes . . . there is someone, for you are turning quite pink,' he said with a sad smile. 'So you see, I am forced to find solace in some other way.'

Taking back his hand, Madeleine squeezed it affectionately; he was everything she should want — a brilliant orator, dedicated to the Revolution and its principles; a thoughtful, generous companion, showering her with little gifts; whilst his physical appearance set most women's hearts racing. Many, Madeleine knew, went to the National Convention just to hear him. How, then, could she love a man with a chin like the toe of a shoe; a man who hated the revolution and their chance for equality? With a sudden resolve and yearning she looked across into the languishing brown eyes, seeking the spark, the explosion which would send her senses reeling, crying out for fusion. Quickly aware of her change, his beautiful eyes filled with excited desire. But he felt the energy dying within her. Lowering her eyes, Madeleine released Charles Barbaroux's hand.

'*Septembriseurs*,' hissed the voice. Furious, Madeleine whirled around, but as usual was confronted with turned backs and averted faces. Georges Jacques Danton might no longer be Minister of Justice but no one was brave enough to openly abuse his wife. Madeleine gave Gabrielle's arm a comforting squeeze as she hurried past the group of women. 'Don't listen to them,' she whispered scornfully. 'They don't know what they're saying. It's a pity Georges resigned. At least in the Chancellerie you were not exposed to such behaviour, even though you thought it remote and impersonal.'

'Yes,' agreed Gabrielle with a miserable little smile, 'I was so happy when Georges was elected as a deputy to the National Convention, realising he would have to resign as a Minister. When he told me he had done so and we were going back to our own apartment, I packed with such speed . . . ! I had no idea what people were saying about Georges . . . all those poor innocent people, massacred.'

'*Septembriseurs*,' screamed the Girondist voices. 'Render the accounts!' These were the arrows of accusation that flew across the floor of the Convention. But their quarry, impassive as a rhinoceros struck by pygmy darts, looked on for a while in silence. Eventually, patience lost, Danton lashed out, drawing blood, causing the men of the Mountain to howl with joy, as progressively isolated from the Moderates, he was driven into the waiting arms of Robespierre and Marat.

It was a struggle which began to affect Madeleine's friendship with Charles Barbaroux. Because he moved in circles which declared war on Danton for his complicity in the September massacres, Madeleine's loyalty and belief in her old friend involved her in furious arguments. Embarrassed and politically ambitious within his party, Charles Barbaroux's attentions suddenly began to cool. Madeleine didn't particularly care; the novelty and excitement had begun to fade. Without love it had all begun to feel quite hollow. Jacques and Annette, who initially encouraged her to go out, seemed pleased when her evening work resumed in The Cordelier. A little hurt by their attitude, she supposed that they had resented her absence. But one particularly busy night she learnt that she had misinterpreted their thoughts. Annette, looking about the busy café with a pleased smile, had shouted above the chatter and laughter. 'You see what you've done, Madeleine, you've brought life back to The Cordelier! It's you they come for and it doesn't matter if you're not in silk with perfume behind your ears!'

'I'm sorry, Annette,' said Madeleine, almost shouting to make herself heard above the click of dominoes and raised voices, 'I feel I've let you and Jacques down.'

'Of course you haven't,' said Annette, coming closer. 'Do you think Jacques and I minded working?

249

No. We were pleased to see you having some fun. But we were beginning to worry for your safety.'

'Safety?' echoed Madeleine in surprise. 'What do you mean?'

'Well, there are many jealous eyes,' said Annette thoughtfully. 'No one has said anything, but I can tell you it hasn't gone down well, your leaving here at night like an aristo.'

Whether Annette's and Jacques's fears were justified, Madeleine didn't know. Her giddy whirl had suddenly stopped and perhaps the envious eyes and wagging tongues were thus directed elsewhere. Nor did she give it a second thought, for occupying all her thoughts was the state of Gabrielle's health. The gossip and the relentless newspaper attacks aimed at her husband, like an insidious poison, had begun to do their work. Dark shadows under Gabrielle's eyes betrayed the sleepless nights; their tortured expression bore testament to her agony of mind.

Madeleine, who was still haunted by the terrible scene at Bicêtre, realised what she was suffering. Often enough in her arguments with the Rolandists and Girondists, doubts within had stirred concerning her friend's husband.

Now, more than ever, when she was expecting another child, was the time Gabrielle needed the reassurance of the man she loved; needed to hear from his own lips that he was not a monster with blood on his hands. But Gabrielle had a powerful rival. France! The mistress that called the tune; sentencing the wife to sit alone, wrapped in her private pall of gloom.

Determined to draw Georges's attention to Gabrielle's plight, and filled with anger at his apparent neglect, Madeleine waylaid him one night at the door of the Convention. But on seeing him, her anger immediately turned to pity.

The big man's face was grey with exhaustion, his eyes red-rimmed from lack of sleep. Chiding him gently, Madeleine saw the weary droop of his shoulders as he silently considered her words. For a moment she wondered if he had understood, for he seemed dazed, almost uncomprehending. As if she had appeared from another world. Then his great hand seized her under the chin, tilting her face so that his eyes stared down into hers. 'Be her friend for me, Madeleine! For I must bind this country into one nation! I must forge unity because it is on the brink of chaos. France must be everything to all of us!'

The energy from his body and eyes consumed her. She felt his will and desperation, recognised that he was operating on a higher level, above family ties, petty politics and self-interest. He could only see France, her unity, her survival under the tricolor.

By November, the intimate circle of Gabrielle's friends had organised themselves so that she received visitors daily. It was as well, for by the end of November, Georges Danton was with General Dumouriez at his winter headquarters in Brussels.

Despite his efforts on behalf of the nation in Belgium, the attacks on Danton at home did not cease. Madeleine and her friends made every effort to see that Gabrielle did not read newspapers or pamphlets, whilst all conversation steered well clear of politics. But the maggots of horror, suspicion, shame, had hatched, consuming the heart of their host. Gabrielle was floundering. Horrified, Madeleine watched the process. No one could reach her – not even the baby boys. It was as if she had taken upon herself atonement for the murders in September; as though she sought to expiate Georges from any guilt.

It was a gloomy time altogether in Paris as New Year approached. In The Cordelier, the only topic was the outcome of the King's trial. Listening to her customers, it seemed to Madeleine that the ordinary people of the Faubourg wished not for the poor man's death. 'We've abolished the monarchy,' she heard a regular customer saying to a rabid Jacobin one day. 'We have him and his family under lock and key. Do we need to take his life as well?'

But then a box containing compromising secret documents was found at the Tuileries and attitudes changed. Louis Saint-Just and the Montagnards's screams for blood grew louder.

On the final day of the six-week trial there was little doubt what the verdict would be. Even so, the inveterate gamblers took the high odds for an acquittal. Whilst small boys, anxious to earn a sou, came flying into The Cordelier with the latest names of those who had voted for death. Hearing the name of Danton amongst them, Madeleine could not resist exchanging a cynical smile with Jacques. 'So our deputy has returned to Paris – impeccable timing!'

'Yes,' replied Jacques, nodding. 'He was shrewd enough to stay away in Brussels until the sentencing.'

'Well, now that he is here, perhaps Gabrielle will recover her spirits,' said Madeleine, slicing a round of sausage for one of the young runners. 'He should spend some time with her at her parents' house at Sèvres.'

'There isn't much hope of that, Madeleine. As head of the Defence Committee he can't abandon everything to take a holiday with an ailing wife. He is one of the ablest men in the Convention: the country needs him.'

'Yes, I suppose you're right,' agreed Madeleine sadly, remembering the summer picnics she shared with Georges and the happy, freckled-faced Gabrielle. It all seemed so long ago.

Jacques was right, the homecoming was brief.

After a few days in the capital, Danton headed back to Brussels to contain the military and domestic problems. He had, nonetheless, stayed in France long enough to excite every French heart with his vision. Newspapers carried to every province his prophecy of the Republic's expansion to nature's boundaries – the Alps, the Rhine and the shores of the ocean. Knowingly, he also left behind a wife who was slipping away from him. For as Madeleine bade him goodbye at the Cour du Commerce she noted the secret terror in his eyes.

When he next returned Gabrielle was dead. It had all happened so quickly. Madeleine, who had thought her friend was with her parents at their new home at Sèvres, was puzzled, when meeting Louise Gély by chance in the Luxembourg gardens, to hear that Gabrielle had returned some days before to the rue des Cordeliers.

'But I thought she would stay with Madame Charpentier until the baby was born!' exclaimed Madeleine in surprise. 'And why didn't she let me know she was back?'

'I think she wants to be left alone,' replied Gabrielle's young neighbour shyly, 'but Madame Charpentier and her husband arrived in Paris today. They are staying with their son.'

Exasperated and a little hurt, Madeleine resolved to visit Gabrielle the next day and try to shake her friend out of the deadly lassitude which had fallen upon her. Perhaps when the baby was born she would put September out of her mind.

It was just after three o'clock the next afternoon when Catherine Motin, one of the Danton servants, arrived at The Cordelier. By the woman's wild expression, Madeleine knew at once that something was desperately wrong.

'Gabrielle?' she asked.

253

Catherine Motin nodded, trying to regain her breath. 'It's the baby, it's early,' she gasped, following Madeleine who was already at the door.

One glance at the blood-soaked sheets and the ominous lack of activity in the bedroom told Madeleine that Gabrielle was dying.

Having met the midwife in the drawing room holding a small, whimpering bundle, she had hoped all was well. But from the grim look in the woman's eyes and the tightening of her lips she realised that neither mother nor baby had long to live.

For a moment Madeleine stood quietly, looking down at her friend. How thin and gaunt her face appeared. What had become of the smiling girl who had served behind the counter of The Parnasse? Unable to control the flood of tears which filled her eyes, Madeleine sank to her knees and pressed her face against the bedsheet to stifle her sobs.

Suddenly she was aware of Gabrielle's hand stroking her hair. She was angry with herself for her lack of control. Swallowing hard she looked up with a bright smile. 'Forgive me, *chérie*, but I was so worried about you and the baby.'

'It's a boy,' smiled Gabrielle.

'Yes, Georges will be pleased. He'll be home soon. Your father has sent word to him.'

'Dear Georges, he works so hard for France. You will look after him, for me, Madeleine – no, don't interrupt me, my dear friend, I know I will soon be with God and I'm glad, I'm so tired. Please don't cry. Look at me, Madeleine, and you'll see at last I'm at peace.'

Through fresh tears Madeleine looked into the serene brown eyes of Gabrielle Danton, recently so tortured and unhappy. 'And now my dear, dear friend – one last favour. Georges must not be alone and the boys will need a mother. I want him to marry Louise Gély. She is a sweet girl and will bend to his ways. You're too strong, my dear; besides, you love another . . . Don't let pride come between you. Search for him, Madeleine! Now kiss me goodbye. Maman will look after me.'

During the night of 10 February, Gabrielle Danton died. For Madeleine it was like losing her mother. From the day Gabrielle had adopted her on the Pont-Neuf and taken her home to the Quai de l'École, she had felt part of a family, knowing that if she were in trouble Gabrielle would be there to listen and help. Now she was gone and it seemed unbelievable.

If the small cortège following the coffin in the parish of Saint André-des-Arts was devastated, so too was Paris. Immediately the politicians seized Gabrielle's tragic death as ammunition against the Girondists. By the time Georges arrived back in Paris six days later, the newspapers were full of wild accusations. The Jacobins screamed that the Girond-ists had persecuted Gabrielle Danton to her grave, and all conveniently ignored her dead baby boy.

Like a whirlwind Georges came to see her, storm-ing into The Cordelier, still splattered with mud from his journey. 'Where is she, Madeleine?' he asked hoarsely. 'Take me to her!' With a brief nod to Jacques to take over the serving, Madeleine threw a cape around her shoulders and accompanied Danton to the cemetery. In silence, she led him to the grave and looked down at the soil, so newly dug. Her small bouquet of flowers, she saw, was already blighted by a heavy frost.

Leaving Georges to mourn alone, she walked slowly between the rows of grey headstones. All was peace, except for the creak of naked branches stirred by the wind, the occasional distant clink of metal hitting stone as another grave was dug.

Upon hearing him call to her she turned to walk

back but Georges waved her away. 'Go and get the grave digger!' he shouted. For a moment she hesitated, not understanding, and he shouted to her again. Still wondering what he could want, Madeleine headed in the direction of the sound of shovelling and found two men digging a grave. Approaching one, standing gingerly on the loose edge, she shouted down.

'*Citoyen*, please come to Gabrielle Danton's grave, her husband wishes to speak with you.'

As they approached Gabrielle's grave, Madeleine could see Georges watching them. 'Where are your spades!' he suddenly shouted. Puzzled and slightly nervous, the grave diggers looked from Danton to Madeleine. 'Well, what are you waiting for? Go and get them! You can't open up graves without spades.'

Both men gaped and then the second man, younger and with a stronger set to his face, spoke. 'I'm sorry, *citoyen* Danton, but a body cannot be exhumed without authority — I'd like to help,' he added nervously, seeing the dark scowl clouding the scarred and pitted face.

'I am your authority!' rasped Danton. 'You will start to dig or I promise I'll have you guillotined before the day is out.'

'But you can't, Georges,' gasped Madeleine, as the two diggers sped away for their spades. 'You can't disturb her, it's been six days.'

But the grief-stricken man looked through her and within minutes the grave diggers had started their grisly work. Horrified, Madeleine fled and leant against the trunk of a tree; eyes closed, her stomach tightening with tension at the thought of what the next moments would bring as metal rapped against wood. There was a moment's stillness, broken by Danton's voice. 'Leave me, but stay within call,' then sounds of feet moving through grass, the forcing of

256

metal, followed by silence. Madeleine pressed her forehead against the rough, sharp edges of bark, not daring to look around. But her ears did not shut out the terrible howl. Forgetting, she spun round in fright.

'Oh dear God,' she whispered, seeing Georges holding the body of his dead wife in his arms. His powerful body convulsed with sobs as he covered the still face and breast with tears and frenzied kisses.

It was a sight both piteous and horrific, paralysing her legs so that she could not fly screaming from the dreadful scene. Sobbing, gasping for breath, she turned, clinging to the gnarled wood of the tree, trying to blot out the white shroud fluttering against the emaciated body. As she had clung to Jacques Metalier outside Bicêtre, so she clung to the tree; finding comfort in its solidity. Eventually as her tears abated, her fingertips explored each groove and indentation in a bid to distract herself, for she lacked the courage to move, fearing what she might see. An overwhelming longing to be with Charette swept over her. To be held tight against his body, safe and secure. When this was all over she would search for him, just as Gabrielle had bidden her.

'Madeleine, Madeleine, please come here.' With a shudder, Madeleine turned back in response to Danton's summons. She glanced around cautiously and saw him moving towards her. Irresistibly her glance was drawn beyond him to the open grave; relieved she saw the coffin lid was closed.

Leaving the sanctuary of the chestnut tree, she walked forward to meet him. He was calmer now, his passion spent. Though like a hurricane it had left its mark. Never had she thought to hear this man weep like a deserted child. His was the voice of strength that urged all Frenchmen to think nationally, the voice that had roared defiance at Lafayette

257

and now at the crowned heads of Europe. Knowing him only for his strength made his grief the more terrible.

Pulling her cloak more closely to her, for the wind had grown stronger, Madeleine waited for Danton to speak as he stood silently by her side. 'There is one more thing you can do for me, Madeleine,' he said at last in a low voice. 'Go and bring Deseine, the sculptor. I wish to have her death mask.'

Nodding silently, Madeleine hurried away to do his bidding. Relieved to escape from the grey, dismal scene.

For two whole weeks the door of Georges Danton's apartment remained shut and locked. He neither went out nor received visitors. When he finally emerged, those closest to him shivered with apprehension, for grief had changed to hate and anger. As witnessed during a late-night sitting of the National Convention in early March, it took just one Girondist taunt to unleash those forces within him. Just one word, spoken by Lanjuinais: '*Septembre*'.

Like a shark breaking surface, drenching hearts with fear, Danton struck, demanding a Tribunal. 'Let us be terrible so that we can prevent the People from being terrible!' he thundered.

Immediately there was uproar. In the public gallery, where Madeleine sat with Jacques, there were elated whoops of joy. 'Yes! yes!' men cried, leaning over the balcony shaking their fists at the deputy, Vergniand, who was speaking against the motion. 'Yes, give us a Tribunal. Yes, an inquisition! We want the guillotine!'

Sitting beside her, Jacques Metalier turned to Madeleine with a grave face. 'Vergniand's right, I fear,' he said softly, so that no one might hear. 'It will be the start of a nightmare in the hands of a

Saint-Just or Robespierre. Let us hope the Moderates here tonight will stand firm.'

But in the stale, vinegar-tainted air of the old royal riding school, the night belonged to Danton. France would have its revolutionary Tribunal. Looking down at the victor, Madeleine realised Gabrielle was right. Georges needed a softening influence in his life – a wife, and soon. At the moment he was soured by sorrow, without pity. Whilst his personal desire for revenge had tonight set in force a machine which might engulf the whole of France.

Six weeks later Madeleine went to the Cour du Commerce to pack away Gabrielle's clothes. With a heavy heart, she secured the last box, understanding better why Georges had not wanted his wife's belongings disturbed. Now, without them, the room looked very empty and stark. Gabrielle had gone. With a deep sigh she wiped the tears from her eyes and, picking up the silver-backed mirror and brush, walked through to the salon.

'Everything is finished, Georges. I've packed the boys' clothes to send to Madame Charpentier. Many thanks for these,' she said, holding up the brush and mirror.

'It's nothing, Madeleine. You were a good friend to her. She would want you to have them. I can't thank you enough ... it's something I could not have done ... Will you take a glass of wine before you go?' he asked abruptly.

Nodding acceptance, Madeleine sat down. 'Georges, I think perhaps now is the right time to tell you. Before Gabrielle died she made me promise to speak to you of marriage. Please hear me out,' she said as his expression froze. 'Gabrielle loved you dearly, Georges, and she wanted you to be happy.

She wished you to marry again and to marry Louise Gély.'

'But she's a child of sixteen,' he cried in surprise. 'Anyway, I'll not take another wife. Gabrielle was enough for me, and were I to do so it would be a full-blooded woman – someone like you, Madeleine.'

'No, Georges, never me,' she laughed gently. 'We would quarrel very soon. But Gabrielle was right,' she added seriously. 'Please consider it, Georges. Louise is very pretty, with a sweet nature. Antoine and his brother need a mother. Besides, you need love in your life. Every day you become more like Marat. Soon you'll hate everyone!'

'What do you mean, like Marat?' he roared, springing to his feet. His scarred lip twisted back into a snarl.

Refusing to be frightened, the girl flashed her beautiful amber eyes at him. 'Just what I said, Georges. When you run a café as I do, you hear a lot. What are they saying about you? Why, the Enragés and the Jacobins are rubbing their hands with glee because Danton has declared war on the Girondists and Moderates. That is what they say, Georges. Would Gabrielle be proud that you are the new head of the Committee of Public Safety, with its Tribunal and its guillotine?'

'We need a Tribunal,' he thundered angrily, the pock marks on his face quite grey against the sudden pallor of his skin. 'We are surrounded by enemies – England, Austria, Prussia, Spain. Whilst internally our enemies threaten our survival even more. Time has run out. I am forced to act. Believe me, I have made overtures to the Girondists; have I not drunk daily that wretched woman's soup at the Hôtel de l'Intérieur? But to no avail. Madame Roland and her disciples want war. You will hear me tell them; I will give them a death!'

Thinking of Charles Barbaroux and his friends, Madeleine shuddered at the clash that was surely to come. She felt dispirited, and rose to go, picking up her bag with its two precious gifts.

'I'm sorry if I upset you, Georges. It's just that when you speak you influence everyone so quickly. Let it always be for good, Georges. All France knows that your efforts are keeping the Republic alive.'

'And that is why my hands must be completely free, to act quickly on her behalf. Why, with a wife like you at my side . . .'

'No, Georges. Besides as soon as I've found a way to pay off my creditors, I shall leave Paris. I need a change; fresh air. Like you I must heed Gabrielle's advice.'

'Gabrielle's advice?' Danton questioned, the line across the top of his nose deepening as he frowned.

'As soon as I've paid off my dressmaker,' laughed Madeleine, shrugging. 'I'm bored, Georges, and there are too many sad memories in Paris for me.'

Together they walked across the salon to the apartment door. But suddenly he restrained her. 'No, come back and sit down. I have a proposition.'

Mildly curious, Madeleine turned about and retook her seat on the couch. 'Once before I asked you to work for me, Madeleine. Indeed, you worked very hard for the Cordelier Club, but it was always your own business that came first.'

'That's how I eat, Georges.'

'Yes, I know,' he said impatiently. 'You now want to clear your debts. Also, no doubt, you've barely made more than a quarter of the repayments on your café. Correct?' Madeleine nodded. 'Well, work for me and you can pay both straight away!'

'Do you wish me to murder someone, Georges?'

'No. I want you to be an *agent provocatrice*!'

'Georges!' burst out Madeleine, seized with laughter. 'You want me to go to England and seduce Pitt.'

'Well, no,' admitted Georges, with a smile reminiscent of the carefree days of The Parnasse, 'although it's not a bad idea. I want you to go to the west. That chap who works for you at The Cordelier, isn't he from the west?'

'Yes, he's from just outside Nantes.'

'Good, I thought so. Get him to teach you the local dialect. With your quick Parisienne wits and that lovely face, you could be very useful to the army. Most of all, you'll be a valuable source of information for me. I can trust you, Madeleine. You'll give me news from both sides. Will you do it?'

'Well, I don't know . . .'

'Think about it, girl! Do you want to see a Bourbon back on the throne? The clock turned back? If we can survive, Madeleine, only think of the reforms that we can bring to the poor. That's why your brother died; why we will liberate other countries! Besides,' he smiled slyly, 'spies don't come cheap. If you do well you'll own The Cordelier within months. Come, will you swear an oath on the tricolor?'

'All right, I'll do it,' said Madeleine, slowly repeating the oath of allegiance. 'But why the west?'

'Because the royalist and religious revolt is gaining ground there. The situation is beginning to look very dangerous. There are two armies in the Vendée. The larger one is centred in Anjou and Haut Poitou, whilst the second force of the Pays de Retz and the Marais, though smaller, is perhaps more dangerous. You, Madeleine, will help to destroy them.'

For the first time in months, Madeleine felt a shiver of fear and excitement as she pondered the challenging role that Danton had thrust upon her. 'But why is the smaller army the more dangerous?'

'Because of its leader,' replied Danton. 'His name is François-Athanase Charette de la Contrie.'

PART II

La Vendée
1793

Chapter One

The yellow flames caught at the edges of the canvas, quickly spreading, leaving behind charred and blackened fragments. Now, only the face remained and just as the first spearhead of fire touched the pretty smiling lips, Madeleine remembered where she had first seen the face. It had been frightened then, peering at her through a carriage window as she marched with the fishwives at Versailles.

Today you would be frightened too, thought Madeleine, as the blue-eyed, laughing face of the Marquise de Lescure crumpled and darkened. Or perhaps anger would overcome fear. For if the Château de Clisson were Madeleine's, never would she forgive the mindless destruction. Nothing was to be saved. Incredulous, Madeleine watched as rooms, luxurious with Aubusson carpets, Fragonards and Flemish tapestries were piled high with brush and faggots and set to the torch.

Not even the sacks of grain in the outhouses were saved. Grain which would feed hungry mouths. It was sheer madness, committed by frightened men. Madeleine could see by the speed at which they worked that the Blues were terrified. By the numerous, vigilant patrols around the velvet-smooth lawns of the château.

Any moment there could be an attack; even worse,

an ambush in the woods. Already it was seven o'clock and the orange flames from the burning building could be seen against the night sky. The local peasants would know republican troops were burning the home of the Saint of Anjou.

It had been a terrible day of fire and destruction. Even now, hours later, she could still hear the screams of the peasant women in the little village of Amailloux. It hadn't taken long to set it alight. In the dry, hot summer the pitiful little dwellings were as tinder. In moments, all was reduced to blackened, smoking debris.

Sick with shame, Madeleine had ridden away, not daring to look at the old men and the weeping women holding on to their children. Within minutes Colonel Westermann, at the head of his column of 10,000 soldiers, had caught her up. 'I hope, *citoyenne*,' he said, laughing brutally, 'you will report we are making a good start in destroying the brigands' lairs. Soon there will be nowhere for them to crawl back to at night!'

'But the old people, the children, how will they live? Must they be punished?' cried Madeleine, her golden-brown eyes dark with anger.

'All who feed and give succour to those wearing the white cockade will be punished. I have advocated to the National Convention total destruction of the Vendée. Today we will destroy one of their leaders' châteaux, tomorrow another – until they are all exterminated!'

The cry 'to horse' rang out. Like the soldiers, Madeleine needed no second bidding. The lurid red of the sky would be seen for miles, and no one shared Westermann's view that fire would cow the spirit of the local peasantry. They moved off as speedily as the surrounding density of trees allowed. Already Madeleine had learnt that speed was the only thing

268

that kept one alive. Although if you were in the sights of a Vendéan gun there was no hope. They never missed.

The ride back to Westermann's headquarters was like a nightmare, with everyone's nerves stretched to breaking point. Every shadow, the slightest noise posed a threat. Inevitably they became quite lost in the local maze of low sunken roads; pitch-black subterranean tunnels where neither sun nor moonlight could penetrate the dense overhanging broom, where frequent crossroads held the menace of an ambuscade, and worse, the growing fear that they would never break out of the bewildering labyrinth.

At last, hours later, they struck the right road to Bressuire, spurring on their weary horses as though the devil were on their heels.

Too exhausted to eat, Madeleine went straight up to her room and flung herself down on the bed. But tired as she was, the distant ringing of the tocsin came between her and sleep. Such a familiar sound, she thought, listening to the low, insistent call drifting across meadows. Soon, no doubt, a second and a third bell would add their voices to the summons to arms. Just like the bells of Paris, calling to the ordinary people to rise and put down tyranny. Except that here in La Vendée the ordinary folk, to her astonishment, were fighting against the tricolor.

They had rebelled against conscription when France was threatened on all sides by foreign powers, whilst their priests had refused to take the Civil Oath, giving their allegiance to Rome before the nation.

For Madeleine, brought up in the hot-bed of Parisian politics, this violent rejection, this willingness of a province to take on the whole might of France, caused her puzzlement and increasing disquiet, which was not alleviated by the tactics of Westermann, nor by the guillotine.

The guillotine was the new attraction in Paris. How glad she was to be away from the excited crowds, craning their fat necks for a better view of another less fortunate neck, their howl of glee when it was parted, dripping blood, from its body. The city had begun to stifle her. There were too many ghosts; too many new sinister faces; too much fear. She had gladly accepted Danton's commission.

Her brief was simple. To link up with the army of the Côté du Nord and render them assistance by gathering information on enemy movements, whilst secretly keeping Georges Danton abreast of all happenings. Before leaving Paris, on his orders she had learnt to use a gun and sword, and how to seat a horse, whilst from Jacques Metalier she acquired a country dialect. It had all been very exciting, and underlying everything was the thought that she would be near Charette. How she had deluded herself, she thought, as a sudden burst of laughter from the republican officers below blotted out the distant bells. In the coach travelling south to Nantes she had not realised that every kilometre bringing her nearer to the man she loved would only widen the gulf between them. Charette had raised the white banner of rebellion and they were on different sides. Not even for him would she fight behind the lilies. Every day she knew she should return to Paris; leave, disengage from the struggle before it was too late to retreat. But the danger, the excitement of their close proximity fascinated her. There was something else, too, which made her stay – a desire to see that proud head bow to the tricolor, as it inevitably would. Yet that would surely mean his death, which was unthinkable. Such confusion, she thought sleepily. Yet somehow I will save him.

The next day Westermann routed the royalist forces, led by the Marquis de Lescure and the

Marquis Henri de La Rochejaquelein, at the woods of the Moulin-aux-Chèvres. The day after he sent a detachment of Blues to burn down the Château de la Durbelière.

'Now we have them by the short hairs,' Westermann gloated to Madeleine at dawn the following day. 'When they see the black smoke rising from the nest of La Rochejaquelein they will have a foretaste of what is to come. As soon as we know where they are assembling we will strike and annihilate them. I believe their assembly point may be at Cholet. I want to know what their strength is and the day and time of their counter-attack.'

'I'll go straight away,' said Madeleine, her stomach knotting with excitement.

'Your zeal is commendable, *citoyenne*. Perhaps first a change of dress? Even the doltish peasants would not be deceived seeing you thus,' he said gesturing to the tricolor sash hanging from her waist. 'Though the sight of you might persuade them to change sides.' As the republican spoke, his cruel, lascivious eyes swept over the girl's long rounded thighs encased in buckskin. His breathing quickened as the sunlight made the thin cotton shirt transparent as she turned. His hands itched to detain her; to unveil the shadowy contours. 'Come back soon, *citoyenne*,' he called after the swinging hips. 'It's time we got to know each other better.'

'I advise you, colonel,' called Madeleine over her shoulder, 'to keep your mind on the job in hand!'

'Oh I will, *citoyenne*, you can depend on it. I will!' he sniggered after her.

Westermann, anticipating an attack from Cholet, had established outposts along the road from Châtillon to Cholet. Thus Madeleine took to a horse, leaving it at the final outpost and proceeding the last kilometres on foot.

Gradually, as she drew nearer to Cholet, so the number of people on the road increased. Many were refugees fleeing from the Blues: whole families, their pots and pans piled high in carts along with grandmother, babies and hens, sometimes an ox tethered behind or being led by father and son.

There were young men too: burly, with muscular brown arms, whose faces were not dazed and frightened, but purposeful, like their stride, as they hastened towards the town. It seemed as if the whole countryside were descending on the town. And as the throng increased, so did the noise and confusion. Eventually, yards from the entrance, their snail-like progress was brought to a halt. The bottleneck Madeleine saw was caused by a group of men whose large, round, black-brimmed hats and white cockades marked them out as royalists. Everyone who wished to gain admittance had to pass before these men. More disturbing was the young man watching these inquisitors. He was quite young, no more than twenty, with blond hair and keen blue eyes. With a sudden feeling of panic she recognised him. The royalist officer, but a few paces from her, was one of those she had faced across the salon in the Tuileries; a companion of Charette's who might not be deceived by her peasant dress of Anjou.

Madeleine's heart and mind raced. To retreat would make her conspicuous. Yet, in a few seconds, she would be face to face with him: already the young men bearing arms were being directed where to go. Next in line before her was a young woman with a baby in her arms and, holding on to her skirt, a little girl who was fractious and crying noisily. Instinctively Madeleine knew what to do. 'Here, let me,' she smiled, reaching forward for the baby. 'It's the heat that is making her cry.'

With a look of surprised relief the young mother

smiled and handed over her baby. 'Thank you,' she said, picking up the crying child.

Quickly nestling the tiny bundle against her averted cheek, Madeleine moved forward, her down-cast eyes seeing only a row of sabots and the black leather boots of the White officer. No one challenged her. They had seen only a young peasant of Anjou comforting her baby. She was through!

The town was like a military encampment, throbbing with activity. Though to refer to the marching columns of peasants as troops would seem something of an exaggeration, decided Madeleine, suppressing a smile. Never had she seen a more comical sight. It was not so much their bizarre collection of homely weapons — scythes, rusty old swords; it was more the expression of pride on the broad rustic faces. As if hoisting a broom handle on the shoulder and cramming a white cockade in an old felt hat had made them part of an élite force. Such clod-hoppers, she and Pierre would have singled them out in a minute on the Pont-Neuf. 'Straight from the farm,' Pierre would have said, watching them gawping around.

Maybe they, too, could spot a stranger, the city dweller. Did she blend in? Instinctively her fingers felt for the little square of brown linen with its red heart, that was so indispensable to the followers of the army of God and King. The young mother, noticing her movement, smiled approval and lifted her white collar. 'The Sacred Heart of Jesus,' she said softly, touching reverently an identical patch. Beaming, she looked towards the marching columns. 'Don't the lads look fine! My Jean-Pierre is with them somewhere. I made him the biggest white cockade and had it blessed by the abbé Bernier himself.'

Madeleine looked at the girl's proud brown eyes

273

shining with tears as she stood on tip-toe for a glimpse of her husband.

'Here he comes,' she suddenly cried, lifting up her little girl on to a low wall for a better view. 'Wave to papa, darling.'

A brawny young man astride a thin nag of a horse, catching sight of the fluttering little hands, waved back. Quickly the young woman, gathering up the little girl, ran forward. For one moment the little family were united and Madeleine saw the father glancing towards her and the baby. Then he rode on.

'Did you see him?' cried the young woman, breathless and laughing. 'Why, he looks like a Prince.'

Smiling, Madeleine held out the baby. 'Yes, he looked very fine,' she agreed. 'I hope your Jean-Pierre will be safe.'

'He will be,' said the young peasant girl, making the sign of the cross. 'God go with you, my sister.'

Madeleine winced inwardly and turned hastily away; whether from the sign of the cross or in the knowledge she was in Cholet to betray, she could not tell. These naïve yokels, like sheep, would soon be ripped apart by Westermann's wolves. Leaving behind their widows and orphans to grieve and fend for themselves.

Eventually Madeleine reached the town's main square. It was obviously the main point of assembly and it appeared from the columns of waiting men that a royalist counter-attack was imminent.

Quickly her eyes ran over the columns, assessing their number. At the top end of the square, mounted on a white stallion, was the fair-haired young man; Charette's companion of the Tuileries. Her heart raced with excitement. Would François be here as well?

'Tell me,' she said to an old woman in black

standing at her side, 'who is the officer on the white horse?'

The old woman lifted her face and peered up at Madeleine. Her brown weather-beaten skin was a mass of wrinkles and furrows; dominating this landscape were two black shiny beads, eyes bright with curiosity. 'Why, that's Young Henri! You're not from these parts or you'd know the Marquis de La Rochejaquelein. The men call him Henri the Fearless.'

'Ah, yes, I see now,' said Madeleine quickly. 'It was the sun in my eyes. I couldn't see his face. Tell me, is Charette here with his men?'

'I've not heard he's here. We're best without him and his black, hairy Maraichins. Young Henri's all we need, and our Saint of Anjou. You know who he is I suppose?' she cackled, her bright eyes slightly narrowed with suspicion.

'Of course,' replied Madeleine confidently, 'everyone knows the Marquis de Lescure.' So, thought Madeleine with a mixture of relief and regret, he is not here!

Deciding she ought to find out the hour of the royalists' offensive, Madeleine moved on. A young boy who was rushing past collided into her. 'I'm sorry, Mademoiselle,' he said, stooping to pick up the rusty iron bar he had dropped. 'I'm in a hurry to join my unit. We're moving off soon to Mallièvre.'

'Mallièvre?' cried Madeleine, seizing hold of his arm as he was about to hurry on. 'Aren't we going to attack the Blues on the Châtillon road?'

'No,' he grinned, making a menacing gesture with the iron bar. 'We're going to take them from behind.'

Stunned, Madeleine watched the small figure thrusting through the people. There was no time to lose if the Blues were not to be caught unawares.

The outposts would have to be warned to relay the news.

Suddenly Madeleine was aware of a profound silence. Startled, she saw that everyone, save herself, was kneeling and holding their rosaries between their fingers. There was no alternative but to follow suit. Slowly she sank to her knees and looked also towards the top of the square.

Now only one man dominated the kneeling assembly. Who he was she did not know, but by his purple ecclesiastical robes she knew him to be a bishop. He was very handsome and from his height in the saddle she judged him to be above average size. Then he spoke, his rich, deep voice reverberating in the stillness. 'Almighty God, bless these, thy children. Give them strength in the coming battle. For they fight in thy name against those who would take away the Catholic religion.' Dramatically, he paused and lifted up the large wooden crucifix he carried. Quite mesmerised, Madeleine looked up at the huge cross, black against the sky. Then the bishop spoke again. 'Merciful Jesus, may those who fall in battle fly straight to thy bosom in Paradise.' Quietly people about her began to sing the Vexillas Regis, as the cleric, making the sign of the cross, moved through the lines of people giving absolution.

Beside the white banners bearing the golden fleur-de-lys, the Marquis Henri de La Rochejaquelein now sprang on to his horse. Then, more slowly, with his arm in a sling, another officer mounted. From the burning portraits at the Château de Clisson Madeleine recognised the face of the Marquis de Lescure. It little surprised her that his peasants had named him the Saint of Anjou. Never had she seen an expression of such sweetness, or such purity. His was not the face of a warrior, rather that of a scholar. And now as he rode amongst his followers, smiling his encouragement, Madeleine could see he was well loved. It startled her to see this open bond of affection between aristocrat and peasant. In Paris there had only been the oppressors — the Vicomte de Cramoisy, the wealthy, irreligious clergy; and the oppressed — the people. She had come to La Vendée believing the poor were being manipulated, coerced. This scene startled her.

The atmosphere had become electric; men were shouldering their weapons, anticipating the order to move off. Up went the great white banner with its large golden words and every throat shouted them out: '*Vive le Roi.*'

It was time for her to slip away. Once out of sight of the town, Madeleine broke into a run. Over the years she had lost none of her speed. Neither did she try to conserve her strength, gambling everything on reaching the first outpost as quickly as possible.

After three kilometres, she recognised ahead the bend of the road where the Blues were. With a final spurt of speed which left her gasping for breath, she neared the spot where they were hidden. But there was no challenge as before. Puzzled, she hovered, and then ran on, thinking she had mistaken the place. But turning round and looking back, she knew she had not. Had the Blues withdrawn? she wondered, alarmed that her horse would no longer be there. It seemed unlikely; Westermann would not recall them until his scouts and she had reported intelligence of the Royal and Catholic Army.

Slowly she retraced her steps, now feeling vulnerable out on the open road. The trees on either side seemed threatening and strangely silent. Gauging the point where she had ridden the army horse up the grassy slope, Madeleine walked quietly into the wood. She had gone just a few paces forward when suddenly, barring her path, was the young volunteer who had earlier led away her horse. The expression on his upturned face was quite calm and free from fear. Obviously he'd known nothing of the bullet which had pierced through his forehead. Nor, apparently, had his companions whom she found a few paces away. There were no signs of a struggle. Evidently the Vendéans, using their usual tactics, had silently moved up on the outpost; each peasant slipping like a shadow between the trees, until he had a Blue in the sights of his gun. Momentarily at a loss to know what to do, Madeleine sat down on a low branch of a tree and surveyed the silent scene. How incongruous and vulnerable the bare white feet of the soldiers looked, stripped of their boots. Gone, too, were their guns and haversacks; as, of course, were the horses. With an exclamation of anger and irritation, Madeleine rose. There was little alternative but to run on. She decided to keep within the fringes of the wood rather than expose herself on the open road.

Her progress was constantly hindered by treacherous tree roots, many hidden like snares in the deep grass. She feared every minute a ricked ankle, but she had to alert Westermann.

This time the challenge rang out.

'*Qui vive?*'

'*Les Bleus!*' Madeleine responded.

Immediately blue-uniformed figures emerged out of cover and advanced towards her. Relieved the outpost was intact, Madeleine looked for the officer in charge. 'I'm here on Colonel Westermann's authority,' she called urgently. 'The outpost outside Cholet has been attacked. They are all dead! Colonel Westermann must be told that the royalists will attack in force today and from the direction of Mallièvre. Have you a rider and a fast horse?'

'Why, there are 10,000 men camped near the

Mallièvre road!' gasped the sergeant. Wheeling around, he snapped out orders. In an instant, horses were saddled and two volunteers were galloping off in the direction of Châtillon.

'Come, *citoyenne*,' said the sergeant, wheeling his horse around and grabbing the reins of another for Madeleine. 'If you've a mind to see the battle, ride with us. With luck we'll be there to warn them before the attack begins.'

Filled with excitement, Madeleine set off with the party of soldiers across country. Their pace was recklessly fast. Every moment she feared a leg would be crushed against the side of a tree, or a low hanging branch would sweep her from the saddle. But bending low over her horse's neck, she urged her mount on, for fear of being left behind.

Eventually they left the wooded slopes behind and entered a series of meadows. Half-way across one, Madeleine's horse reared up in fright as the ground and the air suddenly vibrated.

'Cannon fire,' said the sandy-haired sergeant, turning to Madeleine with a grin. 'Looks like the Whites beat us to it. Come on, to the top of the ridge.'

At full gallop they took the rising ground. Even before she gained the top, the loud rapid outbreak of musketry told Madeleine the combatants were close at hand. Indeed, the sight which met her eyes as she took her place beside the sergeant and his men made her gasp with excitement.

Down below, in a direct line from their position, was a large windmill. Around this the republicans were encamped. Flying figures still running through the tents told the watchers the Whites had succeeded in the surprise of their attack.

Taking in the scene for a moment, the sergeant spurred his horse on for the descent to the battle-ground below. Likewise, Madeleine made to follow.

But as if suddenly remembering her, the wiry young man shouted to a young conscript, 'Stay here with the *citoyenne*. And report to me after we have annihilated these fanatics!'

Catching her chosen chaperon's eye, Madeleine smiled apologetically. But the scowl in return and the red angry flush on the freckled face told her he was far from pleased with the duty of nursemaid. But she was not prepared to argue with the sergeant. This would be her first sight of a battle and here on the brow of the hill she would see it all. Furthermore, she was exhausted after her long run and the fast, hard ride.

Already the republicans were drawn up in battle formation. Their right flank steadily moved forward, each man rapidly firing from the waist. It was controlled and disciplined and a complete contrast to their adversary's tactics. As far as Madeleine could judge, the royalist and Catholic forces had no tactics other than to drive forward. Leading the vanguard, with his sword raised and the Bourbon banner fluttering by his side, was the Marquis de Lescure. Fanning out behind him were the peasants, running forward at great speed holding pitchforks, cudgels and staves. Horrified, Madeleine watched the ragged figures head towards the republican cannon.

'It's sheer suicide,' she gasped.

'Just wait!' said the young soldier and, as he spoke, every man behind the Marquis de Lescure made the sign of the cross and flung himself flat on the ground. Harmlessly the cannon fire flew over them. 'Watch the gunners at the cannons,' continued her unwilling guardian, seeing her puzzled look. 'As soon as the peasants see match applied to powder that is when they dive for the ground. Now, see, they'll run like hares!'

Fascinated, Madeleine watched the homespun

manoeuvre gaining ground for the peasants until, with one mad rush forward, the Vendéans hurled themselves upon the cannon.

These wild, courageous onslaughts were beginning to have an effect on the Blues. Their lines were penetrated and ferocious hand to hand fighting began.

From their elevated perch, Madeleine and the young soldier watched the Vendéans tighten their circle around the Blues. They could see the hunters moving behind hedges and gorse, picking off the lines of Blues like rabbits at a shoot.

'See, they never waste a ball unless they've a kill,' cried the boy with angry, grudging admiration. 'They're getting the better of us, *citoyenne*. I'm sorry . . . I'll not stay here and watch my friends cut to ribbons. I'll live or die with them!'. Before she could stop him, the young soldier plunged down the hill to join in the fray.

It was now no longer a thrilling spectacle below. It was blood and death. Frenchmen fighting Frenchmen. A sense of shame engulfed her that she had found it exciting.

Westermann had no doubt received her warning, for reinforcements arrived again and again. Yet nothing, it seemed, would stop the Vendéans.

Silently she watched the republican lines execute their well-rehearsed drills. But this was a new dance, with no set steps and rules. Before her eyes 9,000 men fell. Blue figures were fleeing for their lives in all directions. The republican horse was running away from mere rustics. She would never laugh at them again.

Chapter Two

The War Minister, Bouchotte, smiled at Madeleine. 'I have read a copy of your report, *citoyenne*, it's excellent. I wanted personally to meet and talk with you,' he said, rising from his desk and walking towards the window. He silently stared out, his fingers drumming lightly on the window sill. Then he spoke again. 'We now have the insurgents in a circle of steel. Our finest troops, the Mayençais, are now at Nantes with Kléber and Travot. It will not be long now before we quell the revolt.' He paused and moved towards a large map. 'Even so, we must be prepared for any eventuality.'

Joining him, Madeleine saw he was studying a map of La Vendée and Brittany. 'My guess is,' he said, thrusting a stubby finger at the long grey ribbon of water which separated La Vendée from Loire Inférieure, 'that they may cross the Loire. If they do they have three alternatives: a march on Paris; capture of a sea port to facilitate an English landing; or a march on Rennes in the hope of inflaming a rising in Brittany. It is the last which is the most dangerous!'

'But do you think the peasants would leave their farms, their own country?' queried Madeleine. 'Surely, the royalists' greatest weakness lies in losing their soldiers to the plough after every battle.'

Bouchotte smiled appreciatively at the girl beside him. 'Yes, you're quite right. It's the reason why they've never held on to the towns they've captured. Still, as I said, we must be prepared for any eventuality!' Once again the short muscular fingers moved upwards over the surface of the map, touching each of the sea ports. 'This is the port they must be encouraged to take ... Granville. It's well defended and it's been heavily fortified. At all costs they must not take Rennes! Your job, *citoyenne*, will be to try and stop them!'

'But I have no wish to return,' faltered Madeleine. The smile left the War Minister's face.

'No wish, *citoyenne*? What could be more important than serving your country?'

'Well, I have a café to run.'

'A café!' repeated Bouchotte in astonishment. 'Come, there must be more to it than that.'

Nervously, Madeleine remained silent. How could she explain the feelings in her divided heart? 'Good, so there is nothing to detain you. You shall start for La Vendée immediately. Remember,' he added on a more sinister note, seeing the suddenly defiant expression on the girl's face, 'the tumbrils carry daily those who have forgotten their loyalty to France. For your sake and all those under your roof I advise compliance. Do I make myself clear?'

Within hours of reporting to the Commander-in-Chief of the republican forces, General Canclaux, at Clisson, Madeleine was donning her peasant dress. And during the following days, the scepticism shown by the Chiefs of Staff upon her arrival quickly vanished, for Aubert Dubayet and Kléber soon found that this latest pest from Paris was an excellent spy. Where their patrols disappeared into the impenetrable Bocage without trace, never to return, Madeleine Fleury did return, and with information.

In fact, Madeleine found it relatively simple. Without Jacques's tuition it would not have been possible. Her Parisian upbringing would have singled her out immediately as an *agent provocateur*, but she had learnt well and moved easily through the royalist towns. For her alert ears, there was no shortage of gossip and whispered snatches of news.

Today, especially, she had information which would make the eyes of General Kléber pop from under his shaggy eyebrows. It had been raining heavily all day and her clothes, by the time she arrived back at Clisson, were wet through. But her news was so vital that she went straight through to the General's quarters.

He was working alone with his aide-de-camp, Buquet, when unannounced, she pushed past the startled sentry into the room. 'Yes, Mademoiselle,' snapped Kléber looking up. 'What do you want? I am very busy . . . and your appearance, if I may say so, might find favour with the Commune of Paris, but not here under my command.'

'Forgive me, General,' replied Madeleine, lifting the dripping strands of hair back from her face, 'but I do have information which will influence your thinking.'

The frowning general growled at the pretty young woman's impudence. 'I hope it's important. It's not often I am told what to think. Come on, out with it!'

'I have learnt the Grand Catholic and Royal Army are to march from Cholet to Torfou.' Madeleine looked at Kléber expectantly, but the reaction she awaited never came. Instead he picked up the document he had been reading.

'Then,' he said, giving it a sharp tap, 'your information is wrong! I have here a dispatch interrupted by one of the patrols. The royalist courier was taking it to Charette. It orders him to rendezvous with the

Grand Catholic and Royal Army at Mortagne-sur-Sèvre; but he will never reach there because we will finish the job we have started. Charette and his army will be obliterated whilst he is unaided.'

'As it was at Légé,' laughed Madeleine.

Jean-Baptiste Kléber ignored the girl's taunt and brittle laughter. Was it not enough to be saddled with a *représentative en mission* who had to get himself wounded in the arm. Now he had this girl babbling nonsense. 'Understand one thing, Mademoiselle,' he said wearily, 'Charette is a very clever adversary. But you and those who sent you will see that cunning and bravery will not save him when the Mayençais move in on him tomorrow!'

His words filled Madeleine with a sudden dread. Until now, it had been easy to laugh, as Charette outwitted every republican force sent to destroy him – but against these troops under Kléber . . .?

'I would like your permission, General, to watch the battle,' said Madeleine gravely.

'So . . . you feel your presence will assist me and my Mayençais?' rasped Kléber, his voice heavy with sarcasm.

'No,' answered Madeleine, forced to smile, for she couldn't be frightened of this grizzly bear. He wasn't cruel like Westermann or Beysser. He was a man proud of his craft and generous enough in defeat to praise his adversary. 'No, my General, I don't think I'll be the slightest help, but I do want to see your face when the Grand Catholic and Royal Army turns up!'

A small spark of amusement shone in the depths of Kléber's grey eyes. Certainly the girl had spirit, but this time her intelligence was wrong. Suddenly, to her astonishment and that of his aide-de-camp, he unsheathed his sword and tossed it to her. 'Well,' he said, gesturing for Buquet's sword, 'if you're going to be no use to me, let's see how you'll manage for yourself!'

The contest was no contest, for she had neither his skill nor strength. Nevertheless, remembering her tuition in Paris, she did her best to parry each thrust; anticipating rapidly and retreating with speed until the huge oak desk barred her way. Feeling out behind her for the corner of the desk her hand came into contact with the heavy silver ink pot. Caught up with excitement, her fingers grasped it and let it fly. There was a horrified gasp from the aide-de-camp and the astonished Kléber let his sabre drop. Seizing the moment Madeleine sprang forward with the point of her sword at his throat.

'Surrender to the nation or die, *mon général*.'

The grey eyes blazed with anger; and the enormity of what she had done hit her. Appalled, Madeleine watched the ink drip from the fierce brows. In other circumstances she might have laughed, but as the dark blue stream reached the immaculate uniform she thought he was going to kill her. Then she breathed with relief; the moment had passed and instead, he burst out laughing. 'Well done, Mademoiselle, all's fair,' he said, slapping her with delight across the shoulder. 'With you by my side, the tricolor plumes will be quite safe!'

Parting from Kléber, Madeleine slowly made her way to her quarters. Her limbs now were leaden and she was very cold. Exhaustion hit her and with it, as she sank down on the edge of her camp bed, the realisation of what tomorrow might bring. She groaned, and pressed her fingers against her temples to try and blot out the horrifying image of his crumpled, blood-stained body lying on a battlefield.

'Oh François, why are you against us, why, why, why? And what am I to do?' she cried. Stricken, she thrust her feet back into her sodden shoes and walked over to the window. Outside, all was blackness: she could see nothing except for the rain driving against the glass; heard only the sound of the wind lifting and battering against the branches of the trees. Where, how? Irritably she thrust aside the impossible task of somehow warning him, and with a weary sigh she threw herself back on to the bed, each heavy thud of her shoes, as they fell to the floor, echoing her gloom. The exciting double game she had played was over; until now her activities had only been directed against the army of the centre, and any intelligence on Charette's little army she had either ignored or misinterpreted. But tomorrow she would be with her own people, and he with his.

When next she opened her eyes, the cold grey light of dawn and the ominous call to arms told her the course was set.

The plumes of the Nation were pinned on Kléber's hat. They dipped and swayed now as he rode before Madeleine across the Sèvre towards Torfou, where he intended to link up with Beysser's column on the right, and the black American hussars.

Alongside Madeleine rode Buquet, whom Kléber had ordered to protect her and never leave her side. From the adoring looks the young officer directed at her, and his solicitude as to her comfort, it was clear he found the duty a pleasant one.

Even Kléber, intent on the day's action ahead, had raised his large plumed hat in appreciation of her appearance. 'My compliments, Mademoiselle Fleury,' he'd said as she'd mounted a large chestnut bay. 'You look most dashing. It would seem you understand our adversary today. The Chevalier Charette is known never to take the field without a beautiful woman by his side. Today he will see her under our tricolor.' The full significance of Kléber's words threw Madeleine's emotions into a terrible whirl. Now the reality was here, she couldn't bear to see Charette's defeat. To be so near him, yet see the chasm open up, parting them for ever. Never had she felt so helpless. Why was he on the wrong side? Was it too late to persuade him, to urge him to come over to the Republic? Kléber, she could tell, admired him, though it was unlikely he could save him from the guillotine, even if he wished to do so. Her heart was heavy with foreboding as she pretended to listen to Buquet's flirtatious chatter.

At nine o'clock they entered the little hamlet of Boussay, where gunfire was exchanged with the first of Charette's outposts.

'Now the King of the Marais will know we're coming,' murmured Buquet as the peasants ceased firing and fled into cover behind the impenetrable broom hedges.

'The King?' queried Madeleine.

'That's the name hereabouts for Charette,' replied Buquet. 'His court was at Légé until we evicted him and his queen.'

Sick at heart at this information, Madeleine forced herself to speak, to ask the question which constantly plagued her. 'Is Madame Charette beautiful?'

Buquet looked at the lovely girl beside him in surprise. Her cheeks were quite flushed and there seemed to be more than casual interest in her voice. But he put it down to a woman's curiosity.

'Ah, it's not the wife who is the queen,' he laughed. 'It is Marie-Adélaïde de la Touche-Limouzinière, the Comtesse de la Rochefoucauld. I'm looking forward to meeting the lady, for they say she is quite a warrior and . . .' But the rest of his words were lost to Madeleine; she was filled with wild jealousy and could hear only her own thoughts.

The going was difficult; the ground sodden with

the heavy rains of the previous days. Many of the *chemins de cruz* were flooded and impassable, making it impossible for the scouts to pinpoint Charette's exact position.

The harsh, dry sound of the drummers began; then the pipes and the 'Marseillaise', and a metallic clash as the long blue lines fixed bayonets. It was a sight which stirred the blood: glorious; terrifying. How then could Frenchmen not be moved? thought Madeleine. Slowly, menacingly, in perfect unison, the war machine which had earned the homage of the Austrians moved irresistibly forward. Waiting for them were Charette's Paydrets and Maraichins. It was the first time Madeleine had seen the peasants named *Mouton noir*. They were fearsome: like wild, shaggy beasts, clad in black goatskins, their faces obscured by masses of tangled hair.

Charette was not with them and, as the Mayençais drew closer, movement began in the peasant ranks. Panic was breaking out; men were starting to break free. Others hesitated, still facing the advancing lines, when a cannon ball exploding in front of them proved the deciding factor. Clutching their rosaries and rusty old weapons they took to their heels. Keeping abreast of Buquet and the colours, Madeleine watched their flight towards the bridge over the Sèvre.

Suddenly he was there! Like a son of Mars he took the field, riding at full gallop towards his fleeing men. Overtaking them, he wheeled his horse around so that it reared up on its hindquarters. Then, raising his plumed hat up on the point of his sword, he plunged forward towards the Mayençais, crying for all to hear, 'If you desert me, I alone will win or die! Those of you who love me will follow.'

His desperate cry pierced Madeleine's heart and she responded. Nothing mattered but her love for this man who faced his enemy alone. She kicked her horse forward, breaking rank, then hesitated, astonished at the sight ahead. But a moment ago the peasant women had been kneeling in prayer before the Calvary at the bridge. Now they were running after Charette, armed with weapons they had snatched from their menfolk's hands.

Behind her she heard the roar of Kléber's voice. '*Citoyenne!* Get back in line, damn you!'

But Madeleine was incapable of hearing or obeying; for overtaking the women and riding up to support Charette were three magnificent women. So, Kléber had not joked. The beautiful amazons existed and they were stunning. Superbly mounted and dressed as though for a royal hunt. One of them, with a reckless, capricious face, was already wounded, the froth of lace at her breast stained a bright red. But she was laughing, one immaculate white gauntlet holding out a smoking pistol before her.

Seeing him so surrounded, Madeleine was consumed once again with jealousy. She felt the humiliation of tears start as, smiling, he acknowledged the presence of a dazzling blonde dressed in white and grey. So that must be the Comtesse de la Rochefoucauld!

Nervously, sensing its rider's distress, Madeleine's chestnut mare whinnied and bucked beneath her. Immediately Charette's quick eye saw the movement ahead of the republican lines. Amazed, he saw it was a girl challenging his attack. Then his thin lips compressed and the blood drained from his face as the hurt of betrayal cut deep. For there was only one glorious head of hair like that, only one girl who would crown it with the Phrygian cap. It was his waif of the Palais-Royal, the beautiful revolutionary.

With a look of icy contempt, Charette rode

towards her. Completely disregarding the hail of bullets directed towards him, he doffed his high-crowned hat and executed a mock bow. Then he was gone, whirling his great sword, rallying his returning men, leaving her with the taste of blood in her mouth from the lip she had bitten to stop her tears.

Now the battle began in earnest. Charette's little force engaged the Mayençais with a ferocious daring born out of their earlier shame. The shock impact of their attacks staggered the Blues. And Kléber, like a lion, roared up and down his lines, cursing and urging his cannoneers on, never stopping for one moment, not even for a bullet in his shoulder. His tricolor plumes rivalled only by his adversary's, he was no lion, but a swift, agile panther, wearing the white plume of the Bourbons, a black plume for mourning and the green of hope.

Like Kléber, Charette dominated his men. Madeleine could see him everywhere, gun blazing, sword whirling. At one point his tall plumed hat was shot clear off his head. Watching him dismount to pick it up, Madeleine saw him glance to where one of his men was surrounded by grenadiers. In a trice he vaulted back into the saddle and, with incredible agility, leaning low from his saddle, he burst through the Blues and seized the fellow by his collar, hauling him clear of danger. Soon he was lost from sight as republican cannon exploded.

The din was terrifying, the air acrid with the smell of saltpetre. Coughing and wiping her eyes, Madeleine waited for the smoke to clear. As it did so she saw moving on to the plateau the banner of the Marquis de Lescure. So too had Kléber; grim-faced at Buquet's side, he ordered up the last of his reserves. Then he swore violently and Madeleine, following the direction of his outflung arm, saw a third royalist force taking the field.

'Now we have that dirty scoundrel, Bonchamps, joining the fight, we're really in the mire,' she heard him growl angrily. Then his growl changed to a bellow and, savagely applying his spurs to his horse, he was racing down the line towards his right flank. Threatened by the Bretons, the grenadiers were falling back on a small wood. But it was too late: like sacrificial lambs they had offered themselves instead to the Vendéan cavalry. With whoops of joy mixed with their blaring pipes and cowhorns, the Vendéans sallied forth out of the trees to the attack.

Throughout the battle, Madeleine had been positioned in relative safety, but a massive counterattack launched by Charette's force had succeeded in breaking through the Mayençais lines. Thundering to the faltering troops to get back in line, Kléber ordered the retreat.

Immediately the well-trained soldiers fell back thirty paces, turned about, knelt and fired. Madeleine marvelled at their coolness and self control. To her, speedy flight from the screaming hordes now seemed imperative. But the Mayençais were not green conscripts; neither were they used to fighting with sharpshooters shadowing them from behind hedges and thickets. One after another, like tin soldiers, they reeled and fell under the deadly accurate fire. Nor could they maintain the disciplined withdrawal over the rough terrain. All about the lines were breaking, the peasants surging through.

'By God, these devils can fight as well as we – and shoot much better!' shouted Kléber, seemingly impervious to the blood still flowing from his shoulder wound. '*Merde!* Now we're really in it,' he cried. 'There's a royalist column marching up the left bank of Sèvre. If they take the bridge at Boussay they'll block our retreat. Come!'

Without knowing whether she should follow,

Madeleine plunged after Kléber and Buquet. The aide-de-camp had forgotten all about her. Their situation was desperate. Without the narrow bridge it would be impossible to get across the deep ravine. They would all be trapped.

Concentrating totally on keeping the tricolor plumes ahead in sight, praying no one would pull her down from her horse, Madeleine tore through the mêlée. When she eventually caught up, Kléber was shouting to the colonel of the troops of Saône-et-Loire, 'Hold that bridge! Die if need be, but save your comrades!'

The fight which ensued was bitter and bloody. Colonel Chevardin and the men of Saône-et-Loire made the ultimate sacrifice. The retreat was kept open. For the first time, the Mayençais, the flower of French military pride, withdrew — leaving behind cannons, mortars and their dead.

The Mayençais had fled and they had fled from the man Madeleine loved.

Chapter Three

The ancient stone walls of the church shuddered with each thunderous boom of cannon, the vibrating rafters shaking a fine covering of dust on to the backs and lowered heads of the supplicants.

All about her Madeleine could hear the same whispered prayer: 'Holy Mary, Mother of God, keep us through this night; Holy Mary, Mother of God, keep us through this night.' Somehow the low, intense intonation was strangely comforting. The soft dismal light and smell of incense gave a feeling of inviolability. Here they were in the eye of the storm.

Sharing this night with the women of the little parish of Beausse, it was impossible not to feel moved by their plight, despite her orders from Republican headquarters. Earlier she had witnessed the heartbreaking goodbyes of husbands leaving wives, sons kissing mothers; perhaps never to meet again. Men who had known only a plough or a loom had resolutely knelt together while the curé had blessed and granted them absolution. They had cried, '*Vive le Roi, Vive la religion,*' and had marched away behind their cross. Now they would be with the Grand Catholic and Royal Army in its desperate bid for survival.

Would Cholet be the decisive battle? Madeleine

wondered. Certainly, if Kléber had anything to do with it. Yet, time after time, against enormous odds, the Vendéans had survived. In fact, to the chagrin of the republican generals and the politicians, they'd won victories. Glorious victories: town after town had fallen to Lescure and Charette. Bewildered, the National Convention saw its finest forces pushed aside, humiliated. Then suddenly there was a split: Charette, leaving the army of the centre, took his small army back into his own country of the Marais. At republican headquarters there was rejoicing and whoops of joy at the good news.

At the front of the church a little girl had started to cry. Glancing up, Madeleine saw the Marquise de Lescure take her daughter into her arms. It was the Marquise whom Madeleine had followed to Beausse. If the Vendéans were to cross the Loire the wife of the Saint of Anjou would be sure to go. The easiest method of anticipating their army's movement was to be near her. Suddenly, from behind, there was a draught of cold air and the metal bolts of the church door crashed against the stone wall. A rider covered with blood staggered in and, without regard to the priest, cried out in a hoarse voice: 'We are lost! Fly, fly for your lives. To the Loire.'

Instantly his cry was taken up as panic broke out. Madeleine, seated at the back, rose swiftly and, supporting the wounded Vendéan, led him outside through the porch of the church. 'What has happened?' she asked, pointing towards the illuminated sky.

'It's the broom on fire on La Pepininère salt marshes,' he gasped. 'Our forces broke through Kléber's and Marceau's centre. We even seized their artillery, but a column of reinforcements arrived and turned our flank . . .' He paused and started to cry like a child, great tears rolling down his grimy cheeks. 'Those who weren't killed by Marceau's cannon fire from La Maillochère ravine were cut to pieces by Beaupuy's horse ... La Rochejaquelein is covering the retreat,' he said wearily as he stumbled away.

So the moment which the War Minister had foreseen was here. In a sense it was with relief that she turned her back on the orange sky and the south. Now she would be rid of him and the sound of his hateful name. Leaving him and his vixen, the Comtesse de la Rochefoucauld, to evade the hounds of the republic as best they might.

Perhaps the rôle she was to play was distasteful. Duplicity had never been part of her nature; cleaner by far to be a soldier. Yet if these peasants were too blind to see the Constitution offered the humblest equality; if they were too stupid to realise that their efforts to restore a Bourbon to the throne would rob all Frenchmen of their hard-won liberties, then, yes, she would do her best to lead them on to disaster.

The first light of dawn was breaking when Madeleine reached Saint Florent-le-Vieil, perched high above the Loire. Early as she was in arriving, the sight below at the river's edge was so astonishing that she sat down to watch.

Thousands and thousands of people stood looking out across the mist-shrouded waters. They covered every foot of the entire shore-line. Every so often tiny boats would appear and within minutes, filled, they pulled away, soon to be lost from sight.

Bouchotte, in Paris, had anticipated a crossing of the Loire by the Grand Catholic and Royal Army and the usual camp-followers, but this surely must be nearly the whole civilian population. Why, there must be at least 10,000 women and children, calculated Madeleine: nearly 50,000 people in total. And all the time hundreds more were arriving.

Many of the rowers were priests, their cassocks fluttering in the October air as they pulled on their oars. Their task seemed impossible to Madeleine and to the thousands still stranded, for their cries of terror were piteous. They could see the opposite bank; safety from the terrible chasseurs lay there. Yet, denying them that refuge was a stretch of icy water. Madeleine had seen the butchery of some chasseurs. Although her peasant dress made her as vulnerable as they, at least tucked into the belt of her skirt was a pistol, not packed with ordinary wads to hold the ammunition in place, but two orders identifying her as a republican agent. They were signed by the Commander in Chief, Canclaux, and the War Minister, Bouchotte, and they ordered all to obey and render her assistance. Comforting though it was to possess these authorities, Madeleine was only too aware that chasseurs did not often wait upon a lady to search out warrants.

Further down the bank there was one who resisted passage. Fighting like a tiger to remain in La Vendée, it was the young Marquis Henri de La Rochejaquelein. Eventually overpowered, she saw him led at sword point to a waiting boat. So, La Rochejaquelein and the Marquis and Marquise de Lescure had crossed. It was time she followed, and the only immediate method of crossing was to swim. To the astonishment of those around her, Madeleine proceeded to strip down to her shift. Carefully she wrapped her pistol and clothes into a bundle, securing them with the kerchief from her head. Just as one of the boats cast off she threw her possessions through the air.

'Monsieur le Curé,' she cried, 'please keep it for me on the other side.' Then, pausing only to see the old man catch her clothes, Madeleine jumped into the Loire.

The icy impact took her breath away, but summoning all her courage she pushed forward for the first stroke. At least it's cleaner than the Seine, she thought wryly, as she felt her legs propelling her forward. Gradually she was gaining on the boat ahead and realised the elderly curé was leaning on his oars waiting for her to catch up. Madeleine was more than grateful, realising the current in the main sweep of the river around the island would be stronger. It was just as she supposed, but another priest – appreciating her struggle to keep on course in midstream – manoeuvred to shield her upstream. And so, keeping pace with a small boat either side of her, she reached the other shore.

Looking back, she marvelled that she had succeeded in crossing, the distance had been much greater than she supposed. But with so many small boats nearby, it had not seemed so frightening. Gratefully she accepted a mouthful of cognac from an elderly man and felt its warmth burning a trail down to her stomach.

'You're a fine swimmer, Mademoiselle, and you're the first woman I've seen able to. Who taught you?'

'Georges Danton,' she replied through chattering teeth. Immediately Madeleine realised her error. 'Well that's what it felt like,' she added quickly, 'when I was just about across and beginning to lose my head.'

At once laughter broke out around her and the shock and disbelief disappeared from the Vendéans's faces.

Dressing quickly she looked back again to the desperate people on the far shore. 'Do you think they'll all get across before the soldiers come?' she asked the curé who was preparing to recross.

'All we can do is try. With God's mercy let us hope so. Pray, my child, that those cannon remain silent.' As he crossed himself and climbed back down into the boat, Madeleine looked up to Saint Florent-le-Vieil and realised that the Vendéans had placed their cannon pointing towards the Benedictine monastery.

'As the good father said,' commented a soldier standing beside Madeleine, 'with 6,000 of their comrades inside the monastery, perhaps the republicans will be persuaded not to attack.'

'Surely our army won't blow up 6,000 helpless men?' gasped Madeleine. 'I thought we only shaved the heads of republican prisoners.'

'Times have changed,' replied the man grimly.

The thought of such mass murder was too horrible to contemplate. Nor was there anything she could do to stop it. With a heavy heart and sense of isolation, Madeleine followed the exodus to the town of Varades across the plateau.

It was a dry, cold day, with a sharp wind, so she walked quickly to try and warm her frozen limbs. For her mission to succeed she had to get close to the royalist leaders. It would not be easy. Even if she managed to do so, to influence their plans seemed an impossibility.

Wondering how best she might achieve this, Madeleine studied a slow-moving party of people ahead. Closing in on them she realised that amongst the group was the Marquise de Lescure, who constantly looked down into a rough wooden cart moving alongside her. Immediately Madeleine grasped this was the cause of their slow pace. Inside would be the Marquis. It was common knowledge he had sustained severe wounds in the battle near the Château de la Tremblaye.

The oxen cart was barely moving; yet every jolt, each rut, caused the man within to cry out in pain. One glance as she passed told Madeleine that Louis de Lescure was mortally wounded. Enemy or not, it was terrible to witness a brave man whimpering like a little child. She turned her head away, feeling embarrassed and upset. Victorine de Lescure noticed her reaction and spoke; her voice almost breaking with grief. 'It's the wind,' she explained. 'The merest breeze touches the exposed nerves in his head ... My poor darling is in agony.'

'Pardon me, Madame, but can I be of any assistance to you?' asked Madeleine.

'Thank you, Mademoiselle,' replied the young woman graciously. 'You are most kind, but I am fortunate enough to have dear friends.' She inclined her head towards two servants and several chevaliers, one of whom was carrying her daughter.

Madeleine nodded and walked on, aware that Madame Lescure's eyes were following her. She suddenly felt anxious, for the despair and unhappiness in them had changed to curiosity. It was four years since Madeleine had seen the pretty, frightened face peering out from the carriage at Versailles, but she had recognised it instantly in the burning portrait at the Château de Clisson. Had Victorine Lescure remembered her too, astride the cannon on that rainy day?

Thirty paces on, the clear, sweet tones of the Marquise cut the air sharp and hard with her order. 'Wait!'

Reluctantly Madeleine halted and turned around, noticing, to her dismay, curiosity had been replaced by suspicion. Furthermore, a cloud of dust, announcing the arrival of Vendéan cavalry, further increased her alarm. If Victorine de Lescure remembered where it was she had seen her then she could expect execution on the spot. 'Mademoiselle, your face disturbs me. I feel certain we have met before.'

'I expect we have, Madame,' responded Madeleine

as casually as possible. 'Was it with the women of Cholet?'

'Perhaps ... but no, I feel it was somewhere else. It will come to me, no doubt,' she said absently, as the first of the horsemen diverted her attention.

But the distraction gave no respite to Madeleine. Indeed, her anxiety only increased. For the chevalier sweeping off his plumed hat in greeting was the second of Charette's companions on that stifling August day at the Tuileries. There was no escape and Madeleine waited for the moment the young man's eyes would rest on her. When it came, the light blue eyes registered for a second and then, to her amazement, the chevalier burst out laughing.

'Why, Mademoiselle, are you here to rescue me? Why aren't you with Charette on his island of Noirmoutier? Perhaps a lovers' tiff?' he teased.

'Noirmoutier? Is it then in Charette's hands?' interjected one of the chevaliers.

'It is, indeed,' responded the young man. 'We learnt the good news when we took the republican letters from the post office at Ingrandes.' Then with a second flourish of his hat, this time directed at Madeleine, he collected in his reins to ride on. 'Forgive me, Mademoiselle,' he said, flashing Madeleine a smile. 'La Rochejaquelein and I owe you our lives. And I must say I am delighted to see you have deserted our temperamental General of the Marais. I am sorry I cannot stay to question you further, but we ride to take Ancenis so that our guns can be brought across at the ford.'

Then, with a flourish of his hat to wave on his column of cavalry, he was gone. So it seemed luck was with her. Charette had obviously never spoken of her, and the merry-eyed Vendéan officer had assumed she had come to La Vendée through Charette. So long as both men did not meet she was safe.

Perhaps the Marquise de Lescure would be less anxious now. Turning towards her Madeleine saw, with relief, that the young noblewoman was smiling at her. 'Forgive me, Mademoiselle,' she said apologetically. 'I must confess I had begun to harbour suspicions against you. We know many republican spies have infiltrated our people – and, well, I thought ... Now I hear Charles d'Autichamp say you have saved not only him but La Rochejaquelein and General Charette as well. You must be a remarkable young lady. When Louis is better you must dine with me and tell me more. Perhaps then I will remember when we met.'

The apology was like a knife thrust, and Madeleine squirmed inside at her deception. It made her feel wretched and unworthy. The oxen pulling forward again set the cart in motion and its wounded occupant cried out in agony. At once the little Marquise left Madeleine and ran across to his side. It provided Madeleine with the opportunity to escape. It would not do to become too close, too involved with these people. Her resolve must not be weakened. Even so, seeing a furniture shop when they reached Ingrandes, Madeleine thought immediately of the suffering Marquis.

On display in the window was a large cane chair, and seeing it she was seized with an idea. Buying the chair and a large white linen sheet, she took her purchases to a carpenter. Within half an hour he had fitted the chair with two poles for carrying, and the sheet was draped over three loops.

Finally, with a payment of extra assignments, she persuaded the man to wait at the entrance of the town for the wounded royalist leader. On no account was he to say who had sent the chair.

Madeleine hoped the canopy of sheets would act as a wind break, for she had seen the merest whiff had caused extreme pain to Louis de Lescure's shattered head. No doubt a Westermann would view such a gift with suspicion. But not a Kléber; he and his Mayençais would understand. It would not give them pleasure to see the man who always led from the front, the man who had earned their respect, in such distress; to see that face, always serene and beautiful, now twisted with pain. With all her heart, Madeleine hoped the chair would give the Saint of Anjou some repose and ease.

After ordering the release of the 6,000 prisoners in the monastery at Saint Florent-le-Vieil, the wounded leader, Charles-Artus de Bonchamps, died. With Lescure near to death, the Vendéans were without a leader. Quickly, by popular vote, Henri de La Roche-jaquelein was elected generalissimo. But did power rest in his hands? From past experience, Madeleine knew that a title did not automatically imbue the holder with total power. Whose voice was the most powerful in the royalist Conseil Supérieur? It did not take Madeleine long to deduce that it was not Henri de La Rochejaquelein. It seemed it was a Prince de Talmond who, now on his home ground, promised soldiers and money for the cause.

Instantly Madeleine disliked the fat, supercilious Breton aristocrat. Most of all she hated the name he bore. The name which had lain dormant, tucked away in the corner of her mind for so many years. Now, tramping in heavy rain through the Breton countryside, past the little cottages, noticing the deluge cascading down on the piles of cider apples heaped beside the doors, the sight matched a treasured childhood memory and sent a name spinning to the surface of her mind.

Madeleine remembered how her brother's eyes had glowed with hate when he had spoken the name of Tremoïlles. Talmond belonged to this powerful family, one of whom had sent her father to his death. Should she ever be tempted to forget why she was amongst these people, the arrogant, haughty Prince would serve as a constant reminder of the *ancien régime* and its abuses.

Since they had arrived at Laval, the Prince was installed in his absent brother's château, where it was rumoured he lived in great style, surrounded by the bevy of young aristocrats who had fled the salons of Cholet. Competing with these spoilt darlings for his attention, in an old ragged peasant dress, did present its problems, thought Madeleine. As for La Rochejaquelein, she wondered if he knew what a woman was. Daily she saw him ride to the back of the long column of civilians to look for pursuers, but he rode with his proud head held high; looking always to the horizon.

Now she sat and watched as he stood with his friend, the young cavalry officer, Charles d'Autichamp. Both men were just out of earshot of a vociferous soldier, Pierre-André Legeay. Like those around her, Madeleine was caught up in laughter as the big man recounted his exploits of the day. The local National Guard were, of course, the butt of his humour. And whilst, initially, Madeleine felt a twinge of guilt as the first smile rose to her lips, it became hard to think of this expressive Frenchman as an enemy. Before long his rolling eyes and mimicry reduced her to a fit of helpless giggles.

Then his manner and voice were aggrieved: '. . . and friends,' he continued, pulling a sad face, 'after our long journey to Laval did we receive a welcome? Did the fearless National Guard stay to offer us a drink? Why, at the sound of the first cowhorn they fled like frightened rabbits!'

'Then what did you do, Legeay?' grinned a young lad with a missing front tooth.

'Ah, it's not what I did, young fellow, it's what our generalissimo over there did. You know how hot-headed Young Henri is. So furiously did he gallop after them, with me following as best I could, that he overran the foot soldiers, grabbing one by the collar with his good arm – somehow without rein he manoeuvred his horse – all the while running the poor fellow this way and that crying, "Go back to the patriots and tell them you've grappled hand to hand with the General of the Vendéans, who had no weapons and only one arm, and yet you were not able to kill him!"'

'*Vive* La Rochejaquelein,' the gap-toothed boy shouted in delight.

'*Vive le Generalissimo!*'

The cries and the merriment had attracted the attention of the young generalissimo who, with d'Autichamp, walked across the square to the little group. 'Now Legeay, you rogue, what are you up to?' asked Henri de La Rochejaquelein, a smile lighting up the serious, proud face. Madeleine noticed how relaxed and easy he was amongst his men.

'Just explaining your new combat tactics, *mon général*,' replied Legeay mischievously. His words were immediately greeted by more whoops of laughter. Once again the shy face broke into a carefree, boyish grin. Then Henri de La Rochejaquelein turned and, in doing so, his eyes met Madeleine's. An impact, a swift mutual instinctive communication passed between them. Surprised by the moment, almost embarrassed, both averted their eyes while he moved past. If they had not been so taken off guard, Madeleine knew that La Rochejaquelein would have stopped to talk with her. She knew Charles d'Autichamp would have made him aware of her presence. But in the weary march to Laval, there had been no time for social pleasantries. Though the Vendéans had met with little resistance, La Rochejaquelein was fully preoccupied, not only with an army, but the immense burden and encumbrance of civilians.

Laval, the Prince de Talmond promised, would provide food, rest, money and men. So far Madeleine had not noticed any great rejoicing on the part of the townspeople at the arrival of the Grand Catholic and Royal Army. Hopefully this indicated a loyalty throughout the province to the republic.

At least for her, whilst they stayed in the town, she was fortunate to have a bed. Until now, in order to pick up gossip and spread her own, it had been important to fare as best she could with the women sleeping out on market squares. But if she were to keep her wits about her she could not afford to fall ill. So she had rented a modest room.

The thought of clean sheets and perhaps hot water was tempting, and there was nothing to be gained by hanging around. Picking her way through groups of peasants who were already selecting and laying claim to areas of the cobbled square, Madeleine saw, hurrying towards her, Charles d'Autichamp.

'Mademoiselle,' he said, sweeping his hat off in a debonair manner. 'The Marquis de La Rochejaquelein regrets that he is detained with war matters, so I am here as a poor substitute on his behalf. Would you do him the honour of going with him tonight to the Prince de Talmond's dinner?'

Madeleine lowered her long lashes to hide the exultation in her eyes. At last, the moment she had awaited! She would be with the men of power. 'Nothing would give me greater pleasure, Monsieur,' responded Madeleine. 'But tell me, do guests at the Tremoïlles château usually dress so?'

D'Autichamp's fine nostrils wrinkled in distaste as Madeleine gestured towards her dress. 'That, Mademoiselle, is not a problem. Tell me where you lodge and Henri and I will call for you at 8.00 p.m.'

The stiff taffeta crackled and rustled as Madeleine withdrew the dress from its box. Rich, jade-green folds spread out, enveloping the counterpane in a mass of glowing colour. Laughing, she held it up against herself and ran over to the mirror. It was the most glorious dress she had ever possessed. Perhaps a little out of date by Paris standards, but the deeply cut neckline and the narrow waist suited her to perfection.

The Marquis d'Autichamp was a wizard — certainly a ladies' man. For also in the cardboard box was a pot of rouge and a flask of perfume. Not for a moment did she doubt him to be the sender. The shy Henri de La Rochejaquelein would never include frothy silk underpinnings and stockings.

The landlady, whom Madeleine felt instinctively was a rabid Jacobin, had looked quite stony-faced when she had taken up the extravagant dress box to Madeleine's room. And when Madeleine informed her that she would be going to the château and therefore would require hot water for a bath, every line of the widow's face had registered disapproval.

It was a situation which made Madeleine laugh. She even sang a few lines of the royalist hymn as she towelled dry her hair. From her background it was amusing to be mistaken for a pampered aristo. And that is what she looked like when her royalist escort arrived.

Whether Henri de La Rochejaquelein's invitation came from the moment their eyes met or from a sense of kindness and past gratitude, she was uncertain. But from both men's stunned reaction to her appearance, Madeleine knew the mirror had not exaggerated.

Henri de La Rochejaquelein became all formality and was distinctly uneasy. Whereas Charles d'Autichamp, easy and graceful, flirted outrageously. 'I do hope, Mademoiselle, you found everything to your satisfaction?' he enquired, his eyes twinkling, clearly thinking of the lace-trimmed undergarments.

'Yes, everything is a perfect fit,' replied Madeleine, boldly meeting his admiring gaze.

Inside the château, amidst a blaze of chandeliers and powdered wigged footmen, it was as though they had stepped back in time and the war was only an ugly nightmare. Yet she must not lose sight of why she was here, nor waste the opportunity La Rochejaquelein and d'Autichamp had put unwittingly in her way. Amidst admiring glances she walked between the two men towards the footmen at the door leading into the salon. Henri de La Rochejaquelein proffered his arm. 'Mademoiselle.'

Unhesitatingly she laid her hand on his, leaving d'Autichamp to fall in behind. Shy though La Rochejaquelein's manner might be, something in those deep cornflower-blue eyes and his tone of voice demanded obedience. Madeleine now understood why 70,000 men marched behind his banner.

The Prince de Talmond, anxious to obtain loans for the Grand Catholic and Royal Army, was surrounded by bankers and the wealthy bourgeoisie of the district. If the Prince was hopeful for a financial coup, the animated, unwed daughters, brought along by their adoring papas, vied for the Prince's attention with minds set on a different kind of coup.

Hearing La Rochejaquelein announced, Talmond, making his excuses, took his leave of the young ladies. He envied the young commander-in-chief of the Vendéan army, but comforted himself with the thought that, but for his gout and a tendency to overweight, he, too, would be able to perform feats of horsemanship and martial arts.

However, when it came to the ladies it was he who was the god. For, he had to concede, they adored him. La Rochejaquelein seemed positively unmoved by the ladies and was rarely seen in the company of one. All the more strange he appeared with one tonight. No doubt she would look like one of his horses.

Taking a glass of champagne from a passing servant, he paused, sipping his drink, allowing himself, like a painter, to study the subject before him. Her back and shoulders were excellent. The shoulders perhaps a trifle wide. But the shapely back tapered to a trim waist; its small span accentuating the rounded swell of hips.

Excited as always by the sight of a new woman, the Prince de Talmond hurried forward. For nothing would give him greater delight than to humiliate the young commander-in-chief by stealing her away.

Talmond's heart sank a little when the young woman turned in response to his greeting. Madeleine Fleury was breathtaking; but hers was not a pretty, empty face. The bone structure was too strong. And although the lips were full and sensual, it was the eyes beneath the thick, winged eyebrows that worried him. They had a watchful intensity. Lynx-like, heavily fringed – quite beautiful, but disturbing. This was not the sort of woman he was used to, one who would easily laugh and respond to a new carriage and a little spoiling. Her movements, though graceful, were too assertive, he thought, as she extended her hand.

'That is a beautiful ring you wear, Mademoiselle,'

he said, struck by a large topaz which seemed like a reflection of her eyes. She smiled, acknowledging his compliment, and he noticed La Rochejaquelein's face stiffening. Obviously it was not a gift from him . . . perhaps a rival. The Prince smiled to himself, deciding to press the matter home a little. 'A family heirloom, or perhaps a gift from a grateful friend?' He noticed with glee the nerve twitching at the corner of La Rochejaquelein's mouth at the implied suggestion.

'How perceptive you are, Prince,' lied Madeleine smoothly. 'It was indeed a gift in return for services which I counted myself lucky in being able to render – for it is not every day one can save the life of the Chevalier Charette,' she laughed, lowering her long curly lashes, hiding the mocking expression Talmond knew would be in the golden-brown eyes. He had meant to steal her away to discomfort La Rochejaquelein; now he wanted her. She amused and irritated him. She was stunning.

'I hope, Mademoiselle, you will honour me by sitting near to me at dinner?'

'Your Highness, nothing would give me greater pleasure. So long as I have our generalissimo by my side,' Madeleine said, turning and smiling at Henri de La Rochejaquelein.

During dinner the Prince was in high spirits. Not only had the bankers come forward with substantial loans, but that very day he had found a large chest, left behind by his émigré brother. It contained a great deal of money.

It is hardly surprising he suffers with gout, thought Madeleine, watching Talmond's fat fingers popping a bonbon into an already full mouth. But she was intrigued, not by the Prince, but the man opposite her at table. There was something familiar about him. Madeleine felt she had seen him before, and

310

quite recently. She studied his profile as he responded to a question from the Prince. Looking at the heavy jawline, she remembered: it had been that very day. Not in the lace and velvet he wore now, but in the tattered rags of a peasant. And the weariness with which he had stumbled towards the château, cudgel in hand, she felt had not been feigned.

'Who is the man the Prince is speaking to?' asked Madeleine of Henri de La Rochejaquelein.

'The chevalier, Saint-Hilaire,' replied La Rochejaquelein casually.

'He has an interesting face. Tell me about him,' requested Madeleine lightly.

'Why there's nothing much to tell. He is a loyal supporter of our cause ... Oh yes, like you, he is a fine swimmer. But he swims from north to south,' he chuckled, then suddenly frowned as though he regretted his last words.

'How did you know I swam across the Loire?'

The young commander-in-chief shrugged and merely smiled.

'At least I was not forced across at sword point,' she teased, enjoying the warmth of his smile.

A sadness came into his eyes; their cornflower-blue now dark in the candlelight, like the night sky. 'It's true,' he sighed. 'I wanted to stay and fight in my own country. I would rather have died on the soil of La Vendée.' His expression was soft and wistful, his tone of voice loving, as though speaking of a dear one left far behind, never to be seen again.

Deeply moved by his tacit acceptance of death, Madeleine reached forward and softly touched his hand. With a start the young Marquis looked at the beautiful girl by his side. He was still dazzled by her, but now, since they had talked together, he felt relaxed in her company. She lacked the cloying, giggling femininity of other women which stifled him. In conversation she actually listened and considered before answering with her startlingly low, musical voice. When he looked at her he enjoyed the same sense of thrill he felt when entering a battle. His pulses raced and he was filled with a heady desire to conquer. A slight tremor passed through her hand, but before she could withdraw it, his fingers closed about it. Their eyes met. In the noisy, glittering throng, suddenly they were alone. Their languorous looks drew the essence of each other closer, until they could almost feel the sweetness of the other's mouth.

'And what is your opinion, Mademoiselle Madeleine?'

It was the braying voice of the Prince de Talmond which broke the spell. Hiding her irritation with a forced smile, Madeleine inclined her head towards the top of the table. 'Forgive me, but I did not hear the question.'

'Well, do you think we should go to Rennes or capture a seaport?' repeated Talmond, his face registering his jealousy at Madeleine's lack of attention.

'I hardly think you need my advice, Your Highness,' laughed Madeleine, 'but I think I would favour a port. Sea air, they say, is very healthy . . . Take a port and you have a line of communication. Besides,' she added coquettishly, 'you owe it to the British to keep them in touch with fashion.'

The Prince de Talmond slapped his fist on the table with delight. 'A good answer, Mademoiselle. I'm more and more in favour of a port myself.'

Madeleine noticed that the man sitting opposite to her was beginning to look anxious as their host helped himself liberally to cognac.

'Of course,' continued the Prince, wiping his womanish lips delicately with a napkin and leaning towards the chevalier, 'there'll be no trouble with the peasants. I understand the fellows. Often listen to them when I'm riding at the head of the columns . . .'

Suddenly the quiet voice of Henri de La Rochejaquelein cut across the loud, boastful voice. 'Prince, when it comes to understanding women, I am sure you do so better than I, but when it is a question of our columns of peasants, I think I know them a good deal better than you.' He rose from the table, his face white and tense with irritation. 'And now, if you will excuse me, we must not forget we have Westermann's cavalry at our heels!'

Pleading fatigue and the onset of a headache, Madeleine, too, took her leave of the Prince de Talmond. As she left the château with La Rochejaquelein, Madeleine took hold of the young general's arm to steady herself, for the cobbles were slippery from the rain. But their moment of intimacy was gone. Both were lost in their own thoughts.

Occupying Madeleine was the Chevalier Saint-Hilaire. Henri de La Rochejaquelein had not tried to conceal his identity, though he had quickly changed the subject to herself and her swim across the Loire and, in so doing, had indiscreetly mentioned the chevalier's swim across La Vendée. There could be only one reason to make such a crossing. The chevalier must be a royalist agent. He had entered Laval in rags and by the deference paid to him he had brought important papers. Where were they now?

They were nearing the royalist headquarters when La Rochejaquelein's companion in arms, Pierre-André Legeay, came running towards them. 'Ah, there you are, *mon général*. I was just coming for you,' he cried, taking La Rochejaquelein on one side so that they might not be overheard. But despite this precaution, his natural tendency to bellow, together with his excited state, did not serve him well, and

313

what Madeleine heard make her freeze with apprehension. She had clearly heard the name General Dannican. Could it be the republican general, drinking companion of Westermann? There was only one way to find out.

The two Vendéans had ended their conversation, and Henri de La Rochejaquelein came to her side. 'Madeleine, I must go. The Blues are mounting an attack. Legeay will escort you back.'

'No, you may need him. I'll be all right,' replied Madeleine confidently.

In the darkness it was not possible to see the expression on his face. But they were so close she could feel the warmth of his breath. Suddenly she realised she might never see him again and the thought distressed her. Her lips parted in a sigh and remained parted as Henri de La Rochejaquelein imprinted a swift, tender kiss. Then he moved away to rejoin Legeay.

The fleeting, lovely moment was over for both of them. He was once more the commander-in-chief of the Vendéans with work to do, whilst she, a republican, had to look for a traitor.

Keeping to the shadows, Madeleine followed both men back to the inn. The entrance, as she expected, was unguarded. For the Vendéans rarely mounted guards; they were usually too busy drinking.

Inside all was bustle. No one paid her the slightest heed, so busy were they cleaning guns and warming up their sword arms. Silently Madeleine slipped up the stairs where she calculated La Rochejaquelein's council room would be. Gaining the top, she waited a moment, straining her ears for the sound of voices. Nor did she have to wait long. With the rise and fall of the nearby conversation came a scraping metallic sound. Cautiously peering around the corner, Madeleine saw Pierre Legeay leaning up against a doorpost with his back to her. The noise came from a piece of flint which he was running up and down the length of his sword.

Holding her breath, Madeleine tip-toed forward, stepping as lightly as possible for fear of creaking floor boards. She had almost reached the open door of a darkened chamber when the soldier suddenly shifted position and the little tune he was whistling under his breath ceased.

Madeleine hesitated, praying that he would not sense her presence or turn around. The moment seemed to last for ever. Then he shifted his weight, reapplied the flint and, as his whistling resumed, Madeleine slipped through the open door.

It was dark inside and she stood quite still, listening for the sound of breathing; but the room, as she had supposed, was empty. Laughter and voices from below drifted upwards as the men prepared for action.

In the next room she could hear Henri de La Rochejaquelein speaking and a deeper voice replying to his questions. Had she heard that voice before? It was difficult to say. Madeleine moved closer to the dividing wall. There was a pause in the conversation as though both men were studying something. Then La Rochejaquelein spoke and Madeleine could hear the excitement in his clear decisive voice. 'So, Dannican, you say the Mayor will lead Westermann's troops here over the heathland of Croix La Bataille?'

'*Oui, mon général.*'

'Good. Then we will be waiting for them. Legeay!' With her ear pressed against the rough plaster, Madeleine heard the big man abandon his vigil in the corridor and enter the next room. 'Legeay, alert the men. We march immediately to meet Westermann's legionnaires!'

Before La Rochejaquelein had finished speaking,

315

Madeleine stole behind the heavy oak door, pulling it open a little further to give herself more cover. All would be lost if anyone entered this chamber. Nervously she peered through the crack of the metal hinges. The first to pass was Legeay. Then, without pausing, La Rochejaquelein left, the gold of his epaulettes gleaming in the dim light of the passage. She noticed he had raised his sling so that the wounded arm would not impede the sword hilt hanging at his right side. Close behind him came Dannican. A large felt hat made it impossible to see his face, but as he moved forward his cloak parted slightly. Underneath was a uniform of the republic.

Remaining concealed for just a few moments more, Madeleine then moved swiftly to the window, hoping to gain another glimpse of La Rochejaquelein's visitor. But there was no sign of him.

Men were swarming into the square from all directions. Below the window, Henri de La Rochejaquelein leapt lightly on to his horse. His white silk banner with the golden fleur-de-lys flapped lightly beside him like a huge silk sail. Under it he waited, watching the assembling Poitevins. Above the sound of horses' hooves, shouted commands and chanted psalms rose the mournful, eerie call of Cotterie's cowhorns directing his 6,000-strong Chouans to their assembly points.

All seemed ready. The fair-haired commander-in-chief of the Grand Catholic and Royal Army raised high the round English hat he favoured and shouted to his army: '*Vive la religion! Vive le Roi!*'

Now, as the army moved out into the night, Madeleine hesitated, wondering what course of action to take. There was no possibility now of warning Westermann's troops, yet here she had the opportunity to look around undisturbed. Of one thing she was certain, the royalists had their spy. The man who had betrayed Westermann's plans tonight must be General Dannican. Though she had not seen his face, the name, uniform and voice indicated it must be Westermann's drinking companion. There was no way she could prevent the royalists' ambush. All she could do, when it was possible, was expose Dannican.

There was little need to light candles in Rochejaquelein's room, for it was brightly illuminated by a large log fire. It was sparsely furnished with a small camp bed on which there was a scattering of used, bloodied dressings, evidently thrown down in haste.

Dominating the room was a large table where, no doubt, the Conseil Supérieur met in session. It was covered with papers, though none were of great significance; certainly there was nothing the Chevalier Saint-Hilaire would have smuggled through republican lines. Did she dare break open the locked military chest? It was the only place where anything of importance would be kept. Any royalist agent would surely hand over documents to the commander-in-chief of the army. Drawing a hair pin from her hair, Madeleine unbent it and was about to apply it to the lock when she paused, struck by a further thought. She had seen the ragged peasant with the cudgel stumbling towards the château. Later, changed, he had attended the dinner; the dinner La Rochejaquelein had left early in anger. Perhaps nothing had been handed on to him after all. This was not the room to search.

In haste she returned to the château, hoping that the Prince would still be at dinner, surrounded by his cronies. Where his apartments were she had no idea. But with a brazen smile on her lips and a knowing lift of her eyebrow, her enquiry to a servant was regarded without suspicion.

His personal suite of rooms appeared to be very

luxurious. But there was no time to look around. Any moment she might be disturbed. She had no explanation to offer for her presence except, perhaps, that her passion for the podgy young man had driven her hence; though even he was not vain enough to believe that, Madeleine smiled.

Her search of the ivory and rosewood desk produced nothing. Where next? The bedroom? Swiftly she ran on tip-toe into the blue and gold room. Immediately her eyes were drawn to the vast canopied bed. There, negligently abandoned on the blue satin cover, was a wooden cudgel.

It seemed to be just a piece of rough wood, except it was lighter than she expected. So she supposed it must be hollow. Sitting down on the edge of the bed, Madeleine turned the club very slowly, holding the handle and keeping the bulbous end uppermost, whilst all the time running a finger-tip gently over the surface. Then, she had it! Two fine, hair-line cracks running around the base and the top of the handle.

Trying to contain her excitement, Madeleine tried to twist the sections apart. But nothing happened. Nor when she pulled. Then it occurred to her to twist them in an anti-clockwise direction. Smoothly the two pieces parted, revealing two hollowed-out sections. Inside each were letters, the seals of which were broken.

Amazed, quite forgetful of her surroundings, Madeleine's trembling fingers laid the letters out on the bed. Her golden-brown eyes blazed with triumph and her full lips curved into a smile.

So immersed was she, it was with a sense of shock that the Prince's laughter reached her from the antechamber. He had entered without her even hearing. Hastily she replaced the letters and made them secure. Quickly she smoothed down the satin cover and looked around for her escape, but there was no other door and now the Prince was coming towards the bedroom. Frantically Madeleine spun around. Then approaching footsteps arrived at the door and in one dive she was under the Tremoïlles bed.

Quite still and tense she lay, listening to the valet undressing the Prince. Eventually above her the mattress descended in an alarming thump, making her want to sneeze as dust choked her nostrils. Impatiently she waited for him to turn out the lights, but instead she heard the rustle of paper. Surely too much cognac had been drunk for reading! Apparently not, for the regular crackle of pages told her the robust Prince was reading a book.

Sticking out her tongue at him in a churlish gesture, Madeleine stared up at the indentation that was his body with tired resignation. Then the excitement of the discovery returned. Three letters bearing the signatures of Pitt, Lord Dundas and, astonishingly, the English King, George III. Money, arms, supplies and troops were promised to the royalists. All dependent on the capturing of a port. The English wanted Saint-Malo. She must make certain it was Granville. At least now they surely would not consider Rennes.

Hours later, when at last the bedchamber was in darkness, Madeleine judged it safe to leave. She was stiff and cold, but the night had been successful. She wondered what the outcome of the battle was and prayed La Rochejaquelein was safe. No doubt soon the Prince would be woken from his snorting sleep with the news. Pulling the wool cloak closely around her shoulders, Madeleine slipped quietly away from the Prince's apartments. But coming towards her, the joy slipping away from his noble face, was the Vendéans's generalissimo. They passed each other without speaking, the cold, cornflower-blue eyes forbidding her to stop.

Chapter Four

Not since the triumphs of early summer had the morale of the army of Anjou and Poitou been so high. They had almost totally destroyed Westermann and Beaupuy's troops on the wild, desolate heathlands of Croix-La-Bataille. Three days later, the Vendéans completely routed Lechelle's army, chasing the troops of Kléber, Marceau, Chalbos and Beaupuy away from Laval and back south beyond the town of Château-Gontier.

Joining the wives and sweethearts at the river to watch the triumphant return into Laval, Madeleine shook her head in wonderment. Here, passing before her, were refugees without boots carrying weapons of the crudest form. Yet, somehow, once again they had apparently put the combined forces of the republic to flight.

Madeleine could picture Kléber's anger at the disgrace, and knew the young dashing Marceau would be stunned by their defeat. But neither general knew of the traitor in their midst. Dannican, it seemed, had betrayed them yet again. When Beaupuy led the advance guard to Entrammes, the Vendéans were already waiting for him on the right bank of the river Jouanne.

Madeleine had determined to warn the Blues, but realising that to travel alone across unknown countryside would endanger her own mission to link up with the republican agent in Fougères and ensure his introduction to royalist command, she looked for a messenger. Trusting her instincts to be right about her landlady's politics, she had sought her help. Now it was obvious her letter had not reached republican headquarters, though she had no doubt it had been sent, for her Laval hostess had eagerly introduced Madeleine to several patriots all impatient to strike a blow against the royalist cause.

A small boy, happily elevated astride the broad width of a burly young man's shoulders, laughed and waved now to the passing men, crying in a high-pitched voice, 'Death to the Blues, death to the Blues.'

Madeleine noticed the face between the little boy's bony legs was grim and stony. And so too was the face of the child's mother. 'Jacques . . . Michel?' she whispered.

The man, unwilling to answer, stared down at the ground, his great hands holding on to the child's little knees. When eventually he looked up his face was ablaze with hatred. 'They're dead!' he said savagely. 'They're all dead. The Blues entered the hospital and butchered them where they lay. Not a man was left alive!'

Even at that moment Madeleine sensed and noticed the change in the army. A brutality was developing which had not been there before. They were not the same people she had watched entering the battlefields behind village priest and crucifix, to fight for God, to save their beloved Vendée. Now, far from home, fear and disillusionment made them cruel.

Cathelineau, the Angel of Anjou, was dead. Now the Saint of Anjou was also near to death. Though Madeleine had never known Cathelineau, nor really the Marquis de Lescure, it was easy to see from her conversations on the long marches, that both men had gained their names from their purity of spirit. Both, leading by example, had held in check the savage nature of men like Marigny and the German troops under Stofflet.

In Laval Madeleine had steered well clear of the Marquise de Lescure for fear of reviving her memory. Nor did the poor woman appear much, so occupied was she with the dying general. It was common gossip that she was more then three months pregnant, but when the march north resumed, Madeleine saw Victorine de Lescure ahead on the road. Despite her condition she was mounted, riding alongside the carriage which bore her dying husband, her head bowed low against the driving, icy rains, and no doubt through grief, too, thought Madeleine. For soon she would be a widow, and the child she carried would enter the world when its father was no more.

When she turned round, Madeleine could see, far behind, the tall hat of Henri de La Rochejaquelein as he followed with a rear-guard. It was a comforting sight, and with protection to drive off the hussars, the women were not quite so frightened. Since Laval, he had neither looked at nor spoken to Madeleine and this added further to the misery of wet and cold.

Any resistance by patriots and National Guards in the villages they passed through was now put down ruthlessly by their advance guard. Since the murder of their wounded, left in the protection of the hospitals, no mercy was shown, no prisoners were taken. The patriots of Ernée and Fougères paid the price of resistance. The roads and meadows were covered with their corpses.

Marching with the civilians along the streets of Fougères, Madeleine noticed the bodies of dead Vendéans, whose ghastly, mutilated faces bore witness to rooftop baptisms of boiling oil; their crimson

322

chests, the sniper's bullet. But oh, how they had been revenged! Before the old fortress in the town, the royalist leader, Marigny, his tunic soaked with blood, his eyes mad from the orgy of killing, was still at work.

Sickened and revolted by these murderous scenes, Madeleine fled along a path which led her higher and higher above the rooftops of Fougères, until she found herself in the gardens of Saint-Léonard on the heights of the town. In a corner, placed before the rampart wall, was a small bench. On to it Madeleine slumped, staring numbly ahead at the weathered green stone, following through a blur of tears the lines of green, velvety moss running between the cracks.

Desperately she strove to erase from her memory the agonised face of the young woman pleading for her husband's life, her piercing scream as Marigny's sabre finished its work. But the brutal scene she had witnessed was still vivid, and she was unable to stop the deep sobs which shook her body.

Gradually, as she was released from the violence of her emotions, Madeleine became aware of a hand resting on her shoulder. Somehow she knew without turning that it was Henri de La Rochejaquelein who stood behind her. They remained thus for some time, gazing ahead beyond the town to the meadows and valley, swathed in the grey mist of the November day. Boy and girl, locked within their thoughts, linked by the touch of a hand.

When at last he spoke his voice was flat, weary. 'I'm glad my cousin died. I should not have wished Louis to see our flag, our cause, so dishonoured.'

'Many tried to stop it happening,' said Madeleine softly, endeavouring to relieve his pain. But her words of comfort were lost to him.

'We should never have crossed the Loire,' he said

bitterly. 'Our people should not have left their own country – yet having done so we should have attacked Nantes when her garrison was empty! Charette has always understood her importance! Nantes is the key to the Loire!'

'And the Conseil Supérieur?' faltered Madeleine at the sudden mention of Charette.

The young commander-in-chief shrugged, 'They, why, they never listen to me ... besides, I've never wanted to be a politician. They're all many years older than I, so I leave the wrangling and decision-making to them. All I ask is to be obeyed on the battlefield,' he added, with a shy, boyish smile. Madeleine returned it, feeling the sudden glow of amusement within her, for she was not deceived by that smile. She had seen La Rochejaquelein in action. In battle he expected total obedience and got it. Even the Prince de Talmond, rebuked for flying his family banner as they left Laval, had hastily replaced it with the simple gold cross and lilies of France. No, when it came to fighting, the boy became master of all.

Now, in a swift easy movement, the young noble hoisted himself up on to the stone parapet where he sat studying the girl's tear-stained face. When she had appeared in the garden he had started to walk away. Solitude was his requirement, certainly not to be with a woman who frequented the private apart-ment of the Prince de Talmond. But he had been unable to leave without casting one final look at the lonely figure. She seemed as desolate as he, her unrestrained sobs echoing the grief he felt, drawing him to her side.

He remembered the proud, defiant expression on her face when he'd passed her in the Château of Laval. No, she was not Talmond's type. Those ladies would by now be installed in some warm hostelry, not here with tears caught like crystals on long thick lashes. He bent forward to brush them away and the girl smiled back at him with such warmth that his heart sang.

Henri de La Rochejaquelein held out his hand, as though requiring assistance down from the wall. In an instant she moved forward to aid him, slipping her cold hand into his. But he held it fast and in a trice, leaping down, he pulled Madeleine to him. What did it matter that she had been with Talmond, he thought, feeling the soft curves of her body close to his. When every day brought death closer, was it so important? But as he nuzzled the soft cushion of her hair, he knew that it did and that the thought would continue to plague him.

Held tightly by the Vendéan, Madeleine sensed his inner conflict. Like him, she was just twenty-one, but her female instincts enabled her to understand quickly the cause of his disquiet. 'Talmond has no claim on me . . .' she murmured. '. . . Only a moment when I contemplated revenge for a father who died long ago . . . that moment passed.'

Henri de La Rochejaquelein did not speak. But she felt the stiffness leave his body. 'Your arm,' she gasped, fearing for his wound as, suddenly, passionately, he crushed her to him. Unheeding, he stopped her mouth with his lips in a kiss that was long and tender. Breathless they pulled apart. Reading the desire in each other's eyes, forgetful of the dead, yet because of them snatching impatiently for love and her elixir of oblivion.

A sudden gust of wind caught the young Marquis's cloak so that it billowed out, reminding Madeleine of another moment so long ago in Paris when a young naval officer, applying spur to horse, had ridden away leaving a small girl with love in her eyes.

Impatiently Madeleine pushed the memory away,

looking at the tall young generalissimo of the Vendéans. He looked quite beautiful as the wind caught his fine blond hair, blowing it back from the classical, proud face. The vivid blue eyes shone with delight and when he spoke his voice was low, urgent. 'Come to me tonight!'

Once more they kissed, high above the town, forgetful of all, lost in the sweetness of each other. Then, with reluctance, they drew apart and bade adieu. He went to the cathedral to arrange a requiem mass for his cousin, the Marquis Louis de Lescure; she returned to the town by way of the path which had led her up to the gardens.

Still warm with the memory of their kisses, Madeleine, humming with joy, skipped down the path, slashing at bushes on either side of the path with a long slender twig, so that the leaves released showers of raindrops down on to the wet, glistening grass. Still high up above the meadows, the river and the church of Saint-Sulpice, Madeleine paused and whirled the switch above her head, releasing it with a flick of her fingers so that it soared upwards, out over the terraces. Admiringly she watched the slender missile trace its curve against the sullen sky, then inevitably topple over into a fast descent. Totally absorbed, following the flight to the rooftops below, Madeleine did not see the man emerge from the bushes.

'A good throw, *citoyenne*.'

Shocked, she whirled around, disconcerted to find she had an audience and one who was a republican officer. 'I am honoured to meet you, *citoyenne* Fleury.'

Madeleine stared, her eyes widening as the officer pronounced her name.

'No, I regret we have not met before,' he said with a short laugh at her reaction, 'but there could be

326

only one beautiful young lady who would be whistling the 'Marseillaise' after kissing the generalissimo of the Vendéans! I had thought your rendezvous was supposed to be with me. Instead, I found you already *tête à tête*, so I retraced my steps and took cover.'

'Then you are . . .'

'Obenheim,' said the man, finishing her sentence.

Flushing with embarrassment at his observations, Madeleine tried to regain her composure. For months their meeting had been planned. Yet she was shocked and disturbed by his appearance. Just a little while ago the only thing that mattered was the touch of Henri de La Rochejaquelein's lips, as desire tore aside their reserve. The heady excitement as their bodies collided making her forget her purpose, so that she did not question, ceased to think, shutting out the words, responding only to her body's needs.

Now reality was before her in the guise of this officer, watching her now through eyes which seemed amused and speculative. Nervously, Madeleine looked back up along the path. 'We'd best talk somewhere more private,' she said, relieved to see no one in sight. 'You'd be cut down if seen in that uniform.'

'I know,' he replied grimly. 'I watched them. I did not think they would be so savage.'

'They've changed,' said Madeleine. 'Since the Queen's execution, since their wounded were butchered in the hospitals, since their homes and villages were burnt, their wives and children slaughtered. Yes, they've changed.'

'So, you're disenchanted with the revolution.'

'No,' replied Madeleine fiercely, 'not with the revolution. Too many of my friends gave their lives for it. I despair only of the assassins who are bringing shame upon it.' Turning away, she led him down to the shelter of a little shed at the corner of a garden.

It was empty and, judging from the strong smell, it probably housed a goat. Safe from detection, she quickly related the content of the letters which she had read at Laval. Obenheim nodded, his deep-set eyes gleaming with approval.

'Good work, *citoyenne*. The arrival of the Chevalier Saint-Hilaire had made our work much easier. Other sources tell me two Breton deputies also carry dispatches from the British government, offering assistance. All I must do is tempt our royalist friends with Granville.'

'Is it really unassailable? The Vendéans hurl themselves into the first assault with great force. I've seen the best troops turn and flee with the shock of their launch.'

'That may be so, but unless they have scaling equipment and are able to sustain a siege of several days, there is no possibility of them succeeding. I, myself, was in charge of the fortifications last year. Granville is well prepared. So, unless your Vendéans grow wings . . .' He shivered and she realised how cold the stocky man must be, for his tunic and breeches were quite wet from hiding out in the undergrowth. 'Now let's go,' he continued, 'for if I stay here either the fumes or the cold will kill me. Introduce me to a fellow who'll offer me a bowl of soup rather than a bullet, my dear.'

Madeleine considered for a moment. Marigny was out of the question. He would unsheathe his great sabre at the mere sight of the uniform. Stofflet, she knew, favoured marching to Rennes to raise the province. And there was no way she could confront Henri de La Rochejaquelein. Donnison, President of the Conseil Supérieur, she knew took little part in decisions.

'I will take you to the man most keen for an English landing at a sea port,' she said at last. 'Once it's known you're familiar with Granville's defences and willing to share that knowledge, you'll soon regain your liberty, especially when you tell them how easy it's going to be. Yes, the Prince de Talmond is your man!'

'So, not our young generalissimo?' Obenheim taunted, and then chuckled. 'You are very young for this work, Mademoiselle Fleury. I hope that your heart will not lead you from the path of duty!'

'I think not,' snapped Madeleine, feeling the blush surging to her cheeks. 'I will accomplish what I set out to do. But there is little point in choosing the slowest or most painful route. Now give me your gun and take my cloak if you wish to stay alive.'

The streets were crowded with the living and the dead. The living were wild-eyed or dazed, searching for a husband, a lost son; while Vendéans reeled, glassy-eyed from looted spirit, too drunk to care about a shivering girl and a man in a cloak.

As Madeleine had expected, the Prince de Talmond was installed in comfortable quarters. Not for him a patch of cobblestones under the stars. No doubt the owner of this fine house, pleased to escape the looters by such distinguished occupation, would have left the Prince the key to his cellar, and a change of linen, too, mused Madeleine, as the front door swung open.

Framed in the opening was . . . Marigny. Momentarily his sharp features registered surprise, then he stepped back so that she might pass. As Madeleine moved forward, out of the corner of her eye she noticed the front of Obenheim's tunic. Anticipating entry, he had already undone the cord of her cloak and Marigny could not fail to see.

Before he had time to react, for he would surely kill Obenheim or fling him into prison, she must take control. Almost casually she raised the pistol, which she had taken from the republican, until it was waist high. 'Monsieur, I have promised this officer safe conduct to the Prince de Talmond,' she said firmly, as she released the safety catch.

Again the quick look of surprise, and Bernard Marigny's eyes flicked a quick glance over Madeleine's shoulder. She could see from the sudden tightening of the man's nostrils that he had seen what she knew he would not miss. The Vendéan officer's exhausted, red-rimmed eyes bore into Madeleine's, but Bernard Marigny had faced guns many times, enough times to know whether the person holding them was steadfast in their purpose or inexperienced – both a lethal combination. Without deigning to comment he glared back into the unflinching, challenging eyes and waved the girl and her prisoner through.

'Ah, Mademoiselle Fleury, what a pleasure,' said the Prince de Talmond as Madeleine entered the salon. 'What have we here? Are you catching prisoners? I am surprised Marigny did not claim him, for he has only just left.'

'I would not dream of letting a subordinate have such a valuable one, sir. I found this officer hiding, fearful for his life. He begged me to take him to the leader of the Grand Catholic and Royal Army. Naturally, I thought of you,' smiled Madeleine coyly. 'He's an engineer so I thought he might prove useful!'

'Er, quite . . .' beamed the Prince, '. . . though, of course, La Rochejaquelein is our commander-in-chief. Nevertheless, you did quite right, Mademoiselle, quite right!'

'Doubtless you will wish to question him alone. So I will bid you adieu,' said Madeleine, casting a look filled with devotion and admiration towards the Prince as she moved towards the door. 'Wait, I nearly forgot,' she laughed coquettishly, holding out

Obenheim's pistol. 'Perhaps you ought to take custody of this, too. I fear it's rather dangerous in my hands.'

The Prince moved eagerly towards her, his soft white face flushed with pleasure. 'Perhaps a little supper tonight?' he queried, arching a thin, fair eyebrow.

'Perhaps. Or maybe we should celebrate in style when you take a sea port!' smiled Madeleine invitingly, her eyes full of promise as she closed the door.

Later that evening Madeleine went to the royalist headquarters. Entering Henri de La Rochejaquelein's chamber, she found the young generalissimo alone. A small table, she noticed, was set for two, and on a sideboard was a cold buffet.

For a second she stood looking at the Marquis, for she had entered quietly and, as yet, he was unaware of her presence. He was standing before the fire, gazing down at the leaping flames, with one boot resting on the iron fender and his left hand against the mantelpiece, but it was not possible to see his face, for he would now have heard about Obenheim. She dreaded looking into the frank, open face, hated herself for deceiving him. But it was done. Obenheim was the bait in the trap and she had set it. And she was thankful now that it was not La Rochejaquelein who decided such issues, for otherwise she could not have kept this assignation tonight. She should not have come, but she had been unable to stay away. Was it possible to separate their relationship from all else?

The logs in the fireplace suddenly shifted, sending a flurry of bright sparks shooting upwards, then a large bright splinter flew out over the top of the young man's boot. He turned round to retrieve it and, in doing so, saw Madeleine. 'Why, Madeleine, you have a light step. I did not hear you enter.'

'The door was ajar ... you seemed deep in thought. I wondered whether I should disturb you,' she added, venturing to meet his gaze. Relieved, she saw a smile light up the serious face.

'Disturb me? Yes, you have, and I am glad of it. For I was consumed by dark and gloomy thoughts and I thought you might not come,' he admitted, pouring her a glass of wine as she removed her cloak.

'Not come?'

'Well, it seemed a possibility. The Prince de Talmond has a reputation second to none with the ladies,' Henri de La Rochejaquelein laughed ruefully, and then his face became serious, his blue eyes intent and curious. 'It seems you have been very busy, Madeleine. You have angered Marigny and given Talmond's English party a saviour. Why did you take this republican engineer to the Prince de Talmond and not to me?'

'Because at the time you were busy with the arrangements for the Marquis de Lescure's Mass. Obenheim seemed unimportant in comparison.'

'But why Talmond? Why not to the President of the Conseil Supérieur, or even to Charles d'Autichamp? Why the Prince de Talmond?'

'Because the man asked for him,' lied Madeleine. 'Besides, there has been so much killing and I was so happy at the time thinking of you and tonight. I just didn't want him to end up in the hands of someone cruel.'

'Well, there aren't many who would have got him past Marigny,' mused La Rochejaquelein, causing another outburst of tiny sparks as he threw more logs on to the fire. 'Come and sit here and warm yourself,' he said, seeing her shiver. 'Your dress is meant for warmer days,' he said, lightly touching the thin taffeta.

'Yes,' agreed Madeleine, 'but it gives me pleasure to wear it.'

'I'd like one day to be able to give you others . . . and I'll take you to my beautiful château of La Durbelière,' he said dreamily, tracing along the ribboned neckline with his finger tips. 'They tried to burn it, but my brave peasants put out the flames after the cowards had fled.'

Madeleine's heart sank, for she had watched Westermann's troops setting out. How nervous they had been at the prospect of entering the deep woods surrounding the château. It had seemed to her senseless destruction and now she was glad to know that they had failed.

With a deep sigh, the young noble dropped his hand down to his side in a gesture of despair. 'Shall I see it again? Will I ever return to ride in the woods of La Vendée?'

There was such melancholy on his face and in his voice that tears sprang to Madeleine's eyes. 'Don't be sad, Henri, not tonight,' she whispered.

Her voice distracted him and the vivid blue eyes, once again aware of her, darkened with desire. 'You're a beautiful mystery, Madeleine,' he murmured, 'and when I'm near you all I can think of is to take you in my arms.'

Madeleine lifted her brows and touched the young Marquis's sling, and boy and girl burst out laughing.

'Well, I'll admit I'm at a bit of a disadvantage at the moment,' he said with a grin. 'Nevertheless it won't stop me.' And he reached forward, kissing her with soft, playful kisses until she responded. Then he suddenly drew back and she saw every vestige of sadness was gone. His face was radiant with joy as he took her hand.

'Come, we must eat some of our landlord's supper. He's an ardent royalist and has gone to some trouble. I would not like to offend him. Nor should either of us miss the chance of a good meal!'

The supper was indeed good, obviously provided by a man who appreciated his guests might not be accustomed to too much food and that the occasion itself demanded only the lightest fare. All was exquisite, laid out on finely wrought silver dishes.

Now Madeleine had reached beyond Henri de La Rochejaquelein's shy reserve, she found him to be of a serious nature, though straightforward. Carefully she steered the conversation to his childhood, speaking of her own only in general terms. But both were restless with conversation. In the soft flickering glow of firelight each longed for the touch of the other. Taking her once again by the hand, Henri de La Rochejaquelein led Madeleine to his couch.

'Come, you must help me!' he said.

It seemed so natural, and an intense excitement flooded through Madeleine as carefully she undid the sling supporting his wounded arm. Momentarily the colour drained from his face and he clenched his teeth, groaning with pain, but he nodded fiercely for her to continue. Swiftly she worked, not daring to look at him, intent upon each task. Then she had finished and slowly she raised her eyes from the floor where his white sash with its black knot of command lay abandoned. With a sense of shock she saw he was fully aroused. Like a bird panicked she looked away, not knowing what to do, her cheeks burning with embarrassment. Only her thin taffeta stood between them; it was no chaperon. Impatiently La Rochejaquelein slid the fabric from Madeleine's shoulders and, as he kissed the swell of her breasts, his hands completed their work and the dress billowed to the ground. Quite naked they clung together, both cast in gold by the light of the fire. Presently, its flames and their bodies were the only movement in the room.

It was already light when Madeleine woke. Beside her Henri de La Rochejaquelein still slept. How different he was from Charette, she thought. His lashes were as fair as his hair and quite straight. His lips full, almost like a girl's. There was nothing complicated in this face, yet he was deceptive. Off the battlefield his manner was modest and restrained and he seemed lacking in confidence. It was no surprise to hear the peasants talking about 'Young Henri', but they also called him 'Henri the Fearless', because of his daring and reckless courage. Softly Madeleine pulled a strand of hair away from the closed eyes. What was it Legeay had told her Henri had said when his peasants first elected him as their leader? Madeleine wrinkled her brow, trying to recall the exact words, then softly she whispered them: '*If I advance, follow me. If I retreat, kill me. If I die, avenge me.*'

He had courage enough to match any leader, whether it be Kléber or Charette. Charette – Madeleine bit her lip, enraged that she should think of him. She imagined how mocking his hateful black eyes would be if he could see her here; remembered with fury the ironical, contemptuous little bow he had made to her at the battle of Torfou. Well, let him stay with his band of amazons. What did she care? She loved the man the Vendéans had made generalissimo of *La Grande Armée Catholique et Royale*. There was no arrogance in La Rochejaquelein, no flashes of temperament and black anger. How glad she was to be in love; to cast away the memory of the Chevalier de Charette for ever. With a smile of triumph Madeleine leant over and kissed Henri de La Rochejaquelein to waken him.

Obenheim did his work well. Offering his services to the Bourbon banner as a republican engineer who knew and would point out the weak points of Granville's defences, he was immediately welcomed. More, he was made a member of the Conseil Supérieur. Cast aside were any suspicions, for with Lescure dead, there was no one who knew anything about siege warfare. Obenheim's arrival proved the deciding factor: Granville, perched high on its rock, was to be taken. Everything was staked on its capture.

Sick at heart, Madeleine kissed Henri de La Rochejaquelein goodbye on the day of attack, thankful for the tears which made his face a blur. Throughout the day and that night she prayed for his safety, but not his victory. A Bourbon standard flying at Granville would bring more than émigrés across from Jersey. Ships of the British fleet would land English soldiers on French soil. They were at war; it was unthinkable!

Obenheim had doubted her intent when first they'd met, but she proved him wrong. France had come first. Now her task was almost completed. As the republicans had foreseen, Granville did not fall. In the town of Avranches where she and the civilians had been left so as not to encumber the army, Madeleine watched the defeated men return. It was what she had hoped for, nevertheless she felt no sense of elation; their weary, dispirited faces showed they knew their cause was lost. Granville had been their last, forlorn hope. With a bitter smile, Madeleine took in the expressions of delight on the women's faces. Her recent propaganda amongst them had worked. In their eyes this meant they could go home; no matter they would be returning to the burnt and ruined villages they had fled from. The cry, for the second time, was 'to the Loire'. The new Jerusalem was Angers, golden gateway to La Vendée. It had not been difficult to nourish the seeds of homesickness. She had powerful allies – the bitter cold weather, dysentery and scarcity of food. But the greatest persuaders of all were the parish priests. Sowing discord and suspicion, they were determined to return with their flock.

And so, under cover of a diversionary attack on the little town of Villedieu, led by La Rochejaquelein and 800 of his men, the main body of the Vendéan column left Avranches for the south and home. It was at the market town of Dol that La Rochejaquelein rejoined Madeleine. He looked weary and was depressed by the general will to return to La Vendée.

'It's madness,' he sighed, slumped in an armchair, his boots and uniform soaked and splattered with mud. 'I also long to return to my own country. But it will be devastated. It is the start of winter. They will all starve, that is if the Blues don't kill them first. Normandy is our only hope; it's fertile. The army needs food and rest; after which we could join forces with Charette. Oh, what's the use?' he said, catching hold of Madeleine's hand. 'All they can think of is going home.'

'Well, it's only natural, Henri. They're exhausted. Things are truly desperate, there's no food and . . . but let's not think of it,' she said, checking her words, for he looked on the point of collapse. 'We found some onions, so eat a little of my soup and I'll try and dry your clothes.'

'Thanks,' he said, giving her hand a squeeze. 'I'll be glad of something warm. But I'll keep my clothes. By now the Blues will have new reserves of men. We must expect an attack any time.'

Madeleine watched him drain back the watery liquid, wishing she had something more substantial to offer. But what food the town possessed had been eaten when they had passed through on the way to Granville. And so it had been with every town and village they had encountered: they had picked them clean the first time. Desperate with hunger, famished men and women gorged on heaps of cider apples, only to writhe in agony hours later with stomach cramps.

Within minutes of finishing the frugal meal, Madeleine saw the young generalissimo's head fall forward in sleep. Gently she placed her cloak over his legs. They might not heed your tactics, she thought, dropping down on to a low stool, but they're all expecting you to get them back across the Loire. It's lucky for the republic, Henri de La Rochejaquelein, that your skill on the battlefield is not carried over into the council chamber. What a mess these people were in; and, for her own part, she was utterly wretched. Granville had broken the royalist cause and she was glad of that, with no regrets. But she had hated her treacherous role and it had left her filled with shame and self-disgust. La Rochejaquelein and his people were doomed, and to atone she would stay.

On entering Dol, Obenheim had ridden up to her and, dismounting from his horse, he'd tried to give her the reins. 'Why are you here? You'll need this to get away. It's only a matter of time before Westermann's troops move in. They will be using the new shells and they'll leave few survivors.'

With a gesture, Madeleine dismissed the reins. 'You have need of the horse yourself, now you have your freedom – I'm going to stay.'

'Then it seems we're both staying.' Obenheim's lips twisted into a small ironic smile. 'Perhaps it's the least we can do for these people – stay and share their fate.'

Madeleine nodded, suddenly feeling less alone. One man understood. He was staying to fight with them because he felt as she did. Then they had shaken hands and parted.

From her position on the stool, Madeleine could see by the clock on the wall that it was just after 6.00 p.m. She yawned, wishing there was a bed in the room. It would be so much warmer to nestle up against Henri. But they were lucky to be indoors and to have a room to themselves.

Suddenly the cry 'to arms' rang out. Immediately Henri de La Rochejaquelein, as though waiting for it, woke and sprang up from the chair. Without speaking, she helped him buckle on his sword belt. Swiftly he kissed her and dashed from the room.

Flinging open the casement window, Madeleine could see at the top end of the street the flash of musketry. From the cries of alarm and clash of steel she reckoned the Blues had penetrated right into the town. Out of every door, soldiers were pouring from their billets, pushing aside the panic-stricken civilians.

Within half an hour it was over. The raiders had been driven half-way back along the road to Pontorson; but the skirmish verified La Rochejaquelein's fears. He returned to the room, his face glistening with sweat, accompanied by his officers: Stofflet, Lyret, Vernet, de Beauvais. 'Gentlemen,' he said, 'we must prepare. This reckless action of the Blues tells me their main army is near and in great force. Place the army in position, we must be ready for the attack.'

At these moments Madeleine saw his authority. No longer the shy, diffident boy, the inexperienced lover. He loved the game of war and his generals acknowledged it was his element.

She could feel his pulses racing as he swept her to him. Once more to say goodbye. If they should never meet again, she knew she would remember him always like this. In a bound he was gone, his spurs jingling as he raced down the stairs. Leaning once more out of the window, Madeleine saw La Roche-jaquelein's groom below, waiting with the four horses which would serve the generalissimo in the battle.

Then the blond head emerged from the doorway beneath, and in a swift bound he was up in the saddle of his favourite horse making, as always before he fought, the sign of the cross.

The onslaught began at about midnight; the main body of Westermann's column moving forward from Pontorson. Well before the troops engaged, order had been established in the town. The main street of Dol was long and wide, so the civilians were ordered to assemble in four lines. In between them were placed the ammunition wagons and caissons.

There was not a sound. Like everyone else, Madeleine held her breath, listening intently for the guns, trying to find courage. She had helped bring these frightened men and women to this and, caught up here in their misery and danger, she felt wretched for the part she had played. This moment of dark and deathly hush now bound them together. As though they had been waiting on the slopes of a volcano, the eruption began. The sky, the window panes, the long silent columns of fearful faces were cast up before her in a bright fiery light. Almost immediately answering the Vendéan thunder came a terrifying whining sound. Were these the new shells Obenheim had warned her of? Whatever they were, the republican gunners were finding their range as the shells burst closer and closer.

For hours this terrible fusillade continued. Then above the boom of the guns an order rang out: 'Forward cavalry. *Vive le Roi!*'

'That means Young Henri must be driving them

back,' laughed an old man, the fear sliding from his wrinkled face. 'They never send for the cavalry unless we're winning. *Vive le Roi! Vive le Roi!*' he shouted.

The ragged cavalry began to move forward, the ribs of their half-starved nags visible in the artificial light; each man's face fearful, yet proud that they had been called. Brandishing their swords and scythes they moved into trot.

'*Vive le Roi!*' they roared. Soon the whole town rang with the cry and Madeleine heard herself shouting with them. She didn't know why, didn't care. She was glad to find relief in screaming, releasing her fear and tension. Any words would do.

Suddenly, above the shouting came another cry. 'Fly, fly, dear hearts, for your lives. All is lost! Fly, fly, the hussars are coming!'

'What is it?' Madeleine screamed, grabbing the arm of a young soldier. He whirled around, his young face in a fury.

'It's Marceau, with a column from Antrain. Those cowards have fled at the first sight of their sabres. Come, we must stop the women from running away, then perhaps the men will stop and fight.' He grabbed her hand, dragging her across the main street which led to Dinan. 'It's no good them running across the meadows to Dinan,' he yelled over his shoulder. 'There's nothing there but republican troops and the sea.'

Screaming with terror, the Vendéans were running past them across the meadows away from the town. Vigorously, with the flat of his sword, the young cavalier hit out at the women. 'Stop, you cowardly women! How will your men fight if you run away? Here, take it!' he cried, thrusting the sword hilt into Madeleine's hand. 'I see General Stofflet, he must overtake them and bring them back.'

Obediently Madeleine carried on the boy's work,

pleading with the fleeing people. 'Stop, stop . . .! For shame, will you desert La Rochejaquelein?' Her words were having some effect, for some of them paused, shamefaced, turning to go back. Suddenly a woman came running towards her and she saw that it was Victorine Lescure, though her haggard feverish appearance made her hardly recognisable.

Showing great courage, the pregnant woman placed herself beside Madeleine, facing a column of soldiers fleeing from the battlefield. 'What, are you trying to escape?' the widow of the Saint of Anjou called to them, holding up her hand. 'Where do you count on going? The army possesses only the terrain it occupies. Once defeated it will possess nothing and your wives and children will be massacred before your eyes.'

Uncertainly, the men halted, and then one of their number suddenly blew the cow horn around his neck. 'Silence,' he yelled. 'Listen to the guns!'

A hush fell and everyone turned and listened.

'They're quieter,' someone cried. 'Young Henri is holding his own. *Vive La Rochejaquelein!*'

Nearby, standing on top of a mound, a priest raised up a large crucifix. His voice was deep and resonant, carrying clearly to everyone within earshot. 'My friends,' he called, 'I will march at your head with the cross in my hand; let those who will fight kneel down and I will give absolution to the brave. Those of you who fall will go to Paradise, but for the cowards who desert their friends and families there can be only death!'

'We will go to Paradise,' cried men and women, sinking to their knees. Then the priest's rich voice sang the first lines of the Vexilla Regis:

'The Royal Banners forward go,
The cross shines forth in Mystic glow . . .'

342

Without thinking, filled with a strange exultation, Madeleine joined the moving column behind the crucifix, hearing only the words of the hymn. Gone was all reasoning; she only knew this was a fight for survival, a fight to save the weak and defenceless from death, a fight to ensure a royalist child might be born, a chance to expunge her guilt, to share their fate.

Steadily she kept her eyes on the moving crucifix as it cut forward like the prow of a ship through the swirling fog. The blessed fog which had hidden from the Blues the panic and flight in the Vendéan ranks.

Ahead was the Prince de Talmond and his men, stoutly maintaining their positions under a hail of musketry and exploding shells. The din of battle cut out all thought save what the next moment would bring. Only the abbé's voice penetrated the brain, 'Forward, dear hearts, to death and Paradise. *Vive le Roi!*'

The Vendéans launched forward into the fog. Opening wide her mouth and throat, Madeleine copied their blood-curdling howl. On and on they ran, seeking the enemy. Then, through the swirling fog came the sound of drums. Her empty stomach knotted with fear; the republicans had regrouped. Steadily the sound grew louder. The insistent roll was nerve-racking; the Vendéan howl made an adversary run away, whilst this – the product of drill and discipline – mesmerised; rooting one to the spot, paralysed with dread.

Suddenly shattering their trance, the Chouan cowhorns blared above the drums. On either side of her, the Poitevins let out their fearful cry and they were racing forward. Now, a wind swirled and parted the curtain of fog and Madeleine saw the lines of soldiers before her.

A scared young face loomed, hesitated, then

343

plunged towards her. The Blue's round eyes rolled in terror as he lunged forward with his bayonet. With all her strength, using both hands, Madeleine swung her sword upwards and outwards. The force was so great the boy's musket flew straight out of his hands. He closed his eyes, waiting for her sword thrust. Instead she leapt away to where a riderless horse reared in panic. Seizing its bridle, Madeleine gradually calmed it. With an intense feeling of relief she hoisted herself up into the saddle. Somehow she now felt safer. It proved a foolish thought, for within minutes she was confronted with two lancers.

Death stared her in the eyes. Frantically she whirled the sword around her head in a desperate bid to keep them at bay. Both men only roared with laughter. All the while circling her, baiting and touching her with the sharp metal tips of their lances.

Hot tears of anger and humiliation spilled down her cheeks. Oh, that she could strike one blow, but it was useless. Any moment they would tire of the game and run her through. Thrusting out her chin, Madeleine glared in defiance towards a laughing face. But its expression had changed. Now the face was contorted with pain; its owner, with blood spurting from his neck, was falling from his saddle. Spinning around, Madeleine saw the second lancer slumped over his horse's neck.

Reloading his gun, Henri de La Rochejaquelein galloped towards her. 'I need you, but not here,' snapped La Rochejaquelein, his blue eyes blazing with a strange fire. 'How can I fight knowing you are here? Monsieur d'Allard,' he said, turning to the chevalier beside him. 'I cannot leave the field or the men will panic and retreat. Make sure Mademoiselle leaves.' He then stood up in his stirrups and leapt on to a fresh horse which his groom had brought forward. Quickly lashing its reins to the pommel, La

Rochejaquelein, raising his sword high, plunged towards the fray, his voice drifting back to her as he disappeared. 'We'll meet again at Antrain. *Vive le Roi!*'

Bordeaux-en-train, taking his sword and running towards the li.y. by your order his chief to terrible disappeared. "We'll even, again at Antrain, I saw beat.

Chapter Five

For fifteen long hours the battle continued. Unbelievably, the starving, scarecrow army was victorious, driving back the might of the republic beyond Pontorson in the east and Antrain to the south-east.

Completely routed, Westermann, Marceau and Kléber went away to lick their wounds leaving behind their dead. Hundreds! They covered the streets, so deeply that the weary peasants were forced to tread on the corpses. Never would Madeleine forget Antrain – the terrible waste of life; the cost of their survival.

From Antrain they trudged on to Fougères, Ernée, Sablé, La Flèche; each town deepening their despair and horror. For they found no food, only those they had left behind – the wounded in the hospitals, children with their nursing mothers. All were dead! Savagely butchered by Westermann's troops.

Every day now men fell out of the column because of frost-bitten feet covered with abscesses, clutching their bellies as they crawled behind a bush. The stench of dysentery and despair clung to bodies and minds alike.

The nights in the desolate countryside were frightful; long hours of either torrential rain or cruel, bitter frosts. Shaking with cold, they huddled in front of great bonfires; fearing every moment would bring the dreaded cry of 'hussars'. There was little sleep until morning. Then, stretching out stiff and frozen limbs in the dreary grey light, they forced themselves back on to the road, leaving behind those too weary to move. Huddled figures stared after them with blank eyes, often frozen in the welcome release of death.

Yet, even amidst this misery, Madeleine and Henri de La Rochejaquelein found some bliss; precious moments which gave escape.

At last the silver-grey of the Loire joining the Mayenne was sighted. The Seine was Madeleine's river, but like those around her she felt deeply moved. It was a sight which spread hope. Even those in the last stages of collapse found a final spurt of strength.

On the approach to Angers, the air was filled with the old familiar battle hymns. They were going home. They'd take the city just as they'd done on 19 June. Then, on to La Vendée! Listening to the confident chatter and reminiscences of summer triumphs, Madeleine remained sceptical. How could these people not see the pitiful state they were now in? How could they expect their exhausted army to breach the massive walls of this ancient city? Without scaling equipment it would not be possible.

They found the city was prepared for them! Granville had set its suburbs alight; Angers left them empty of food, and the massive walls of the city proved impregnable. There was nothing to do but go away. To see the broken-hearted despair on the faces of young and old alike as they turned their backs on the river, and on their homes in La Vendée, overwhelmed Madeleine with pity.

At least for herself it was different. She was with them by choice. At any time she could leave. Packed away still in the gun hidden in her little sack were the republican authorisations. All she had to do was present them to the authorities and she would be on her way back to Paris, back amongst its streets and cafés and away from this freezing wilderness. The Cordelier was paid for. It was time to sell; buy something larger in a better area. It was tempting, but though she longed to escape, she could not run out on Henri de La Rochejaquelein.

He and his officers were now under the most terrible pressure, trying to keep at bay the shadowing packs of hussars from the weary, straggling column. Hour after hour, like sheep dogs driving away wolves, the young officers and their men galloped up and down the column. Their efforts were heroic, but how long could they keep it up? pondered Madeleine.

Then news, filtering down the line as it always seemed to do, told them that by a brilliant action La Flèche was in their hands. They must make all speed. Once into the town the bridge would be destroyed, cutting off the hussars for hours. It was welcome news. At least now they could march the ten leagues to Le Mans free from harassment. And Le Mans, in the department of Maine, would have all the food they needed.

Royalist headquarters at Le Mans were at the Cheval Blanc on the Place des Halles. They were comfortable and warm and, joy of joys, upon enquiry Madeleine learnt they possessed a bath. Indeed the anxious landlord seemed eager to provide one, for like everyone else she had suffered her share of dysentery and knew she stank.

Eagerly she watched as the jugs of steaming water were carried into Henri's room. It was easy to see from the hostile servants they were not welcome in Le Mans, but then what city would want hundreds of starving, disease-ridden refugees taking over?

348

Even now, an hour after she had arrived, the tattered column still kept coming; with hundreds yet to come. And following them tomorrow or the day after would come the inevitable military action and its destruction.

Ah well, she thought, stripping off her filthy clothes and stepping eagerly into the water, it is for the good citizens of Le Mans to weep and wring their hands. For the moment, Madeleine Fleury, you will lie back, relax and enjoy. The large tub had been placed in front of a cheerful log fire and, around it, giving some privacy should anyone enter, was a screen. It was the most delightful arrangement! The warmth from the crackling logs and the hot suds gradually eased away the cold ache in Madeleine's bones, lulling her into a luxuriant state of drowsiness. Contentedly she savoured the peace, feeling the film of grime and dirt lifting and floating away from her body. Almost with regret she recognised La Rochejaquelein's footsteps entering the chamber. Briefly he looked down at her over the top of the screen, a faint smile touching his lips. Then he withdrew and she heard him fling himself down on the bed. His exhaustion made her feel selfish and, though sorry to end her bath, Madeleine stood up and started to dry her body. It surprised her to see how thin she had become, for the flesh had fallen away from her ribs and hip bones, making them ugly and skeletal. But her new-found state of cleanliness felt glorious! Humming, she wrapped a towel into a sarong and went and stood beside the young Vendéan.

'Come, Henri,' she said, shaking him gently by the shoulder, hoping that he had not already gone to sleep, for he looked grey with exhaustion. The long straight eyelashes fluttered open. 'Come, you deserve a bath more than I. I'm afraid the water is far from clean.'

'Perhaps later,' he murmured wearily.

'No, now,' she said firmly. 'You'll feel much better and the water is still hot.'

Henri de La Rochejaquelein looked up at Madeleine's determined face with amusement. Chasing off the 3,000 defending Blues here was easier, it seemed, than to escape her bath. Idly he slipped his hand beneath her towel and stroked the back of her leg. The curve of her knee was warm and still slightly damp. She leant over him to undo his sword buckle and as she did so, playfully, he tugged on the towel pulling it away. Laughing, she stepped back.

'No, Henri, not until you're bathed!' she teased, readjusting the towel. But the brief sight of her had been enough. Magically, the exhaustion slipped away from the young Marquis.

Later, each wrapped in a sheet, they sat before the fire sipping cognac. As he watched the girl fluffing out and drying her hair, La Rochejaquelein swirled the fiery liquid around the base of his goblet. The light from the fire shone through the crystal. It was the colour of her eyes and hair; a rich, living, golden-brown. He loved to see her so, with her hair falling free, a wild mass of tangled curls; especially when she stood or walked towards him and it fell over her creamy shoulders, masking the beautiful breasts swinging provocatively above the tiny circle of her waist.

Tenderly he stroked the nape of her neck and looked sadly at the bent head. Oh, for another time and place. There was so little time to talk, so many questions about her still unanswered. He sighed – what did it matter now?

'Madeleine,' he said softly, 'I've often wondered why you came among us, but I'm glad you did.

You've given me such joy. It is likely soon we will part. Always remember how much I loved you!'

The words sent the blood rushing to Madeleine's face in a flood of shame. She remained still, despising herself. This Vendéan would never engage in duplicity. And because he was steeped in honour it had never occurred to him that she could be an agent for the republic. There were times when he had come near to asking about Charette, but his restraint, she sensed, was not only from good manners but the desire not to know. Please, God, she prayed, never let him know my part in this: it would destroy him.

The feline, laughing face of Charette slipped into her mind. Could she have let him ride to Granville? Would she have broken her oath to the tricolor for him? Trembling, she dared not answer.

Abruptly she raised her head from the heat of the fire, the tawny tresses crackled and swirled about her shoulders. 'Is it hopeless?' she whispered, her face glistening with tears.

'Yes, I'm afraid it is,' replied La Rochejaquelein, wiping away her tears. Silently he looked at her and she saw the expression of sadness and regret in the blue eyes change to anxiety. He picked up the cognac glass, swallowing back its contents. 'All I pray is to be killed on the battlefield, not to be wounded!'

Desperately Madeleine searched for an answer. If she could travel to Paris, had Danton still power enough? Anxiously she spoke. 'If I go, go to Paris – beg for a pardon – take a letter from you,' her words trailed off as the blue eyes widened with surprise and the long serious face flushed with anger. Springing to his feet, Henri de La Rochejaquelein moved to the corner of the room where his banner stood, its white silk and golden lilies softly gleaming in the firelight. With a proud defiant gesture the young Marquis touched its silken folds.

'When my peasants asked me to lead them I swore this oath before them. *Si j'avance, suivez-moi. Si je recule, tuez-moi. Si je meurs, vengez-moi.* Nothing has changed!'

Westermann launched the Republic's attack on the second day, bringing their recuperation to an end. Throughout the long, tense day couriers raced back and forth with news of the battle. Everything depended on them holding the Pontlieu bridge, a quarter of a league from the town. The numbers against them were overwhelming. Two of La Roche-jaquelein's horses had been shot from under him but somehow he, Monsieur d'Allard and Forestier had managed to hold and rally their fleeing men.

It was towards sunset when news came that the Blues had managed to ford the river. Moments later the first rush of Vendéan cavalry came racing back. 'Run, run for your lives,' they shouted. 'All is lost.'

Like the women around her, Madeleine was stunned and terrified. So many times they had anticipated defeat, yet always the army had somehow managed to throw back the Blues – at Laval, at Dol. What were they to do? Where were they to run?

Fear galvanised her into action. Racing back into the Cheval Blanc, she snatched up the small sack which she had already packed. Outside, the square was already a mass of seething people. At its entrance she spotted two of La Rochejaquelein's officers setting up a gun and ran, pushing her way towards them.

'Where is Henri?' she cried desperately.

'He is commanding the rear-guard. They're trying to hold back the Blues. You're all to take the road back to Laval.'

Around her the panic and tumult was deafening. Trying to remain calm, Madeleine pushed her way along to the Place de l'Eperon, tagging on behind a column of people marching down a main street. Ahead she could see General Stofflet and, as more people were falling in behind her, she felt confident she was heading in the right direction.

The light was rapidly fading. She tried to picture Henri and his brave men, fighting desperately to give them the chance to escape. Or were he and the brave already slain? Would the Blues at any moment, thirsty for their blood, rampage into the town?

In the flickering torchlight, Madeleine noticed the street was gradually narrowing to little more than an alley. A terrible clamour broke out ahead. Like those around her she halted, thinking it must be the Blues. However, the press of the crowd behind her soon forced her on again. Ahead the sounds of panic were increasing, the shrill whinnying of horses mingling with screamed oaths.

Then din and movement erupted, engulfing her and those around her. Desperately she strove to retain her balance as the men and women in front fell backwards against her. Someone slipped and Madeleine felt for a moment a hand clutching her cloak; heard the agonised screams as the unknown was trampled underfoot.

'It's a dead end,' a man shrieked. 'Turn around, you fools.' But wedged between two opposing forces it was impossible to do so. Tightly clutching her sack, Madeleine tried to think calmly, as elbows and bodies jabbed and pushed against her. Was it better to stay here or try to get to the edge, near the wall? Neither course seemed safe. Then her mind was made up for her.

'Stop, stop, you're crushing my little girl!' the shrill voice of a young woman cried out. 'Please help me, someone.'

Unhesitating, Madeleine responded to the sobbing

voice and fought and pushed her way towards it. The terrified young woman was pressed up against a wall, a screaming bundle in one arm and a weeping child encircled in the other.

'Come on, little one, you'll be safe with me,' said Madeleine, taking the child. 'Now hold on to my cloak and don't let go,' she snapped harshly at the mother in order to mobilise her.

'Can't we stay here?'

'No. Stay here and we'll be crushed by people and horses or the ammunition wagons.'

Slowly, a few footsteps at a time, they progressed until they were clear of the mêlée. They found themselves in a small square.

'We're to go to Laval,' said Madeleine.

'Yes, I know,' replied the young woman. 'I think it's this way.' Together they hurried from the town and were soon struggling across the water-logged meadows. It was hard going. Their skirts, soon drenched, became heavy, impeding their movements. They made slow progress, but fear drove them on.

After about two hours, Madeleine became uneasy, sensing they were going the wrong way. It was true they were not alone: in all directions she could hear movements. But where was the road and the main body of their army?

Not wishing to alarm her new-found companion, she said nothing. For the moment all that mattered was to put as much distance as possible between them and the sound of the guns. Once they'd taken Le Mans it would not be long before the Blues started their mopping-up operations in the countryside.

Gradually, as the night sky lightened to the first grey glimmerings of dawn, Madeleine glanced across to the woman trudging wearily by her side. There seemed nothing to distinguish her from the countless other unhappy young women who were following the army. Her clothes were in tatters and her feet wore makeshift shoes of sacking.

For a moment, Madeleine paused, and hitched up higher the brave little soul clinging to her back. Since Le Mans the little girl had uttered not a cry. But she had become a dead weight. 'We'll soon be there little one,' she murmured. 'Just keep on holding tight.'

But where, she thought, staggering on. It was increasingly clear they were quite lost. She was separated from Henri La Rochjaquelein with no way of finding him. The realisation filled her with an empty misery. He needed her now, more than ever. How could she have been so stupid to have missed the road? On her own she could have made better time. Silently she cursed the hindrance of the small, helpless family who were obviously going to depend on her for all future plans. She cast a fierce look towards the young mother, but immediately her anger dissipated at the sight of the forlorn figure driving herself on in the bitter November drizzle. 'Let's stop and rest for a little,' she called, indicating a fallen tree trunk. 'At least we have breakfast,' Madeleine said cheerfully, setting down the little girl.

Stooping so that the child could slide down from her back, Madeleine's eyes caught the dark clump of thicket to their left. It would afford them better protection, she decided, and turned to suggest it. But the weary young woman was already sitting listlessly, her baby greedily sucking on a small white breast. Another hundred yards for her at the moment was as far as many leagues.

They sat for half an hour, eating the rolls and cheese which Madeleine had thrust into her sack. The little girl, she learnt, was named Marie, her mother, Marguerite. The baby, Armand, was just six months old.

It was amazing how some food could so quickly restore children's spirits, thought Madeleine, listening to Marie's happy prattle. This life of roaming through open countryside had become normal for her. But the silent, withdrawn mother who had lost her man, her home, her country – she barely existed, willing to be led this way and that by others. And where was she, Madeleine, going to lead them?

Carefully Madeleine weighed up the three possibilities open to her. To find and rejoin the Vendéans was fraught with danger; whilst to report back to Republican headquarters and be party to the inevitable final annihilation of Henri and his people was inconceivable. At least in Paris she had friends. And there she might be in a position to ask for clemency for the families to return to La Vendée. Women like Marguerite were no longer a threat to the Nation. She would make Camille speak for them in his *Vieux Cordelier*.

'I think we'll go to Paris,' she laughed, suddenly feeling everything would work out. Startled, she saw Marguerite's face was a mask of terror. Whirling around to see what had so disturbed her, Madeleine froze with horror. Coming towards them at great speed was a party of hussars.

'Quickly, make for the wood. It's our only chance,' she shouted. 'Now hold on tight, Marie,' she said, as the child straddled her back. The little hands dug into Madeleine's shoulders as she leapt forward. Frantically she tried to avoid the water-logged ground and keep to the frozen clumps and ridges. Given dry flat ground and no burden she might have made it, but the pounding hooves and the yells of the men told her it was hopeless.

Madeleine stopped running and turned around. Marguerite was about 25 yards behind. Her eyes were no longer blank, but wild with terror. From her mouth, breath came out in great spurts, condensing in the cold air; the sound of her panting echoed by the advancing horses as their hooves cast up great sprays of water and clods of mud. Their only hope was the War Minister's letters, packed in the barrel of her pistol. Quickly Madeleine set down the little girl and ripped open her sack. The first two hussars had reaching the staggering girl. Leaning low, the first of the riders struck her across the shoulders with the flat of his sword; screaming, she fell forward as the baby in her arms flew upwards.

Horrified, trying to steady her shaking hand, Madeleine withdrew the gun. Already the dismounted trooper had dropped his breeches and had fallen upon the struggling girl. A red rage exploded within Madeleine as she saw the frail white limbs threshing against the muddy ground. Raising the gun, she fired and the fat white buttocks of the trooper instantly stopped their frightful heaving.

The letter had gone up in flames. Now, with a roar of anger, the second hussar was spurring towards her. With a mighty blow he hit her across the temples, spinning her across the earth. As she fell, her head whiplashed back and as she plunged into darkness she felt his hands ripping open her bodice.

The pain in Madeleine's head was like a pulsating drum, each beat regular and excruciating. She tried to go with it, to float above it, but it didn't help. Movement was impossible, to raise her head meant waves of nausea. So she remained still, keeping her eyes shut.

The sheet drawn up to her chin smelt clean and carried the gentle perfume of lavender. She wondered, who had made this bed? And who had carried her into the darkened room? Perhaps it was the rider who had brought her here. For she had regained consciousness hanging over a saddle. But she had been unable to see anything beyond the moving ground below. Her brain had ceased to function. Gradually, as the pounding lessened, Madeleine felt able to think. She remembered the wet brown earth, the screaming baby sailing through the air and Marguerite's wild-eyed terror. Those images were still with her; horribly real and vivid. Thereafter, all she could recall was the hussar coming at her as though in slow motion.

She sat up, trying to free her mind of the unbearable, instantly crying out as the pain attacked. But supporting herself with her hands, she remained upright, fighting off the nausea and dizziness.

At once there were heavy footsteps on stairs and a man entered the room. She watched the barely visible silhouette move towards the window recess. Filled now with curiosity and excitement, Madeleine waited for the shutters to open. As the wintry grey light washed into the room, the man turned about. To Madeleine's joy and amazement she saw the hussar was Thomas Adams. She flung back the sheet to try and get up, but in one bound he prevented her. Laughing and weeping, they clung on to each other.

'Oh, Tom, I can't believe it,' she laughed, clasping the red-headed giant. 'Is it really you? Where am I?'

'You're at the house of my friend, Suzanne Guillet.'

'And your uniform? Why? How?'

'Well it's your fault really.'

'Mine . . .? Oh, yes,' said Madeleine uncomfortably, recalling her cruel words as he'd fallen from her cart. 'I knew you'd enlisted.'

'Yes,' said Thomas, taking hold of her hands and not seeming in the least embarrassed. 'I made a fool of myself that day. Besides, it was time I stopped playing dominoes all day. I'd always liked riding, so it was the cavalry for me!'

'Oh, it's so good to see you,' sighed Madeleine. 'The old days seem so long ago. So many dear ones are gone – Pierre, Gabrielle, little Paul. But did you know Annette is married to Jacques?' she said, not wishing to dwell on sadnesses. 'And Georges, too, to Louise Gély. What of him? I've not seen a newspaper for months.'

'I fear things are not good for Danton,' replied Thomas, lighting a pipe. 'And if you've not seen a gazette you'll not know the Girondists were sent to the scaffold. It was very moving by all accounts,' he said, drawing softly on his pipe. 'Twenty-one were taken together. They sang the "Marseillaise" right to the guillotine, not stopping as the blade fell; until at last Vergniand alone stood singing. Then he too died.'

'But they were the revolution!' gasped Madeleine astounded. 'And Charles Barbaroux, was he amongst them?'

'No, he escaped from Paris in time. But I expect they'll hunt him down. Times have changed, Madeleine. I fear storm clouds are brewing for Danton. Robespierre will have his head, mark my words!'

'Guillotine the King of the Cordeliers? They wouldn't dare!'

'A Saint-Just would! Where have you been, Madeleine? You're out of touch with Paris – and that's Georges Danton's problem, too. Doubtless life with a young bride at Arcis is very pleasant, but it won't protect him. He has lost his influence in Paris.'

'Well you can't blame him,' she sighed. 'He grieved so for Gabrielle. Just like poor Simone Evrard grieved for Marat.'

At Marat's name Thomas looked thoughtful.

'Be very careful in Nantes, Madeleine. Carrier is proconsul here and, believe me, he's a mad dog! His execution squad call themselves the Marats. Steer well clear! You're safe here, this house belongs to a friend of mine. I'll call her up presently to meet you, but I wanted to see you alone first. You're going to need a good citizen's certificate. Getting that for a rebel isn't going to be easy. In hell's name,' he suddenly blurted out, 'why did you get mixed up with royalists, Madeleine?'

'Because a War Minister named Bouchotte and a commander in chief called Canclaux ordered me to. Perhaps you've heard of them?' teased Madeleine, enjoying the look of anger on the stolid features turn to one of surprise and relief.

'How glad I am to hear you say that. Why, if I hadn't seen that medal round your neck and been so fond of you, I'd have left you just where you were ...' He looked down, flushing crimson. They had carefully avoided the subject. But like the pain in her head it would not go away completely. 'I stopped him, Madeleine, before he ...' the big man said in a choked, thick voice.

'And the mother and her children?'

'I don't know. She ran off. I hadn't much time. Other troopers were near. All I could think of was to get you away as quickly as possible.'

'Tom, why are men such monsters?'

Tom shook his curly head in despair. 'I don't know – it's like a madness coming over one. A sort of revenge. We've seen friends and comrades die; heard how young volunteers were killed in the villages of the Bocage, women and children clubbing them to death, burying them alive. One fills with hatred and forgets. It's war.'

'Then let us pray it soon ends,' said Madeleine despondently.

'I'm afraid it's likely to go on for some time yet,' sighed the American, 'and it's not to my taste, this civil war. Defending France against the Austrians was different. I'll be no part of this new terror.'

'Are you going to stay in France?'

'No, Madeleine, I guess it's time for me to go home. The heady days are over, and I shall never forget them. Whenever I pull a cork on French wine, I'll see the lovely goddess under the apple-green leaves of the Bois de Boulogne; I'll see you racing into the Bastille by my side. Oh, my darling,' he suddenly uttered, his voice shaking with emotion. 'Come home with me. Let me take a part of this lovely land with me!'

Madeleine did not push her old friend away, instead she clung to him, much moved, remembering the happy times of laughter, their eager hopes. After a while her embrace slackened and she took hold of Tom's massive hands.

'My dearest friend,' she said softly, looking up into the earnest grey eyes.

Hopefully Thomas waited for the caressing timbre of her voice to continue, but she said no more, merely tightening her grip on his hands, the beautiful oval of her face diffused with love, the kind of love a sister shows. With a sad sigh of regret he acknowledged that, for Madeleine, nothing had changed.

Tom's friend, Suzanne Guillet, was a large and curvaceous young woman. The bulk of her body seemed to be composed entirely of breasts and hips. Yet, incredibly, this body was not what made the greatest impression on Madeleine. Tiny hands, exquisite in shape, lively in movement, demanded the attention of the onlooker, whilst a row of small perfect teeth, like the loveliest of pearls, left one hoping for another smile. Her skin, Madeleine noted, had the dazzling translucency which painters liked, and when she moved she glided with the serenity and grace of a swan. Would she be a devastating beauty without the body, Madeleine wondered, watching the girl's lovely fingers smoothing back a wisp of black hair into her chignon? Or would an essential part of her being be lost?

It was now her second day in Nantes and Thomas had already returned to his company. He had been absent without leave and had taken a great risk bringing her to Nantes, so he had stayed but a few hours.

Suzanne Guillet's brother had been a trooper with Tom and, when he had been killed in action, it was Tom who had brought Suzanne her brother's personal effects. Since then a great affection had grown between them. Madeleine did not doubt this was true; she had not failed to see the soft looks the pair had exchanged. And her willingness to shelter a girl she did not know under her roof demonstrated to Madeleine the extent of Suzanne's love for Tom. She was glad for them, but envied their happiness.

For the next few days Madeleine was content to rest. She had been badly concussed and bouts of dizziness still affected her when she stood. But as her strength returned she grew restless. The fate of the Vendéans, especially of Henri de La Rochejaquelein, plagued her. She had to know what had happened before she returned to Paris. For return she would. There was nowhere else left to her. She was rid of foolish dreams. Paris must be all she needed.

But when she mentioned to Suzanne her desire to see the town, the small head turned to her in alarm. 'Oh you can't go out yet, Madeleine. Not until I've organised papers for you. While no one knows you're here, you're safe . . . I promised Thomas I'd look after you – I don't want him to return and find we're both in Bouffay prison, or worse,' she added darkly.

'But how can you obtain them, Suzanne, without endangering yourself?'

'Have no fear of that,' Suzanne Guillet replied, smoothing down her dress around her capacious hips. 'I have a good friend, Proust, who's a member of the Revolutionary Committee. I'm afraid the poor man is the only good one amongst them and there's little he can do for people, but he can help us, Madeleine! Because, you see, he is responsible for issuing certificates of civism.'

As Suzanne Guillet promised, they experienced no difficulties in obtaining the necessary documents. With hundreds of captured Vendéans flooding into the city daily, the bloodthirsty members of the Revolutionary Committee and its hired assassins, the Marats, were fully occupied.

Suzanne had burnt Madeleine's filthy clothing and seemed in no hurry to go out and buy new, lending her lodger a warm, voluminous dressing gown. Filled with gratitude for what she had already accomplished, Madeleine tried to hide her impatience. Nor could she say why she wanted to go out. Suzanne, she knew, would not understand or approve of her desire to stand for hours looking at Vendéan prisoners entering Nantes. But this was the cause of her sleepless nights and impatient fretting. She had to know if Henri had been taken prisoner.

At last Suzanne responded to her sighs and restless pacing. 'I can see, Madeleine, you'll give me no rest until you've walked along the quays. Although it's no time to go out; with all the filthy disease-carrying royalists infecting the air, it's best to keep indoors and not catch typhus. However, if it will make you feel more comfortable to wear a dress, I'll buy one for you today.'

'Oh will you, Suzanne? I'd be so grateful. I'd like to get out each day. I feel I need the exercise.'

'I should have thought you'd had enough exercise by the look of you,' remarked her hostess drily. 'Now is there anything else you require, Milady?'

'Nothing,' replied Madeleine, flashing back a wicked grin, '. . . well, I'd like a gazette to see what's happening everywhere.'

Not for a moment did Madeleine consider she would be disappointed with Suzanne Guillet's choice of clothes. She might be indolent – that and her easy, relaxed manner went with her size – but she was elegant, and the plain grey wool dress with a white fichu and a matching grey bonnet and cape were perfect. Of good quality, they were inconspicuous. Just what Madeleine wanted. Politely she expressed her delight, but it was the gazette she really wanted. Trembling, her fingers spread it out on the table before her. The black type stared up at her. There it was. It was over! On 23 December at Savenay the Grand Catholic and Royal Army was defeated. Anxiously she scanned the bulletin, but no mention was made of the Vendéans's generalissimo.

'They're finished then,' said the dispassionate voice of Suzanne over her shoulder.

'Yes,' replied Madeleine, looking up.

'Good, now perhaps Nantes can return to normal,' commented Suzanne gaily.

The next day, looking like a respectable young matron of the town, Madeleine ventured out. She would have much preferred to go alone but Suzanne insisted on going with her. Gradually, as their route took them towards the Place de Bouffay, Madeleine could see a long line of figures.

'I see they're bringing in today's batch of rebels,' said Suzanne distastefully. 'Shall we turn off?'

But Madeleine was hurrying ahead, her heart

beating violently. A mixture of emotions flooded over her as she drew closer. These were the people she had stood beside in the awesome silence of the street of Dol, waiting for the onslaught to begin. She had marched with them behind their crucifix to live or die. To see them now, roped together like cattle brought to market, was unbearable. Hundreds of wretched creatures shuffling along. Their scant, filthy tatters exposing gaunt limbs, wracked by dysentery. She turned away, unable to look at the crushed and broken spirits.

'So this is the glorious army of Anjou? The troops which made our proconsul fly for his life!' laughed a young man derisively, then immediately casting a fearful look around after his indiscretion.

'He's certainly right,' remarked Suzanne, moving alongside Madeleine. 'I can't imagine these ragged yokels beating our Mayençais. Oh do look at him, Madeleine! Why he's a real gladiator!' she said bursting into helpless laughter.

Madeleine followed the gloved hand towards a shivering young Vendéan soldier who wore only a woman's skirt, a small shawl and a battered bonnet. Such a pitiful scarecrow, the sight tore at her heart and she whirled on her companion. 'Never laugh at them! Never. They fought like tigers for their banner!'

Surprised by the girl's anger and embarrassed by the curious stares it had attracted, Suzanne moved away. Regretting the violence of her outburst Madeleine followed. 'Forgive me, Suzanne,' she urged, 'but I cannot bear to see these brave people laughed at. They may be misguided, but they have suffered for it.'

'And so too has Nantes!' replied Suzanne. 'They have tried time and time again to bring us to our knees. Don't think the bread roll you ate this morning came easily, Madeleine. We are near to starvation in Nantes and their rebellion is to blame! Now if you wish to remain to admire this scum, by all means do so. I will see you later.'

The huge figure, with her cloak billowing out like a sail catching wind, dipped from sight into the crowd. Disturbed by their brush, Madeleine turned back to look for a familiar face amongst the prisoners. If that was a decent, reasonable woman's opinion, thought Madeleine, scanning the gaunt faces, there won't be much mercy in this city for you all.

After the last prisoner had entered the prison, Madeleine, quite dizzy from looking at so many people, returned to the little house on the rue Félix.

Nothing more was said about the incident earlier in the day, although Madeleine detected a slight change in Suzanne's manner. It did not surprise her that the following morning, when she tied on her bonnet, there was no offer to accompany her. As she was about to leave, the Nantaise blocked her entry into the hall. Her restraint, Madeleine could see, had been replaced by a nervous anxiety. She gestured for Madeleine to be seated.

'Forgive me, my dear, if I have been somewhat abrupt. It has upset me greatly to think there were differences between us. Tom wanted us to become good friends. But I must confess your sharpness yesterday and evident admiration for the royalists upset me. You see, Madeleine, here in Nantes we have experienced first hand what it is like to be cut off from the rest of the country and surrounded by those devils. Last June they penetrated right into the city. Fortunately one of their leaders, Cathelineau, was shot and they fled. But many good patriots were killed and we were all starving. We were lucky,' she reflected. 'Somehow all their forces didn't link up and that great rascal Charette remained across the Sèvre. Do you know, before leaving with his army he had the impudence to hold a ball out in the open, within sight of the city walls?'

'Really!' responded Madeleine, hiding a smile. How typical of his reckless nature, and doubtless he had no lack of partners, she thought – her amusement fading at the memory of the Comtesse de la Rochefoucauld and the amazons.

'But I'm not reaching the point. I don't know what your work for the army has been, nor do I wish to, but please be careful of how you look and what you say. Carrier's spies are everywhere! Terrible things are happening at the Entrepôt . . .'

'The Entrepôt?' queried Madeleine.

'It's a coffee bonding house down at La Sécherie port. It's been turned into a prison. All the Vendéans they're rounding up are being taken there. It's certain death then,' she whispered. 'I can't tell you more, it's too terrible, but that is why I'm fearful for you and what you may bring on me.'

'Don't worry, Suzanne,' said Madeleine. 'I'll be very circumspect. As soon as I have the information I want I'll be on the first coach to Paris.'

'Oh, I don't want you to feel unwelcome,' replied the young woman swiftly, though not without relief showing on her face. And part of that relief was in knowing that when Thomas returned, a possible threat to her own happiness would be gone.

Relieved that their relationship was once again friendly, Madeleine embraced Suzanne and departed for the prison of Bouffay.

The day was very cold and overhead the sky hung heavy, a yellowish grey portending snow. It was no weather to hide out in the countryside. How many of the survivors of Savenay and Le Mans were still dodging the Blue patrols? Was Henri among them? To her surprise, as she walked into the Place de Bouffay, where the guillotine stood, she saw a ragged column of women and children were coming out of the prison.

'Are those people to be released?' she asked a young soldier standing on duty.

'No, *citoyenne*. They're being transferred to the Entrepôt, the prison is too full.'

'Thank you . . . that's very sad,' she added.

'Yes, it is.'

So, like the Conciergerie, Nantes had a death house. From the soldier's reply and the miserable expression in his eyes, she knew Suzanne had not exaggerated about the Entrepôt. Incredible as it seemed, this slow-moving line of fragile humanity was going to be murdered. Why are you feeling surprised? she asked herself bitterly. We should all be used to massacres by now. She wanted to run out to the soldiers leading the miserable cavalcade and shout, 'Stop! Stop! Leave them! What are we ordinary people doing? Why have we let the cruel, the monsters steal the liberty and equality we fought for?' But she didn't. Fear had castrated all of them, including herself.

Unable to bear the sight of the guillotine any longer, Madeleine walked quickly in the direction of the Quai de la Fosse to which the procession was moving. Calming herself and breathing in the keen air of the river, she waited. There were over 200 unfortunates. Rapidly she scanned the dishevelled figures, looking for a familiar face. It was no easy matter, for many were caked in mud and grime.

Then suddenly she saw the little girl, Marie, walking along next to a National Guard. And beside her, holding a baby in her arms was her mother, Marguerite.

On the way to the Quai de la Fosse she had been considering what she might do should she see someone she recognised. Now she knew. Praying that Marguerite would look in her direction she waited. But instead it was the child whose glance she met. Quickly she smiled and waved, realising in her new clothes she was as unrecognisable as they. For a moment the little face stared back at her and then, to Madeleine's intense relief, she pulled on her mother's skirt and pointed. The expressionless eyes of the Anjou peasant girl followed the pointing finger of her daughter. Vacantly she looked at the well-dressed young woman in grey who rocked her empty arms as though holding a baby and pointed and smiled towards her child.

At last Madeleine saw the young mother begin to understand her meaning. A look of acute agony appeared on the emaciated features. Furtively, so that the escort would not notice, Madeleine frantically signalled once more and pulled back her bonnet so that the peasant girl might more easily recognise her. One moment longer it would be too late, they would pass. Still the mother hesitated, her features contorted with grief. Then she acted. As though it were a parcel she threw her baby to Madeleine. Like the Nantaise onlookers, the soldier had seen, but like everyone else he looked away. Tears flooded Madeleine's eyes and she swallowed rapidly to control her emotion as she and the mother exchanged one final look. Then, over the baby, Madeleine made the sign of the cross to show she would bring him up a Catholic. With a sad little smile, Marguerite moved on.

Suzanne's coolness of the previous day became positively icy when Madeleine returned carrying a rebel's baby, but as soon as the filthy, soiled shawl was unwrapped a miracle occurred. The little toddler, sitting on Madeleine's lap, waved his little fists, gurgled and laughed across at the terrified woman. His laughter was irresistible and infectious. Immediately the filthy rags were on the fire and the little brigand was cooing with delight in a basin of warm water.

'If only I could get a pardon for his mother and little sister,' sighed Madeleine, watching the long deft fingers of Suzanne towelling dry the little pink body.

'You'll never get her out of the Entrepôt. In there you're doomed. There's only one man who can do that. Oh you little miracle,' she laughed, lifting the little boy against her shelf-like breasts.

'You mean Carrier?'

'Yes, but don't even consider it if you want to live.'

'I cannot leave them there without trying, Suzanne. There must be a spark of humanity in the man.'

'I tell you, he is a man without mercy. To go will be to throw your life away for nothing,' she sighed, seeing the determined glint in the beautiful lynx-like eyes and the stubborn set to the girl's rounded chin. 'What shall I do if you don't return?' she asked gravely.

'I have friends who are running my restaurant in Paris. They will take care of Armand. I'll give you the address. Unless you feel you could adopt him?'

Wistfully Suzanne rocked the child in her arms. 'I'd like to,' she smiled regretfully, 'but I'm a spinster, and Goullin from the Revolutionary Committee also lives on the rue Félix. He'd know immediately it was a Vendéan orphan and this little fellow might not survive. But Proust, he's powerful enough to adopt. He has five children of his own and five adopted – one more won't make much difference. Let me talk to him – I think the mother would not like her son to lose sight of the Loire,' she added impulsively.

'Yes, there you're right,' replied Madeleine. She, too,. had come to recognise the hold the wide, beautiful river had on those born near to its shores. 'But if all goes well he'll be reunited with his mother and sister and I'll look after them all!'

The Hôtel Villestreux, requisitioned for the Republican Conventionals, was situated in Petty Holland on the Ile Feydeau. The sentry on duty showed no surprise at Madeleine's request for an audience, merely jerking a dirty thumb towards a dark staircase.

With a fast-beating heart, Madeleine ascended to the first floor where she found she was not the only petitioner that day. Feeling uncomfortably conspicuous, she was forced to remain standing. Like everyone else she strained her ears, hoping to hear some encouraging sounds from Carrier's chamber. Instead there was only a menacing, deathly silence. And then, as though a bull had been loosed from a stall, an enormous bellow of rage followed by something crashing against the door turned the tension to terror. Nervously, the occupants of the ante-room exchanged glances and, after a moment's hesitation, several ladies rose to leave. There was another bellow followed by a yell of pain and the door flew open. On the floor, protecting his head with his hands, was a grey-haired man. Besetting him with furious blows with a sheathed sword was a small man with spindly legs. 'Get out of here, you bloody bugger,' he shrilled, 'or I'll have your bloody head.'

Without rising the terrified man scurried out on all fours, emitting another howl as the sword fell across his buttocks.

Somewhat calmer, the small man looked up from the retreating victim and his eyes fell on Madeleine.

'Well don't just stand there, come in!' he shouted in a bitter, unpleasant voice.

It was not her turn, but no one was going to object; no one wanted to be next, she thought, trembling as she followed Nantes's consul into his room. From behind, Jean-Baptiste Carrier was unprepossessing; Madeleine relaxed a little, running her eye over the slight, fragile body and thin bowed legs. Then he turned around and her stomach contracted with fear and distaste. Set deep within a face of coppery skin were narrow eyes, their bloodshot whites threaded with red veins crossing through to the lids, whilst the black irises mirrored a soul consumed with hatred and suspicion. In that instant, she knew Marguerite and her daughter were lost.

'Your name?' Carrier asked, picking at a long sharp nose.

'Madeleine Fleury.'

'Your petition?'

'The release and pardon for a young widow and her small daughter from the Entrepôt.'

'Is this widow pretty?'

'Er . . . yes,' replied Madeleine, startled by the question.

'Good, then we shall have to give her a republican wedding. She won't be a widow then!' he laughed, tossing back stringy hair.

Madeleine, not understanding, smiled nervously. 'I knew you would understand. She and her child committed no crime, unless it be a crime for a wife to follow her husband and a child to be with its mother.'

'But it is!' cried Carrier, starting to pace up and down. 'There are no innocents at the Entrepôt; only filth, scum!'

'But a young mother and child; I beg you, consider!'

'Yes, you beg. You're very pretty, let me see you beg. Come on, down on your knees,' he said, waving encouragingly to the floor before him. Sick with dread Madeleine slowly knelt.

'I beg for a pardon for Marguerite ... and her child,' she gasped, as the mad eyes thrust forward down to her level.

'And your interest ... What is your interest?' he breathed, his fetid, sour breath poisoning the air she breathed.

'The interest of a patriot in begging for the lives of two French souls who are clearly innocent.'

'Clearly innocent! A whelp, innocent? Do you say the 500 we shot yesterday were innocent? The nation is better off without their canker!'

'Five hundred children,' cried Madeleine, aghast.

'Yes, children, you bloody fool. What d'ye think I meant – sheep?'

Unable to speak, Madeleine's mind reeled, disbelieving the words the man had spoken. No one could ... but as she rose to her feet she knew it was true. This monster in front of her could.

'Why, you cowardly, evil wretch,' she snarled. 'You dare vilify the name of the nation for your murder. You, who fled the battle of Cholet have dared to kill children ... By God, I'll rid France of you myself!'

Like a rat he scurried from her, his coppery skin glistening with sweat. The mean little eyes filled with a sudden fear and his whole body began to shake. At first Madeleine thought it was his fright, but the movements became too violent. Shocked, she realised that he was in the grip of a kind of fit. His bloodshot eyes rolled with rage and as his writhing body fell to the floor, instead of words, a brown foam issued from his twisting lips. Petrified and nauseated, she looked down on his wretched body as he snarled

373

and snapped. What was it Thomas had called him? A mad dog. Instinctively she backed towards the door; but with a shriek of fury he leapt towards her and grabbed both her ankles. She fell heavily and, in a trice, she felt Carrier's hands transfer to her throat. Desperately she lashed out but, small though he was, he was possessed of great strength. She was back in the alleys of her childhood, fighting off her brother's friends, but this was not horseplay, it was life and death. She remembered Pierre's training. With all her strength she pulled up her knee into his testicles – hard! Screaming in agony, the proconsul fell away. At once the door burst open and Madeleine felt her arms grabbed from behind.

It was useless to struggle. Closing her eyes and gritting her teeth, she prepared for Carrier's attack and death. But it did not come. As suddenly as rage fell upon him, so too did calm. Upon opening her eyes, she saw he was smiling. A terrible, calm smile directed at her over the rim of a water glass.

'I won't offer you refreshments, *citoyenne*,' he said, winking at the guards beside her. He waved towards the window which looked out onto the Loire. 'Out there, tonight, you will be able to quench your thirst. You'll be able to drink as much as you like . . . You see, I'm going to organise a little bathing party for you and your friend. Take her away to the Entrepôt!'

Roughly Madeleine's hands were pinioned behind her and she was pushed out of the room. With a wry smile, she saw not a single petitioner remained.

As Madeleine watched the governor's lamp disappear, she tried to stifle the scream of terror which rose within her. In this black hole of despair she had seen by Dumais's lamplight hundreds of prisoners in the coffee bonding house. Though there was nothing to suggest it had housed beans, for the air smelt sweet and sickly. A smell which caught in the throat, making her want to retch every trace of it away. She had smelt it before in the Hôtel Dieu in Paris. It was the smell of death.

Gradually, as her eyes accustomed themselves to the darkness, the restless shifting and low sighs materialised into the faint outlines of figures; though they were hardly visible at all, there was so little light. Marguerite was somewhere here, she realised, although it was unlikely that she would ever find her. But she must try. At least she could tell her that her little boy was safe. Cautiously she moved forward and, in doing, so, immediately bumped into someone.

'I beg your pardon,' she whispered.

'That is quite all right, Mademoiselle,' replied a cultured voice.

'I'm looking for a friend.'

'That will not be easy without a candle – I will give you mine. I was conserving it for later – but no matter; it may be better not to see.'

In a sudden glow of light, the disembodied voice became a person. Instantly Madeleine felt better and saw that her generous benefactor was an elderly priest.

'That is very kind of you,' she said with a smile. 'Have you been here many days?'

'No, my child. I was brought here last night. I was at the fall of Savenay.'

'What of Henri de La Rochejaquelein?' she asked.

'Why, he was separated from us at Ancenis. He crossed the Loire in a small boat to bring back a barge, but it was chased off by Blues when he was unloading it. I expect by now he has joined forces with the King of the Marais.'

'The King of the Marais . . .? Ah, yes, Charette,' she said, realising whom he meant.

'Though which one of them will bow the knee to the other I cannot tell,' chuckled the old man. 'Charette, he's always been his own man, and our Young Henri expects to lead. Ah, but that is not for us to know,' he sighed. 'God go with you, my child. There are many women and children lying down over there.'

Thanking him, Madeleine slowly progressed in the direction the good abbé had indicated, her small sphere of light revealing scenes of the utmost misery and horror.

After half an hour, she gave up. The candle stub was at an end. It was hopeless. She sank down, too weary and sick at heart to care whether she sat beside dead or living. The heavy sense of doom dissipated all hope. She would die and no one would know.

How glad she was Henri had escaped. She thought with pleasure of the love they'd shared. It comforted her to conjure up his boyish face, the moment when he had looked into her eyes and the cornflower-blue of his eyes had darkened with desire. She remembered their kiss on the heights of Fougères, with the wind whipping back the blond, straight hair. Now he was with Charette. Tears sprang to her eyes and her heart contracted with pain; no, not even now could she let herself think of him. Wrapping her cloak tightly about her, Madeleine tried to ease her mind with sleep, but it was not possible. It was too cold and she was hungry. Though unlike the wretched souls around her who had barely eaten for weeks, she, at least, had enjoyed a roll and coffee for breakfast.

It was towards ten or eleven o'clock when the dismal monotony was broken. Coarse laughter and swearing could be heard outside the building. Moments later the door was flung open and four men, bearing lanterns and heavy coils of rope, entered.

'They've come for victims,' whispered a well-dressed man next to Madeleine. 'If you've anything valuable you'd best hide it.'

Quickly, acting on his advice, she slipped off the topaz. Though she wore it with the gem turned inward, nevertheless, the gold band alone would attract a thief. Impulsively she pulled out a skein of hair and, sliding the circle of gold along it, secured it with a knot. Then, fluffing out her thick curls and waves, Madeleine tied back on her bonnet. She was just in time, for one of the four men, his uniform smothered in gold braid, had turned his gaze towards her. Jauntily he swung a coil of rope in one hand, whilst his hand rested on the hilt of an enormous sabre, so long that it trailed along the ground when he walked. 'I shall move amongst you and choose 300. There will be no favourites, but we can only take 300. You will need to bring with you everything you have – food, travelling clothes, everything for a journey.'

At his words, spoken in a light clear voice, everyone started to speak and ask questions. But he held up his hand. 'You will be told your destination once you are on board. Now, will Madeleine Fleury step forward!'

Nervously Madeleine moved forward out of the shadows into the lamplight.

'Ah very charming! No wonder our proconsul chose you to lead the party. Now let's see if I can find a fine young fellow for you.' Laughing, he moved away, threading his way through the throng, returning with a strapping peasant soldier. 'You see what a pretty fellow I've brought you. What a pity there isn't time to give you both a republican wedding!' Laughing, he grabbed hold of Madeleine's wrists, piniong them tightly behind. As the line grew longer, Madeleine and her partner were led outside on to the quay.

It was bitterly cold, the sky clear with frost, a huge silvery plate of a moon sailing high. Shivering and trying to loosen the tight bonds which were cutting into her flesh, Madeleine turned to speak to her partner. 'What did he mean by a republican wedding?'

'He wanted to bind us together, face to face, then throw us in the water,' said the boy abruptly.

'And what is going to happen now do you think?'

'I expect they're still going to throw us in the water, but with company,' he added ironically.

Slowly they moved forward as the roping went on behind. Ahead on the side of the quay were two men waiting beside a gang plank. As they reached it, one of the waiting men stepped forward. 'Right, that's far enough,' he snapped. 'Take off hats and clothes. Where you're going you won't be needing any.' Roughly he undid Madeleine's bonds and grabbed at her cape.

'It's all right, I can manage,' she said.

It had been over two hours since they'd been marched outside on the quay. Madeleine's fingers were numb with cold. But she tore savagely at the fastenings on her dress rather than have the wretch beside her do it. But she was not able to escape the humiliation. As soon as she was down to her shift, the man slipped his hand under it.

'Just making sure you haven't got Du Barry's diamonds up there, sweetheart,' he laughed.

Shuddering with revulsion at his searching fingers, Madeleine turned away. The peasant soldier caught her eye.

'You see my trousers were so ragged that even they don't want them,' he said, exposing a set of magnificent large, white teeth in a swift grin. Madeleine smiled back, realising he was trying to cover her embarrassment.

'You two. No talking!' shouted the second man. 'And I think this is mine,' he laughed, snatching the medal of a *vainqueur de la Bastille* from Madeleine's neck. She stared back, silent and contemptuous that anyone could be so base. These were not patriots but common criminals. Again bound to her partner, only this time left separate from the column with only one wrist bound to one of the boy's, they were waved on.

Immediately they were hustled up the planks which led over two ships to a *gabare* where two more men waited with lamps. Seizing hold of her partner's arms, they flung him down into the hold and, as she was bound to him, Madeleine followed. Shocked and winded by the fall, she lay sprawled on her back as other couples crashed down beside her.

'Come on, get up,' the Vendéan said, tugging at her wrist. 'Now listen to me, your life will depend on it! They're going to drown us. My guess is they'll tow us down towards the basin above Cheviré Island; it's very deep and wide. These boats are just slapped together with planks so I expect they'll sink. First, we've got to free our rope.' With that, he pulled her wrist towards his mouth and began to gnaw. Madeleine thought of the large white teeth and thanked the fates for tying her to such a man. Like a mad dog he worked on the rope, often nicking her flesh, but she didn't care. More and more bodies continued to fall and crash against them in the darkness. 'It's beginning to fray; give it a good pull!' Following his bidding she jerked away her wrist. Above them the hatch was slammed down with a thud. Once again the boy applied his teeth and as the vessel shuddered and moved forward, the last of the fibres parted. 'Well done. Can you hear me?' he whispered, his lips touching her ears.

'Yes.'

'Feel with your fingers above your head for a gap in the planks. Somehow they let water in here. I expect through port holes. When the water rushes in, hold on. Don't panic. As soon as it reaches your chin, take a deep breath and try to find a port hole. They're very roughly made. With luck it might hit a sand bank and break apart.'

'What's your name?'

'Michel.'

Madeleine leant forward and kissed him tenderly. 'Thank you, Michel, my friend. God protect you!'

From the other side of the hold came a loud scraping sound, as the *gabare* caught against the lighter moored alongside. Then it was free, and the terrible journey downstream began: the terror of anticipation making every breath seem the next but one from death. Above the wails and cries of despair, Madeleine suddenly heard the crash of heavy mallets on the wooden timber.

'Port holes!' Michel shouted.

Immediately there was a terrifying roar, and torrents of icy water burst into the hold. Desperately she dug her fingers into the narrow gap between the rough wood. Already the swirling, bubbling water was up to her thighs. 'I must hang on,' she repeated, as bodies crashed and tossed against her. Then her words changed to frantic screams like those around her as, in the blackness, water swept up to her armpits.

'Oh, François my love, help me!' she sobbed. Her face brushed against her hand and she realised buoyancy had lifted her body up level with her raised hands. Now with the water swirling around her neck she felt above for another gap. Finding one, she hauled herself higher. Again the water level reached her neck, her chin. Once more Charette's compelling black eyes flashed into her mind. Calmly she filled her lungs with air and let the water close over her head.

Touching along the inside of the vessel, Madeleine swam towards where the water had gushed in. Unseen hands and bodies bumped and slapped against her. Horrified, she pushed them away, knowing they were dead. Groping forward, her right hand contacted the end of wood and, with a strong kick, she was through.

Resisting the frantic urge to surface into the fresh air away from the stinking coffin, she swam towards the bows. Every stroke she made as powerful as she could, putting as much distance as possible between her and the *gabare*, until a sharp pain in her lungs and pounding temples forced her to surface.

It was bright with moonlight. Behind she could see the *gabare* had completely vanished. Yet the nightmare continued; terrified she dived again and hurled herself forward. Such was her fear that on the next ascent she paused only long enough to suck in air, diving again immediately. When, finally, she surfaced for the last time and looked back, there was only the moonlit river. Gone were the imploring hands, the men in the small boats, hitting the swimmers with oars, slashing at their raised arms with sabres. All was still. Wearily she turned on her back, floating to regain her strength. She had not surfaced like the others in the barge had; Georges Jacques Danton's lessons in the Seine had saved her life. Madeleine felt the ebb tide carrying her downstream towards Paimbeuf. There was only one man she would turn to now. She rolled over and struck out towards the left bank.

PART III

The King of the Marais
1794

Chapter One

The almost naked body of a girl lay sprawled on the river bank, her arms outstretched before her, the lower part of her legs and feet still immersed in grey lapping water.

With a grunt of pain, René Larivière bent his arthritic limbs and knelt beside the stranger. He could tell she had been there since dawn from the dusting of snow covering her body and the little drifts caught up amongst her tangled coils of hair. Whether she was still alive he could not tell. Though, by the feel of her icy flesh, as he rolled her over, it seemed unlikely. Yet, indeed, she was: marble white, cold as the Madonna in the church; but still breathing.

With another grunt of pain, René pulled the girl completely clear of the water and lifted her into his arms. Casting a cautious look around to make sure no one was in view, he stumbled back through the woods towards the cottage.

Set deep within a screen of gorse and broom, René smelt, before seeing, the woodsmoke, which told him Brigitte was preparing his soup. He had gone out to inspect his lines and traps; she would be amazed to see this morning's catch, he thought, kicking open the stout oak door.

Immediately his wife's hands flew upwards in

alarm and surprise. Then, collecting herself, she ran from the pot suspended over the fire to the kitchen table where, with a sweep of an arm, she sent two hens squawking and fluttering to the floor. Gently René laid the girl down on the rough wood surface.

For a moment the elderly couple stared down at the still form. 'I fished her out of the river,' he said, looking significantly at his wife. She nodded gravely and crossed herself, needing no further details. Carrier's National Bathing Parties could not be kept a secret from anyone living near the river.

Swiftly she removed the wet, torn shift from the girl and, with a rough napkin and the palms of her hands, tried to imbue the icy flesh with some warmth. After about half an hour, she gave a little nod of satisfaction and with the help of her husband, wrapped the thin young body in a soft linen cloth. Next she turned her attention to towelling the wet mass of hair, but as her fingers took hold of the girl's head, they made contact with a hard, small object. Curiously, Brigitte Larivière parted the dripping hanks. There, glittering and winking up at her, was a ring. Gasping, the old lady called out to her husband. 'René, René, come back quickly!'

At once the grey head of the woodsman looked over the manger door which divided their living quarters from the animals. 'I've found a ring,' she cried, trying to unknot the hair which secured the thick gold band. 'Here, give me your knife!'

With the ease of slicing the stalk of a mushroom, the old woman freed the skein of hair and held up the glittering prize. It was as though the girl had felt the severance, for she stirred. Her lips parted and as soft as a sigh she whispered a name, 'Charette'. Then again, as though making a supreme effort, she repeated the name with more force.

So, that was it. She must indeed be a survivor of

the royal army and, even rarer, a survivor of *noyades*. Husband and wife looked at each other in fear. They were isolated, but troopers now roamed the whole countryside. The penalty for harbouring a rebel would be death.

For the rest of the day and part of the evening they discussed what to do, both sitting before the fire, silently contemplating the ring. Never in his life had the woodsman seen anything like it. He could tell it would fetch a fortune, more than he could earn in a lifetime. From one to the other they passed the jewel, marvelling at the glittering diamonds, the glowing warmth of the topaz. Never once did the wife think to place it on a roughened finger. Never did they think to keep it for themselves.

At dawn the next day, with a cape made of sacking wrapped about his bent and knotted body, René Larivière set out south through the winter snow to find the King of the Marais; their own General Charette.

For four days Brigitte watched over the delirious girl. On the fifth, she heard men's voices. Fearfully she rushed through into the stable and flung hay over the girl, covering her completely where she lay on the little platform above the cow's head. Then, praying that she would not cry out in one of her terrors, Brigitte crept back towards the window. Cautiously she peered around the shutter to see how many Blues had arrived. She sighed with relief. Coming towards her was her husband. The waiting group of men wore the black skins of the Maraichins but it was their leader, striding alongside René, who took the old lady's breath away with excitement. Every peasant in the Pays de Retz knew of the Chevalier François-Athanase Charette de la Contrie.

And though she had never seen him, she knew that this was the King of the Marais.

Snatching up a clean apron, she hobbled to the door and went outside to greet him. Greedily her sharp eyes examined him. He was tall, at least two heads higher than her René, and this height was accentuated by a magnificent high crowned hat, the brim of which was pinned up at the front, securing three large ostrich feathers as white as fluffy clouds. Under the hat, knotted creole style, was a white handkerchief embroidered with fleurs-de-lys. Slowly the peasant nodded her head approvingly as she noted the cross and badge of the Sacred Heart pinned to the violet, embroidered velvet jacket. Here was a remembrance, indeed, to while away long winter evenings – the gold-hilted pistols tucked into his gold-fringed white sash and the delicate lace at the throat and wrist. This indeed was their General.

Humbly she dropped to her knees in front of the great hero, but a hand, on which she recognised the girl's ring, stretched forward and took hold of hers and raised her to her feet. Then, with his thin lips curving into a smile, the General raised her rough brown hand to his lips as though it belonged to the noblest lady in the land.

Like a young girl, the blood rushed to the old woman's face. In a mixture of embarrassment and pride, she beckoned her illustrious visitor to enter. Straightaway, without being told, Charette strode through the dark, low-ceilinged room into the stable. And within minutes returned with the girl in his arms. His face, she saw, was still calm and impassive, but now the black, magnetic eyes glinted with excitement and the stranger was held against his chest as tenderly as a baby. Once more the old peasant nodded. Here was the force! The reason why a soul, who should have died from exhaustion and exposure, had clung to life. Now indeed, she would live.

Like a humid, dark swamp suddenly warmed by the sun, Madeleine felt his presence through the fever. Later she would remember little of the journey to the forest of Gralas; the sensation of a horse in motion, the feel of furs against her cheek, a strong arm around her body. But the inner knowledge, the instinctive recognition that she was home at last with him; this joy spread like an antidote throughout her weary body.

The nightmare turned to sweet dreams of him sometimes stroking her head or spooning warmed milk into her mouth, until one morning she awoke to find him sitting smiling down at her. No longer hazy and out of touch, but clear and real, his expression tender and grave.

Without understanding where she was, or how she had come there, Madeleine felt only a great happiness and the desire to cry, to nestle within his arms and purge herself of pent-up grief. He leant forward and she smiled, closing her eyes, waiting for the warmth and strength of his encircling arms. But it did not come. Instead he had risen and walked towards a rough wooden chest on which was a tray. 'Come, you must eat,' he said, offering her a little bowl of soup. He raised the spoon encouragingly to her lips, just as she remembered in her dreams, but now a mask of politeness concealed his emotions.

Quietly Madeleine took the bowl and spoon from him, aware of the change. Not daring to speak, an awkward silence fell between them and she sensed he was impatient to leave. 'I must not detain you, François,' she said, glancing around the rough wooden cabin. 'But where am I? How did you find me here?'

'You're in my camp, deep within a forest where

the Blues cannot find us. An honest Peydret brought me the ring,' he said, holding up his hand. 'Forgive me if I do not stay to answer more of your questions, but my men wait for me. The ladies will look after you.' Reaching the door, he paused and turned his head and she saw his eyes gleamed black mockery. 'A word of warning, my dear Madeleine. I should not mention your revolutionary tendencies here, not if you wish to live!'

His words and manner were disturbing, but soon her attention was diverted by a visitor. There was a brisk rap on the door and a small brunette in scarlet flounced into the room. 'Ah good, I see you are up at last,' she trilled, seeing Madeleine sitting on a chair.

'Yes,' replied Madeleine. 'I'm weaker than I thought. Just carrying the tray to the chest has quite exhausted me.'

'You must not be impatient, Mademoiselle. By all accounts you have suffered a terrible ordeal, but soon, if we look after you, you will be strong enough to leave.' She gave a harsh little laugh. Her hands, Madeleine noticed, were small and beautiful, just like Suzanne Guillet's. But unlike Suzanne, they set off arms and a body perfect in symmetry. However, there was a fierceness about this miniature doll-like creature, and from the moment she had entered the room, Madeleine was aware she herself was being assessed from head to toe. Nor did it make her feel better when her visitor gave a dismissive shrug of her small rounded shoulders. 'But I forget my manners. Allow me to introduce myself. I am Madame de Monsorbier. Since François took me under his wing,' she continued, 'I try to see things run smoothly . . . I suppose I've rather taken over from Marie-Adélaide. Do you know Comtesse de la Rochefoucauld?'

'No Madame,' replied Madeleine.

'She is very beautiful and of such a noble family. What a Queen she must have made for François at Légé. I fear he must miss her terribly. I must be a poor substitute,' she sighed, affecting modesty which was belied by an arrogant little smile. 'And you, my dear, should I know your family?'

'No, I think not. My name is Madeleine Fleury.'

'Fleury,' repeated the brunette, rolling the name slowly on her tongue as though trying to conjure up some connection.

'Would that be the Fleury family related to . . .'

'No,' said Madeleine, bringing Madame de Monsorbier's attempt to embarrass her to an abrupt halt. 'My parents are dead. They were poor people. Now, if you will excuse me, Madame, I feel rather tired.'

'But of course,' replied the dainty woman, arching fine black brows in an anxious solicitude. 'We will talk another time. Let me know if there is anything you require – François expects me to look after all his waifs and strays; the happiness of all his peasants is most important to him.' Picking up the tray she departed, leaving Madeleine the memory of a superior smile and a sense of irritation.

Was she really just one of his waifs and strays? Brought here not out of love but pity? She recalled the intimate tone in which Madame de Monsorbier had referred to François; remembered his cool, distant manner. Madeleine felt the stab of jealousy. She would leave, for she could not bear to see him with another. And if the Comtesse de la Rochefoucauld had left, might she not return? That thought was even worse. How could she compete with a woman not only beautiful, of a noble family, but one who in the past had fought fearlessly by his side. Perhaps it might have been better if she'd gone down with the rest in the *gabare*.

In such a morbid frame of mind she slept. Hours

later she woke with a keen sense of hunger, though she did not relish the appearance of the little brunette. When a tall, older woman entered carrying a supper tray, she was much relieved.

'Good evening, Madeleine Fleury. I am Céleste de Bulkeley. I was simply longing to see you, so I have just snatched this tray from Madame de Monsorbier. I declare she was not pleased at all!' she laughed, setting the tray before Madeleine. 'Now before I inspect you, I shall need more light. I'm sorry, we only have these resin candles. What a foul smell they make. Well, that's better,' she said, turning back towards Madeleine. Suddenly she tossed back her head, releasing a merry peal of laughter. 'Now I see why a certain lady has been in a frightful temper all day,' she chuckled, sitting down on the stool beside the bed. 'It's clear, too, why our dear General has been playing nurse these last days, allowing no one but Pheiffer to enter.'

'Pheiffer?' asked Madeleine with a smile, immediately warming to this grey-eyed lady. She was not, however, a stranger to her. Here before her was the amazon who had ridden, gun blazing, at the battle of Torfou.

'He is François's bodyguard. He'll slit your throat if you so much as scowl at our General. But I am not here to answer your questions. I expect you to answer mine, for I am consumed with curiosity.'

At a loss for words, Madeleine could manage only a wan smile. Kind though Madame de Bulkeley might be, her energy, like that of Madame de Monsorbier, was exhausting. It was like having bright, strident parakeets loose in the room. But the affable lady proved highly sensitive.

'François was right to keep us all from you,' she said in a voice suddenly soft and tender. 'You've suffered greatly and here I am babbling on like a great fool. We must do our best to help you forget . . .'

'Forget, how will I ever forget what happened on the Loire?' a silent voice from within Madeleine shrieked. Dumbly she stared back at the woman holding her hand, no longer having the strength to hold back the flood of silent tears which spilled over her lashes. Suddenly the woman had her held tightly in her arms while she sobbed, consumed with terror and disbelief.

'There, there, my dear. You're safe now with us. Cry away your pain . . . Weep for me, too, for I have no more tears to shed.'

Gently Madame de Bulkeley rocked the girl like a child in her arms until, exhausted, Madeleine fell asleep. A savage light shone in the grey eyes of the amazon as she looked down at the grief-stained face. 'Tears today, Madeleine,' she whispered, 'but tomorrow, give death in remembrance!'

The next day, feeling much stronger, Madeleine, supporting herself on Madame de Bulkeley's arm, ventured outside the small wooden cabin. The sight which met her eyes was astounding and her astonishment brought forth Céleste de Bulkeley's already familiar peal of laughter. 'Did you think to find us all cramped in a dozen sheds, my dear?'

'Well, I'd no idea what to expect,' confessed Madeleine. 'Certainly not so many. Why it's a town, there must be over 300!'

'Yes, it would make the Blues very unhappy if they knew we were so comfortable.'

'And I suppose this area in the centre is meant to be the town square.'

'Yes, it's used as an assembly point, but we also grind the wheat here, that's why it's paved with stones. François had them brought here when the Blues started to burn down the windmills. He said our survival depended on self-sufficiency. We all help to grind; the whole area can be covered with wheat or dancers. Do you enjoy dancing?'

'I've never really tried,' admitted Madeleine, blushing.

'Never tried!' exclaimed her companion, her grey eyes widening in disbelief. 'Where have you been all your life? Well you'd better learn before François returns or he'll throw you back in the Loire.'

'It seems strange for an army to hold dances in the forest,' said Madeleine quickly, before Céleste de Bulkeley should realise the insensitivity of her last remark. She need not have worried, for, slapping her thigh in an almost manly way, the older woman hooted with laughter.

'We dance everywhere. It's one of François's rules. This is like the Hall of Mirrors compared to some spots we have cavorted in. I assure you it's quite exhilarating executing a figure with Blues sniping at one from the walls of Nantes – we danced too that night on the Ile de Bouin. Oh, how we danced . . .' she said dreamily. 'So many dear friends lost.' For a moment the grey eyes became bleak and distant, then the amazon shrugged and continued in a brisk voice. 'The republicans had launched a huge offensive to capture François. He assembled us all before him, the whole army, and told us how desperate our situation was. The Blues had blocked all four bridges leading to the mainland. We were trapped, our backs to the sea, our forces of 1,500 completely outnumbered. It was the end! We knew death for all of us was but hours away. So what did François do? Taking the arm of his lieutenant's wife, Madame de Couëtus, he opened the dance. Then everyone joined in. I cannot explain, Madeleine, how our blood raced. To feel a man's arm around you when every hour the brink of death draws nearer. There was no fear, no remorse; just joy! Every smile, every touch was sharp, intense. Finally, in the small hours, we all embraced and went to our posts to meet General Haxo's attack. We were ready to die with honour. But then one of the soldiers brought forward an elderly man who had lived in the area all his life. He said he knew of an exit through the marshland which would not be guarded because it was thought impassable. He vowed he could get the army out. At first François hesitated, not willing to abandon the women and children. It was impossible to smuggle them out over such terrain; nor would we save them if we stayed. Then he had a clever idea. He ordered the women and children to seek refuge in the church. Yes, I know what you're thinking,' she exclaimed, 'wouldn't that be the first place the Blues would look! That's what François counted on. When the Blues looked into the church and found it empty they would look elsewhere. So, leaving the main body of the church completely empty, everyone crammed up into the steeple and the stairway into the tower. It almost worked too,' she said sadly, shadow falling across her features. 'We learned later, just as François foresaw, that the Blues marched in and marched out. Then, upon finding the whole town empty, they supposed somehow the women had escaped with the army. Unfortunately a more imaginative soldier ran back to the church and opened the door to the tower. All was lost. Madame de Couëtus was executed, and her daughters, Sophie and Céleste, are now prisoners.'

'And the army?' enquired Madeleine.

Madame de Bulkeley's grey eyes glinted. 'Over 1,000 crept out under the very noses of the Blues. Naturally we lost all our equipment. We had to abandon the horses, all our cannon, ammunition . . . In complete silence we followed our guide who navigated a network of little paths running through the canals. You may be interested to know, Madeleine, that muskets make very useful stilts on such occasions.' She tossed back her blonde curls and laughed. 'When I say silence, that isn't really true. It's the only time I've seen François inept at anything. Time after time he fell into the water, laughing so loud you would have thought we were out on a picnic – somehow he always takes our fear away. Eventually we reached the village of Château-neuf. We were exhausted but in high spirits. For then, of course, we didn't know the fate of those hidden in the church. So when our General ordered an attack on a republican convoy, we required no urging; it provided us with everything we needed. The Blues were devastated! Not only had we man-aged to escape and hoodwink them once again, we'd had the stamina to tweak their tail. But I am tiring you. I'm afraid, like most seasoned warriors, I like recounting our moment of triumph – you must rest. Perhaps you'll call on me tomorrow.'

Smiling her acceptance, Madeleine watched the imposing figure stride away. Did one perhaps leave calling cards at these little rustic huts; would a white-wigged footman open the door? The thought made her giggle out loud.

'Good, I see Madame de Bulkeley has amused you.' Quickly Madeleine's merriment faded as the small figure of Madame de Monsorbier hurried towards her. Immediately she felt foolish and gauche under the scrutiny of the woman's challenging eyes. 'I've brought you some clothes. I think they should fit you and you will find them suitable. You can't walk around in a nightdress and a blanket. What was Madame de Bulkeley thinking of?'

'We were only outside for a few moments,' replied

Madeleine. 'Besides it was I who requested to see the camp.'

'I see. Then no doubt you know where the mess is. Now you're obviously feeling stronger, you may wish to eat with the rest of us. Another time you'll be expected to help prepare the meal.'

'I'd be pleased to,' replied Madeleine. 'In Paris I ran a restaurant so I'm quite experienced with such things.'

'Really! How ... extraordinary,' exclaimed the brunette with a shocked note of disapproval, her lower lip curling contemptuously. 'General Charette will be most interested to hear of such experiences,' she added, her black almond eyes gleaming triumphantly.

'Your General is well aware of such things, Madame. You see, he has known me since I was a little girl. There's little he does not know about my life.'

'Really?' replied Madame de Monsorbier in a tone of silky sarcasm. 'He seemed most surprised to hear of your friendship with La Rochejaquelein – but then, Mademoiselle, you have not perhaps had the time to bring him up to date with recent happenings as I have.' The dainty woman laughed, seeing the girl's startled look of surprise. 'Of course, you don't know La Rochejaquelein is a friend of mine – I understand you made him very happy, and no doubt you will be pleased to be with him,' she added, her eyes glinting maliciously.

After she had gone Madeleine picked up the dress left by Madame de Monsorbier. It was of the coarsest cloth, quite shapeless and the colour of mud. Casting it down, Madeleine threw herself face down on the bed, filled with anger and hurt as she recalled the other woman's smile of superiority. How typical she was of her kind. Born to privilege, smug and self-satisfied, without having herself earned anything – merely a parasite. She had sneered at The Cordelier; if Madeleine owned every restaurant in Paris she would still sneer. For her, personal achievement didn't count, only birth. No wonder the King had to go, she thought. Yet here I am in the company of those who would put one back on to the throne of France.

Later, just after midday, Madeleine made her way to the long, low building which was used for communal meals. Like her cabin, it was roughly made and simply furnished. On either side of the long row of trestle tables, tree trunks served as benches, whilst at the top of one of the tables, placed beneath a banner, was the rounded stump of a large oak. Presumably this was where Charette sat when in camp. Madeleine looked up at the tattered white silk noticing the blackened edges of a large hole.

'Quite a cannon shot, Mademoiselle,' remarked a voice.

'Yes,' smiled Madeleine, acknowledging a priest who had come forward to greet her.

'We are pleased to have you amongst us, Madeleine. I am abbé Remaud, personal chaplain to our dear General. Come and sit by me and Madame de Bulkeley and Madame de Monsorbier. Like you, she sought our protection in the forest of Val-de-Morière.'

Aware of curious, though friendly, stares, Madeleine followed the priest. Rather disconcertingly, Madame de Bulkeley, after acknowledging her with a wave, suddenly dissolved into laughter. 'Forgive me, Mademoiselle Fleury,' she spluttered, 'I am embarrassing you. I just couldn't help admiring Madame de Monsorbier's efforts on your behalf. Tell me, my dear,' she said, turning to the brunette,

398

'did you make a special journey to Cholet to find something so attractive?'

'Well, it is a little plain,' flushed Madame de Monsorbier, 'but I thought Mademoiselle Fleury would feel more comfortable . . . more at ease . . .'

'More unnoticeable!' chortled Madame de Bulkeley.

'Ladies, ladies, please,' interrupted the abbé Remaud. 'I would like to say grace.'

The meal was very frugal. But it didn't seem to matter. There was such a feeling of warmth and unity amongst those in the long cabin, though it was evident from the glances directed towards the empty place at the head of the table that a vital presence was missed.

The next morning, Madeleine awoke early. There was no one stirring in the camp as she stood at her cabin door. Even the birds were silent; the whole forest seemed wrapped in a white cloak of silence. For a while she walked around, gazing at the orderly rows of cabins, the shelters for the livestock and horses, the water butts and rubbish pits. If one never met the man, just to see this organisation told everything. Here was will, a force, a determination.

Approaching the smithy, Madeleine saw someone else was also up. Outside the lean-to hut, saddled and waiting, was a large bay mare. As the blacksmith appeared, Madeleine saw the rider was Madame de Bulkeley. Curious as to where she would be going at such an early hour, Madeleine quickened her step. 'Good morning,' she called. The grey-eyed blonde, armed to the teeth, wheeled the prancing mare around and trotted forward towards Madeleine.

'I'm going to see if I can do a little better than Madame de Monsorbier,' she said, laughing down from her excited horse. Then, smartly applying her crop, she urged the mare forward at a furious gallop towards the spiked fence and entrenchments which surrounded the camp; and with a whoop wild enough to disturb the whole forest, rider and horse disappeared from view.

It was not until the next day that she returned. Both she and the horse were splattered with mud, and though she entered the camp walking, leading her horse, it was evident by the weariness of her mount that she had had a long, hard chase. 'It's very busy out there today!' she grinned, untying a parcel from behind her saddle. 'Come and see what I found under a bush.'

Intrigued, Madeleine followed. Céleste de Bulkeley's cabin, like hers, was quite bare but for a crucifix on one wall and a Phrygian cap pinioned by a dagger to the door.

'See,' said Madame de Bulkeley, holding up a bottle of Armagnac. 'Something for François on his return. And for you . . .' With a flick of her wrist, she sent a length of velvet billowing across the trestle bed. Madeleine gasped with pleasure as the rich material shimmered softly in the dim interior.

'It's beautiful,' she breathed, holding up its softness against her cheek. 'But to risk your life for a piece of material!'

'It's nothing,' shrugged the blonde. 'Life, death, what does it matter? On the second day of January the beasts murdered my love at Angers.'

'Oh, Madame, I had not realised.'

Unemotionally the round grey eyes of the amazon stared at some inner scene. 'My William was the handsomest officer in the whole army. At six foot six, he towered over everyone. He used to call me his darling girl . . .' Suddenly Céleste de Bulkeley's face crumpled and her body was racked with deep, hollow sobs. Madeleine made no move to comfort her, realising the woman's need to expunge her grief.

Gradually the blonde's sobs diminished and after wiping her eyes she looked up. Her eyes were red and swollen but her expression had regained its brittle brightness.

'Forgive me, my dear, buried grief sometimes catches one unawares. As to the velvet – well I can't bear to see our General in a bad humour. He cannot abide ugly women around him – the sack you're wearing is the surest way to bring on a black mood. Besides, he needs a new banner. I thought you might like to start work on this.' Carefully she unwrapped another parcel and withdrew a piece of white silk and a quantity of gold thread. 'Are you clever with a needle?' she asked. Madeleine nodded. 'Good! I'll send two of the girls to help you. You can work on the banner during the day and your dress by night. It will be a nice homecoming for François to see his court adorned with such a lovely lady. It will be a surprise for Madame de Monsorbier too,' she added impishly.

'Perhaps by then the Comtesse de la Rochefoucauld also may have returned,' said Madeleine, trying to keep her voice casual.

The older woman stared at the girl in surprise. 'Why that she can never do,' she replied sadly. 'Marie-Adélaide was captured on 15 January and both she and Thomazeau were taken to Les Sables d'Onne and shot on the beach.'

'Oh Madame, I didn't realise. Madame de Monsorbier spoke as if . . .'

'Madame de Monsorbier should put things more clearly,' said Madame de Bulkeley crisply. 'Though it's so recent, it's difficult to think she's no more.'

'Who was Thomazeau?'

'Why, Thomazeau was Marie-Adélaide's squire. They fell deeply in love. Always in battle they fought at each other's side. They left with their followers to operate independently.'

'That must have made Charette very sad.'

'Yes, it did. François loved her — no, Mademoiselle, it's not what you're thinking,' she laughed, seeing the flash of jealousy in the girl's eyes. 'There is a great love for every one of us if we are fortunate enough to meet them. For the Comtesse, it was her squire. For François — well, it's true he needs lovely women as he needs danger and the dance. Even so, in the lives of such men as he, there is always only one great love. Perhaps it's time for Diana to catch him,' she said with a smile.

The following day Madeleine started work on the white silk banner with the help of two young orphans. The sisters, Prudence and Henriette, were quite young and very quiet and withdrawn, but gradually, as the days went by and the golden lilies of France took shape, so they relaxed. Their story was a sad one. Like so many villages in La Vendée, theirs had been visited by one of the incendiary columns which were burning and laying waste to the whole province. Their parents, though loyal patriots, thought it prudent at the approach of the raiders to hide the girls in some bushes bordering the village. Then they had run back for the girls' baby brother and a few possessions. They never returned. For three hours the girls, crouching in their hiding place, listened to the screams of the villagers, watched the flames and smoke pouring up to the sky as every house was set alight.

'We were so frightened, Madeleine,' said Prudence, the older of the girls, pausing in her work as she told the tale, 'that long after the soldiers departed, we sat paralysed with fear. At last we plucked up courage and went back. It was horrible ... everyone had been killed ... even our brother.'

402

The girl, no more than thirteen, swallowed as if to steady herself and her voice shook with emotion when she continued. 'They left nothing alive.' Henriette, the younger of the sisters, started to cry. Filled with pity, Madeleine put down her needle to comfort her. 'No,' snapped Prudence. 'She has to learn not to cry. We're here to help General Charette kill the Blues.'

'I think he would be very sorry to hear that,' said Madeleine, putting her arm around the weeping child and kissing her cheek. 'You're young, Prudence, in time you'll learn to forget and forgive.'

The little girl did not answer. Only her eyes spoke, and Madeleine saw there would never be forgiveness.

Madeleine fitted quickly into the routine of the rustic village. During most of the evenings the women sewed; patching together as best they could garments which had already seen a year of war; or altering republican uniforms from intercepted supply convoys. But the desperate need was boots. Just like the peasants of the army of the Centre, Madeleine saw frost-bitten feet in the camp. It made her feel uncomfortable; not only had Madame de Bulkeley provided her velvet, but suede gloves and riding boots too. One evening when they were sitting together quietly sewing, she mentioned her reticence.

'Mon Dieu!' laughed her companion. 'You are a puritan, Madeleine. It gives the men great confidence to see women looking glamorous. We may have little food, next to no ammunition and a spartan village, but when the Blues see us poised on the crest of a hill they are quite demoralised. Why do you think I'm ruining my eyesight in this dreadful light, sewing this?' Laughing, she held up a piece of gossamer lace. 'Because when our General waves his hand for his men to take republican cannon they see only his lace and not death facing them in those barrels . . . and

403

because François loves fine things . . . and we all love him,' she said quietly.

'Then I must sew at twice the speed if I am to be ready before he returns. Where is the army now?'

'Who knows?' replied the older woman. 'Charette marches and countermarches over great distances to confuse the Blues. If our intelligence reports the Blues are going to burn a village he intercepts and prevents it.'

'Are there many other camps like this one?' asked Madeleine, dipping a silk thread into a bowl of tallow to prevent it knotting.

'That is not for me to say. It is not advisable to ask such questions, Madeleine,' said Madame de Bulkeley smoothly, as she began to pinch the fine lace into small pleats.

'Don't you trust me, Madame?' Madeleine asked, flushing.

'I neither trust nor mistrust. I know little of you, Madeleine. You were brought here by our General who has a great weakness for pretty women. Even worse, he trusts them. You're very beautiful and he obviously cares for you. There's no need to look so hurt, my dear. I like you very much. You're pleasant, amusing company. Even so, you could still be in the service of the tricolor.'

'But if I were I could leave and betray this camp.'

'You would not get beyond the entrenchments, my dear. If the sentry didn't kill you, I would.'

A cold shiver ran down Madeleine's spine. The hostility from Madame de Monsorbier was as nothing compared to the threat from this handsome woman smiling over her lace. She had risked her life to bring back something pretty for Madeleine to wear, in order to please her General. Not for a moment did Madeleine doubt she would keep her threat. Nor was this woman's regard for Charette unique. Everything was for the General. All must be ready for his return.

The feeling was infectious and Madeleine raced to finish her velvet jacket and skirt. Already, golden lilies gleamed on the white silk banner. Now, with help from the little sisters, she had started to work on Charette's motto: '*Combattu: Souvent; Battu: Parfois; Abattu: Jamais.*' It was typical of the man: he fought many battles and was sometimes beaten; but never would he be vanquished. Often they could not couch the gold threads, their fingers were so stiff with the intense cold. Then they would jump up and down, vigorously beating their arms against their sides, or dance the steps of the *bourrée* around the cabin, until they collapsed in a giggling heap, their limbs tingling.

It was on such an occasion, when Prudence and Henriette were tickling Madeleine, that Madame de Monsorbier entered. Briefly the alert black eyes swept over the disorderly group on the floor and then rested on the silk on the table. 'You have made rapid progress,' she said, picking up the soft fabric. 'And the work is quite excellent,' she murmured appreciatively, turning towards the light from the open door. 'I had planned to work the new banner myself but Madame de Bulkeley has forestalled me. We have heard the sentries' calls; the army will be back within the hour. If you can all spare the time, we have much to do!'

Madeleine staggered to her feet, feeling foolish, and quick to notice the thinly veiled sarcasm. The banner, she could see, had been an awful shock to Madame de Monsorbier, even though she had tried to intimate she knew they were working on it. Now, as the woman handed her back the completed work, Madeleine saw her look of envy was almost agonised in its intensity.

Tension was high. The air charged with excitement and anxiety. Wives kneaded bread, hoping with every thrust that a loved one was safe and free from wounds. As darkness fell, a great fire was lit on the stones and the last bullock killed for the spit. Then, suddenly, the young boys snatched up burning torches and were off running towards the palisade. Prudence and Henriette, each catching hold of one hand, were dragging Madeleine along after them.

'Come on, Madeleine, can't you hear the jingle of the harnesses? They're here, they've come home!'

With all her heart Madeleine wished to run back and hide within her cabin. The thought of seeing him and La Rochejaquelein together was unbearable. It was the thought which caused her sleepless, anguished nights, for though her mind refused to think of the nightmarish sailing down the Loire, she had not forgotten the priest's words in the Entrepôt: 'La Rochejaquelein has gone to join forces with Charette.'

Now the sound of many feet, horses, and men's laughter drew nearer and, appearing from out of the blackness, she could see the white plumes of his hat and the white sash of command. She knew his line of approach would bring him close to her and her stomach knotted in anticipation.

'Who is that lady with General Charette, Prudence?'

'Why it's Madame du Fief, Madeleine. She always fights with the army and is as good as any of the men with a gun.' The horses were now passing them and little Henriette, running forward, patted the black stallion.

'Welcome home, *mon général*,' she piped in her shrill young voice. Immediately Charette broke off his conversation with the woman at his side and looked down at the little girl. His face, Madeleine saw, was tired and as white as the cravat around his neck, but still his thin lips curved into a beautiful smile and he stretched down his arm and whirled the delighted little girl up before him on the saddle. As he did so his eyes caught Madeleine's. Only for the briefest of moments he held her gaze, and she wondered if he, too, had remembered another little girl in Paris; but without speaking or acknowledging her, he passed on.

In the dim light of the resin candle, with Prudence's help, Madeleine put on the velvet jacket and skirt. It was a rich golden-brown and even without a mirror she knew it matched her hair and eyes to perfection.

'Oh, Mademoiselle, you look glorious,' breathed the young girl, adjusting the honey-coloured lace cravat. 'May I brush your hair?'

'Yes, I'd like that,' laughed Madeleine, twirling so that the skirt whirled about her.

'I hope you'll never wear that ugly dress again,' said Prudence, firmly pushing Madeleine towards the stool. 'And if you don't mind me saying so, I think you should wear your hair loose tonight. It's the prettiest hair of all the ladies.'

'And if you don't stop pulling it so hard, I'll be the baldest lady in the camp,' laughed Madeleine.

Outside her cabin the paved area was filled with peasant soldiers. Many were wearing large black hats, the turned-down brims of which cast their faces further into shadow, making it impossible to judge their ages. Others wore coarse woollen bonnets, the pompoms on the pointed ends giving a merry, cheerful look. Over long waistcoats of russet or white, they wore large woollen belts of red or blue. All, she noted, wore the beige badge with a red heart surmounted by a cross. Though she could not see the words under the point of the heart, she knew they would read *Dieu, le Roi*. Laughing, the men stood warming their hands before the fire. The fearsome *mouton-noir* in their great black skins sniffed the meat on the spit like wild beasts, whilst others were breaking open casks of wine taken from a republican convoy. And all the while still more men poured into the camp.

'I didn't think Charette had so many men,' said Madeleine to abbé Remaud.

'Tonight you see the troops of old Joly, Couëtus and Guérin du Cloudy. All three chiefs are fiercely independent but they have acknowledged Charette as their Generalissimo. Like Stofflet who now leads the Angevins, Joly begrudges Charette the title, though it's obvious to all that Charette is the superior tactician. He treats his soldiers better, too.'

The name Stofflet made Madeleine start – so the German ex-gamekeeper and devotee of the Prince de Talmond had survived Savenay.

'And La Rochejaquelein. I don't see him here. I was told he was joining forces with Charette.'

The abbé chuckled and patted the head of a child carrying a screaming baby. 'No, not yet. But put two roosters together, and feathers will surely fly!'

'*Si je recule, tuez-moi,*' she murmured, remembering the proud young Vendéan's words as he stood before his banner.

'So you know Monsieur Henri?'

'Yes,' replied Madeleine. 'One could not meet more honour or courage in a man.' But as she spoke, in her heart she knew it was a fiercer métier which magnetised her whole being.

Together with the priest, Madeleine made her way to the long, rough mess. Inside Charette was surrounded by a group of young officers and ladies. Amongst them was Madame de Monsorbier, who had evidently just said something amusing, for the group burst out laughing and Charette, catching hold of the little brunette's hand, raised it with mock gallantry to his lips. The smile of pleasure on the scarlet mouth faded, however, as the Breton noblewoman caught sight of Madeleine, and the girl saw her making a supreme effort.

'Ah, Madeleine,' she said, springing forward. 'How charming you look. I've been telling the gentlemen how busy you've been making a new banner – and wrestling, too!' she trilled, her almond eyes gleefully malicious. Madeleine ignored the jibe and smiled to hide her irritation, for she had intended the banner to be a surprise. With a defiant toss of her head so that her hair swung out about her shoulders, Madeleine advanced. The effect was not lost on the circle of young men. They knew of this newcomer – the survivor of the *noyades*. Indeed some of them had ridden with Charette to the banks of the Loire to bring her here. But was this the wretched creature their General had carried in his arms? There was a luscious warmth about this girl recalling the golden days of autumn, when the sun touches fields and leaves, stamping them with bronze and gold. Yet her youth and springy step seemed the herald of green spring and hope. Eagerly each man looked at the soft golden velvet clinging to the swell of shapely breasts and the curve of a long supple waist; each one of them imagining the warm, sweet smell of the girl's creamy flesh.

Madame de Monsorbier, used to being the centre of the stage, was immediately aware of the impression Madeleine was making. Anxiously she tore her eyes away from the voluptuous young girl to study Charette's reaction; but his face was an impassive mask. Reassured, the dainty brunette threw herself into her role of hostess, sparkling with gaiety as she made the introductions.

It was hardly a feast they sat down to, but it was served with such élan on the rough wooden platters that it seemed so. Up and down the long trestle tables, Charette moved like a solicitous host. Laughing and teasing, stealing little morsels of the coarse flat bread from plates, just as though it was the finest fare in the land, served on the porcelain of Sèvres. No wonder when he was away they all glanced towards his empty seat, she thought, for he infused the atmosphere with his energy and gaiety. Everyone sought to catch his eye and win a smile. Somehow he imbued each person with a sense of value, whether they were a pretty young woman or an elderly matron, of noble or humble birth. This tall elegant man had a word for all his courtiers in his forest kingdom. Madeleine marvelled, seeing him thus for the first time; saddened that she alone received no word or smile, only a dark brooding stare when once she caught him watching her.

But it was not to be a night for inner reflections. Out came the fiddles and the pipes, joyously shattering the silence of the dark forest. Under the starry winter sky, Charette and Madame de Monsorbier, silhouetted by the leaping flames of the fire, opened the dance. They were well matched, their bodies lithe and graceful, their black eyes flashing as the tempo increased.

'Come, it's no time to stand admiring others, Mademoiselle,' cried a cavalier with shoulder-length wavy hair and a grin which stretched from ear to ear. Taking her by the hand Hyacinthe de la Robrie whirled Madeleine out on to the expanse of flat stones. They danced a *bourrée* which was fast and furious, and soon all sadness, all memories, all pain was forgotten. There was only laughter and wine, the clash of sabots on stone as the chain of dancers stepped to the pulsating music.

Madeleine was whirled from partner to partner, then on to him; the brief touch of his hands, his head thrown back, his black eyes sparkling with joy as he laughed down at her. Then on to the next partner and the next, until, laughing with exhaustion, she was led off the floor by Hyacinthe de la Robrie's brother, Prudent, who had his brother's grin but lots more freckles and whose short muscular legs were as nimble as a little bull's. And so it continued until the small hours of the morning. Never had she experienced such *joie de vivre*. In Paris it had been all politics and with the Vendéans there had been psalms. Here, there was fun! Trembling with fatigue, dizzy with the memory of all her partners and new-found friends, Madeleine left the last revellers to the dying embers of the fire.

She walked along the dark row of cabins to her own; tired and almost content. Ahead she recognised the dark massive bulk of Pheiffer, Charette's body-guard. The moon sailed out from behind a cloud, illuminating the scene with its cold silvery light. A man and woman, arm in arm, walked ahead of the bodyguard. They stopped outside Charette's cabin, then the moon slid behind a cloud and all was dark, but she still heard a woman's soft, low laugh and the slam of a cabin door.

Though the pangs of jealousy tried to keep her awake, Madeleine soon fell asleep. When she woke it was in a state of alarm, hearing footsteps and the creaking of the uneven planked floor.

'Who is there?' she whispered.

'Don't be alarmed. It is me, François. Get dressed and come with me!'

It was more of a command than a request and she responded to the urgency in his voice. Without bothering to light the candle, she felt for her dress which she had draped over the bed for extra warmth.

His physical presence in the darkness bore down on her. She felt the tension mounting between them as she thrust her feet into the soft leather riding boots. Then throwing a fur skin about her shoulders she whispered, 'I'm ready.'

Quickly, he opened the door. Outside it was the half-light between night and day. Standing just a few paces away was Pheiffer with two saddled horses. One, she saw, was Charette's black stallion and the other a grey with a side saddle.

While Charette mounted, the fierce bodyguard threw Madeleine up on to her horse as though she were a small child. As they moved off, the man made to follow, but Charette with a swift look dismissed him. Filled with curiosity and misgivings, Madeleine followed swiftly behind in the tracks of the black horse. The silence was awesome; every sound they made, like their tracks, seemed to violate the white, still landscape through which they moved. From above, cascades of fine powdery snow showered down on to their heads and shoulders as their horses disturbed the lower branches of the trees; sometimes, the snow would drop moments after they had passed, causing Madeleine to whirl around to look for followers.

After the camp had been left far behind, they came out of the trees into a clearing through which ran a sparkling stream. Above, the dawn sky tinged with mauve was changing to a vivid pink as the winter sun rose, its weak rays providing no warmth, merely playing on the frosted covering of dew so that blackened bark and evergreens glinted and shimmered, reflecting a thousand tiny jewels.

Before her, Charette jumped down from his horse and threw the reins over its head. Quickly Madeleine dismounted before he had time to render her assistance and, to calm herself, attempted to shake the snow from her hair.

'So!' he said, striding up to her. 'Here we have *citoyenne* Madeleine Fleury, *vainqueur de la Bastille*, attacker of the Tuileries, friend of the Mayençais. I am deeply honoured that you sent for me!' he said, bowing with a mocking smile. 'Tell me, how can I help you?'

Madeleine turned away, feeling the anger rise within her at the taunting tones and his scornful expression.

'Come, my dear,' he continued, 'don't be reticent. We are far away from prying eyes and ears and I am most interested to hear of your exploits with the Catholic and Royal Army in Brittany. Tell me, what persuaded you to abandon your tricolor for the lilies? Perhaps the stunning looks of the young generalissimo?'

Desperately Madeleine groped for words, still not daring to meet his eyes, which she knew would be hard and unrelenting. She had known this moment would come ever since Madame de Monsorbier had entered her cabin. Yet she had not anticipated how awful it would be, or the sense of shame she would feel. It was useless to lie to him, nor did she want to deceive. She raised her long lashes and looked fearlessly at him. 'You have guessed correctly, Chevalier,' she said, knowing each word would damn her in his eyes forever. 'I was an agent of the Republic. My orders were to cross the Loire with the Vendéans; to influence, if possible, an attack on a heavily defended sea port rather than Rennes, by making close contact with the leaders of the rebellion.'

'Well, you certainly succeeded with La Rochejaquelein,' snapped Charette, in a voice like a whiplash.

'That is not so ... Henri was different,' she faltered. At her words, spoken with such tenderness of feeling, it was as though something snapped

413

within the man before her. His face blazed with a sudden fury; like a panther he sprung at her, seizing her by the throat, slamming her head hard against the tree behind her.

'I should squeeze the last breath out of you,' he snarled, 'for you are beneath contempt. Was it not enough to betray, to witness their defeats at Granville? Did you have to stay until Le Mans to gloat upon your efforts?'

'No, no,' she gasped. 'After Granville my life was theirs. I couldn't leave them. Please, François, at least believe that.' But his fingers retained their vice-like grip and his eyes their murderous quality, and when he spoke his voice was harsh and cruel.

'And now, after your republican friends rewarded your efforts by throwing you in the Loire, you are here to betray me, to ingratiate yourself to them once more, by crawling into my bed as you did into La Rochejaquelein's!'

It was too much! Indignation, anger and outrage exploded within Madeleine. Wildly she lashed out and dealt him a stinging blow across the temples. Surprised, he shook his head, relaxing his grip, and she pushed him violently from her.

'I shared La Rochejaquelein's bed because I cared for him and loved him,' she shouted, her golden-brown eyes dark with anger. 'And I turned my back on Paris and the tricolor when I swam to the left bank of the Loire. Not for the lilies of France, or Henri, but for a man, the only man I have ever . . .' she choked back the words, her pride and her tears overcoming her. 'Now kill me if you wish,' she said dully, 'for I no longer care to live.'

The rage and scorn had slipped away from Charette's face and he stared at her, as though caught in an internal, agonising conflict. Then, in one bound, he closed the distance between them and his arms were around her. Fiercely he crushed her body to his in a savage, hungry embrace. His lips were hard and demanding as they found her mouth. With all her being she responded.

'Oh my chevalier, never leave me again!' she cried, her tears spilling on to their lips. Unable to speak, overcome by the strength of his feelings, Charette drew her closer and stroked Madeleine's hair, just as if she were the little waif of so long ago. But now it was the woman in his arms, and the feel of her body quickly set his blood racing again. Purposefully, he walked away towards his horse and, taking the thick fur from his saddle, threw it down in a little hollow near the stream. He held out his hand to her.

Together they sank down on to the soft fur and she abandoned herself to the hands of a practised lover. She ached for him, but as she brought the black curls, glinting with tiny icicles, down to her, felt the warm sensuous lips lingering on her throat and breasts and lips, she knew this was no impatient boy but a man well versed in the art of love, who would relish every step of their journey.

'Ah, my love, my dearest love,' he murmured, 'I've waited so long to enjoy you and I shall make every part of you sing with pleasure!' Hungrily his mouth sought hers once more and, gathering her to him, he took possession. Savagely they unleashed their desire: he thrusting upward, she opening, holding; their bodies racked with urgency as they consumed each other. Until at last the fury abated, and, purged, they fell apart.

Drunk with love, they rode back to their forest village, reining in to kiss every few yards; he shouting, 'I love you,' until the forest echoed. It seemed impossible to stay apart, so acute was the need, so sweet the delight in touching. All sensuality had slipped away from him. Like a boisterous student he raced back and forth, whipping up great flurries of snow, leaving the tracks of acrobatic skill across the virgin snow as he showed off his horsemanship among the silent trees.

Charged with emotion they re-entered the camp, suddenly conscious of the wetness of their clothing as they dismounted.

'I suppose you should dry off, though I can hardly bear to part from you,' said Charette, drawing back the wet hair from Madeleine's face. 'I need to make love to you soon, *chérie*, very soon. You've set me on fire, you know that, don't you?'

Madeleine smiled up into the dark, expectant eyes.

'Your fire branded me long ago!'

'*Mais oui!*' he murmured as understanding dawned. 'Could I forget the Tuileries; I was so close to killing you . . . is the scar very large?'

'Enormous!' teased Madeleine, wanting to chase away his sad concern. 'It's as big as a monkey's paw!'

Charette bent down and swept her up into his arms, his shout of laughter with its unique note of utter joy reverberating in the clear air; contentedly Madeleine basked in its warmth as he carried her to her cabin. She felt like a bird that had been long out at sea, battered and buffeted by storms and wind. Now she was home, and safe.

It was a little after noon when the arrival of a visitor was announced to Charette. Immediately his lips tightened with vexation and he frowned, wondering what effect this visit might have on Madeleine. Quickly he finished signing the letters placed before him by his secretary, Auvynet. 'See that couriers take these today,' he said. 'And tell the Marquis I am ready to receive him.'

Thoughtfully, François-Athanase laid down his

quill pen. Had La Rochejaquelein come to offer his sword, or had he come for Madeleine? His teeth clenched together as he thought of the girl with the Marquis, and a murderous surge of jealousy erupted within him, the like of which he had never known: his eyes widened in wonder at its force ... No matter, it was better so, now he would see what this man meant to her.

'Marquis,' he said, concealing his emotions with a cold, polite smile as he rose to greet his visitor. 'This is an unexpected pleasure. And you have come on foot,' he said, his quick eye observing the other's sodden boots. 'You must take a cognac, for you must be perished!'

'Yes, Chevalier, I am,' responded the young man. 'Even with a guide I began to think your camp would never be found.'

'That's good to hear,' smiled Charette, giving a glass to La Rochejaquelein. 'For the Blues regularly try to search it out.'

For a moment a silence fell between the two men and, although neither betrayed his interest, both seemed to be taking the measure of the other.

Eventually it was La Rochejaquelein who spoke. 'You have been very successful in sustaining your attacks against the Republic for so long.'

'Yes, but not without the loss of many loved ones!'

'It is ever so,' replied the Marquis bitterly. 'Many times I wished I had died with my friends at their last stand at Savenay.'

'Fate did not intend it ... perhaps,' added Charette somewhat drily, 'that is why she abandoned you on the opposite shore to your army. Besides,' he added quickly, seeing the other's offended expression, 'La Vendée needs you and I will gladly furnish you with equipment and a horse, for I need gentlemen of courage to follow me.'

417

Just as if he had received a slap, Henri de La Rochejaquelein started, and threw back his blond head in the haughtiest of gestures. 'Chevalier,' he said coldly, 'I do not follow, I lead!'

'Lead, Monsieur Henri!' laughed Charette. 'And pray, where would you lead my men? Another wild goose chase to pick cider apples in Brittany? To capture back a few towns in La Vendée? No, if you stay here, you will follow! And learn tactics and the art of retreat!'

At the word retreat, the younger man's hand lifted from the hilt of his sword and his full lips curled in disdain, but the gesture was lost. He was already dismissed, for Charette had turned away.

Just then the door opened and Madeleine entered. Like statues the occupants of the cabin remained motionless, each one desperately trying to hide their emotions. If she could have fainted, Madeleine gladly would have done so. Her mouth went dry, leaving behind a bitter taste; and panic paralysed her mind. Vaguely she became aware Charette was speaking to her.

'. . . Your arrival, Madeleine, is most opportune. You and the Marquis, I know, are old friends, and no doubt have much to discuss! So,' he said, saluting La Rochejaquelein as elegantly as if he were at court, 'I bid you adieu, Monsieur Henri. God go with you.' Then, with a parting glance at Madeleine, Charette departed.

It had been the briefest look, but it enveloped the girl with its intensity. For her there could only be him! Nor was this silent communion lost on La Rochejaquelein: immediately he recognised a rival. Anxiously, he studied the girl. Never had her golden eyes looked more beautiful, more hypnotic: their dilated pupils glistening liquid black, as though she had recently made love . . . His blood ran cold: was this why she was here, rekindling the ashes of an old love? As always where Madeleine was concerned, La Rochejaquelein silenced his inner voice. He didn't want answers: he only knew that this beautiful girl had given herself to him lovingly; he could not believe anything had changed. And now, as she approached with tears in those eyes, he did not doubt she was much moved by his presence.

As always when he was with her, his shyness and reticence fell away and he smiled, holding out his hands to her. 'Ah, my love, my dearest love, thank God you're alive. I thought I'd lost you.'

Hardly able to see for tears, without the courage to meet his eyes, Madeleine felt for his hands. Their warmth closed on hers and she could hardly breathe, knowing what would come. Gradually, as she calmed herself, she raised her eyes. How weary Henri looked, the beauty of his classical features marked by sorrow and fatigue.

'It seems a lifetime since Fougères,' she said softly, as memories of their meeting and the moment he had kissed her flooded back. '. . . and your eyes are still as blue as the cornflowers.' The words had somehow slipped out and she regretted them immediately; for the young noble's anxious face relaxed into a delighted smile and the beautiful curve of his lips moved down into a kiss.

It was then that La Rochejaquelein knew.

'You do not respond?'

Sick at heart, Madeleine fingered the threadbare cloth of Henri's jacket, wondering how she would ever find the words. For he had lost everything! Another time, she could have dreamed of life with this gentle, uncomplicated boy: borne his children; grown happily old together in his château of La Durbelière; but the man who had claimed her in one brief, passionate look, had made it otherwise.

'Oh Henri, it's not to be,' she whispered. 'Don't ask me to come with you. I've belonged to François since I was a little girl!'

Pale as death, Henri de La Rochejaquelein stared at Madeleine as though he had received a knife thrust. Then a surge of colour flooded his ashen face. Abruptly, the Marquis turned away and picked up his hat. Unable to speak, averting his eyes, he walked past Madeleine out into the snow.

Distraught with grief, she ran to the door and gazed after the retreating figure. She knew they would never meet again – dear God, they could not part so! Swiftly she ran to overtake him and, facing him, barred his way.

'I do not ask forgiveness,' she uttered gravely. 'Only believe in what we shared!' The blue eyes rested on Madeleine an instant, their expression bleak and full of pain. Miserably, she stepped aside and let him pass, for there seemed nothing else to do.

Long after the crunch of footsteps on snow had faded, Madeleine remained leaning against a tree, filled with guilt and a sense of desolation. She needed to feel Charette's arms around her, but she knew she would have to search him out: he was too proud to come to her. He had left her with La Rochejaquelein on purpose, that was plain: there had been no plea, no parting entreaty in his eyes.

Slowly, Madeleine turned to walk back. Beside the last line of cabins, elevated on the rise of ground, a solitary figure stood looking down on her. Motionless, yet attentive, like some wild creature, she saw as she drew nearer that the dark, feline features of the man were set in tight concentration as he examined her face. So, after all, he could not stay away. Charette had come! Surprised, she halted. Her heart began to pound; joy and energy flooded her being.

420

Suddenly, like children, their arms outstretched, they ran towards each other.

'I was afraid,' he said.

'Never be,' she said fiercely, holding him tight.

The hurt she had done La Rochejaquelein plagued Madeleine intermittently throughout the remainder of the day. Nevertheless, it was impossible to suppress the effervescent surgings of happiness within her. And by evening, when she entered the mess, her face flushed pink, her brown eyes dancing with pinpoints of gold, the smiles of the young officers grew wider as they watched their young generalissimo try to extricate himself from conversation with an elderly dame, each impatient glance directed in their direction becoming darker and more scowling as they teasingly flirted with Madeleine.

The only person not to smile was Madame de Monsorbier. Proud, intelligent, she at once recognised her reign had come to an end. Whatever feelings she had remained concealed beneath a lofty air of unconcern and the sudden onset of a headache.

Under the canopy of stars, which surpassed any chandeliers, Charette led out Madeleine to open the dance. Their happiness was infectious and the whole company danced in celebration of their joy. Smiling, she moved through a graceful gavotte with an elderly Chevalier de Saint-Louis. She could not help but think of her dead brother who'd lifted her up so often on to his shoulders to watch the bejewelled ladies enter the Opéra for a ball. 'Are you angry now, Pierre,' she whispered, 'to see me partnering those whom you so despised? Yet even you who fought for *égalité* must see in this particular White camp only brothers and sisters in arms. This is a place where birth bows before courage.'

Just as the night before, they danced until the

small hours. Always his eyes sought hers; and each and every parting in the dance seemed far too long, so that they longed to renew physical contact.

'Come, Mademoiselle Fleury, I feel quite ignored,' complained the sturdy chevalier with the freckles and broad grin. 'And to punish you I shall not let you return to our General, but make you partner me in the next dance!'

'Prudent, I cannot manage a *bourée*,' gasped Madeleine, as the fiddles changed tune. 'I'm far too breathless.'

But grinning from ear to ear, Prudent de la Robrie stamped his short muscular legs to the rhythm of the music and tightened his hold on Madeleine; he was not going to let this lithesome lady go just yet, not even for his General.

With an amused smile of submission, the girl acknowledged her determined partner with a curtsey. 'You will see, Chevalier,' she said flirtatiously, 'my whole attention will be for you alone, and by the end of this dance, I shall have counted every freckle on your face.'

'Then I am most fortunate in possessing them,' cried the sandy-haired man, whirling Madeleine around so that her velvet hem lifted from the ground.

At the end of the dance, laughingly resisting all other hopeful partners, and Prudent's efforts to detain her, Madeleine slipped across to rejoin Charette.

'Are you happy, my darling?' he asked, handing her a small mug of wine.

Madeleine nodded, her eyes sparkling. 'I think I'm going to enjoy living here.'

'Good,' he said with a small grave smile. 'I want to see the dark, terrible look which sometimes touches your eyes disappear for ever. Dancing and fun, my love, will help, but you will need more than that to erase the memories you have of the Entrêpot, and forget what you will see outside this camp. Talk to our abbé Remaud. He is a remarkable man, Madeleine. Let him bring you closer to God.'

Together they sat down beside others on a tree trunk and watched the dancers perform a minuet. Like pale, beautiful moths fluttering against the blackness of the forest, the women moved gracefully to and fro, executing the stately figures of the dance.

'Was it like this at Versailles, François?' she murmured, leaning her head against her lover's shoulder.

'Almost as elegant,' he quipped. 'But they never danced like this!' he said, springing up to his feet and holding out his hand to her as the fiddlers changed into a strident rhythm.

Fatigue forgotten, Madeleine ran after Charette on to his forest dance floor. Like pagan spirits, Versailles forgotten, everyone threw themselves into another wild, fast *bourée*. This is what Céleste de Bulkeley meant in her story of Bouin, realised Madeleine. Tomorrow death might make its claim, so this dance, this night, this touch of a partner's hand, was a bonus which heightened and intensified all pleasure.

The next day, as though to establish her position of trust, Charette invited Madeleine to sit in on one of his war councils. 'Gentlemen,' he said, beckoning for his secretary, Auvynet, to spread out a map on the table. 'As you know, the Blues have burnt many châteaux and villages. However, the position is now even more serious. The National Convention has advocated the total annihilation of the Vendée. All villages, forests, crops and habitation are to be completely destroyed. They intend to leave not a blade of grass. Our intelligence reports that twelve republican columns will operate for this purpose under General Turreau. They will be based here at these posts – Cholet, Tallud-sur-Maine, Le May,

Pouzauges, La Flocellière, Les Epesses, Saint-Laurent, Caillère, Jallais and Sainte-Christine. Their point of communication will be Cholet. In total, these troops will number 10,000.'

At his words there was a stunned silence. Then the abbé Remaud spoke. 'But they cannot mean to do it. Their own loyal patriots live in these villages.'

'That means nothing to Barère or Robespierre,' replied Charette bitterly. 'Anyway, look around at our men. Are not many of them disillusioned patriots?'

'But, François, their numbers. How can we hold out against such strength?'

'We can't if we try to meet them in pitched battle,' replied Charette. 'We must learn from the past, study our failures and successes. What do we do better than the Blues?' he asked the young man who had posed the question.

'Why, we aim better,' he laughed.

'Precisely,' smiled Charette. 'We shoot better, and we were born and raised on this earth. The marshes, the forests and the Bocage are our friends: we must use them! Unless we are convinced our number can bring success, we will not fight in the open. We will run away!'

'Never!' shouted the men in one breath.

'Yes, Messieurs!' cried Charette, slamming his fist imperiously on the map. 'Yes, we will run away! Like morning mist we will appear and then disappear. Then, as lightning, we will strike! From behind, on their flank, at night, during the day. Always when they are unprepared.'

Like the officers in the room, Madeleine sat mesmerised by the force and energy unleashed from Charette. 'The army of Anjou,' he continued even more excitedly, 'took towns; but we will take roads!'

'Roads?' exclaimed Hyacinthe de la Robrie in disbelief.

'Yes, roads!' cried Charette, with a dramatic gesture of hand and lace. 'Along roads pass communications, troops, supplies. Cut them and no army can survive. Above all, because we are few, we have speed, mobility. We have surprise! And, Messieurs, we have right on our side!'

Every day, spies left and entered the camp with news of Republican positions. Many of them were orphans like Prudence and Henriette, whose hatred of the Blues and love for Charette inspired them to surmount all personal fear and daily risk death.

Anxious to prove herself, Madeleine begged to be given a mission, but Charette, as though soothing a wilful child, dismissed her request instantly. 'The marshes are no place for a stranger, Madeleine. You would be lost within the hour. Then I would have to search for you. It's enough for me to return and see your lovely face,' he said, catching her by the waist and pulling her to him. 'I know you want to share our fight, but until you can shoot straight and, even more important, defend yourself with a sword, I'll not let you endanger yourself, or my men.'

'Then will you be my teacher in combat as well as love?' she teased. Charette shook his curly head, and whirling her up into his arms, carried her across to the couch.

'You're an excellent pupil, Mademoiselle,' he murmured, nibbling her ear and covering her throat with rapid kisses, 'but I fear you need many more hours of tuition; but for armed combat I suggest you see Madame du Fief. She is a veritable Mars.'

It was like being circled by a wolf, decided Madeleine, as Victorine du Fief prepared to attack. This green-eyed redhead was obeying Charette's orders a little too seriously, thought Madeleine, looking down at the scarlet weal on her forearm. Immediately her agile teacher scratched her arm a second time.

'There'll be no time to inspect scratches, *chérie*. The Blues give no quarter to women. Remember you can't use strength against a man, only speed . . . skill . . . and treachery. Now, let's try it again, much faster. Footwork . . . footwork, Madeleine.'

For the third time, Madame du Fief, with a supple flick of her wrist, sent Madeleine's sword flying through the air. Sighing with frustration, the girl moved to retrieve it. As she did so she remembered Kléber and the ink pot. Swooping down, she grasped a handful of snow and flung it into Madame du Fief's face. Then, catching hold of the startled woman's wrist, she twisted it up behind her back.

'How is that for treachery, Madame?'

Both women laughed, and Madame du Fief patted Madeleine affectionately. 'Don't worry, you're learning. I know you had a little tuition in Paris, but it's not a school out there. We're women against soldiers. We have to be twice as fast and that means practice every day. It's your sword arm which will save your life, not your gun. Once you've discharged your first ball there is little time to reload. Nevertheless, you still must practise that too!'

Sheathing her sword, Madame du Fief walked away and pinned a marker on the trunk of a large oak tree. As she returned, Madeleine saw she, too, was ramming home a ball down the muzzle of her gun.

'Madame,' said Madeleine, 'I know you have fought in many battles. Are you never afraid of losing your life?'

'You can only lose it once, and when those whom you loved have been murdered, what does life mean anyway? For every Blue I kill I avenge my child . . .

Besides,' she said, preparing to take aim at the marker, 'like François and Céleste, I thrive on danger, it gives that extra frisson to life. Now let's see what you can do. Hit the bull's-eye and I'll recommend your promotion to active service. Then you'll be able to start your own collection of Blues' scalps.'

Scalps were not what Madeleine sought. She wanted only to be with Charette and share his danger. But within the first day of riding out, her attitude changed. They had ridden out to defend a village from attack by an incendiary column. Just half a league away, the spiralling plumes of black told them they were too late. Still they carried on in case there were survivors. There were none. All was silent, save for the roar of flames, consuming the little cottages. Filled with an indescribable horror, Madeleine saw even the unborn had been put to the sword. Quivering with an emotion that was beyond rage and fury, she spurred her horse on.

'Will we be able to overtake them?' she gasped, coming alongside Charette. He turned to her, his face drained of colour, his large magnificent eyes filled with agony.

'No, we will not pursue the fiends,' he said quietly.

'In God's name, why not?'

Charette took in the bewilderment on the girl's face and understood by the trembling of her lips and heaving of her chest her inability to cope with the monstrous sights around her. 'Madeleine, this is happening every day. Carrier and the murderers in Paris mean to leave here an uninhabited wasteland. Our little army is all that stands between the people of this province and genocide. I must be governed to act with my head and not my heart.'

There were to be many days for retribution as

throughout the harsh winter months they rode out against the death squads of General Turreau.

Accompanying Charette's small force to take part in her first ambush, Madeleine had been full of fear; born of the thought she would not have the stomach to thrust her sword into a living body. So, wedged between Céleste de Bulkeley and Victorine du Fief, who were chattering casually as if on the way to a shopping expedition, she too tried to appear nonchalant; all the while checking the security of the white sash holding her gun, and feeling for the hilt of her sword.

'For pity's sake, Madeleine,' said Victorine du Fief, 'do stop. You're beginning to make me nervous, and that will take all the fun out of things. Just remember, a boot in a Blue's face or a trooper's horse always provides a nice element of surprise.'

'I'll bear it in mind,' replied Madeleine drily, watching the red-haired amazon demonstrate a quick punch-kick from the leaping head of her side saddle.

Once again the women continued their conversation until they reached the outskirts of a burning hamlet. Then silence fell upon the whole company as they moved past the burnt-out, smouldering shells of buildings. There was nothing new about the sight, yet the impact of the horror never lessened with familiarity, nor blunted the senses. Breaking the deathly pall of silence, a shutter hanging from its burnt-out frame clattered back and forth in the wind and, unseen, a dog howled its grief and loss.

Expectantly, Madeleine looked towards the village church and saw the usual horror. But this time she did not close her eyes or look away. She stared at the butchered villagers, wishing to etch them on her mind, so that they would rise up before her when the time came to kill with steel.

After some six kilometres, the rising black incense

of death pin-pointed the path of the Republic's Avengers.

'Does that mean we won't be engaging them?' asked Madeleine of her companions, noticing that Charette, who was at the head of their column, was turning off the road into a meadow.

'No, quite the opposite,' replied Céleste de Bulkeley, with a cruel expression in her round grey eyes. 'François intends to come up ahead of the devils and take them by surprise. It will be the last village that these particular fiends will lay waste to.'

Gradually, as they drew closer, skirting the burning hamlet, dreadful wails and cries for mercy drifted towards them with the smoke.

'Mon dieu,' gasped Madeleine. 'Can't we stop the killing now?'

Madame du Fief glared at her, her eyes glittering and staring hate. 'We are too few – you must learn control, as our General has taught us. When we strike, we must be stronger than they. Come, we are to ride down on to the road.'

The amazons rode down the steep bank leading to the narrow track below, and Madeleine waited with them as Charette deployed their sharpshooters behind the broom hedges on either side of the track. Next he positioned the bulk of the cavalry at each end of the concealed firing squads.

'Now, ladies and gentlemen,' he said, when all others were hidden from view. 'If you have a mind to lead murderers to Hell, follow me. The moment they take the bait, turn and make all speed beyond the last of our Horse!'

Strangely, as Madeleine followed the white banner on its approach to the billowing flames, she felt no fear. Ahead she could see the black mounted figures emerging from the inferno and, like those around

429

her, she discharged her gun and cried, '*Vive la religion!*'

'Turn, *mes enfants!*' commanded Charette, as ahead the soldiers began to return fire and give chase.

With some 200 troopers now on their heels, the road back suddenly seemed ominously empty and Madeleine lashed her horse on to greater effort.

Riding beside her, Charette glanced at Madeleine's frightened face under her large plumed hat. 'You're quite lovely,' he called, blowing a kiss to the astonished girl as she glanced towards him.

'And you, *mon général*, are crazy,' Madeleine gasped and then laughed; suddenly feeling elated and as reckless as he, as she took his outstretched hand. Together, hand in hand, they raced down the narrow track until, just past the last of their cavalry, they turned, as if to make their stand.

'Pick some of them off from here if you can, *chérie*, but stay clear of the hand-to-hand fighting. Look after her, Céleste!'

Now, as Charette and his party of cavaliers spurred their horses forward to meet the oncoming troopers, his voice shouted the order, and the waiting peasant guns assaulted the ears with a furious discharge. Then followed absolute panic, as the republican soldiers, fired at from every direction, fell from their horses; while others strove to fire back at their hidden assailants.

'Well, don't just sit there admiring our wily General, Madeleine. Help him with a little target practice,' laughed Céleste de Bulkeley, pouring powder into the breach of her gun. Carefully Madeleine took aim and fired, feeling a cruel glow of satisfaction as she saw the man in her sights reel back in his saddle and fall to the ground. Soon her movements became regular and smooth as she reloaded, aimed and fired.

Gradually, however, the fight came closer as the Avengers strove to break free from the impossible situation they were in. The only means of escape from the relentless fire was through the royalist cavalry blocking each end of the track.

Suddenly, without warning, Madeleine was facing a spearhead of troopers who had broken free. With no time to reload, she thrust her gun back into her sash and withdrew her sword.

'We'll work as a team,' yelled Céleste de Bulkeley. 'Cover my back and I'll take care of yours.' Madeleine nodded, tightening her grip on the hilt of her sword as Victorine du Fief, leading their defence, let out a bloodthirsty scream.

The moment her sword engaged another, a total calm fell upon Madeleine; and a dissociation from the man wielding it. Her hours of practice with Madame du Fief had made her fast, and within seconds she had slashed through the tendons of her opponent's wrist. Then, leaning forward, she lunged at a trooper coming for de Bulkeley's back.

Throughout the fight, the two women maintained their position of horse's head to the other's tail. It provided two lines of attack, two lines of defence and guarded their stirrup legs. At the end of the fight both were unharmed and, though Madeleine was totally exhausted, the revenge she had taken left her with a fierce feeling of exultation.

One day, after another particularly fierce fight, when not a Blue was left alive, Charette picked up the bloodied tricolor and brought it over to her. 'I know at heart you're a patriot, Madeleine. Does it make you sad to see it so?' he asked quietly, so that none might hear.

'Yes, François, it does. At the moment it's being dragged by monsters through a sea of blood.

Whether one is a monarchist or for the Republic, it matters not: we must all fight to rid France of this Terror.'

But their resistance against the Terror was not without cost. Many died, including the Marquis Henri de La Rochejaquelein, and she learnt of it from Charette.

They were camping out within the stone walls of a ruined abbey. It was bitterly cold and everyone was exhausted by the day's march of thirty kilometres. It was not unusual; daily they covered such distances, countermarching until Turreau and his troops were in utter confusion as to their whereabouts.

It was unbelievable what he expected of them, thought Madeleine, watching Charette refuse a handful of crushed wheat. Though she was out of earshot, she knew he would be saying he wasn't hungry. It wasn't true; they were all hungry. Yet no one would say so. No one wanted to see the look of hurt which would cloud the smiling, serene face of their General. For he tried so hard for them all and would see it as his personal failure. As a man he was such a mixture: worldly and sensuous; yet pinned on his coat, above the little brown patch with its red Sacred Heart, was a crucifix and golden medallion inscribed with the words: 'You who complain, consider my suffering.' Was this the source of his inspiration, she wondered, as Charette's strong baritone launched into the first notes of a madrigal? Whatever it was, physically and mentally he inspired even the weakest and most timorous to follow out of love.

Slowly Madeleine walked over to the camp fire and warmed her hands, then handed out some shrivelled frozen root vegetables and bulbs, which she had dug up from the old monks' garden.

Chewing on a bulb herself, she squatted down in front of Charette and leant against his knees, enjoying his singing. Song after song he sang, and sometimes they joined in with him. Until at last he sprang up and clapped his hands. 'Are you cold, *mes amis?*'

'No, no!' protested everyone, knowing what would follow.

'But ladies, you are shivering – come, one dance to warm the blood and your fingers and toes!'

'François, are you never tired?' laughed one of the women, as wearily everyone struggled to their feet.

'Ah, but you'll thank me soon,' he cried gaily, as the pipes began to play.

Later, with a warm, glowing body from her exertions in the dance, Madeleine lay down in Charette's arms under a sheepskin. Like so, she was always reminded of the nights she had sheltered with La Rochejaquelein: it was then Charette told her.

'There, there, *chérie*,' he whispered, holding her tight. 'Henri would not wish you to grieve,' he said, trying to calm the flood of sorrow and guilt.

'I couldn't help loving you more,' she choked, her words muffled against Charette's chest, thinking of the hurt she had caused in abandoning the young Vendéan.

'It is the way of love,' murmured Charette. 'La Rochejaquelein was one of our bravest leaders. La Vendée will always remember him. He has saved hundreds from death and he was shot in treachery by a prisoner he had given grace to. We must honour his vow, "*Si je meurs, vengez-moi*".'

But some grief Madeleine bore alone. Later, when others laughed with joy, she shed secret tears alone for her friends in Paris. Georges Danton, King of the Cordeliers, who was guillotined. Camille Desmoulins and pretty Lucille, mourning for him, were also guillotined. Madeleine's heart was set fast on revenge.

Under Charette's leadership they became expert exponents of the ambuscade. Painstakingly he chose his ground and time. The life was exhausting. He demanded so much of them; taking for granted that others possessed his endurance. Nor did the Blues' numerical supremacy prove to be an advantage, for Charette refused to be drawn by the Blues or the elderly chevaliers in his army who thought along the traditional concepts of war.

'No, we'll make them fight our style of war,' he would say firmly.

Time and time again they slipped away from Haxo's frustrated columns or, hidden, watched admiringly the manoeuvres of what often looked like tin soldiers. As the incendiary columns left their trail of fire, so the flames of hatred spread: royalists and patriots alike gathered information for the little army. Soon they knew thousands more soldiers were being sent in. Troops of the line under General Haxo were going to encircle them.

'Are they expecting us to go down and play with them, François?' laughed Céleste de Bulkeley one morning when the Republicans were preparing for battle. 'See, they've even brought a band, but it's not cheering up these grim-faced gentlemen.'

From the ridge where they were looking down on the enormous republican army, Madeleine followed the direction of Céleste's hand. 'Those grim-faced men, Céleste, are Representatives of the People. I expect they're here to see our demise,' commented Charette with a mischievous smile. 'Well, ladies, do not disappoint our friends. They've all heard how beautiful you are. The least you can do is acknowledge them.'

Moving forward, Madeleine, Céleste and Madame

434

du Fief rode to the very edge of the ridge. Then, in unison, they took out their blunderbusses and fired; after which they swept off their large plumed hats in a dashing salute. Then, with the white banner and its Bourbon lilies, the gentlemen joined them.

Down below, the tricolor plumes swayed as officers and officials looked up. The drums were beating, the grenadiers, the Cuirassiers, the cavalry were waiting.

'What a marvellous sight,' sighed Charette regretfully, then he shrugged. 'Remember gentlemen and ladies, we are foxes. Leave the republican hounds to howl their disappointment. It's time for us to go to earth!'

Turning, they dropped from the skyline and, riding hell for leather, disappeared like the morning mist, seeking the forest of Touvois.

435

Chapter Two

It was spring. The snow had left the trees and hedges, and the landscape, fresh and green, bore the white and pink of May blossom. Somehow they had survived the rigours of winter and the relief on every face was plain, for, though Charette had imbued them with hope, there had been within every heart the niggling thought that, like the Grande Armée at Savenay, they were doomed.

Along with the harsh winter, the brutal General Turreau had gone too; somehow, incredibly, they had totally exhausted him and his troops. Now the black ashes under which he had buried the province were cold, but La Vendée was aflame with hatred. Daily hundreds of new recruits arrived to join Charette and his leaders: Sapinaud, Couëtus, Guérin, Stofflet, Joly and Savin. Combined, these forces numbered nearly 10,000.

Early one morning, when everyone was asleep at their camp at Saint Philbert-de-Grandlieu, Madeleine and Céleste de Bulkeley slipped past their sentries, went down to the shores of the Lac de Grandlieu, and got into a small rowing boat.

'My dear, I had no idea you were so skilled with oars,' marvelled Céleste de Bulkeley, trailing her fingers in the water.

'Tell me that tomorrow, when I've got blisters,'

laughed Madeleine. 'And don't forget to keep a lookout for the Blues.'

'Ah yes, tomorrow! Let us hope our dear Boëtz has something to earn Charette's forgiveness. Once he discovers we've gone, all hell will break loose. Still, it will break his black mood of gloom.'

'I hope so,' said Madeleine. 'I've never seen him so low ... though I can't think a new coat from his tailor is going to help him forget Challans.'

'You don't know your man,' laughed the grey-eyed blonde. 'The defeat at Challans is only a temporary setback. I know he wanted to shine before the Prince's emissary and he feels humiliated that the Blues sent us packing; but he is the eternal optimist. You'll see, the moment he throws away his blood-stained, winter-worn clothes for the new velvet and lace, he'll be talking of tomorrow, and not thinking of yesterday. Besides,' she added thoughtfully, 'the Chevalier Tinténiac is no fool: he saw the ferocity of our attack, and recognised the strength of the republican defence. No, he'll report favourably to the Prince.'

At her words, Madeleine gave a vicious pull on the oars which sent the boat hurtling forward. Like her grief for Georges Jacques Danton, she had to keep her thoughts about the Prince to herself. Every day her gallant friends risked their lives for the prisoner in the Temple; and what were his uncles risking? Nothing! They had done nothing to assist their supporters at Granville; would they keep their promises any better now? Madeleine frowned with anxiety, remembering Charette's trust and happiness when the envoy arrived.

'At last, a Prince of the royal blood acknowledges we have a rebellion,' he'd confided. 'And he and Provence, the Regent, wish to fight by our side.'

'But do they mean it, François?' she had asked.

'You've been fighting for over a year and they didn't appear.'

'Yes,' he replied with a sigh. 'Their presence has always been important, but now it's essential. If they will come to lead in the name of Louis XVII, Brittany, Normandy and Maine will rise. Over 300,000 Frenchmen will fall in behind our banners. All we need the British to do is to land the Comte d'Artois with 10,000 émigrés on the Vendéan coast.'

'And what if they should land English troops, would you use them?'

'No! I must make that quite clear to the Chevalier Tinténiac. This is our fight. It must be Frenchmen against Frenchmen.'

He was right, thought Madeleine, pulling more gently on her left oar, and sending the small craft towards a gap between tall rushes on the approaching shore: the last thing we want are English soldiers on French soil.

After concealing their boat from the eyes of republican patrols, Madeleine and her companion set off for Nantes. In their peasant dresses they passed through the republican outposts like the other countryfolk, and entered the tailor's shop safely.

'Ladies,' said the tailor, all smiles. 'If you will follow me upstairs, perhaps you'll accept some refreshment. The door is locked, so we won't be disturbed.'

Intrigued, Madeleine followed the short, plump man upstairs. With his spectacles on the end of a pinched nose, a tape measure dangling around his neck and a profusion of pins in his lapel, there was no mistaking his work. Yet in the charming yellow salon it would have been hard to place his trade; except for one item which she noticed hidden behind a screen.

'So you've found it straight away,' laughed the

tailor, returning to the salon with a tray. 'I have what every soldier dreams of capturing: Le Grand Brigand.'

'Monsieur?'

'It's a dummy made to the exact measurements of our dear General,' laughed the tailor at Madeleine's puzzled air. 'So you could say I have Charette here.'

'Well, I hope you've something under the white cover to cheer him up. You know we tried to take Challans,' said Céleste de Bulkeley.

'Yes, I heard. The republicans were forewarned. Hundreds of reserves were rushed in. I couldn't get word to the General in time.'

The tailor turned to refill Madeleine's glass. 'I hope, Mademoiselle, that you are enjoying wearing my velvet.'

'You mean the length of golden-brown?' enquired Madeleine.

'What else? The moment you walked into my shop I knew to whom it had gone. I only wish I could have made it up for you. Still I can take your measurements now. Please, don't refuse me, it is an honour to serve ladies as brave as you. Besides, you may all be needing new gowns soon.'

'Why so?' asked Céleste, peeping under the white covering on the dummy.

'Well, Robespierre can't last for ever,' said the tailor, lifting away the dummy. 'One by one the monsters gobble each other up. People are tired of bloodshed ... the guillotine no longer amuses.' Setting down the headless figure, he removed the cover with a flourish. 'There, what do you think? It's been ready for quite some time.'

'It's magnificent!' said Madeleine, touching the heavy gold epaulette on the jacket of hunting green. 'Why, this gold thread embroidery is exquisite.'

'I'm glad you think so,' said Boëtz, beaming with

pride, almost caressing the red brocade collar and cuffs.

'I think he might forgive us,' laughed Céleste, 'especially if there are silk breeches and a new cravat.'

'Naturally I have a complete outfit ready for the chevalier,' replied the dignified little man, his pride evidently ruffled, 'including the soft leather boots he loves so.'

'Ah, my dear Flamand, forgive me!' cooed Madame de Bulkeley. 'Now what can you tempt us with? What are they wearing in Paris, for we are quite out of touch!'

Immediately recovering his humour, Boëtz nodded and walked across to a heavy oak table on which was a large box.

For the next hour all thoughts of war disappeared as Madeleine and her companion handled lengths of the finest muslin they had ever seen. 'Why, Céleste, I've never seen such material. It's like the wings of dragonflies. Surely, Monsieur, it's for a fichu?'

'One would think so,' agreed the tailor, pushing up his spectacles on his shiny dome of a forehead, 'but I think you will find the dressmakers on the rue Saint-Honoré will create a new line with these materials from India. Let us hope it will herald a new liberty for us all.'

After making their goodbyes to the tailor, Madeleine and Céleste made to leave the city. Madeleine was relieved to go. The remembrance of the Entrepôt and the sight of Bouffay prison filled her with terror. As they passed its grim walls and the guillotine falling and rising on that day's batch of victims, Madeleine knew she had been right not to visit Suzanne Guillet. All she could hope was that her brief residence with Suzanne had not endangered her, and that she and Thomas had found a decent home for the little boy, Armand.

For a little while in the delightful yellow salon they'd escaped from grim reality and giggled together at the prospect of wearing anything so revealing as the new fabrics. But the next day, seeing the guillotine at work, knowing that the sentries at the post had only to lift up the coils of rope on their baskets to see clothes that only one man would wear, they both moved with caution. If caught, they might be lucky to die; they were more likely to be tortured in an attempt to discover the whereabouts of Charette.

'Are you making an early escape from Nantes?' an impudent voice suddenly called. Startled, both women looked around apprehensively.

'God protect us, it's a republican sergeant!' gasped Céleste de Bulkeley.

Trying to conceal her fear, Madeleine stood still and smiled broadly as the horseman drew close.

'Yes, there's nothing to keep us here. We sold our goods yesterday and spent our money, too,' she said, patting her basket.

'Well, as you're early birds, you can have the benefit of a lift – hop on one of those wagons.'

'Oh no, it's quite all right, really,' demurred Madeleine, her agitation increasing.

'Don't be shy now,' grinned the soldier. 'Who wants to walk when they can ride – get on before I change my mind!'

Anxiously, the two friends darted a look at each other and moved towards the wagon which the soldier was pointing at, for there seemed little else to do without arousing suspicion.

'At least we'll pass every sentry post,' muttered Céleste, as she sat on a sack of grain. 'Look out. Here comes your admirer again.'

'Where are you bound, girls?'

'Les Brouzils.'

'Well, it's your lucky day. We're going to Montaigu,' he said cheerily.

'What possessed you, Céleste?' asked Madeleine, when the soldier was out of hearing. 'Les Brouzils is right out of our way.'

'I'm sorry, it just popped out.'

'Well, we can slip down when no one is looking,' said Madeleine.

'I don't hold much hope of that,' replied Céleste wryly. 'Our trooper is much too interested in those pretty legs of yours. All we can hope for is an ambush.'

But there was no ambush and the opportunity to slip from the wagon never arose. Highly nervous, fearing every moment an attack by the Grand Brigand, the escort was constantly on the alert. Whilst the further south they travelled, the more attentive became Madeleine's admirer. For her part, Madeleine responded to his regard with wide-eyed admiration, answering coyly in the broad local dialect which Jacques at The Cordelier had taught her. So thick was her accent that the trooper, she saw with a smile, had the greatest difficulty in understanding her.

By the time Montaigu appeared in the evening twilight, both parties felt the journey a huge success. The sergeant felt certain of having the firm young buttocks beneath him that night. Whilst, by flattery and subtle questions, Madame de Bulkeley had extracted the date and destination of the next convoy out from Nantes. But it was what he said as he dismounted to help them down from the wagon which made their hearts beat in alarm. Quite politely the Blue reached up for their heavy baskets and helped down Céleste, but with Madeleine, instead of releasing her, slyly, with familiarity, he swung her down against his chest. Retaining his hold, he grinned at her, his close-set eyes glinting with lust. 'Better stay here tonight, sweetheart. It's dangerous for women to wander the countryside alone. Let's have some fun, there'll be plenty to drink and eat. And tomorrow we can drop you by Les Brouzils on our way to the forest of Gralas. We're going to catch the fox in his lair,' he chuckled boastfully.

Somehow Madeleine managed to hide her dismay, her thoughts racing wildly. Seductively she parted the pouting fullness of her lips as though she were about to kiss him. Through her lowered lashes she saw him start. 'I'd like that,' she sighed softly, pressing herself against his body, 'but my sister and I must return home tonight. We have an elderly mother. You understand, with so many brigands roaming the countryside, how mothers fret, but if you could escort us there, well I'd be very grateful. You could rest for a few hours in my bedroom.'

The sergeant's small eyes gleamed as he took her meaning and his ruddy face became even redder, but as he let her slip to the ground, he looked uneasily over his shoulder. 'It's not possible for me to leave,' he said.

'Oh, come on, sergeant,' said Madame de Bulkeley, divining Madeleine's intention. ''Tis but a little way. Who's to know? Don't you have the authority to borrow one of your men's horses?' she taunted.

Whether he had or not, the sergeant, wishing to appear in the most favourable light before the admiring golden-eyed sister, hurried over to his men. 'I'll be shot for this,' he grumbled, returning with two horses. 'I only hope you'll be properly grateful.'

'You can count on it, sergeant,' smiled Madeleine as the man leapt up behind her on the saddle.

At a brisk trot the little party crossed the bridge over the Maine. Now that he had made his decision, and being in such close proximity to Madeleine, the soldier was in high spirits. Riding some paces behind, as though to give them privacy, Céleste de Bulkeley hummed the 'Ça ira'.

'Tell your sister not to do that,' said the sergeant, nervously. 'These woods are full of brigands; we don't want to bring them down on our heads.'

For a while they rode on in silence. Impatiently, Madeleine waited for Céleste to strike as the sergeant's advances became more bold. Already his hand was clumsily groping under her blouse. Nauseated, she pushed it away.

'Later,' she whispered promisingly. 'We'll soon be there, then I'll really spoil you, soldier.'

'Well, I don't see why you can't start now,' he complained. 'It would make the ride far more interesting.'

'Oh no, not with my sister so near,' she giggled, wondering what was delaying Céleste. They were now in isolated countryside: it was ideal. Had she understood what she was meant to do?

As though in answer to her question, the man behind her suddenly groaned, the full weight of his body slumped against her back, and his hands fell from the reins.

'At your service, Mademoiselle,' smiled Madame de Bulkeley, riding alongside. 'Knowing how sensitive you can be to killing, my dear Madeleine, I resisted the temptation of putting a bullet through his disgusting head.' With a sigh, she lowered the raised gun butt and, leaning sideways, pushed the trooper so that he fell off the horse.

Quickly, Madeleine slid to the ground and, with Céleste's help, lashed each of their baskets to the cruppers of the horses.

'The last thing we want is to lose François's jacket,' joked the blonde, pulling on the basket to test its security. 'He'll be furious enough when he hears about tomorrow's search.'

'Do the Blues know for certain there is a camp in Gralas?' asked Madeleine.

'Yes, I think they've suspected it for a long time. They've tried many times to find it. It sounds as though they may have found a guide . . . No peasant would betray us for money . . . they must have used other means of persuasion.'

'At least no one is there.'

'Quite, but there is ammunition – damn, it was so secure there. We must get back to Charette as soon as possible, he may wish to try a diversion.'

Before departing, Madeleine, being the taller of the two, slipped on the unconscious trooper's uniform. They intended to steer well clear of villages, but in the event of bumping into a Blue patrol, perhaps the disguise might help them bluff their way out of danger.

They rode northwards in the direction of Vieillevigne. The going was extremely tough and Madeleine, like Céleste, put her faith in her horse's natural instincts. Although at times, in alleys of dripping darkness, down steep ravines beside the froth and thunder of waterfalls, it was necessary to dismount and pull their quivering steeds on.

At last, just as the birds started to announce the dawn, they reached the river Boulogne which flowed between them and the royalists' camp at Saint Philbert-de-Grandlieu.

'Shall we ride further down and look for a place to ford?' asked Madame de Bulkeley.

'No,' shouted Madeleine, 'it's quicker to try here. Give me the rest of the rope. We'll tie one end to a tree trunk and the other around my waist and if the current is strong I won't be swept away. Then it'll give you a line to cross by. Don't look so worried,

Céleste,' she laughed. 'Remember you're with a swimmer! Oh, one last thing – be sure not to drop François's clothes in the water!'

With the rope knotted securely around her waist and made fast to an oak, Madeleine kicked her horse forward and slithered down the river bank. The impact took her breath away as the icy water surged over the lower part of her body. Desperately she clung on to the saddle as the water swirled about and the current began to pull the floundering horse sideways.

'Come on boy, steady!' she said, trying to calm the struggling animal, but they were moving fast and she felt the rope spinning out behind. 'Come on, swim!' she screamed, slapping the horse's flanks. With a loud snort the animal steadied itself and, turning its head, plunged forward towards the opposite bank.

The moment her mount launched itself ashore, the rope around Madeleine's waist began to tighten. Swiftly, she pulled on the reins and halted, and for a while looked for somewhere to attach the line. But as every tree of substance was out of reach, she decided the only means of holding the line steady for Céleste was to tie it to the saddle, and let the horse take the strain. So, dismounting, she fumbled with the knot at her waist, striving to undo it with her cold, icy fingers. So absorbed was she in her task, she did not hear the approach of horses until they were encircling her.

Their riders were a frightening sight: wild and dishevelled, their eyes glaring with hatred.

'Prepare for Hell, you republican dog,' snarled a young man, levelling his gun at Madeleine.

'No, it's too quick,' cried another. 'If he's a scout, we'll make him sing first. String him up by his heels.'

With a blow which sent her reeling to the ground, Madeleine felt a rope being tied around her ankles.

Mute with fear, she tried to speak as, upside down, her body was suddenly hoisted up into the air. For a moment she swung back and forth, and the large blue eyes under shaggy blond eyebrows confronted hers.

'I'm going to rid you of a hand first, in memory of my mother,' snarled the youth who had threatened her. He thrust the gun into Madeleine's face and then he moved away.

'No, wait,' she screamed, at last finding her voice. But it was too late, there was the report of a gun; she screamed and waited for the pain to start, but there was no sensation. Only the continuing feeling of coldness in her hand. Perhaps it was as the wounded described, one doesn't always feel the bullet.

'Why, it's Madame de Bulkeley,' a man's voice cried.

'And that is no lad,' laughed another, as Madeleine's cap finally dropped away. 'Cut her down quickly.'

By the time Madelèine's pounding senses cleared, Céleste de Bulkeley, surrounded by the mass of armed men, was laughing and chattering to the one she had obviously disarmed.

'I do hope they won't pain you too long,' she said, as her victim sucked his fingertips, more with injured pride than hurt.

'Well, I'll say this, Madame, you are certainly a fine shot.'

'Just tell Madame du Fief,' chuckled the blonde.

'And you, Mademoiselle Fleury,' he said, looking down at Madeleine, who felt as weak as a baby. 'Don't ever wear a trooper's uniform if you wish to live. Oh, and ladies, a further word of warning. The General is in a fearful rage.'

Chapter Three

François-Athanase Charette de la Contrie rose from his camp bed and stalked proudly towards Madeleine and Céleste de Bulkeley. His expression was as cold as ice and his brows met in a black threatening line. Worse, the small nerve pulsing near his tightly compressed lips forewarned of an imminent explosion.

'So, you decided to return?'

'Yes, we . . . er,' faltered Madeleine.

'Before you give me your explanation, I hope you will consider how greatly you have let me down. By breaking the rules of camp you endangered every man, woman and child under my protection and you endangered and wasted the time of those I ordered to search for you. Do you have any conception of what would have happened to you if you'd been taken? You would have betrayed our position before they killed you.'

'No, never!' cried Madeleine.

'Yes, Mademoiselle! You have seen what they can do. Now if either of you ever disobey our rule again, I will have you shot!'

'My dear General,' said Céleste in a faint voice, 'you know we would follow you to Hell and back. But . . . there are times when, as a woman of fashion, I must keep in touch with what is happening in the world. You mustn't blame Madeleine, it was I who persuaded her. Please, François, forgive me.'

'Céleste,' protested Madeleine, unwilling to let the older woman take the blame; but ignoring her, Madame de Bulkeley walked over to the wicker baskets.

'It was Madeleine's idea while we were in Nantes to call in at your tailor's. By good fortune, dear loyal Flamand had this ready for you.' Smiling now, sensing the moment of crisis was over, Céleste held up the magnificent green tunic.

Silently Charette looked at the luxurious clothes the two women were happily displaying. Still his face was grave, but his black eyes, which but a moment before had been narrowed in anger, were now large and lustrous. Visibly moved, he picked up the velvet jacket and touched the gold embroidery on the red collar. Then the curious inverted bow of his mouth lifted into the sweetest smile.

'My dear friend,' he murmured, lifting Céleste's hand to his mouth, 'this is not the first time you've risked your life in order to give me pleasure. It grieves me to see someone so lovely denied of elegance; enduring the privations of our nomadic life.'

'Nonsense, François,' replied Madame de Bulkeley, her face pink with pleasure. 'A gilded salon would be dull indeed. All I require is your forgiveness.'

'That you have willingly, so long as you never endanger yourself again.'

Watching them as they tenderly embraced, Madeleine could not help but feel a stab of jealousy. But she brushed it aside for she loved them both and understood the feelings which bound comrades together.

'And you, *chérie*,' he said, turning and taking her

into his arms, 'it is not the first time you have placed yourself in danger for me. Never, never leave me again!' he whispered, pressing his warm lips against hers.

The news that General Vimeaux – the Republic's new commander-in-chief – intended to search for their camp in the forest of Gralas threw Charette into a furious temper. Watching him flexing and warming up the muscles of his sword arm, Madeleine was relieved they had kept this news till last.

One by one his officers filed in for their briefing. 'Gentlemen,' he said, holding up his hands for silence. 'A few days ago, a party of republicans, waving the white flag, tried to parlay with a patrol of Couëtus. They endeavoured to persuade them to lay down their arms, to put their trust in the Republic! Quite!' remarked Charette drily, as hoots of laughter met his words. 'We have replied to this General Vimeaux. We have told him that until a king sits on the throne of France, until our priests and people are free to practise their faith, we will never lay down our arms! Madame Bulkeley and Mademoiselle Fleury have reported that Gralas is to be searched. If we have been betrayed, the village is lost to us. We will have to find somewhere else.'

'But where, General? Nearly every village and town has been burnt.'

'I know,' replied Charette sadly, 'but our cause is just. We will find somewhere. What we must show is our determination. Their swords and fire have not defeated us. False promises are more dangerous. We must hold fast for God and King. Today we will strike Légé. It belongs to us!'

To take Légé, defended by the troops of the line, was madness, thought Madeleine. But then they were all mad, she decided, looking at Madame du Fief and Madame de Bulkeley riding each side of her. Their faces, glowing with excitement, mirrored the expressions of the cavaliers surrounding them. And behind, proud in their uniforms, came the army, each face under its white-cockaded black hat confident and fearless.

The source of this madness rode ahead. Visually he dominated all. The tips of the white Bourbon plumes could be seen fluttering above the tall crown of his hat, whilst the cut and elegance of Boëtz's hussar-type jacket emphasised the straightness of the chevalier's back. With a mass of lace at throat and wrist, his muscular legs encased in silk breeches and soft, brown-topped black boots, it was not hard to see why the sober Protestant Stofflet viewed him with suspicion and jealousy. Yet even the leader of Haut Poitou had to acknowledge that beneath the trappings of finery was a warrior of steel.

No, it was more than lace and velvet. Just to be near him, even the sight of him, calm and smiling, infused everyone with hope and the courage to rise above bodily needs. This was what had sustained them throughout the winter. He was like thunder and sun. And now, thankfully, the sun shone and everyone was basking in the warmth, as merry as if riding to a fête.

Certainly, they would not be out of place at one, she thought, touching the soft, creamy ostrich feather on her large brown hat. 'Don't worry, Mademoiselle Fleury, you look magnificent!' cried Prudent de la Robrie, riding up from his cavalry. Madeleine laughed with pleasure. The brown hat and dress were the perfect foil for her colouring. The sun had lifted strands of her hair to gleaming gold and tinged her skin with a light tan. Over her eyes the velour brim cast its shadow, making them seem darker and mysterious, whilst her soft, full lips were rivalled only by the luscious curves of her body. She was teeming with health and happiness, and seeing Charette's eyes earlier, when she had given him a lace kerchief for luck, she knew she had been made for the King of the Marais and he for her.

They moved south: crossing over the river Logne to gain the route to Nantes and then the heights of Blignière.

Like skilled poachers, the sharpshooters glided through the trees and found their positions, whilst the infantry, armed with billhooks and scythes, moved forward in column. Ranged around Charette and the colours were the chevaliers, ready to launch the attack. For a moment there was the faint sound of leaves rustling in the summer breeze and bird song. Then Charette's cry, 'For God and Louis XVII.'

The earth shuddered as their six-pounder launched a shot. Eight hundred voices emitted an ear-piercing scream and at a gallop the fleur-de-lys swooped down on Légé. From her vantage point, Madeleine could see the Blue sentries panicking, many dropping their guns and racing from the barricades back into the town. Within seconds the republican call to arms rang out and a defending column of Blues marched out to support their hard-pressed soldiers.

Spurring on her horse to where Charette was directing the fire, Madeleine saw there were now literally thousands of troops pouring out of the town.

'Had you anticipated such numbers?' she yelled to make herself heard.

'No,' answered Charette, his black eyes gleaming. 'And their entrenchments and fortifications are new. They seem very determined to retain their hold on *my* town,' he grinned. 'Tell the ladies to bring up their stone-thrower.'

Wheeling her horse around, Madeleine galloped back to the waiting women and waved them forward. Guiding them to a position which would do the most damage to the lines of the republican infantry, she dismounted, and together with Marie Lourdais and Prudence and Henriette, she passed along the stones to fill the sling. Their first throw fell short. So, heaving and pushing, they moved the wooden machine closer. Compared with cannon it was primitive, but it did the job of killing. Already the Blue artillery was returning a retaliatory hail of fire, but not one woman moved until every missile was fired.

Clearly the battle was not going their way, for many of their 800 were lying dead or wounded, and Madeleine estimated there must be near on 4,000 Blues. Following the other women, she picked up a stretcher. Together they ran out on to the field and picked up their wounded. It was hard work ferrying the wounded back and forth to the ambulance wagons at the rear of the lines. They were under fire throughout, and the men were heavy and often in terrible pain. As they set forth on another trip she heard, above the din of battle, a man's voice. 'Aid to Charette,' he cried.

At once she dropped her end of the stretcher, terror possessing her. Ahead was a riderless horse and she sprinted towards it, hurling herself up into the saddle. Unsheathing her sword, she felt consumed with a fierce savagery which lent her a strength she had never known. Her man was in danger and no one would stop her reaching the waving ostrich plumes.

'Aid to Charette! *Vive Charette!*' she cried to galvanise more support. At a wild, erratic gallop, swerving and evading Blue uniforms, she reached their colours.

Guarding Charette's back was Pheiffer, who stood fighting, surrounded by a pile of republican dead. Fighting beside Charette, holding off at least a dozen hussars, was the wild, independent Guérin. To Madeleine's amazement, she saw that, in the midst of this danger, both men were laughing like school-boys. Suddenly Guérin cried out as a hussar lashed out with the butt of his gun.

'Ah, my friend,' cried Charette, with lightning reflexes, dealing the hussar a tremendous blow, 'that was mine!'

Losing consciousness, Guérin slumped forward as the men of Bas-Poitou surged forward to the support of the two chevaliers.

Légé was not taken, but there was no dishonour in defeat. The ferocity of their attack had justified the excessive precautions the Blues had taken to defend the town. It told everyone in the army, too, how effective their resistance was and how much they were feared.

For Madeleine it was a disappointment, she had wanted a glimpse into the past; to relive with Char-ette his happy days at the court of Légé.

The discovery of the camp in the forest of Gralas by General Vimeaux's adjutant, General Ferrand, was a terrible blow. Whilst it was possible to replace the impounded ammunition and stores with raids on republican convoys, it was imperative to find another base and shelter for the women and children before winter came.

Mercifully, Belleville was waiting for them and they found it together. On a hot, airless day, slipping away from the others, Madeleine and Charette sought the relief of the Boulogne. In the crystal-clear river, they cooled off, floating aimlessly on their backs, letting the water lap over their bodies.

'Did you know I was once a tight-rope walker on the Pont-Neuf?' she teased, gazing up at a network of tender young leaves.

'Really! Then you should have no difficulty following me,' laughed Charette, pushing her head under water. Spluttering and choking with laughter, Madeleine saw as she surfaced that Charette had reached the bank and had started to climb a tree. Swiftly she hurled herself forward in pursuit, realising what he intended to do. As a child she had scaled alley walls and trees in the Bois de Boulogne with Pierre, so the gnarled oak proved no problem. Already Charette was balancing on the outflung branch which partly spanned the river. He had reached the delicate stage where the branch narrowed and began to dip with his weight. With her arms outstretched, Madeleine ran forward lightly on her toes and pushed. At once Charette, unbalanced, fell but, quick as lightning, he twisted and grabbed hold of her ankle. Shrieking out loud they fell together into the cold water below. 'Come on, let's do it again!'

'No, my little mermaid,' he said, hauling her back. 'you're coming with me. I have other plans for you.'

'But I have my own plans, Chevalier,' she laughed, breaking free and swimming towards the bank. Laughing, they both scrambled up the grassy slope, and Madeleine ran off to climb the tree again. As she reached up for the lowest bough, Charette grabbed her waist from behind. His hands, sliding upwards, found her breasts. Sinuously she leaned back, her lips parted, her eyes closed as his hands massaged and stroked, making her breasts swell full with desire. He pressed her close against him and she exclaimed with excitement, feeling the hard line of his body. Swiftly he spun her round and clamped his mouth on hers in the fiercest of kisses. 'Ah, you are a savage!' she moaned, feeling the rough bark graze her back as he lifted her up to him.

'And you are going to kill me,' he retorted through clenched teeth.

As the hot rays of the sun burnt into Madeleine's satiated body, she sighed contentedly and nuzzled up against Charette. 'I wish every day could be like today,' she sighed, languorously.

'Have patience, *ma petite*. One day we'll live in my lovely manor of Fonteclose, and every day will be filled with hunting and dancing. But for the moment we must find a new headquarters; and I think, Mademoiselle, it's even more urgent to remove your pretty derrière into the shade. It's becoming very pink, and you'll not seat a saddle with any pleasure.

Through her eyelashes, Madeleine squinted up at the sun, red as an assassin's gown – like the one Charlotte Corday would have worn to the guillotine. If only she had had her resolve and courage, had struck down Carrier, hundreds would still be alive. But then, of course, she would not have seen this lovely day or ever known the joy of the last few months.

Half-regretting, half-relieved, they dressed and, forsaking the sun-drenched bank for the cool and shady trees in the woods of Essart, they rode towards the Chemin de Palluau. So absorbed were they in conversation that they unintentionally found themselves on the Salligny road leading into Belleville. Recklessly, they ventured further into the bourg.

'Why, it's completely intact. Not one house has been burnt,' remarked Madeleine in surprise, as they rode together along the main street.

'Yes,' answered Charette, looking around with delight. 'Evidently the avengers overlooked this charming little spot. We have found our new head-quarters, my little republican. This will be our new Légé!'

456

The move to Belleville was filled with happiness. The Manor of Jarriette was chosen for Charette's headquarters, but Madeleine had other ideas as well for their general. Across its large courtyard, nestling amongst trees, was a small pavilion. 'Oh do let me have it, François,' she pleaded, her heart singing at the prospect of them having their own little house.

'But it's filthy and vermin-ridden ... But if it makes you happy,' he said with a smile, 'it shall be your Trianon.'

'No, that would be unlucky,' she said hastily. 'I shall simply call it the Pavilion.'

'Well, so long as you don't make it too grand, my love. Remember I live and eat as my brothers-in-arms.'

It felt just like when she'd taken over The Cordelier in the Faubourg Saint-Antoine, only more so. Every minute of her day, and even at night, her thoughts dwelt on refurbishing the little building. With the help of Prudence and Henriette she threw out timber, broken bits of furniture and scrubbed floorboards, walls and ceilings. One morning she even found Pheiffer up a ladder mending a hole in the roof.

Her Pavilion for General Charette amused and interested everyone, as though by its establishment a permanency, a stability would enter all their lives. They were all weary of the nomadic life. Belleville was perfect: it was as if it had been slumbering, waiting for them. Ideally placed in the centre of their operations, it would reinforce Charette's speedy mode of warfare.

For strangers, it was virtually inaccessible: it was surrounded by vast areas of desolate marshland; hidden to the south-east and north by a seemingly endless belt of trees and to the west by expanses of uncultivated land. At the vulnerable spots, Charette placed his battery of guns: at the north-west, and at the meeting of the three roads of Saint-Denis, Salligny and Lucs. Here also entrenchments and a high palisade were erected to block entry into the town.

This new-found security did not lessen Charette's expectations of his small army. There was training and drilling and reviews on the square outside the church. Up and down the ranks he rode, his sharp eyes examining each man. At other times he would be closeted away with his secretary, Auvynet, or abbé Remaud.

As the weeks sped by, so, too, Madeleine found her duties increasing. Like Légé, Belleville became known as a safe haven. Weekly the sentries brought to her young ladies seeking sanctuary and chevaliers offering their swords to Charette. It fell on her to find them accommodation and to make them feel welcome. Every week there were dances and fêtes to organise as well as dinners in honour of invited guests of Charette. For all the revels the fare was simple and basic. There was no crystal, silver or porcelain at table; but there was music and laughter, there was conversation, a repartee she had never experienced before. Not like the heated debate of the old Cordelier quarter or the sober conversations of La Rochejaquelein and his officers. This was fast and frothy, where only wit survived.

With the increasing influx of newcomers, it was rare she found herself alone with Charette during the day, but Madeleine accepted this; nor did she feel jealous watching him, as now, surrounded by a group of young women vying for his attention. He loved to flirt. A stranger might take him for a court dandy in his lace and velvet and by his polished, frivolous dalliance; but, like a diamond, he had many facets and, though he revealed a few to her alone, Madeleine doubted she would ever completely know this complicated man. There would always be new surprises.

July was marked with celebrations, when a courier brought news of Robespierre's execution. 'Let us hope the Parisians will follow it up by finishing off that fiend, Carrier,' remarked a Vendéan.

With the ending of the Terror, Charette increased the intensity of attacks against the republicans. Their couriers and convoys went out through the wooded countryside in fear of their lives. Very few ever made it to their destinations. On 6 September the republican camp of La Roullière was taken and burnt to the ground. Next followed the camp of Frérigné. The fighting was bloody and the peasants, losing control, massacred almost every Blue. A few days later the camp of des Moutiers was also seized.

Throughout the autumn and the first chill winds of winter, the countryside belonged to the Whites. It was extraordinary so few could dominate so many; yet living at Belleville it was easy to see why. Charette had welded them into a cohesive force. They were trained: every man knew what to do and believed in what he was doing. Impassable and threatening as the countryside might be for the Blues, for them marsh and forests were the allies who masked their attack and shielded their retreat. Added to this, Charette was a perfectionist: his mischievous sense of daring and razor-sharp, swift mental agility made him, as generalissimo directing operations, the deadliest of foes.

One day, just as Madeleine – together with Charette and a few others – was about to eat in the dining room of the Manor of Jarriette, the distant howl of a sentry was heard. A little later the warning was louder, as it was taken up further along the line. 'Strangers approaching,' remarked Charette's uncle, Fleuriot.

'No matter, be seated,' remarked Charette. 'If it's anyone of importance we'll soon know.'

Following his example, everyone sat down, and had barely taken a few mouthfuls of soup when the door burst open. 'Forgive me, General,' cried Hyacinthe de la Robrie, striding up to Charette. 'I have brought here gentlemen wishing to speak with you. One of them is a Representative of the People.'

'Indeed,' said Charette calmly, 'then show these gentlemen in.'

Fascinated, wondering what it meant, Madeleine fixed her eyes on the door. Two visitors entered the room, with Pheiffer following close on their heels like a great shaggy dog. As Hyacinthe had forewarned, one wore the tricolor plumed hat of an officer of the Republic. With him was a civilian, an imposing elderly man with grey hair, whose skin was brown, mottled with age. It was he who spoke first.

'Monsieur de Charette,' he said, using the old form of address, 'we have come to discuss peace for La Vendée. To prove my good faith, I bring greetings from your sister who is known to me. It was Mademoiselle Charette who arranged for us to meet with an officer at the first outpost so that we could journey safely to discuss with you the pacification of the Vendée. The National Convention wishes for peace.'

'Where is my sister now?' asked Charette eagerly.

'She rests with her companion, Madame Gasnier-Chambon, at Roche-Boulogne.'

'Monsieur,' cried Charette, his face ablaze with joy, 'I beg you remain and enjoy the hospitality of Belleville. Come, Madeleine, I want you to meet my sister.'

Before either of the two strangers could speak, for in truth, like everyone else in the room, they were stunned by Charette's words, he had departed.

'François, wait!' called Madeleine, rushing after

him. 'You can't just leave a Representative of the People who has travelled all this way to discuss peace.'

'Yes I can, for my sister,' he called gaily over his shoulder. 'If they want peace, they'll wait!'

Her eyes were large, black and lustrous like those of her brother, but there the similarity ended. The rest of her features were small and regular. There was no trace of the shoe-like chin, the sharp upturned nose which gave an air of bravado and dash to Charette's face. Here was the balm to soothe the volcanic temperament of the chevalier.

A little apprehensive of her greeting, Madeleine watched brother and sister embrace. 'Only sixteen months,' laughed Charette, lifting his small, dark-haired sister off her feet. 'Why it seems more like years. Come, Marie-Anne, I want you to meet someone dear to my heart.'

'Ah, yes, Mademoiselle Fleury. I'm so happy to meet you, Madeleine – I've heard so much about you,' added Marie-Anne Charette, moving quickly forward and embracing Madeleine as if she were a sister.

'I am pleased to meet you too, Mademoiselle,' said Madeleine, puzzled by the young woman's familiarity, 'but how have you heard of me?'

'Ah, I would embarrass François if I told you that,' Marie-Anne replied with a sweet smile, 'but, of course, there is another gentleman who gave me a detailed account of you . . . Boëtz!' she laughed.

At that moment the door into the salon of the old château at Roche-Boulogne opened. An extremely beautiful woman, whom Madeleine judged to be in her early thirties, entered.

'François, I would like you to meet my protector,

461

Madame Gasnier-Chambon. Madame, my brother, General Charette, and Mademoiselle Fleury.'

'Madame,' said Charette, taking hold of his sister's hand, 'I owe you my sister's life. Words cannot express my gratitude.'

'Then, Monsieur, do not try, for it was only what Marie-Anne would have done for me and what I believe you, Mademoiselle Fleury, did for a little Vendéan child.'

Once again Madeleine expressed her surprise.

'Perhaps you do not know, Mademoiselle, that my apartment is in the Hôtel-Villestreux. One meets many people at Republican headquarters. A certain Monsieur Proust told me about his adopted children, including a little Vendéan boy whose mother had thrown him into the arms of a young woman. This woman, who resided with a friend of his, was subsequently thrown into the Entrepôt when trying to obtain a pardon for the mother. It was you, Mademoiselle, was it not?'

'So,' exclaimed Madeleine, 'Suzanne Guillet kept her word and poor Marguerite's little Armand found a home.'

'Yes, and a good one. I was much moved by Proust's story, and your name stuck in my mind, so when our dear friend Boëtz told Marie-Anne and me of your visit to his shop with Madame de Bulkeley, I decided it must be the same young lady.'

'But tell me, Madame, how can you bear to live in the Hôtel-Villestreux, after Carrier?' asked Madeleine, remembering the sinister atmosphere of the mansion.

'Since Carrier's recall to Paris in February it is much changed, Madeleine. Besides, the screams and laughter of my little daughter, Zizi, have chased all terrors and ghosts away.'

'Yes, from what I hear she should be our top

agent, for I understand she uses the entire house as her playground, including meeting rooms,' laughed Charette.

'Yes, open doors left ajar by little hands can be very useful,' remarked the Creole, for by her easy grace of movement and speech Madeleine identified her as such.

'Now, tell me about the two visitors you sent me,' said Charette, turning to his sister.

'They were sent to you, François, by Ruelle, a Representative of the People in Nantes. He wishes to open a line of communication between you and himself. He is a decent man, François.'

'Yes,' interceded Madame Gasnier. 'I have had many conversations with him in the evenings. Of course, he had no idea I was sheltering your sister as my cook, nor an ex-magistrate as my butler. I became convinced of his desire for peace, so I told him I had the means of contacting you. In short, he agreed that the only way was to send to you someone you completely trusted: your sister. With her, besides an official of the Republic, should be a man of intellect and a neutral known to Marie-Anne as being trustworthy. The obvious choice fell on my footman.'

'Monsieur Bureau de la Bartardière is completely honourable, François. He is neither for the Blues nor Whites, only peace. You must speak with him,' urged Marie-Anne Charette.

For a moment, Charette stared at his sister, then he turned to Madame Gasnier. 'But this man, Ruelle, can he be trusted? Was he not amongst those who voted for the death of the King!'

'Yes, that is correct,' she replied, 'but I have his affection and I know his heart. He speaks ardently of peace, as does General Canclaux.'

'Peace,' mused Charette. Then, as though quickly

weighing up issues in his mind, he strode to the door and flung it open, revealing Pheiffer on guard. 'Tell two of my bodyguards to ride back to Belleville and bring my visitors here.'

For many hours Charette spoke alone with the elderly Breton magistrate and Bertrand Geslin, the Representative of the People. Undoubtedly there would be many on both sides who would do their best to sabotage any early negotiations, so Madeleine offered to return to Nantes. 'Let me do this for you, François,' she argued when they were alone. 'Let Marie-Anne stay with you, enjoy your reunion. If I go with Monsieur de la Bartardière to take your letter there, I can return with Ruelle's reply. My going is less obvious at this stage than your sending ambassadors; besides, they'd never think a mere woman would be entrusted with such a mission,' she said provocatively. 'You need only say I've taken advantage of a safe escort into Nantes for a new dress.'

'I'm not sure, it's dangerous; I don't want to be parted from you,' he said unhappily.

'Please François, let me play a useful part. No one could be more loyal to you,' she said persuasively.

'Even though a republican at heart,' he teased, putting an arm around her shoulder. 'Very well, if it is what you want. But don't delay there a moment longer than necessary, or I shall come and look for you.'

Madeleine was glad Charette consented to her request, and found she easily identified with the ex-magistrate's neutrality. As she, Madame Gasnier and Monsieur de la Bartardière spoke on the rough, difficult journey to Nantes, so many things he said reminded her of Danton. Yet, fearing if she said such a thing he would shrink away from her in horror, she used instead Georges's words as she replied to one of his questions. 'Yes, Monsieur, none of us belongs exclusively to this or that province. We now belong to all of France.'

'Mademoiselle, you are quoting Danton,' smiled the magistrate. 'You are right to do so. Much can be levelled against him, but I truly believe he did save France from the foreign wolves. And now we must try to stop Frenchmen killing Frenchmen. You will see when we arrive at the Hôtel-Villestreux that there are many republicans who wish for this too.'

When Madame Gaşnier led Madeleine into the salon overlooking the Loire to meet the Representative, Ruelle, she could not help but repress a shudder, remembering the scene which had taken place on her first visit to the mansion; but the ex-judge, with a lawyer's knowledge of the human heart and a quick turn of mind, soon established her at her ease – so much so, she found herself speaking of the journey from Paris to the Vendée and from the tricolor to the lilies. He listened attentively, all the while his grey, thoughtful eyes never leaving her face. At last he spoke.

'As a *vainqueur de la Bastille* you are indeed on a different road now, Madeleine, but things cannot stand still, not for us or France. I voted for the death of Louis ... Would I do so now?' he said, sadly shaking his head. 'You have put your love for one man before your love of France. And I think that makes you feel guilty. Yet, that man has saved the honour of your country.'

Surprised by his words, Madeleine looked up sharply. 'How do you mean?'

Ruelle smiled, enjoying, once more, the sound of her low, husky voice. 'Because he prevented the mother eating her baby. He saved La Vendée from total destruction and thus, the honour of the Republic. Now we must bring both sides together and forget past bitterness.'

'But how can the politicians in Paris forget? Or will they let Charette and the other Vendéan leaders disband their armies and then destroy them?'

'No!' replied Ruelle. 'There will be a guarantee: the armistice will apply to the leaders.'

'And what of the émigrés and the priests? Will the armistice cover them as well?' she asked, knowing this was one of Charette's concerns.

Ruelle's grey eyes were averted and she knew her question had embarrassed him. 'That must be discussed as a separate issue,' he murmured. 'We are dealing only with those who took up arms in France.' He rose, indicating that the discussion was at an end. 'I entrust you, Mademoiselle, with this,' he said, handing her a sealed envelope. 'I think I need hardly tell you to guard it with your life. There are many who wish this war to continue.'

Before leaving Nantes, to establish her supposed visit to the town, Madeleine collected some lengths of cloth from the tailor, Boëtz, and a number of the large, red handkerchiefs which the officers, like Charette, wore Creole style under their hats.

Boëtz was not surprised at her visit for, as one of Charette's agents, he was in Madame Gasnier's confidence, but Madeleine had a special request to make of him and, when he heard it, the tailor's gold-rimmed glasses nearly fell off his nose.

'You wish to have such a dress edged with ribbons?' he gasped.

'Yes. Do you have a needlewoman whom you can trust to be absolutely discreet?'

'Is there such a woman?' asked the tailor, with a mischievous smile. 'Whatever it is you wish, Mademoiselle, I will attend to myself. For where fashion is

466

concerned I trust no one . . . and this is obviously a matter of some delicacy. Tell me, will you require this dress soon?'

'Yes, yes, I think quite soon,' replied Madeleine gaily.

Behind the glasses, Flamand's eyes glinted knowingly. 'Then it seems perhaps prudent for me to start work on something appropriate for a generalissimo!' he smiled.

After Madeleine's visit to the Hôtel-Villestreux, events moved quickly and the New Year of 1795 brought the hoped-for armistice. On 9 January, in front of 8,000 republican troops, three Representatives of the People declared the Amnesty of General Canalaux at Nantes. But despite the release of prisoners from the grim prisons, and the freedom to wear the white cockade on the streets of Nantes, the registers opened by the Republic throughout the parishes remained empty of names. Unheeding of their free pardons and compensation for their ruined homes, the men waited steadfastly for their general to sign.

'As General Charette wishes, so do we,' they cried.

He did wish. Madeleine knew from his sleepless nights just how much he wished to end the suffering of his people. The plight of La Vendée was desperate. The peasants were almost starving and so, too, were the citizens of Nantes. Both sides were very anxious for peace. But Charette's ambassadors, the Chevaliers de Brue and Bejarry, negotiating on the issue of the émigré and refractory priests, received only the assurance that the Republic did not wish for their blood. Eventually, realising Charette was not going to give way, the Republicans proposed a meeting between General Canalaux and Charette himself.

* * *

Madeleine stood back and inspected the man who had brought the might of France to the negotiating table. Next to the crucifix and badge of the Sacred Heart, he was pinning on to his jacket the inscribed gold medallion. There was no emotion on his face, but she knew he was tense and nervous. It was not a time for conversation; turning, she picked up his high-crowned hat, pressing her lips against the green ostrich feather of hope pinned next to the Bourbon white and black for mourning. 'Good luck, my darling,' she said softly, passing it to him. 'We're all so proud of you.'

Down below in the courtyard of the Château de la Jaunaye came the sound of restless hooves as 300 chevaliers waited for Charette. Madeleine moved to the window and saw him appear in the new red-trimmed beige coat. With his usual easy grace he mounted his horse beside the banner which she had worked, and the cavalcade moved off.

It was 13 February, the second day of the conference between the republicans and the royalists. Certainly no efforts had been spared to make them comfortable. The château had been furnished with paintings, rugs and beautiful furniture whilst, in the evenings, the wines and food were of the highest quality.

On the first day of the talks, Madeleine, together with Céleste de Bulkeley, Victorine du Fief and Madame de Monsorbier, had positioned herself to watch Charette's entry on to the fields of Gibraye at Lion d'Or on the route between Nantes and Clisson.

The sight had been spectacular. Outside the marquee where the leaders would meet fluttered the tricolor, whilst row upon row of troops, vivid, immaculate in their red, white and blue uniforms, waited at attention. Then the silence was broken by the sound of approaching pipes and cowhorns. The golden lilies of France, the white banners of the Bourbons appeared and beside them rode the man every Blue was waiting to see: the invincible King of the Marais, the Grand Brigand. Through her tears of pride, Madeleine watched the column of mounted peasants ride in behind their officers. Compared to the uniformity of the republican ranks, their appearance was extraordinary. Perhaps a stranger might have laughed aloud to see such nags harnessed with string and twine, but not the youngest drummer boy, not one man in the blue, white and red laughed; for these were the men who, for two years, had stood firm against the finest troops in Europe.

Now the courtyard below was empty, the rest of the day was hers. There was much for her to do, for in the evening they were giving a ball. Amongst their many guests would be all the high-ranking republican officials and families from Nantes. Madeleine wanted everything to be perfect, especially as the bill was eventually to be settled by the Republic. Though the nation need not have incurred such a debt, thought Madeleine, running her finger along the guest list; for such were the eager acceptances, it was clear the Nantais ladies would mortgage their homes to meet and perhaps dance with the Vendée's generalissimo.

Madeleine had kept the dress from Boëtz well hidden, so that no one, not even Charette, should see it; nor did she intend him to see it until she made her grand entrance down the staircase.

'You'll see,' she teased, wearing only a light wrapper when, hours later, he returned. 'It will quite take your breath away.'

'Don't be late down will you, *chérie*? I'm counting on your support. Have you had any problems?' he asked, tying on a fresh cravat.

'No, they sent us everything; except we're short of

bread of course. So I arranged for only the ladies to receive bread rolls.'

'Ah, discrimination,' he laughed, fastening the gold-fringed white sash around his slim waist.

From down below came faint sounds of the orchestra tuning their instruments. Impatiently Madeleine waited for Charette to depart. Then, as soon as the door closed behind him, she rushed to the cupboard and removed the black and gold striped box. Impatiently her fingers shook free the layers of tissue from the folds of the muslin. The dress was indeed breathtaking: the embroidered gold fleurs-de-lys gleamed as if suspended in a night sky, so fine was the midnight-blue material, whilst binding the delicately draped sleeves and neckline and edging the hemline were ribbons – in the colours of the tricolor! Breathless with excitement, Madeleine slipped the diaphanous folds over her head. How skilful Boëtz was, for though this cobweb flowed and caught at her body, Madeleine saw the clever cut and draping had been designed to reveal no more than a tantalising glimpse of her body. 'Monsieur, Paris and the rue Saint-Honoré would be at your feet,' murmured Madeleine, replacing the lid on the box. In doing so she noticed the corner of a flat box submerged beneath the layers of tissue. Wondering why she had not noticed it before, she withdrew it. Inside was a band of white satin, the front of which made her laugh with delight. It was like a tricolor, exquisitely worked with narrow rows of rubies, pearls and sapphires; and in their centre was a large, gold fleur-de-lys.

'It's glorious!' she cried aloud, running across to the mirror. 'But do I wear it around my throat or forehead?' She chose the latter, arranging it so that it caught back the folds of her hair at the temples. Also, in the box, she recalled, had been a card. It was from Boëtz. He'd written just four words, 'To salute your courage'. It did need courage to wear this dress, daring in its line but even more outrageous in its combination of tricolor and Bourbon lilies.

Down below, the sound of wheels on gravel told her it was time to take her place beside Charette. Let the war party think what it liked, she, Madeleine Fleury, was for peace.

Descending the great staircase, she saw that, as luck would have it, three of the most vigorous critics of the negotiations were standing near to Charette, whose impatient upturned glance had directed their attention to her. Others, too, had noticed her and she heard murmurs of admiration as the dark blue dress, clinging, revealed the outline of her long legs and the swell of her breasts. She knew her body was superb and she moved with pride.

As she descended and the design became clearly visible, the murmurs changed to an exalted hum. The faces of Messieurs Poirier de Beauvais, Launay and Moële stared at her with cold hostility. They mattered not to Madeleine, her large golden eyes swept over them disdainfully to find those of Charette. His brows were arched in surprise whilst his expression was a mixture of disbelief and amused irritation. Then he threw back his curly black head and laughed. 'I see, Mademoiselle Fleury, you have already made our minds up for us. Perhaps you are party to information I have not yet had,' he said, taking her arm.

From those who feared an outburst, there was relieved laughter. Then a cool voice spoke out. 'The dress is quite charming, Mademoiselle, and must have taken considerable time to make – perhaps during the long winter evenings at Belleville, in anticipation of this day? It does bear out my suspicions that we have not been brought here for our opinions, but merely for our signatures.'

'Oh, that I possessed such skill with a needle,' retorted Madeleine. 'Even so, Monsieur, because one prepares for summer, it does not necessarily follow the sun will shine!'

Beside her Charette's face was still angry as he glared at the man Launay, and she felt his hand tremble on her arm as he fought to control his temper. Nervously Launay stepped back, but with a disdainful shrug of his shoulders Charette turned away from him. 'Come, Madeleine. You symbolise the hopes of both parties! You shall greet our guests.'

Like her dress, the evening was a brilliant success. Introduced by Ruelle as a *vainqueur de la Bastille*, known by all to be Charette's mistress, the symbolism she had dared to introduce on her gown filled the Nantais guests with optimism.

'So, General Charette is anxious for peace, Mademoiselle Fleury?' queried a merchant, interrupting a conversation Madeleine was having with a group of young ladies.

'As much as all of us, Monsieur. It grieves him to see the people starving and homeless.'

'Yes, things are desperate indeed,' agreed the man. 'Our warehouses are empty and trade is at a standstill. Soon we'll all be ruined. I hope you'll tell the General we are all counting on him. Nantes needs bread and business.'

'Oh Papa, Papa, please don't trouble Mademoiselle about such matters,' cried one of the young women, clicking her fan impatiently. 'Do carry on, Mademoiselle Fleury. You were describing the shops on the rue Saint-Honoré.'

'Was I?' laughed Madeleine.

'No, you were going to tell me how you learnt to fight and if you always carry a gun!' said a brunette who turned adoring brown eyes on Madeleine.

'Well, I'll be bound there is no hiding place under

that dress,' whispered Céleste de Bulkeley in Madeleine's ear, as she joined the giggling group.

As best they could, the two friends dealt with a bombardment of questions. Nor was Charette having an easier time, observed Madeleine, watching him disappear within a circle of Nantais matrons and their daughters.

'I see every lady wants to boast she has danced with the great bandit,' she teased later, meeting him during the figure of a dance.

'And every republican officer wants to claim he's held you in his arms,' he retorted with the merest tinge of jealousy in his voice, as he bowed to her curtsy. Their eyes met and they laughed, acknowledging that, despite the adulation around them, just one glance between them was enough to set their blood racing.

Tirelessly throughout the evening, she danced and smiled, using all her feminine skills to captivate and influence. She wanted the negotiations to work, wanted peace for herself, for children like Prudence and Henriette, for the young republican boy who'd fought like a tiger to protect his dead father at the camp of Frérigné. Most of all she wanted peace for François, who carried the burden of command.

Later, when they retired to bed, Charette did not speak of the negotiations, nor did she press him. So far he had remained deaf to all questions, refusing to discuss the negotiations with anyone; nor would his secretary, Auvynet, the generals Fleuriot, Sapinaud, Couëtus and the chiefs of the divisions, Messieurs de l'Espinay, de Bruc and de Bejarry. Also party to the negotiations was commissaire general abbé Remaud and his brother, abbé Jagault, and the Chevalier Baudry d'Asson. All remained silent, to the frustration and anger of the war party.

On the night of the 16th however, just as she was

slipping the beautiful topaz ring on to her finger, Charette entered. By the expression on his face she knew he had good news. 'You shall be the first to know,' he said, resting his hands on her shoulders and smiling at her reflection in the mirror. 'We have received the set text of the proposals from the Republic. It seems very favourable. They have met most of our demands.'

'So it's to be peace, my love,' she cried, springing up and flinging her arms around him.

'Yes, it must be, for reasons which I cannot tell anyone; nor will I burden you. Yet to you only will I say that when I sign the peace treaty of La Jaunaye, it will be to achieve what is dearest to my heart. This is why I have carried the white standard throughout these years. But many will oppose the signing of the treaty.'

'But why?'

'Because I will ask them to swear an oath recognising the Republic and its laws!'

Madeleine nodded, acknowledging the effect this would have on those bent on war.

As he changed into fresh clothing, she watched; it always fascinated her to examine his lean supple frame, the curve and swell of compact muscles, and wonder how such power should lie so easily under finery. Yet it did, and all his movements were light and graceful.

Before he could put on the fine cambric shirt, she moved across to him and ran her hand over the hard contours of his sword arm.

'I wish I were a sculptor,' she said, following along the width of chest down to the taut muscles of his stomach. Wistfully she traced her fingertips along the top of his breeches: immediately the black eyes gleamed in response but, as he bent forward, Charette checked himself and, giving a little shake of his curly head, he chuckled and pressed a finger against her lips.

'If I kiss you now I am lost,' he declared. 'And tonight I must not be a minute late at dinner. I need you, my temptress, to charm and influence those who would think I have betrayed the royalist cause.' His face grew sombre as he buttoned his tunic and made the final adjustment to his cravat. 'They must trust me! Could I forget those who died beneath the Lilies? Those I have loved? How could I let their sacrifice be for nothing?'

'No one could think that, François. Only perhaps . . .' she hesitated, thinking aloud, 'that perhaps you have made a secret arrangement with them.'

The black eyes glinted and a flicker of a smile touched the corners of his lips. Grasping her by the chin, he stared at her in the same way as he had when she'd appeared in her dress: half-amused; half-irritated.

'That thought, my little revolutionary, you must keep entirely to yourself,' he said, covering her mouth in a swift parting kiss.

The uproar in the dining room that night was enormous. Throughout Charette's reading of the proposals there had been deadly silence. Most of the Vendéan claims had been met in respect of religious freedom for the refractory priests, compensation for the ruined province, termination of the process of sequestration against returned émigrés. Republican troops would be withdrawn from Montaigu, Machecoul and Challans. Whilst the Vendéans would be free to set up territorial army units within the province. It seemed to Madeleine, as Charette sat down, that he and his commissioners had achieved considerable success.

Then an elderly Chevalier de Saint-Louis stood up.

'Surely,' he cried haughtily, 'these are matters for the Princes to decide!'

'And Stofflet! He should be here, too,' shouted a man of Anjou.

Immediately Poirier de Beauvais rose to his feet, his face flushed crimson with rage. 'These proposals say nothing of the liberation of our little King. Has his liberation been refused? Have you made our feelings towards our Sovereign known? It would seem, gentlemen,' he said, turning to right and left, 'that we have been brought here purely for signing agreement to Monsieur Charette's wishes.'

Now everyone was on their feet, shouting and thumping the table. Madeleine saw the colour drain from Charette's face until it became white with rage. Silently he surveyed the disorder, the small nerve pulsating beside his compressed lips, warning of the volcanic outburst which would surely come.

The room had become stifling, and suddenly Madeleine had to leave; escape from the noise and rancour. Slipping from the table she walked out on to the terrace. The tumult within increased, voices all echoing the same words: 'Never, never will we swear loyalty to the Republic.'

Then, like a whiplash cutting through, Charette's voice, harsh, determined. 'We have been given forty-eight hours. I will sign and not lose this opportunity!'

Madeleine smiled grimly as the dissenting voices rose to a crescendo. Let them shout; Charette would have his way. He was not like Henri at twenty-one, willing to shrug his shoulders before age and experience. The war party here were dealing with a man of thirty-two, used to command at sea long before the rebellion.

Gradually, as she walked over the velvet-smooth lawns, the angry voices faded. It did seem odd the republican proposals omitted to mention the future of the boy king. She recalled the red face of Poirier de Beauvais, how he'd trembled with rage when he'd noted the omission in the treaty. Yet, in her room but an hour ago, Charette had told her that in signing the treaty he would achieve the dearest wish of his heart. That was it, of course, she thought, leaning against a stone sundial. She had stumbled across it when she'd suggested he had a secret arrangement; and that was why he'd told her to keep such a thought to herself. What fools they are, she thought, glancing towards the château. Was it likely that the man who had answered Louis XVI's summons to defend the throne at the Tuileries, who had carried the Bourbon flag for so long, would neglect the rights of Louis XVII? She shivered and started to walk back, thinking how foolish it was to come out without a wrap.

Against the lighted doorway on to the terrace she saw the outline of three men, doubtless needing — like herself — fresh air and peace. Yet their movements did not have the casual slowness of diners taking the air. The thought made her pause, instinctively draw behind one of the neatly trimmed boxed privets which lined the length of the lawn. She felt absurd, and made to move out on to the gravel path when the sixth sense once more restrained her. The men had chosen the same path as herself and she could hear their boots crunching on the gravel as they drew nearer. Now their voices were audible. They had paused behind the privet.

On the other side of the evergreen she recognised the cold, haughty voice of Launay, and his words filled her with anger and alarm. 'He must be prevented from signing the treaty. There is no alternative; I will call him out into the garden and shoot him for the traitor he is.'

'Then we will ride to Clisson and write a protest against peace,' said a second voice.

Without waiting to find out who the other men were, Madeleine lifted up her skirt and prepared to run for the terrace. There wasn't time to do a detour around the grounds. The men must see her the moment she emerged, but that didn't matter so long as she warned Charette. Taking a few deep breaths to fill her lungs with air, she shot forward. As she expected, she only covered a short distance between her hiding place and the next box before she was seen.

'Quick, stop her! Cut her off before she reaches the terrace!'

Throwing her head back and cursing her silly little heeled slippers, Madeleine tried to ignore the sound of pursuit. She decided they would not risk bringing her down with a gun or within seconds every man in the dining hall would be outside. No, they would have to catch her. Out of the corner of her eye she caught a glimpse of white cloth behind. Immediately she looked ahead at the point she wanted to be, widening her eyes as her mind released an ultimate spring of energy. With a wild feeling of exhilaration she shot forward. She knew she couldn't sustain it for long but it would get her to the terrace. Just as she'd held off the Vicomte de Cramoisy's men at the Palais-Royal so long ago, now, over this short distance, she outstripped the men behind her. Only this time it was she, not Charette, who was to play the rescuer.

Calm had not descended over the dining hall and she saw Charette had left. Straightaway she ran away from the uproar to the library. Flinging open the heavy door, she saw Charette was standing before the fireplace.

'Launay plans to kill you and take command,' she

panted. 'He's in the garden now with two others. I think they are Moële and de Beauvais.'

'Do they know you're here now?'

'Yes,' Madeleine replied, bending forward, her hands on her thighs, drawing in great gasps of air. 'They plan to ride to Clisson with the rest of the war party to send a protest before the treaty is signed.'

Charette turned round and looked at the Chouan leaders, Cormatin, Solilhac and Richard. Then at his friends Couëtus, Savin and his uncle Fleuriot. 'We must act with speed! My friends, I cannot reveal the motives which compel me to sign the peace treaty, only believe that they are pure and honourable! Please sign along with me.'

Never had Madeleine seen such desperate appeal on the proud, resolute face. Responding to it one by one, the leaders stood up. 'We will sign,' they declared.

'What of the assassins?' asked Madeleine.

'They'll be long gone, *chérie*. Come, my friends, let us sign before they can do their worst!'

On 17 February at 2.00 p.m., the deadline for signature of the treaty of La Jaunaye was reached. Unable to extend the time limit so that Stofflet might yet be prevailed upon and brought to sign, Charette, together with the Breton delegates, his generals and divisional leaders of the armies of Anjou, Bas-Poitou and the Centre, signed their peace with the Republic.

With tears of pride and relief, Madeleine and her companions watched the *ci-devant*, Marquis Canclaux, embrace their King of the Marais under the tricolor.

For once I am a leader of fashion, decided Madeleine, thinking of her lily and tricolor dress.

Chapter Four

The quays and streets of Nantes were packed solid. There wasn't a space in the twenty-deep ranks facing each side of the procession. Even the leafless branches of trees were filled with young boys, like excited clusters of birds, chattering and shrieking at each new sight, whilst from upper windows and leaning low over balconies, young girls threw down handfuls of tricolor and white cockades, turning to each other with giggles and blushes when a soldier looked up and waved.

The din was deafening. An ear-shattering medley of military music, cannon salutes and cheers. Oh, how they were cheering him – just like she and Pierre and the Parisians had cheered Lafayette's return from the Americas; so the Nantais were greeting Charette.

'*Vive la paix!*' they cried. '*Vive Charette! Vive l'Union!*'

Laughing with excitement, Madeleine looked amongst the crowd hoping to spot Suzanne Guillet or perhaps the tailor, Boëtz. But there were so many upturned, smiling faces it was an impossible task. Amused, she saw two small boys on the edge of the crowd leave their mother's side and dart towards her.

'Look, Maman, at the ladies' guns,' they shrieked.

Smiling, she tossed down two white cockades and

watched them catch their prizes with screams of delight.

'Let us hope, Madeleine,' laughed Céleste de Bulkeley, 'they won't trample them underfoot when they grow up!'

Nodding, Madeleine stroked her nervous horse as another salvo of cannon fire caused the air and ground to vibrate. 'Steady boy, you should be used to gunfire by now.'

'It's not the guns, Madeleine. It's the sound of republican cheers which is giving all our horses the jitters.'

Madeleine flashed a grin at the grey-eyed blonde beside her. She and Madeleine were both in their large plumed hats, a suede gauntlet glove resting casually on the hilt of their sheathed swords, their gun butts clearly visible above the white sashes around their waists. It was little wonder the Nantais citizens were oohing and aahing with pointed fingers as they rode by.

Behind them, on this day of 26 February, rode hundreds of republican and royalist horses; riding together like brothers-in-arms. Ahead, in a flurry of Bourbon plumes, rode their divisional leaders and, wedged between them and the Vendéan generals of command, were adjutant generals of the Republic, magnificent in their shiny buttons and snow-white gaiters. But no one rivalled the leader of this martial column.

He had almost reached the forbidding, grim Bouffay prison. Madeleine prepared to rein in her horse as she saw him stop, and gradually the long procession came to a halt. As Charette raised his white plumed hat in salute to the dead, Madeleine – like those around her – bowed her head, praying for the hundreds who had died beneath the blade of the guillotine and perished in the icy waters of the Loire.

Then, as the procession moved off once again, fresh cheers broke out. '*Vive Charette! Vive le Roi du Marais!*'

'François has certainly taken Nantes by storm,' shouted Madame du Fief.

'Yes,' declared Céleste de Bulkeley. 'They were expecting a Brigand; instead a king rode in.'

Nothing could be truer, thought Madeleine. He looked superb, heading the cavalcade on a magnificent charger. As usual, the narrow brim of his hat was pinned back against the tall crown and bore three white plumes, whilst under it was a kerchief of the finest gold thread. His spurs were gold, too, and gold glittered on his boots, shiny as jet, and on the hilts of his pistols and sheathed sword. Around a tunic of sky blue was fastened his white silk sash of command, gold-fringed, gleaming with the golden fleur-de-lys of France. No Sun King could have dazzled the spectators more. Yet, overriding this finery, was an aura of virile masculinity; and the face above the snowy lace cravat was sombre and grave. Riding to make his submission, to pay his homage to the Republic, Charette entered Nantes, justifying the words on the banner beside him: '*Abattu: Jamais*'.

A magnificent reception followed the set formalities before the Representatives of the People. It was to be the first of many given for the man who had brought peace. The man on the street missed his bread, the merchant his commerce; all wanted to fête the one who could revive the heartbeat of their city.

Wherever they went, the acclaim was effusive. There were dinner parties and balls when Madeleine found herself unable to sit out a single dance to catch back her breath, so many handsome young republican officers wished to dance with her.

And there was one who especially sought her company, and she in turn felt drawn to him; for his carefree charm and flippant, outrageous gossip put her in mind of Philippe of the Palais-Royal.

'Oh, do stop being so secretive about where we have met,' she scolded one evening when they were dancing together. 'For I swear I have never set eyes on you before!'

The republican officer tightened his hold on Madeleine's arm and stood still. 'I fell in love with you at Légé,' he said dreamily. 'And ever since my life has been in turmoil.'

'How could that be, Captain?' Madeleine enquired, enjoying the flirtation.

'At the time I was occupied with the positions of your soldiers when, through my field glass, I found your lovely face and forgot everything.'

'You didn't even consider shooting me!' teased the girl.

'I wanted to make you my prisoner,' murmured the young officer, his grey-green eyes speaking love. 'Why did you desert your flag, Madeleine Fleury?'

The unexpected question took Madeleine by surprise and, disconcerted, she allowed her partner to lift her hand to his lips where, unhurried, he pressed a long lingering kiss on its palm. 'So, there's my answer,' he said, jealously following Madeleine's look. 'Ah, if ever I had Charette in my sights I would wish to be holding a gun!'

'Then understand, Captain, you will have killed me too.'

She thought no more of the incident until the next day when, upon returning from a visit to the little orphan Armand at his adopted home, she found Charette's bodyguard mounted outside the Hôtel-Villestreaux and her own horse saddled and waiting beside Charette's stallion.

Anxiously she ran upstairs to their bedchamber. 'Has something happened?' she cried.

At her entrance, Charette ceased his restless pacing and picked up his hat. 'We're leaving,' he said flatly.

'Leaving, but why? Everything is going so well!'

'Is it?' he said sarcastically.

'Why, yes. Every night the crowds cheer for you and never cease until you go out on to the balcony.'

Charette shrugged. 'Crowds are notoriously fickle,' he replied. 'Tomorrow they might shout for my head.'

'That's not so – I just don't understand. You are within the republican sphere of influence here; they are getting to know and like you.'

'Me? I rather thought it was you, Madeleine, that everyone adored.'

So, that was it. Jealousy. 'Did you not order me to use my charm on these republicans!' she flashed, angered by his childishness.

'Not on captains!'

'I see, it's all right for me to flirt with generals. And presumably if a royal prince declared an interest, you'd hand me over in ribbons; white ones of course.'

Like lightning he swooped and seized her wrist in a vicious grip which made her cry out.

'Understand me, Madeleine. I have never wanted to live in Nantes, and spheres of influence sicken me. I love you, and no man shall take you from me. We leave for Belleville!' and swinging her up into his arms he carried her downstairs.

Charette set a furious pace on the return to Belleville; it suited Madeleine's mood. She was throbbing with anger at his high-handed treatment, and for several miles the memory of the men's uproarious laughter when he threw her up on to her horse made her grit her teeth and thump the pommel of her saddle with fury. And when he tried to ride alongside her she glared fiercely. 'Don't speak to me!

484

I hate you!' she cried, spurring her horse on faster as Charette started to laugh.

Many hours later her anger, like her energy, had drained away. She was saddle-sore and her horse, like the rest, was lathered in sweat.

'You'll soon be home now,' she said, giving her mare a comforting pat.

'And glad of it, like me!'

Madeleine looked up at Charette, who had slowed his pace to hers; but she did not smile.

'Come now, my love,' he said, stretching out for her hand. 'Will you not forgive me? Don't make me unhappy. I know I behaved badly and I'm sorry if I've spoilt your fun; you're still so young and the months of hardship were long. But I had to leave, for with every passing day I become more doubtful that the republicans will honour the treaty, and in Nantes I was defenceless. One can only bargain from strength.'

Madeleine squeezed his hand and then once more. 'Well, it wasn't Paris,' she said softly.

Wearily, a member of the cavalcade answered the call of the unseen sentry and they passed beyond the fortifications into the little bourg. At once an officer ran up to Charette.

'Sir, Launay is here in the officers' mess. He came, he said, to pay his respects to friends. Do you wish to place him under arrest?'

'No,' answered Charette. 'I accept his reason for being here.'

'But, François,' protested Madeleine as they continued along the main street. 'He threatened your life!'

'My dear, men say things in anger. He is here to see old friends. As a gentleman I cannot doubt his word.'

Unhappily she watched him dismount. 'Take him

with you to the Pavilion,' he said, passing up his horse's reins. 'I'll be over soon. First I want to see Auvynet, to draft a letter to the Comte de Provence – there will be those who will try to cast shadows on what I have done.'

Filled with disquiet, she watched him walk towards the Manoir de la Jarriette. The voices of the war party that night in the garden of the Château de la Jaunaye had been filled with menace; certainly Launay had not been jesting when he threatened to shoot Charette. Who knows what disaffection he might now be spreading in the officers' mess?

Leaving their horses outside the Pavilion for Pheiffer to take to the stables, she wearily unlatched the door. Inside the tiny hallway she slipped off her cloak and was about to enter the salon when she heard a slight noise, as though a door had closed. Immediately she paused, an alarm bell ringing within her. She tiptoed towards the oak door and pressed her ear against it, but all was quiet save the beating of her heart. Deciding her nerves were getting the better of her, she gently opened the door. The room was empty. Relieved, she walked in. Suddenly, from behind, a hand caught hold of her mouth and she was pulled backwards against a man's body. Unable to scream, she struggled, fiercely kicking against her unknown assailant's legs, but he merely grunted and lifted her up off the ground. Before her the door into the bedroom opened and the figure of Launay emerged. Horrified, she saw he was carrying a blunderbuss. 'So we have the she-wolf first,' he said in a cold, contemptuous voice.

'What do you want me to do with her?' slurred a voice which exuded the reek of brandy.

'Keep her quiet. How you do it, my dear fellow, is up to you. Have a little fun if you wish, she's only a

486

commoner – no more than a slut; but kill her quietly if she attempts to scream.'

Wild with terror, Madeleine stared at the royalist, but his eyes, like those of a dead fish, were cold and empty of emotion. Glaring fiercely at him, she was bundled past into the bedroom and, as the door shut, she knew, no matter what this unknown man might do, it would be a matter of no interest whatever to the man waiting to kill Charette.

Almost paralysed with fear of what was to come, she searched for a way to deal with the situation. The window was her only means of escape. But how to reach it? She ceased struggling, hoping by doing so to lure her captor into a state of false security.

'Ah, that's more sensible,' he said; but as he lowered her to the floor his grip on her mouth did not relax. 'Now I'm going to remove my hand and, when I do, if you scream, I shall run you through with my sword. Do you understand? Good!' he said in a pleased tone, as Madeleine nodded. Slowly he moved his hand and, remaining silent, she turned around and somehow forced herself to smile at the man. She had never seen him before. His face was heavily flushed, which indicated that he had probably been drinking in the officers' mess for some hours, but though there was a lascivious gleam in his eyes, his face was not cruel and she doubted he would kill her.

'I would be obliged if I could have some cognac. I'm very cold after the journey,' she said, pouting her lips and flashing the man another seductive smile. She could see he was quite startled by her response, and pleased by the prospect of another drink for himself.

'With pleasure. I can see you and I are going to get on, Mademoiselle, just as long as you remember to keep quiet. Now, where is it?'

'In the cabinet. Shall I get it?'

'No, you sit down there.'

Compliantly, Madeleine sat down on the couch before the fireplace and watched the man return with the cognac bottle and one glass. He was not a heavily built man, but she noticed his movements were slow and a little unsteady. Patting the sofa beside her, she flashed him an inviting look and he perched on the edge beside her.

'Here,' he said, thrusting an enormous measure into her hand. 'You're a disloyal little thing, aren't you?' he said, his eyes resting briefly on her face before sliding their gaze to the neckline of her dress. He swung the bottle up to his thick lips and took a large swig from it. As he did so, she sprang forward and pushed, catching him full force behind the shoulder. Before he could recover, she dealt him a second blow, which sent him staggering forward. Quick as lightning she ran to the window and, flinging it open, screamed with all her might.

'You bitch,' roared a voice behind her and she was immediately dragged back from the window; but she had done enough, her cries had been heard. Under a hail of heavy blows she heard shouts and running footsteps. '*Merde*,' gasped the man. 'You've done for us.' Savagely he thrust Madeleine away from him and made towards the open window.

As he disappeared from sight, she heard the report of a gun from the salon. But it was not Charette who stood facing Launay's smoking gun but Pheiffer. White-faced, the assassin dropped the weapon to the floor. He had missed, and knew the mistake had cost him his life.

Outside came the sound of more footsteps and then the white, scared faces of Sophie and Céleste de Couëtus appeared in the entrance of the salon. They were just in time to see Pheiffer spring at Launay as he endeavoured to withdraw his sword. With a howl of fury, Pheiffer lifted the terrified man up in his arms. Just like a bear lifting a small prey. 'No, no,' shrieked the sisters as the huge man transferred his grip to Launay's throat. It was too late for anyone to intervene. With another ferocious bellow of rage, Charette's devoted bodyguard tossed the man like a rag doll to the floor.

A few days later, with Launay's treachery and death still on their minds, Charette completed his submission to the Republic. Many could not bear to watch, and broad, muscular soldiers hung their heads to hide the tears running from their eyes. Stony-faced, Charette handed over two banners to be conveyed to Nantes and thence on to the National Convention in Paris.

It was a terrible moment. They were but tattered strips of silk, marked with mud, singed with cannon shot and rent with musket ball; but beneath these testimonies of resistance, hundreds had died, making the last supreme sacrifice to save them from Republican hands. Now, without uttering a single word, Charette handed over the lilies of France.

The pain Madeleine felt for the desolate figure walking from the parade ground outside the church was physical. Somehow she had to help him, but she had to give him more than the temporary relief of their lovemaking. In her arms she knew she could make him forget, but only for a while. It would not last.

Anxiously she hurried after him, racking her brain for a way to distract him from the scorn and criticism which would follow this action. Suddenly she thought of a way. 'François,' she said, gently touching his arm. 'I have something to show you. Please will you come with me?'

He turned towards her, his black eyes dull with

misery. 'Why not, I have nothing else to do,' he said bitterly.

Taking his hand she led him, not to the Pavilion as he expected, but to a clearing surrounded with trees. 'This is it,' she said mysteriously. With a puzzled frown, Charette shrugged uninterestedly and made to walk away. But grasping his arm, she restrained him. 'Here, François, you will build your small palace.'

Startled, the black eyes widened with surprise and stared fixedly into Madeleine's for some time. 'So ...' he whispered, with something resembling relief showing in his eyes and voice, 'you have guessed!'

'Yes, it was not hard,' she smiled. 'All those who know and love you should have guessed. You did not gallop alone at Frérigné to retrieve a banner in the midst of grenadiers merely to hand it over to republicans in Paris; nor did you sign the Treaty of La Jaunaye for peace alone. You, my dear Generalissimo, have played for much higher stakes. For the prisoner in the Temple. For Louis XVII!'

Like sun piercing through heavy sullen clouds, a beautiful smile transformed the downcast features. 'Oh, you Parisienne minx,' he cried and, seizing her by the waist, he whirled her round and round until, breathless, they both collapsed laughing to the ground. Delighted with his response, Madeleine watched him roll over and inspect the site, his chin resting on his hands. Always the view of his profile made her smile. The sharp upturned nose, combined with his curly black lashes and inverted bow-shaped mouth, gave his face such a look of vitality. Sparkling with excitement, his eyes reinforced the impression. 'You're right, *chérie*, I must have somewhere worthy to receive him. We must start today! But no one must know why we build. Absolute secrecy must be maintained. If the regicides learn the secret clause of the Treaty, all will be lost! Only to you, because you are me, can I speak my thoughts aloud. Here, in this little glade on 13 June, we will receive into our care Louis XVII and his sister, Madame Royale. It is for their safety and for the restoration of the French throne that I have laid down arms.'

'Well,' said Madeleine, holding his hand and walking across the springy turf to the centre of the glade. 'The Palais-Royal in Paris brought a salt smuggler's orphan and a naval officer together; perhaps a Palais-Royal here might bring the little prisoner of the Temple to his throne.'

Madeleine had indeed found the distraction Charette needed to absorb him. As work progressed and the stone walls of the house rose higher, so, too, did their hope that the little dauphin, Louis XVII, would soon be the new occupant.

To allay suspicion, Madeleine made it known that the new house was for herself and the costly furnishings arriving from Nantes were for the comfort of the visitors who now flocked to Belleville. Indeed, it seemed the whole world had heard of Charette – Parisians, émigrés from England, Americans; all came to pay homage.

Much to Charette's embarrassment, and to everyone else's amusement, songs were even written in his honour. Singing them proved the most delightful way of teasing him.

But there was one letter which even the naturally modest Charette could not conceal his delight in receiving. It came from the famous Russian, Marshal Suvorov. Like a small, pleased boy, he had shown it to her. 'See, Madeleine, this is from one of the greatest generals of all time.'

Intrigued, she took the stiff parchment. ' "Hero of the Vendée",' she read, ' "illustrious defender of the faith of your fathers and the throne of your kings, I salute you!"' Delighted by the opening text, Madeleine looked up with an amused smile at the man before her and laughed at his expression of studied nonchalance. 'It's no good trying to appear modest, François. Your famous marshal pays you too many compliments. Why, here he says, "the Universe is filled with your name. An astonished Europe is watching you and I admire you and congratulate you." It is a marvellous tribute to your courage my darling,' she said, after reading the rest of the letter. 'And one thing is assured, you have made a powerful friend; perhaps one day we'll visit this general.'

'Yes, we'll do that,' smiled Charette.

Now, for the first time, it was possible to ride out without fear of an engagement. The whole of the wild and desolate region was under their command. To pass through it, the Blues now sought permission and safe conducts. So the spring and summer days were mostly carefree and filled with laughter.

Instead of war they made excursions. Visiting the châteaux of friends; going often to Légé; riding through what seemed never-ending woods, to burst suddenly upon the Château du Bois Chevalier and the surprise of its ornamental waters. Even now, after so long in the west, the Château of La Vendée never ceased to startle Madeleine. Jealously guarded by woods, one came upon them unexpectedly, like finding a jewel under a pile of leaves.

With the mellow beauty of the topaz Charette had given her so long ago, Fonteclose, when she saw it, stole her heart away. His beloved manor was just as he'd described, set amidst a spinny of ancient oaks. Without the grandeur and pretensions of a château, its rustic simplicity seemed an extension of the beautiful trees, merging as part of nature.

'Oh, François, let's hide away here for ever,' she had breathed.

'One day we will,' he'd smiled. 'I'm so glad you like it. To me it has more beauty than Versailles. One day we will live here with our children. There will be time for you to draw: of course I shall order you then to make drawings which do not make fun of my profile,' he said, flashing a grin at her, 'and I shall show you that mathematics is as beautiful as music, for music is mathematics.'

Yet there was no time to hide away. Charette was thought the man of the moment, perhaps the future. Newcomers with clever eyes and smooth tongues showered Madeleine with gifts, but she did not allow herself to be drawn by subtle questions and flattery. If not by birth, by upbringing she was a Parisienne, where quick wits meant the difference between life and death. It would not be from her lips that they would gain access to Charette's thoughts and plans.

Disappointed, also, were those who arrived seeking a return to the *ancien régime*. There was elegance and courtesy, but there was the new spirit of the age, too, embodied by Madeleine herself. She made no pretence of her humble origins, and those who thought to topple her because of it floundered under her lively wit. Whilst the allure of a beautiful amazon who had fought against the grenadiers of France secured her a place no timid little marquise or provincial comtesse could threaten.

Throughout this time she indulged herself, deluding herself that the Treaty of La Jaunaye had brought lasting peace into their lives. But the couriers who arrived from Verona in the name of the Regent, the Comte de Provence, and his brother the Comte d'Artois in England, only foretold the struggle was far from over.

Sensing the storm clouds were gathering, she threw

her sword and gun into a chest, as though by doing so to stretch out the precious moments of peace. The whole of her attention was given to the Palais-Royal, to flirting and dancing, poetry and songs. All she wanted was for things to stay as they were. Never had she been so happy. So many friends had died, could they not live?

Filled with such thoughts, she lay one Sunday morning in the Pavilion, watching Charette as he slept. Tenderly she touched the scars on his arm and the slight grazing made by a ball in his cheek. Even in repose there was a vibrancy about him. Energy emanating as though he might be dreaming of leading a charge or stepping a country dance.

At her insistent caress, his black lashes fluttered and his eyes opened, and two pinpoints of light gleamed from their black depths.

'How many women have you made love to?' she suddenly asked.

François-Athanase Charette widened his black eyes with surprise, and pondered; it was a question with no easy answer. Thoughtfully, he ran his finger down the girl's straight nose and playfully tapped its rounded end.

'Fifty – a hundred,' he said speculatively.

'One hundred!'

'At least!' he laughed, enjoying the jealous blaze in Madeleine's eyes. Why was it women were always curious about such matters? When you told them they became angry; and if you didn't, they usually sulked.

'Did you make love to the Comtesse de la Rochefoucauld, your Queen at Légé?'

Charette sighed, took the intent oval face between his hands and contemplated the brown eyes staring into his.

'*Ma petite*,' he said, trying not to laugh at the

naked emotion in their golden depths, 'a gentleman never reveals a name. Only the base or the impotent would stoop so low. And certainly one should never be so discourteous as to think of other women when one is accepting a lady's hospitality, no matter how plain she may be – or how beautiful,' he cried, ducking away from a slap.

Sinuously, Madeleine stretched out, arching her back so that her nakedness pressed against its covering; slowly, Charette pulled away the thin linen sheet, and ran his eyes over her. In a swift, easy motion he rolled over, straddling her, his knees gripping tightly against her body. For a little while he remained so, gazing down at her. 'You're the loveliest creature I have ever seen,' he said wonderingly, 'and every time I look at you I want to take you as urgently as the first time.'

Then he lowered himself down and she felt him enter and possess. Joined as one, in body and soul, they abandoned themselves to a rhythm as old as the world, their desire lashing and peaking like waves against rocks, surging back with the undertow, then hurling them forward once again in a desperate ecstasy. Until, at last, they were flung over the reef on to the strand: exhausted, sated, content.

Later they rose and walked to the simple stone house, the Palais-Royal. Though small, each room was now exquisite. Proudly Madeleine led Charette into the main salon. 'Do you like this soft green? I thought it was restful, yet like spring – perhaps not too regal.'

'Yes,' said Charette, replacing a small portrait of Marie-Antoinette on to a small polished table. 'You've shown excellent taste, Madeleine, but you've not made it too grand to arouse suspicions. Our little King and Madame Royale will adore what you've done. God help them, anything would be better than the years they've endured in the Temple. I fear Louis will be much changed – not the merry little boy we all knew. Our agents in Paris report the fiends have abused and debased him; for months he has been boarded away like an animal, seeing no one, not even light.'

'Well, soon he'll be here,' she said swiftly, before his mood could change. 'Then all will understand why Charette sheathed his sword and . . .' she added with a rueful smile, gesturing to the brocade-covered walls, 'Madame de Monsorbier will no longer be talking about Du Barry when I enter a room.'

Charette frowned at her words and Madeleine could not resist a small smile. She knew how he hated disharmony amongst his followers. The little Breton noblewoman had had no alternative but to accept Madeleine's position, though it was not without some resentment. Since the erection of the Palais-Royal she and her sister, Madame Voyneau, had made very pointed remarks. They hadn't worried Madeleine, but she would be glad when the purpose of the Palais-Royal was revealed, for it did concern her that others, like the La Robrie brothers and Céleste and Madame du Fief, might think her venal.

Satisfied that all was ready in the orphans' little palace, they walked towards the church for Mass. Belleville was overflowing with peasants and they smiled and saluted familiar faces. It seemed just like the bustle and activity before a campaign, but the couriers had not roused the parishes for war, only for the distribution of food. The Republic had promised help to all the starving families, but already these promises seemed forgotten. Over 3,000 peasants had marched to Belleville, to their leader, who would somehow always provide.

Entering the dim coolness of the church ahead of Charette, Madeleine knelt in prayer. Her thoughts still dwelt on the wretched little boy wasting away in his cell in Paris. She prayed for his safety and asked for forgiveness; for she, along with the fishwives, had helped put him there. Camille Desmoulins with her persuasive pen, Georges Jacques Danton with his thunderous rhetoric, had put him there. Those sprigs of green, the oak leaves of the Palais-Royal, had been the green of hope which had filled every heart with courage; a courage to topple the grimmest fortress in the world and a courage which had set France spinning towards the Terror: that hope had put him there. Soon, unbelievably, he would be in her care. Fervently she raised her eyes to the statue of Mary and the baby Jesus and made her silent vow.

As Mass drew to its close, above the voice of abbé Remaud came the distant howl of a sentry. Strangers were approaching. Whoever they were, they must feel a sense of fear at such a sound. The disembodied voices were unnerving, nor was it ever possible to spot the tree-top sentinels. They perched in the topmost branches, often with their rope-ladder drawn up with them.

As Charette had requested, the peasants formed up in orderly ranks outside the church. Like them, Madeleine looked curiously towards the palisade. No one ever came to Belleville without an invitation, and she knew no guests were expected. Suddenly she gasped with surprise as a peasant guide appeared at the head of a party of Blues. There was no threat for there appeared to be only about thirty of them, but the thousands of peasants looked as stunned as she felt, for it was unheard of for a peasant to guide republicans right into royalist headquarters.

Not a man moved as the Blues approached. The rap of hooves and jingle of harness seeming extraordinarily loud in the watchful stillness. Then the captain of the party, seeing Charette, spurred his horse forward. Protective as always, Pheiffer drew nearer to Charette, and Prudent de la Robrie's hand flew to his sword hilt.

Wisely, over a sword's length from Charette, the captain halted and drew a package from his wallet. 'General Charette,' he said in a voice filled with respect. 'My name is Captain Marion. I am under orders to deliver this package to you and to await your reply.'

Charette stepped forward and took the package. As he opened it, Madeleine saw that it contained two letters. As he read Charette frowned, then his expression became livid with anger and the small pulse, the barometer of his mood, began to beat. He is about to explode, thought Madeleine. So, too, did the captain, for he nervously moved his horse back several paces. The coal-black eyes lifted from the creamy parchment, their expression sending a cold shiver down Madeleine's spine – never had she seen such a look of murderous anger. A mere nod and the 3,000 peasants flew forward, encircling the republicans.

'You will be spared your lives,' said Charette quietly to the terrified Blues, 'for you have come here with sealed orders; but you are now my prisoners. For the man who brought you here, there is only death!' With a terrible expression, he looked down at the trembling wretch already prostrate before him. 'You have betrayed your brothers and sisters. Make your peace with God.' Then with a curt nod to Pheiffer, he continued to speak. 'The moment has come to tear aside the veil which has covered, for so long, the secret clause of the peace treaty . . .' Out of the corner of her eye, Madeleine saw the condemned man kneel before the priest. Instantly she whipped her head around so as not to see. She had killed men herself, but only in the heat of battle – somehow it was different. Never had they executed someone in cold blood.

Charette, she saw, was now trembling with passion and almost unable to speak. Dear God, she thought, what can have happened to make him so? She saw him breathe deeply and then, regaining control, he continued speaking, his voice thick with passion. 'Our little King is dead! He has been poisoned by this ungodly sect of barbarians!'

Like those around her, Madeleine made the sign of the cross. Tears flooded her eyes as she thought of the little boy and his horrible, lonely death and of their hopes and the Palais-Royal. The door would now never be opened by its young master. He had followed his mother and father and all the other murdered innocents. All hope drained away from her as she turned to go, anticipating Charette's next words.

'Messieurs,' he cried, unsheathing his sword and holding it up before him. 'The war recommences. Long live Louis-Stanislas Xavier, Louis XVIII.'

Filled with despairing anger, her eyes blinded by tears, Madeleine returned to the Pavilion. Taking the blue diaphanous dress from its box of gold and black, she ripped it from end to end till the gossamer fabric was only a mound of frayed silk, the tiny embroidered fleurs-de-lys covered by ripped lengths of tricolor ribbons.

It was a long time before he returned to retire for the night, and her eyes were still red and swollen from weeping. Questioningly he looked from Madeleine to the torn dress. 'Why?'

'Because it's over!' she replied bitterly, and saw his eyes widen a fraction in alarm.

'Do you mean the truce?' he asked in a tense, quiet voice, as he started to undress.

'Yes. Now the killing starts again, and for a

cowardly Prince who ran away from his country!'
The words were spat at Charette, and with a deep
feeling of satisfaction Madeleine anticipated the reaction. She was waiting to draw more blood. But as
though sensing her mood, the man before her
remained calm, his face impassive, as he knelt and
picked up a fragment of her dress.

'We do not choose our King, we merely serve,' he
murmured matter of factly, looking down at the
small golden fleur-de-lys between his fingers.

'And what if he be a madman, what then?' she
taunted, relishing the change of emotion now on his
face. 'Well, so much for our Constitution. For this
Prince will want things just as they were before; you
nobles in your châteaux, and we poor kept firmly in
our place.'

'Then perhaps you wish to go?' His quiet words
brought her up sharp and the misery on his face
nearly tore her apart.

'Oh François, François,' she cried, falling upon
him with tears streaming down her face. 'Why? You,
who treat the humblest of your men as a brother and
wait until last to eat; how can you help bring back
the old ways! A boy King would have been schooled
under your protection, but Provence and his syco-
phants in Verona . . .! Do you think they care about
Égalité?'

'The *ancien régime* can never return!'

'But it will, it will!' she cried hysterically, raining
furious blows against his chest. 'Damn you, and your
Bourbons!'

Livid with anger, Charette's patience snapped, and
suddenly they were fighting; both filled with the
desire to inflict hurt; both hating what the other
represented. Like some wild creature, Madeleine
threw herself at Charette who, losing his balance, fell
backwards on to the bed, pulling her with him. So

close; she smelt the virile maleness of him, and her immediate response angered yet excited her. Straddling him, she thrust herself upon him; wanting physically to dominate, to destroy somehow the thread which bound them together; the thread which had shackled her like a slave to live his dream. Looking down, she saw that Charette's eyes blazed with amused delight. His response fuelled her fury, driving her on to obliterate her bitter passion, until at last his eyes closed, and she knew she was taking him beyond the brink. And as she heard his cry, a fierce exultation swept through her.

Drained, she remained over him, the shaft of her thighs and the curve of her back glistening with sweat, her hair falling forward in thick, damp strands. Silently, she studied his face; the firm line of the mouth, the stubborn chin and, about the whole, an intangible aura of honour. No, he would never change. Just like the fervour of La Rochejaquelein before his banner at Le Mans, so too was Charette's devotion to the Lilies of France. His belief, his sense of duty, born of past generations, were an integral part of his being. To destroy them would be to destroy the man. And what of her own beliefs, sown so recently?

Under her touch, the thick curve of Charette's lashes fluttered, and he gazed up dreamily at her. Then, taking hold of a darkened coil of hair, he pulled her forward and down until her lips met his.

'I'll never let you go,' he said.

'No,' she affirmed, pressing her lips against his, renewing the pledge she had once made. Never, never would she leave him; only death might part them.

Tenderly they made love; each caress, each kiss, a silent, sacred vow; handling each other as though for the first and the last time; their eyes speaking what no words could express; moving on back through time, reviving that precious moment, so long ago, when their souls touched.

At last Marie-Antoinette's brothers-in-law made their move: troops and arms were to be landed on the French coastline, a Breton landing led by the Comte de Puisaye. It was a slight; the greatest insult to the Vendéans. In public Charette hid his feelings, but in private Madeleine witnessed the extent of his anger and frustration.

'Why have they ignored my advice?' he snarled, pacing up and down like an angry cat, his eyes glaring with hurt pride. 'Can't they see the dangers of landing at Quiberon? Why, even Stofflet and Sapinaud agree, the only place is La Tranche or Aiguillen on the Vendéan coast!' Angrily he threw himself into a chair, his long elegant fingers drumming on its carved arm. 'And why the Comte de Puisaye – the man's inexperienced and a fool!'

'Perhaps,' replied Madeleine, resting her needle against the silk of a new banner she was working, 'perhaps the English have picked a less able man to ensure failure! Or maybe their highnesses are punishing you for signing the Treaty of La Jaunaye.'

The restless black eyes widened as they stared at her. 'Yes, that's what many of the officers think. Do any of us trust the English? It suits them if France is in turmoil. As for the Princes,' he said bitterly, 'neither of them have known necessity. For three years I and the Maraichins, the Paydrets and the people of La Vendée have suffered and died to keep their cause alive. The honour should be ours!'

Despite his anger, in the ensuing days leading up to the landing of the émigré force Charette threw himself into the task of creating a diversion in the south, thereby occupying the troops of General Canclaux and preventing them linking up with the Army of Brest under the republican general, Hoche. But as he had foreseen, the expedition was a complete disaster, and hundreds of royalists were taken prisoner.

A few days after this terrible news, just as they were entering the church at Belleville, a royalist courier arrived. Quickly Charette snatched the gazette from the agitated man. Straightaway his face became as pale as the rider's. He turned to an officer standing near. 'The 300 prisoners we captured at Les Essarts,' he said, in a cold, hard voice. 'Take them into the wood and execute all but six.'

Horrified, Madeleine clutched at Marie-Anne Charette's arm, hardly able to believe what she had heard. He couldn't mean it! He had never allowed brutality towards prisoners. It had happened at Frérigné, but then it had been beyond his control. Now, in cold blood, to kill . . . She rushed forward.

'François, please, I beg you . . . why?'

'Because I must teach the Representatives of the People and the republican generals of France a lesson they will not forget.' He slapped his hand against the gazette. 'They have murdered thousands of royalist prisoners at Quiberon. After formally giving an undertaking of clemency to all who laid down arms, Hoche betrayed his promise and they have all been executed. They will learn today that for every royalist man, woman or child they kill, I will retaliate!' Before Madeleine could speak, he swept past and entered the church.

'It is useless, Madeleine,' said Marie-Anne at her side. 'He's doing what he thinks is right. No one will dissuade him – they've slaughtered hundreds of Catholics. François is only trying to save our people's lives.'

Unconvinced, but without resisting, Madeleine

allowed the gentle girl to lead her into the womb-like comfort of the church. As they sang a psalm, she listened for the sound of the muskets, straining her ears while dreading to hear. Kneeling, she stole a quick glance across at Charette, but his face, though pale, was calm. The bell rang out for the Holy Office and in the distance she heard faint cries. They had begun! Not a flicker of emotion showed on Charette's face and a flood of helpless anger and hatred consumed her. For the rest of the service she dug her nails deep into the palms of her hands, to shut out all sounds and thoughts other than the eight points of pain.

In a subdued silence they filed out of church into the sunshine. Waiting outside were six Blues, their faces strained and fearful as Charette walked up to them. 'You are free to go,' he said. 'Before you do, you will each eat a good meal, after which you will travel separately to each of the republican camps. Once there, you will tell them how you have been treated these last few months as my prisoners, and how, today, with sadness and grief, I was forced to commit a barbarous act and execute your comrades. I did not wish to do it, but the actions of your leaders at Quiberon forced me to avenge those who died, and to prevent, if possible, the recurrence of such barbaric acts.'

As he finished speaking, a young officer, an émigré who had recently joined them at Belleville, marched smartly up. Nauseated, Madeleine saw his hands and uniform were smeared with blood. 'The executions have taken place, General. To conserve ball and powder I ordered most of the prisoners to be killed by club and sword.' He waited, as though expecting a compliment. Instead, with a snarl of rage, his eyes slits of black fury, Charette made towards the terri-fied man. 'Sir, get from my sight!' he cried, his lips curling back from his teeth. 'You're not fit to wear the uniform of an officer. Never let me see your face again!'

The man fled in terror and the reprieved republican prisoners hastily followed the chef to eat before the long journey.

'Go to him, Madeleine,' said Marie-Anne, watching her brother stride away. 'He shouldn't be alone.'

'I can't ... I won't,' faltered Madeleine. 'Don't ask me to, not after ...'

At her side, the fingers of Céleste de Bulkeley gripped her arm like pincers. 'Do you think it was easy for him? Have you forgotten so quickly the corpses in the villages? Well, I haven't forgotten William, and Sophie and Céleste haven't forgotten their mother, or their miserable days in prison.'

Madeleine, startled by the vehemence in the amazon's voice, looked at the young girls whose mother had been executed at Bouin. 'Yes, Madeleine,' said Sophie de Couëtus softly. 'They punished our country after Savenay. Now after Quiberon, François is telling them to keep their hands off La Vendée. It had to be terrible to make them heed. Don't turn away from him, I beg you.'

'It's true, Madeleine. You know he's not cruel,' said Marie-Anne.

Nodding, choking with varying emotions, the girl kissed and embraced her friends and left to do their bidding. Deep within, she knew what those executions had cost him. And for him to learn that some of them had not been given a soldier's death, but one of dishonour, would be more than he could bear. Not hurrying, she walked after him, beneath the soft green leaves of summer. She wondered whether she should leave him to be alone with his grief. A monster – a Carrier, a Robespierre, a Turreau – would not grieve, but for Charette, these

505

executions carried out under his command went against the nature of a soldier. He had always saluted the courage of an adversary and mourned a brave man's death, whether he be a Blue or a White; for months all 300 prisoners had been fed as everyone else, had been free to wander during the day, even to join in the dancing at eventide. Their only restriction was to be locked up at night. Nor was it his fault they had remained prisoners, for he had tried, without success, to exchange them for the Chevalier Allard and six royalist prisoners at Les Sables d'Onne. Now he had caused their deaths.

Parting the chestnut leaves which formed a barrier of seclusion around the Palais-Royal, Madeleine found him standing before the simple stone house. He was quite still. He usually stood so erect, but there was a tiredness, a drooping in the line of his shoulders. She padded quietly up to him, her soft riding boots making no sound on the smooth moss. Moving alongside, she slipped her hand into his and stood beside him. Not speaking, not daring to look at him, for she knew with the terror and helplessness of a tiny child that this strong man, so daring and fearless, was crying.

Desperately seeking to comfort him, she brought his head down to rest on her chest, pressing it closely to her, murmuring softly as she stroked the curly head. All the time praying he would not ask her whether he had been right – for she had no answer to give. She dared not think beyond being with him. But he did not ask. He was not weak.

After a while she went and saddled their horses and together they rode in silence out of Belleville, feeling the wind tearing away the pall of death as they galloped mile after mile. When, at last, they returned, they were both spent. Side by side they lay together, listening to the evening bird song from the trees around the Pavilion.

'You've never once asked me about my wife,' he said suddenly, gently touching her cheek.

'No,' she replied.

'Why?'

'It didn't seem important. Besides, last time I mentioned her, outside Paris, we quarrelled.'

'Ah, yes. How foolish we were.'

'And there is another reason,' she said archly.

'Oh?'

'Céleste told me how old and unattractive she was and you are quite separated – so there!' she laughed.

'So, you rogue, you are just as curious as other women,' he laughed, for the first time recovering his humour. 'Yes, it's true. We never see each other. I wonder now why I married her, things are so different, but then I had no prospects. Because of the revolution the Navy was more or less in ruins. I resigned my commission and, like many other impoverished nobles with lineage but no money, I married a rich widow.'

'Well, it doesn't matter now, François.'

'But it does!' he flashed. 'I can never make you my wife or give you my heir.'

Madeleine looked at the earnest, sad face. It seemed so small. 'True, you can't make me Madame Charette,' she said, giving a savage tug to his hair, 'but, *mon général*, you have given me your heir!'

Madeleine did not confide their new-found joy to anyone. It would be quite some time before it began to show. For the present she and Charette enjoyed their secret alone. Always attentive to every woman, now his eyes were always on her and she was forbidden to ride out against the republican convoys. Adding to their joy was a visit from the Marquis de

Rivière. Time and time again this brave chevalier had risked his life passing through the republican lines to deliver letters from the Comte d'Artois into Charette's hands. This time, the Marquis, always the diplomat as aide-de-camp to Charles Philippe, did not conceal his happiness as he faced Charette in the salon of the Manor of Jarriette.

'Monsieur Charette, reaching your camp – as you will appreciate – can at times be hazardous, but any dangers which I have encountered on this mission have been met with a happy heart. Knowing that I carried you an honour long-deserved.' With a smile, he picked up a grubby bag of sacking and withdrew a red leather box on which the arms of France were engraved in gold. Excited, Madeleine watched the slim, white fingers, which belied the rough peasant clothes, dip once more into the bag – again the arms of France on red morocco leather but on a flatter, larger wallet. This he handed over to Charette who, opening the clasp, withdrew a thick cream parchment.

'As you will see,' said the Marquis, 'it is your commission as Lieutenant-General of His Majesty Louis XVIII's forces. And this, brave Charette,' he said with a smile of charm and pride, 'is from Their Majesties for your courage and your faithful heart.' Between his fingers hung the Order of Saint-Louis.

Both Madeleine and Marie-Anne, who alone were present at the interview, clapped their hands in delight as the Marquis stepped forward to pin the order on Charette's chest; but before he could do so, the chevalier held up his hand. 'Marquis, I cannot wear the Order of Saint-Louis; not until my army receive the compensation they merit from His Royal Highness. I will give you the names of the officers and soldiers who are to be decorated and presented here to His Royal Highness.'

Nodding in understanding, the Marquis de Rivière bowed and replaced the ribbon in its box, and Madeleine noticed the gleam of approval in his eye as he did so.

'And now,' he said, 'I have completed my mission. I have already called at Stofflet's camp with Their Highnesses' commission. He has been made a Marshal of the Camp,' he said, responding to Charette's raised eyebrows. 'Though worthy, His Majesty felt you alone should receive the highest honour. Now, Mademoiselle Madeleine, perhaps for this evening you could provide me with a change of linen and one of Monsieur Charette's fine cravats?' he said, touching his soiled rags with disgust.

'Certainly Marquis – perhaps a bath too,' she laughed, teasingly holding her nose, 'but first a glass of wine. What shall we drink to?' she asked, filling four glasses.

'I think I know what Monsieur Charette would like the toast to be,' replied the Marquis, his intelligent eyes twinkling. 'Let the toast be, Louis XVIII and Charles Philippe d'Artois on Vendéan soil!'

'Yes,' said Charette, setting down his glass after the toast. 'My letter for His Royal Highness will insist his brother, Artois, lands on our coast. If our brave hearts are to continue to give their lives for the House of Bourbon, then they must have, *deserve* to have, a Prince to lead them!'

On 16 September the Marquis again returned to Belleville. Madeleine was not present to welcome him as she was resting in her tiny bedroom, but as soon as Charette entered she knew! 'The British Government have accepted my plans for an invasion,' he cried, his face ablaze with joy. 'At this moment, my darling, Charles Philippe d'Artois is on board one of His Britannic Majesty's ships, the *Jason*; what is more, it lies off the French coast.' He grinned down at her, his teeth white against the summer bronze of his skin and laughed boyishly, patting her stomach. 'With luck my son will be born with a Bourbon on the throne.'

'Will a Bourbon recognise a bastard?' she suddenly snapped. There was silence. She was as surprised as Charette by her venomous outburst, but it still bubbled inside and she could not hold it back.

'And whose name will he bear when you tire of me and go back to your wife?'

A shadow fell across Charette's eyes and his thin lips compressed in impatience. 'I am talking of our child!' she snapped, as he walked away. 'How can you leave without discussing something so important?' With his hand already reaching for the door-knob, Charette halted in his tracks. Slowly he turned around.

'At a time like this, you wish me to discuss domestic trivia! When the destiny of France lies in the balance!' His withering look and words wounded her deeply, and she dropped her head to hide the colour flooding her face. But he had seen her distress and quickly knelt before her.

'Don't cry,' he pleaded, taking her hands. 'I can't bear to hurt you – forgive me, but your doubts wound me! If I cannot marry you, Madeleine, rest assured you and our child will be honoured and cared for. You are the love of my life, now, always! Now, my rogue,' he said, tenderly pinching a tear-stained cheek, 'you will not sadden my day. We have much to do and you have yet to finish my new banner.' And with an ebullient wave of his hand, he was gone.

For a time, Madeleine made no move to do anything; as though mesmerised she stared into space, her thoughts turned in on herself. Never before had she displayed jealousy towards the elderly

wife living at Nantes. Charette never saw her, and
Marie-Anne confirmed their relationship was quite
severed. The fact that divorce was impossible had,
like her own future, never worried her before. But
now, with a baby on the way . . . what if Charette
were killed? The thought was too terrible and she
dashed it from her mind.

Purposefully she rose from her chair and walked
briskly over to a carved oak chest. Before lifting out
her workbox, she looked at herself in the gilt-edged
mirror above.

'Madeleine Fleury,' she said coldly, 'you are
becoming cowardly and clinging!' Administering this
admonition made her feel a great deal better and she
was tempted to repeat it; instead, her eyes slid down
to examine with curiosity her figure; her waist still
slender and, turning sideways, her stomach quite flat
. . . well, perhaps there was a little more curve.
Impulsively, she pressed her hands against it and
smiled down reassuringly.

'Don't be frightened, darling – I'm a Parisienne at
heart. I'll always find a way!'

Humming a little tune, Madeleine shook out a
length of pure white silk on to a long table. There
was a knock on the door and she looked up expecting Bossard, Charette's valet. Instead the elegant
figure of Céleste de Bulkeley appeared.

'*Mon Dieu*, we've just been told of our Prince's
arrival, and already I find you working him a
banner,' she laughed.

Madeleine smiled; she loved to hear her friend's
silvery laughter. 'And now you've arrived in good
time to help me,' she teased, searching out another
needle.

'You know my needle is always at your disposal,
especially when you start work on a layette!'

Madeleine looked up in astonishment as the light,

merry peal of laughter echoed again in the room. 'Oh Céleste, how did you know? François told you?'

'No, my dear. He has been just as secretive and just as pleased as you. We all guessed days ago. The bloom of parenthood is on you both. Now, which section do you want me to work?'

For a while they worked in silence, couching down the fine gold threads, just as they'd done so often in the forest in Gralas. It made her think of Prudence and Henriette and she hoped they were happy in their new home in Nantes.

'Marie Lourdais returned today,' murmured Madeleine's companion. 'She brought news that General Hoche has deployed 2,000 men to Noirmoutier to assist their General Cambrai should the British attack the island. More serious, 23,000 troops have been sent to destroy us.'

'There's no need to sound so cheerful, Céleste.'

'Well, François always manages to get us out of such scrapes. Besides, now he's about to have an heir he'll be even more skilful at outwitting Hoche. Although,' she added, looking up, her face becoming more serious, 'this General is no Traveau. He's a Kléber, a military man. I think we'll have to watch our step with this one. Did you know he hates the English so much he calls his dog Pitt? Perhaps I shall call my horse Hoche.'

During late September, events escalated. To draw attention from the British expedition, Charette moved their forces south to tempt Hoche to follow. On Friday 25 September, leading 900 horsemen and 10,000 foot soldiers, Charette attacked the bourg of Saint-Cyr-en-Talmondais, to try to take the river Lay so that communication between the Comte d'Artois, the shore and the interior might be achieved.

The engagement was fierce, the losses appalling, including the death of the reckless Guérin. But there

512

was no time for Charette to mourn the death of one of his dearest friends. On 30 September their spies warned that 8,000 Blues were marching towards Belleville. In Madeleine's mind, though, there was no possibility of their little bourg being taken. Fired by the prospect of meeting his Prince, Charette's energy spilled over, touching them all. No generals of the Republic were going to rob him of this moment; and so it did not come as a surprise to Madeleine to hear, hours later, the returning men singing their favourite song:

> 'Admirons la Vaillance
> De Charette, homme de coeur.
> Il est né pour la France,
> Il fait voir sa Valeur.
> Jusque en Angleterre
> On parle de lui,
> Aussi sur les frontières,
> Même à Paris!'

'Même à Paris,' responded Madeleine, wondering what plump Annette had made of La Vendée's Grand Brigand.

The whole province had to be raised. Day after day, together with the Couëtus sisters and Céleste, Madeleine rode through the bourgs spreading the news of the assembly points. Always their message was the same, as men ran in from the fields at the sound of the tocsin. 'The Prince is coming. Take up your arms for Charette and Louis XVIII!' Then they would gallop on to the next parish and the next, cutting across meadows and fording rivers when they saw a republican patrol. And so, on 12 October 1795, 15,000 men marched forward from their assembly point. Forsaking their families and their pardons, shouldering, once again, their weapons, they followed the white banners south through the land of Nesmy to La Tranche.

It was unusually hot for the time of year, and Madeleine removed her white suede gloves. Turning round in the saddle, she looked at the chevaliers behind her. It was the most spectacular sight she had ever seen. Elderly chevaliers, officers of the *ancien régime* were there; their old elaborate uniforms contrasting strangely with the skins of the *moutons noirs*.

Smiling, she acknowledged the salute of the Chevalier L'Espinay de la Roche, whose thin sardonic face hid a kindly, sensitive nature. With him were Charette's brother, Louis-Marin, and Barbot de la Tresorière; and they, too, swept off their hats, acknowledging her work on their behalf, for she, like every lady, had been busy mending and smartening-up battle-worn clothes so that each man felt worthy of greeting his Prince.

Facing about, Madeleine patted her horse, admiring its mane which Pheiffer had plaited for her. She had to admit she was just as excited as everyone else, but also curious. Unlike many of the army, she had never been close to royalty. Of course she had glimpsed the Comte d'Artois many times as a child, but today she would meet him and perhaps better understand the fanatical loyalty which he and his family inspired in the people around her.

Ahead she could see the sea, as blue as the dress of Victorine du Fief who rode beside her. Her own habit was new for the occasion, given to her that very morning by Charette as a surprise, together with pearl ear-drops and necklace. It was exquisite in its simplicity and clearly made by Boëtz himself. Apart from the chevron design of seed pearls worked down the front of the jacket, it was entirely grey. A soft shade, like morning mist, and her hair, now darkening like the bracken and autumn leaves, added a warmth and vibrancy to the total effect.

Now, as they reached the exposed shoreline of La Tranche, playful little breezes tugged at the rim of her grey hat. Anxious not to lose it, Madeleine readjusted her hat pins. It was her first long glimpse of the ocean and she thought it magnificent. Even their boisterous drummers and pipers did not drown the crashing of the white-tipped breakers. She breathed deeply, enjoying its smell and the sight of seagulls wheeling and mewing. Already many of the battalions were waiting, formed up along the silvery sand-dunes. Madeleine shaded her eyes from the glare as the sun's rays bounced off hundreds of pikes and scythes, polished as brightly as mirrors.

The clamour was intense as different divisions rivalled each other with their songs, increasing the moment Charette appeared. Just as always before a battle, he rode along the length of the ranks. Was life tame for those who returned to their homes after the pacification? wondered Madeleine. Here in the lines, farmers' and weavers' faces glowed with excitement and pride. She knew many had come despite weeping, protesting wives, women who had fallen to their knees in despair when Madeleine had ridden in to call their men once more to arms. Nevertheless, feminine fingers had been busy. Many of the woollen hats of the Bocage with their pompoms were new, and every man here today sported a new white cockade and the little lint badge of the Sacred Heart.

Sweeping off his hat in a salute to the valiant grenadiers of Loroux, Charette wheeled his horse around and galloped out on to the strand to face the whole army.

Trying to view him dispassionately, Madeleine stared down at Charette. This was his day. The sash of Lieutenant-General of the King's army was around his waist, paid for with his blood and indefatigable courage. There was no worthier leader, nor more modest, she thought, looking at the gold-trimmed burgundy tunic where he had pinned not his Grand Order of Saint-Louis but a simple white flower: the Lily of France.

Smiling, Madeleine watched him raise up, with a theatrical flourish, the Shield of France for all to see. His face, shining with pride, scarcely concealed his deep emotion at that moment. Like the fierce men around her, her heart reached out to him. Laughing, unable to hear her voice, she cheered with the soldiers.

'*Vive Charette! Vive Charette!*'

'*Vive le Roi!*' Charette responded.

With the answering roar for Louis XVIII, Charette returned to take his place beneath the Bourbon white banner. With a sweet smile, he took her hand and raised it to his lips. His large dominating eyes glistened with tears of joy. This was the moment which had carried him forward through the long years of suffering and deprivation.

'Well done, my brave chevalier,' she whispered.

Gradually quiet fell upon the assembled army as they scanned the ocean. It was an expectant silence – reminding Madeleine of the wait for dawn in the faubourgs of Paris. She had stood beside her brother, Pierre, on that hot, sultry night. It had been his moment, too; the ousting of a king from his palace. And before the windows of the Tuileries palace he had died for his hatred of the monarchy. She tried to conjure up his face, but could not. There seemed so many dear, dead faces to remember. How ironic that many of her companions now had defended the palace on that day in August.

The breeze from the sea was freshening and she

could taste salt on her lips. The banners, which had been lazily flapping to and fro, suddenly streamed out, and the motto which she had embroidered, '*La religion, le Roi ou la Mort*', blazed out its bold message in the bright autumn sunshine.

Half an hour had passed and, beside her, Charette's large black stallion began to paw impatiently at the ground. She narrowed her eyes, scanning the horizon for a small speck of white, but there was no sign of the *Jason*. The stretch of blue water ahead was empty. Anxiously she glanced to the left and noticed a tiny boat pulling towards them along the shoreline.

Others, too, had seen it. Prudent de la Robrie, detaching himself from his cavalry, was cantering over the fine sand-dunes.

Within minutes of reaching the water's edge, the young cavalry commander had returned, with a ragged peasant mounted behind him. Straightaway Madeleine saw by his noble, haughty countenance that he was no fisherman. Though Prudent had set him down some thirty paces from Charette, the stranger did not speak or move. Almost curiously he stared about, taking in the white cockades, the fleur-de-lys banners, the black goat skins of the Maraichins, the mangy horses of the proud cavalry, their ancient pieces of armour and swords polished, glittering like new. Madeleine felt his gaze resting on her and the other amazons in their plumed hats and velvet habits; and then on the hundreds of chevaliers. Slowly his face turned a deep scarlet and he staggered towards Charette. He tried to speak, but so gripped was he with emotion, he seemed unable to do so. Now the angry red had drained from his face, leaving it a deathly white. In a low voice, barely audible, he spoke.

'Monsieur Charette, I am the Marquis de Grignon, aide-de-camp to His Royal Highness, the Comte d'Artois. It is with the deepest regret I bring a message from the Prince. He is unable to join you here today. The British have advised him to return to England. There are reasons.'

'It can't be true,' shrieked a silent voice within Madeleine. 'He must come! No man, least of all a Prince, could abandon an army which had risen to his summons; men who had thrown aside their pardons! Could any man be such a coward, to abandon them – and the man who had given all in his cause?'

Hardly able to breathe with anger, she glared with hatred at the Marquis; but the wretched man, she saw, was consumed with misery and shame, looking as if he wished Charette would plunge a dagger in his heart. The silence was ominous, at last broken by Charette's voice; not raised in anger, but quiet and terrible, thick with disdain. 'Monsieur, you have brought me the sentence of death!'

Madeleine did not hear the rest of his words, as she fought to control the blind rage which swept upwards within her, remembering the orange flames and smoke in the devastated villages. Yet here they were today for their Prince. She thought of Dol and Le Mans and of La Rochejaquelein, the Marquis de Lescure, Marie Lourdais; all risking death every day. Yet this Prince was running like a coward. Oh, how right we were to guillotine them! They are not fit to rule, she thought savagely. Thomas Paine was right – how can we leave it to nature to choose a king?

Chapter Five

Sire,

The cowardice of your brother has lost everything. His return to England has settled our fate. All that remains is to perish uselessly in your service.

Le Chevalier Charette.

Wearily, Madeleine laid down the letter.

'It's the same as the others. Was it nailed to a church door?' Prudent de la Robrie nodded. Sighing, she crumpled it up and threw it on to the fire. 'It would only anger him,' she said, watching the paper blackening and bursting into flames.

'Yes, I know his loyalty to the crown would not permit him to write so to the King,' said Prudent de la Robrie, 'but it's the truth, even if its author is General Hoche. He has been clever enough to write what is in our hearts. Our cause is doomed!'

'His cleverness lies in taking no reprisals to make the men fight on through fear,' said Madeleine.

'Yes,' agreed Hyacinthe, who was also present with his brother.

'Where Turreau spread murder and fire, this general's weapons are conciliation and money. Did you know, Madeleine, the price on François's head is now raised to six million louis-d'or?'

'That's why we must bring a stop to this fighting before it ends in death for all of us. You know we love him dearly,' blurted out the young cavalry officer, his broad, generous face colouring with embarrassment, 'but we must think of the future. Every day thousands of new troops are arriving . . . We're going to meet with one of Hoche's generals tomorrow,' he said slowly.

'Will you break the ice for us, Madeleine? Tell him we are going with Couëtus and Auvynet to discuss terms for our submission with General Gratien at the Château de la Grange. We will bring back the document for his approval,' added Hyacinthe.

'I'll tell him,' said Madeleine sympathetically, knowing instinctively what Charette's response would be.

It did, indeed, take all her powers of persuasion for Charette to agree to talk to his officers on the subject. But on 25 November he gave them an audience.

Usually so relaxed and friendly with his men, Madeleine watched him sit statue-like through the reading of Gratien's proposals. Upon reaching the end of the report, the spokesman for the group, abbé Remaud, looked up expectantly. There was no response, and a cold, uncomfortable silence descended on the room. When at last Charette spoke, his words did not relieve the tension, but increased the strained atmosphere.

'Is that all?'

'Yes, my General,' replied abbé Remaud.

'Eh bien! Throw it on the fire!'

Then, with eyes hard as ebony his mouth as tight as the expression on his face, he looked slowly from one man to the next. 'It's really something, *Messieurs*, that you, who have sustained for so long an honourable war for religion and for the throne, bring to me a cowardly proposition – and especially you, Monsieur de la Robrie,' he said, his eyes finally resting on his friend. 'You who were covered in glory in the many combats, will you lose in an instant the prize of your courage and your exploits?'

The cruel words brought the blood rushing to the broad, good-natured face, and Prudent de la Robrie sprang up. 'I will prove to you on the first possible occasion that I haven't changed!' he flashed back, his face aflame with anger and hurt.

'Don't be long,' responded Charette coldly as he left the room.

Once more a terrible, embarrassed silence pervaded the room. Madeleine squirmed, not knowing whether to leave or stay as the cavalry officer slammed his fist into a cupped hand in a gesture of anger and frustration. Then, sweeping up his hat from the table and ignoring comments and attempts to make him stay, la Robrie followed on the heels of Charette. Deeply upset by the incident Madeleine rushed after him.

'Prudent, wait!' she cried, coming up behind him and seizing hold of his arm. The short, square-framed officer took no notice of her and she pulled vigorously, her fingers pressing into the rock-hard muscle of his upper arm. This time he stopped and swung around to face her, his strong reddish brows drawn together in a frown and his usually cheerful face set in an angry scowl.

'My dear friend,' she said, trying to reach through the anger, 'you know that he loves and admires you – you are one of his main supports. He only spoke in anger.'

'It's too late, Madeleine,' replied Prudent de la Robrie. 'The words have been said! I'll not let him think I'm a coward. You will see in our next engagement, I will hand him the tricolor soaked in my blood!'

'No, Prudent, no!' gasped Madeleine, desperately trying to hold on to her friend, but with an impatient shake of his head he broke free and strode away until she could hear no more the sound of his step or the jingle of spurs.

Helplessly she leant against a tree, a tight constraint in her chest making her breathing shallow and fast. Just for one moment she had hoped the deep affection which Prudent held for her might have allowed her to assuage the hurt of Charette's words. But his love for his General showed in the pitiful hurt in his eyes, and she knew that she would never see, or be whirled off her feet in a dance by Prudent again, for there was only one step beyond his usual reckless mode of fighting.

Two days later, shouting, 'This is my last day,' he hurled himself at the Blues. In the first minutes of the engagement the freckle-faced cavalry officer was dead.

Convulsed with grief and remorse for the words which had sent his reckless friend headlong to death, Charette shut himself away from everyone.

But there were to be many more deaths: such heinous crimes as the murder of the silver-haired Chevalier de Couëtus, cut down with bayonets when under the protection of a safe conduct to discuss peace terms. Outraged, the gentle Sophie and Céleste left the ambulances and took up arms to avenge their father. The fast-dying embers of the rebellion in Bas Poitou burst, once more, into flames, but it did not last long.

Gradually, their numbers decreased as there were more and more defections. An absent king and a prince who had failed the test of courage and devotion inspired no loyalty. Many stayed to protect Charette, but day after day friends and comrades were killed. By the start of the new year, Belleville was lost and they were being chased from village to village.

Seven months pregnant, Madeleine suffered greatly, but she refused to go into hiding in Nantes. If she had to give birth on the forest floor she would do just that rather than leave him.

Once again, just as they'd done the previous winter, they were forced to dig up roots and bulbs out of the icy ground, to shelter in the forests of Touvois and Gralas, always on the move, living on the handouts of the peasants.

Then one day, when they were sheltering in a farmhouse in the little hamlet of Montorgueil, a letter arrived which gave her hope. It was from the curé of Rabatardière. Anxious to bring the fighting to an end, he was offering to act as an intermediary between Charette and General Gratien, whose proposals for peace he included in the letter.

'It seems, Madeleine,' said Charette, throwing a log on to the fire before which they were drying off, 'that our latest republican generals are tiring of wandering in our country. So they propose I go to England. Or if England does not suit, General Gratien says General Travot will escort us all to Switzerland, so long as we do not go via Paris!' He threw back his curly head and laughed derisively. 'Can they be afraid I might seize the Tuileries?'

Madeleine did not speak, for she did not want to influence him. Yet her emotions were plain to see. His laughter died and he stared with concern at her strained white face. 'You want me to say yes, don't you?'

Silently, she nodded, unable to restrain her tears. 'I want you to live, François! I want to have our baby in safety. If we go on fighting it will only be a matter of time before you are . . .' she choked, unable to say the word. For a moment longer he studied the

523

girl's unhappy, tear-stained face. Then, his hand resting against an oak beam, he stared down into the fire. For a long while he remained so, his face brooding and dark. Then suddenly he looked towards her with a forced, gay smile.

'I have decided, *chérie*, we will accept that offer. We will go to Jersey! They promise to send money from my estate, so we will not starve.'

'But what if it's a trap?' asked Madeleine who, delighted by his decision, was yet suddenly fearful, remembering the fate of the émigrés at Quiberon and the execution of Couëtus. 'Will they keep their word, François?'

'That we shall have to chance, or make our own way across the Channel,' replied Charette drily. 'But my mind is made up. Tomorrow we will go to inform the divisional officers.'

There was no sleep for either of them that night. Throughout the long hours, Madeleine tossed and turned, disturbed by the sound of Charette's footsteps below as he paced back and forth. She knew his decision had been made for her sake and she was filled with guilt. But she was also anxious lest he change his mind. They had to leave if they were to live. It was true the peasants still rallied to their aid in moments of dire distress, but they were tired of fighting; nor had the poorest man thought to claim the fortune set on Charette's head – but one day . . . Shuddering at the thought, Madeleine buried her head under the pillow and willed herself to sleep.

The next morning as they rode to rendezvous with the divisional leaders of the army, she knew from his hard, resolute expression that his decision stood.

Most of the officers were already waiting when they entered the house at Begaudière. What a shock they were going to have, thought Madeleine. Each one of them, she knew, was expecting to hear the planning of a new action. At last, when all were present, Charette held up his hand for silence. Straightaway, without preamble, in a harsh, bitter voice, he delivered the blow. 'Messieurs, I have asked you to meet me here in order to inform you that I have the intention of going to England!'

It was as though a cannon had gone off, so stunned were the listeners. No one spoke. The room was quite still as every officer stared uncomprehendingly at Charette. Finally Lecouvreur, the divisional commander of Légé, spoke, twisting his cap nervously between his great hands. 'And what will happen to us, *mon général?*'

'I will receive all those who wish to follow me, but it would be better, and that is my advice, for you to remain in France and submit to the law. In this way you will be more use to me and the royalist party. I will be able to correspond with you and thus take advantage of better circumstances in the future.'

Once again there was a long silence, and then Lucas Championnière, the faithful, brave leader of the country of Retz, stood up. 'You are right, *mon général,*' he said. 'The country during your absence will be harassed by the Republic, but it can easily be returned to you later. In this way you will avoid the useless death of many brave men. In England you will be able to prepare a landing with a body of émigrés for the spring.'

'Emigrés! Bah, neither they nor the Prince will come,' shouted a young officer, springing to his feet.

At once the floodgates of stupefaction burst and everyone tried to speak at once. 'We are lost, lost without you!' someone cried.

Madeleine found she was sweating with tension as the arguments raged in the room. Throughout, Charette sat listless, his eyes dark pools of misery, his expression stony. Seeing him so, she realised just what he would be like in Jersey. Life would be impossible! He had always despised émigrés for fleeing France. Now she willed him to speak, and he did. With a lightning change of mood, he sprang up, slamming his fist down on the gleaming oak table. 'I'm not leaving! I do not have the right to abandon my soldiers! Nevertheless, any of those who wish to opt for peace are entirely free to submit. Each person is free to make his own choice. As for myself, even if I am abandoned by all of you, as long as I retain a single breath in my body, I shall fly the white flag. The symbol of the old French honour.'

His eyes were no longer dead, but sparkling; his movements full of verve and vigour as he withdrew from its sheath the beautiful silver sword sent to him at La Tranche by his Prince. Holding it up before him he cried in a voice resonant with passion, 'I will never surrender!'

The next day, as if to throw down the gauntlet, a courier galloped away with a haughty rebuttal to General Gratien's proposals. Whilst the army rode out to attack the vanguard of General Travot, Madeleine did not go, for she found it difficult to keep up and only endangered those around her.

It was late when they returned. Horrified, she saw they had been routed as never before. Lifelessly draped over two of the officers' horses were the bloodied figures of two women.

'*Mon Dieu*, what has happened, Hyacinthe? Is Sophie dead?'

'No, Madeleine, but she and Céleste are badly wounded. They were both surrounded by hussars and near cut to death.'

'Bring them both inside, Hyacinthe. I'll go and get some bandages, they're still losing a great deal of blood.'

Both women were in agony and crying piteously

526

and Madeleine worked swiftly. The wounds were clean sabre cuts, but deep, and she applied meadow-sweet to help staunch the bleeding before binding them up tightly. Then she gave Céleste and Sophie a sleeping draught.

'Tell me what happened,' she said to the exhausted officer.

'Well, our spies had correctly told us where to find Travot's column. As usual Charette chose the most advantageous position to launch our attack. Like a rocket, we shot out from the trees, taking them completely by surprise. We were outnumbered by almost four to one but the day was almost ours . . . when, suddenly, almost from nowhere, 400 hussars appeared. It was terrible . . .'

'Here, drink this.'

Gratefully the young chevalier took the bottle of wine from Madeleine. 'It was a massacre . . . I saw Charette's brother, Louis-Marin, and his cousin cut down. We left many dead behind – we're lucky to return at all.'

'And François?' she whispered, at last daring to ask.

'He's supervising the wounded. He's not speaking to anyone. He's just like when Prudent was killed.'

'I'd best go to him,' she said. 'Will you stay with the girls?'

With a deep sigh, Hyacinthe nodded and accompanied Madeleine to the door where they embraced, then clung for a moment longer in silence, each thinking of Prudent.

'Remember all the dancing, Hyacinthe?' she whispered, not really knowing what to say.

'Yes,' he replied in a voice hollow with sadness. 'We have to make our submission, Madeleine. We cannot win without help from the Princes, and the Marquis de Rivière brings only empty words.'

Outside, the scene which confronted Madeleine was harrowing, for nearly everyone, it seemed, had sustained some injury. She found Charette kneeling beside a chevalier, who did not seem to have any visible wounds, but who was clearly dying. Quietly she waited, listening to the low murmur of Charette's voice comforting the weeping boy. She had witnessed such scenes many times before, but it seemed even more painful this day. After a while the boy quietened and, kissing his forehead, Charette beckoned for the abbé.

'What can I do to help?' she asked quietly as he stood up.

'It's nothing,' Charette said, as Madeleine reacted to the blood on his brow. 'Just a graze, that's all. Come over here, I must speak with you.'

Terrified, Madeleine followed him, wondering what he wanted of her, for his manner was very grave. As soon as they were a little apart from the rest, beside the slender trunk of a birch, he spoke. 'Tomorrow, *chérie*, you must go with the rest of the women into hiding. There's an isolated farmhouse where you'll be safe for the next few months. And when you've had our baby, if things are no better . . . or should I be killed, arrangements have been made to get you out of France. What money I have will be yours.'

Madeleine stared at him, appalled.

'No! I stay!' she said firmly. 'You are keeping the oath you made before your peasants, when they asked you to lead their rebellion; never to submit until the rightful monarch of France was on the throne. I, too, will keep my oath!'

'Your oath, *chérie*?'

'Yes,' said Madeleine, slipping off the topaz ring and holding it up before her with a smile. 'Do you remember giving it to me on that cold, starry night when I was so frightened? Well, as you galloped away, I clenched it in my fist like this, closed my eyes, and said for all the street to hear, "I swear I will find you again, and never will I leave you!"'

Opening her eyes, Madeleine slipped the ring back on to her finger, laughing lightly to conceal her feelings. 'So you see, as long as I, too, have breath in my body, I will not be parted from you.'

March came in with cold, icy winds and rain which drove into the face and penetrated through clothing to the skin. Others before Hoche and Travot had given up the chase, exhausted by the speed and energy of their prey. But as Céleste de Bulkeley had foreseen, Hoche was cunning. He poured men, spies and gold into the Marais.

There were betrayals, but the courage and loyalty of the poor people more than made up for the perfidies. Under the very noses of the Blues, they slipped into the woods with food and news of troop movements. And brave little children played their own game of 'spot the Blue', giving the alarm from high up in the trees when troops were arriving.

At dawn on 23 March, just as the cocks were crowing at the farmhouse where they were sheltering, the alarm, as it had been so often, was raised. 'Quick, Madeleine,' said Charette. 'There's little time.' Springing from bed as quickly as she could, she followed him down into the kitchen. Like herself and Charette, everyone was ready to leave. No one now undressed; they did not even remove their boots. 'Come, my children, take courage,' said Charette, putting on his plumed hat.

'*Mon général*, I beg you, leave the hat – you know it always draws their fire to you,' said Pheiffer urgently.

'Then that's how it should be, comrade,' said

Charette, with a reckless laugh. 'Besides it makes them realise what bad shots they are,' he said, gesturing to two recent wounds which Madeleine knew grieved him piteously. 'Now let's go. We'll have to cross the river. Open the door, Pheiffer!'

As soon as the heavy door swung open, everyone ran out towards the river bank. The grenadiers were arriving as they left the shelter of the farmhouse of Pellerinière, and as Pheiffer had foreseen, the heaviest fire was directed at Charette. Out of the corner of her eye, Madeleine saw several of their small party fall, but she dared not stop. To her right, Charette and the Chevaliers L'Espinay and de la Barre were firing and reloading as they ran. Suddenly Pheiffer came racing up to Charette and, in a swift movement, snatched the distinctive hat from his General's head. Then, placing it on his own, he raced away from the river. At once Charette made to give chase.

'No! Don't let him die for nothing,' Madeleine screamed, seeing Pheiffer stagger with the impact of a ball, then lurch onwards in a wild, erratic flight.

Without further delay they ran down to the water's edge and crossed over the tiny bridge to the Moulin de Gate Bourse.

'Are you all right, little one?' asked Charette, giving her hand a squeeze.

'Yes,' she replied, forcing a smile to her lips. 'Perhaps we can rest when we get to La Guyonière.'

But they had no sooner reached the outskirts of the little hamlet when they saw, emerging from it, another column of Blues. Now they were caught between two forces – their escape ahead was barred and to go back would land them into the hands of the grenadiers.

'Oh François, what shall we do?' she sobbed in terror.

Hesitating hardly a moment, Charette whirled her

around. 'We'll have to cross over to the farmhouse of Sableau. Can you manage it, my love?'

Madeleine nodded, hiding her anxiety as he shouted instructions to their companions. Realising her friends were slowing to keep pace with her, Madeleine pushed herself as hard as she could; but all she could manage was a lumbering trot. She cursed, realising she was endangering everyone. Anxiously she looked at the test ahead; it was the second branch of the river with no bridge over to the other bank. Surprisingly, as Bossard and Charette lowered her into the water, she found that though the water was icy, it took her weight. She could not swim fast, but it proved much easier than trying to run.

Once they had gained the shelter of the farmhouse, she leant against a wall to regain her breath, while the men took up their positions; but the respite was brief.

'They're still coming,' shouted Barbot de la Tresorière, 'and will soon be on us, *mon général*.'

'Right, then we'll have to head towards Boulaye and the wood of Essarts; but first let's give them something to think about. Abbé, start out now with Madeleine.'

Immediately a furious discharge broke out as the men fired at the advancing grenadiers. Under cover of the diversion, Madeleine slipped away with the abbé Remaud.

'I fear we are done for, Father,' she gasped as they picked their way over the rough, marshy ground.

'Nonsense, my child. Have faith. We've escaped before. See, here come the others.'

Glancing over her shoulder, Madeleine saw their companions running towards them at great speed. They had been forty last night, now she saw their numbers were no more than twenty. Gritting her teeth, she pressed on. Ahead was safety – if they could just reach the woods of Essarts.

Suddenly everyone stopped in their tracks. Cutting them off from the deep, dark wood, was a third column of Blues. Desperately they turned around, seeking shelter, but it was too late; in the distance they heard hurrahs and yells. They had been spotted.

'Where to now?' Madeleine gasped, biting her lip to stop the terror which was rising within her.

'No need for alarm, my love,' said Charette, with a calm smile. 'We'll go up to the little wood of the Chabotterie, then, after losing them, we can retrace our steps to the sanctuary of les Essarts.'

Childlike, she placed her hand in his, wanting to be reassured by the smile; but as the sounds of pursuit grew louder, she knew their situation was desperate. They were now between three columns.

Like a kaleidoscope of horror, the pictures of corpses slaughtered during the Terror flashed into her mind. Would these troops be as cruel?

'Oh, please God,' she prayed silently, 'don't let them rip my baby from me, let them shoot me.'

Fear gave her the strength to carry on and Charette, steadying her with his arm, inspired her with the courage she lacked. Casting a sidelong glance at him she saw, however, that his face had become anxious. He stopped and, shading his eyes, looked back. Though he spoke softly to the Chevalier L'Espinay at his side, she caught his words. 'They're still following. We should have lost them by now. Damn – there must be a peasant guiding them.'

'Leave me,' she gasped. 'Please ... François, go on, I'm finished!'

'No!' he snapped. 'We'll die together, for I'll not abandon you. Take your time. We are but yards away from the Chabotterie.'

Slowly, as her senses cleared, she saw that the trees

were indeed becoming more dense. Making a supreme effort, she lumbered forward towards the sanctuary of the wood. Though not large, it would enable them to lose their pursuers. Then they could retrace their steps to the immense wood of les Essarts.

Relieved to have survived, Madeleine paused and wiped the sweat from her face. Oh, for one of those hot air balloons, she thought, that would lift them clear. Laughing at the thought, she moved off with the others. Struggling, they pushed their way through a barrier of holly, when all at once all hell broke loose and they were caught by a heavy fusillade. Around her, figures spun and reeled and she saw the young Roche-Davo fall dead.

Beside her, Charette started to return fire at an amazing rate. As she was reloading her own gun, she saw him start suddenly as a ball took him in the shoulder; his eyes widened a fraction as he absorbed the shock. Then as he had done so many times on the battlefield, he was fighting on. Bearing down on him were three republicans, braving all to be the one to take Charette. Like a tiger he took the fight to them, slashing and wheeling his sabre with furious energy. With a cry of alarm, she saw two of his fingers were severed by a blow from a republican sabre. Taking careful aim, she shot the man through the head. Then, as Charette left the other two reeling from their wounds, they ran on.

Now soldiers were running towards them from all directions. Their only avenue of escape was a large thorn hedge ahead. With a little reassuring smile, Charette turned and grabbed hold of her hand and pulled her towards it. Suddenly he clutched his head. Terrified, she screamed as he fell away from her. Blood was pouring from his temple. Immediately the massive Bossard, following them, caught him up in his arms like a child and ran on, lifting him over his shoulder.

'Quickly, Madeleine!' gestured abbé Remaud, standing before the barrier.

The thorns of the hedge ripped and tore at her clothes, but as bullets crashed into the trees around them, the abbé pushed her body through it. Waiting on the other side to help her was the Chevalier L'Espinay.

'Come on,' he said.

'François.'

'Bossard has him.'

Madeleine turned to check. As abbé Remaud struggled through the dense hedge she saw the whole thicket shake as the big valet started to force his way through. With relief, she saw his face appear but then his expression became anxious and he started to struggle furiously. 'It's the General's coat, it's caught,' he shouted, fighting to free himself. Suddenly his face contorted in agony, screaming out in pain, and he fell backwards from view.

'François!' screamed Madeleine.

There was a sharp blow against her temple and all went black.

When she came round she found she was lying amongst hay. From somewhere below came the sound of animals moving and eating. Waves of pain gripped her body and, though it was her first time, she knew the contractions indicated her labour had begun. The baby was early; it was hardly surprising, she thought. Gradually she became aware that she was not alone. In the dim light she saw two men were sitting near to her. As she struggled to support herself on an elbow, they crawled towards her, and she saw they were the abbé Remaud and L'Espinay.

'François?' she whispered.

'He's alive,' replied the abbé softly.

'Is he here?' she asked eagerly.

'No. He's been taken prisoner by Travot. Don't worry, they are treating him with great respect. Now, no more talking,' he said, seeing her face contort with pain, 'you have work to do. We dare not bring a midwife. As it is, this farmer and his family are taking a great risk sheltering us. They are billeting six republican soldiers; you can hear the horses down below. I'm afraid you'll have to keep very quiet, my child.'

'I'll try, Father. Perhaps you could give me something to bite on.'

With a shy smile the Chevalier L'Espinay undid the cravat around his neck. 'It's a little soiled, Madeleine,' he said, folding it into a wad. 'I must confess I'd rather face Travot than the next hours,' he said ruefully.

For more than twelve hours throughout the night, Madeleine worked to bring her premature baby into the world. Covered in sweat, she hung tightly on to the two men's hands in the darkness, biting into the wad of linen and lace to drown the agony. Later, as the first hours of dawn introduced a dim light into the stable, the abbé, kneeling under the low roof, held up before her a tiny, red-faced boy.

Exhausted, she fell back against the hay, experiencing a fierce, exultant joy. Beside her, the autocratic chevalier, his face glistening with sweat, was, like herself, laughing and weeping. 'That was really worse than any battle,' he murmured, leaning down to kiss her on the cheek.

'My dear, dear friends,' she said sleepily, as the priest laid the little child beside her.

'Sleep now, my child,' the abbé Remaud said. 'We'll be gone in a few hours because we must make arrangements to move you from here as soon as possible. It's too dangerous to stay in Chevasse.'

When Madeleine next awoke it was with a feeling of having had a deep, luxurious sleep; something she had not experienced for months. As she opened her eyes she was aware of a small mewing noise beside her and, laughing out loud, she reached out, remembering she had a son.

'Are you hungry, darling?' she crooned, placing the little creature against her breast. In wonder she felt the little mouth lock on to her nipple. Totally absorbed she studied the little being who was her son. 'Such tiny nails – and dark curls like your daddy,' she murmured joyfully.

Suddenly a ladder slammed against the side of the loft. Terrified, Madeleine came back to reality. She thrust her hand under the cape which covered her to see if there was a gun, but there was nothing. Then a man's head and shoulders came into view. Horrified, she saw it was a republican soldier. For a long moment they stared at each other; he taking in the baby at her breast and the badge of the Sacred Heart pinned on to the bodice of her dress. A look of understanding flashed across his face.

'I'm lost,' she thought, but suddenly the trooper smiled, then put his fingers to his lips and disappeared. For a while she wondered what to do. Should she try to escape? There seemed little point; if he had wanted to raise the alarm he would have done so immediately. Relieved, she lay back, knowing that she had been fortunate in being discovered by a decent man. But the abbé Remaud was right, they must move quickly. It would not be possible to keep a baby quiet. Hiding over troopers' horses was not safe.

Though she tried to stay awake, she gradually succumbed to sleep. When she awoke several hours later, abbé Remaud and the chevalier were sitting smiling at her. Quickly she related what had happened earlier.

'Thank God, you were lucky to meet a good man,' remarked the abbé.

'It does seem strange the soldiers haven't ridden out today,' she said.

'There's an easy explanation for that – they're all celebrating the capture of Charette,' said L'Espinay. 'I doubt whether there is a sober Blue in the whole district. That's why we must move now, if you think you can manage.'

'Yes, with your arm I think so. Did you find out any more about François?'

'Yes, they're going to take him from the Manor House of the Chabotterie to Angers.'

'Then we must try to snatch him from them!' declared Madeleine fiercely.

Through her tears, Marie Lourdais watched the beautiful Parisienne run her fingers along the ornate silvered sheath, pausing to read out loud the inscribed motto.

'I will never cède. Never,' she repeated in her low husky voice.

In love with Charette herself, the little pastry cook had not wanted to part with the sword. But now, as the lovely amazon took her into her arms and held her close, she was glad.

'Thank you, Marie – you took a great risk bringing it to me.'

'It was nothing, Madeleine,' flushed the girl. 'You know the men tried to hide our General under a pile of logs. One of them escaped with the sword, knowing our General would not wish it to fall into republican hands.'

'He was so close to escaping ... poor Bossard. Like Pheiffer, he laid down his life for Charette.'

'So would we all,' said Marie Lourdais, bursting into tears.

'Come, be brave, Marie. François would not wish you to be unhappy,' Madeleine said, taking the young woman into her arms. How she wished she could cry like the girl, but tears were no good if she was to save him. Only ten of them had escaped from the Chabotterie and they, like the other old campaigners, were as if mesmerised. The impossible had happened. Charette was taken. 'Now, no more tears,' she said, patting the young woman. 'You are amongst the bravest. We must not waste time if we are to rescue him.'

'Rescue?'

'Yes,' said Madeleine, turning to Lucas Championnière. 'That's why I sent for you!'

The leader of the men of Retz shook his head in disbelief. 'You don't know what you're saying, Madeleine. The republicans have captured our King of the Marais. Marie will tell you they're guarding him like a king. Why, four generals and hundreds of troops escorted him to Angers. It's impossible.'

'Nothing is impossible,' she snapped. 'I will not let them shoot him in some dark corner like they did Stofflet and all the others. We must try – I will go alone if no one will help me!'

Lucas Championnière looked at the angry face of the girl and knew from the defiant glint in the lovely golden eyes that she would, indeed, go to Angers. He sighed heavily and motioned her to sit down. 'Look, we do know that he has been well received. The senior officers even held a dinner for him at the Hôtel-Lamberty. The fact that they did means they are treating him differently from anyone else. He's famous, Madeleine. Remember our song:

538

> *'On parle de lui,*
> *Aussi sur les frontières,*
> *Même à Paris!'*

'Then do you think they may send him to Paris for trial?' she asked hopefully. 'Marie-Anne has spoken to Madame Gasnier-Chambon who, as you know, moves in republican circles, and she says if the trial were moved to Paris he would probably be acquitted. I'm sure that's right. The Parisians love a hero. Besides, he has never tweaked their tails,' she said with a small smile.

'Whereas your Nantais,' said Lucas Championnière, developing her thought, 'are still smarting for revenge because he took up the sword again. But there's no way we can influence a move to Paris, Madeleine. And if Madame Gasnier's friends think Paris is the place, our General's enemies will make sure he doesn't get there.'

'Oh, if only there were more time – if only I knew someone with influence – but there isn't even time to travel there and back. They're bound to act quickly before the people can rise in his support.'

Despondently Madeleine sat and thought, her feeling of helplessness reflected by Lucas Championnière as he sat with his bowed head in his hands. As if to organise her thoughts, she spoke aloud. 'We have to assume if François is taken to Paris he has a sporting chance. If he is tried at Angers we know Generals Travot, Valentin and Guérin are for him and do not seek his life, only his submission to the Republic. The danger then lies at Nantes. Madame Gasnier says General Duthil has threatened to shoot him. Therefore our plan must be to rescue him on the road from Angers to Nantes, if they should decide to move him there. Agreed?'

'Agreed!' said Lucas Championnière.

All through that night, Madeleine tried to think what Charette would do. She remembered how he used to advise the various partisan leaders. 'Always choose the terrain least favourable to your foe – use surprise,' he would say in his clear voice. There would, of course, be hundreds of soldiers. So, somehow they would have to attack when numbers were at a disadvantage. A narrow passage where chaos, similar to that in the street at Le Mans, would break out. Then, at great speed, they would lift him clear.

The next day, Good Friday, Lucas Championnière returned with a party of loyal men. Madeleine put the plan to them.

'We'll need some barrels of gunpowder, of course,' she added.

'That's going to be difficult,' said one of the men. 'We're left with nothing and we haven't the strength to attack a Blue camp.'

'Perhaps, then, I should seek help from Charles d'Autichamp who has taken over Stofflet's command. I do know he's brave and would help.'

'No! No!' shouted the men, jumping up in fury. 'He's our General and we will save him!'

'Good,' said Madeleine, turning away lest they should see her triumphant smile.

That day she left her hiding place and with her baby set out for Nantes. Straightaway she went to Boëtz's shop.

'Flamand,' she said, using the name which those closest to him used. 'I need you to find a good wet nurse for little François for about three days. Can you do that?' Solemnly the tailor nodded. 'I also want you to find a trustworthy boat-owner who will take Charette and me down the Loire and, more difficult, passage on a sloop.'

'So, I see you intend to snatch our General away

to England,' said the tailor, his eyes twinkling approval behind the lenses of his glasses.

'No, I wouldn't dare,' laughed Madeleine. 'I'm going to accept General Suvorov's invitation. We shall go to Russia!'

Quickly Madeleine explained the plan of the intended ambush. When she had finished, the tailor nodded. 'Madame Gasnier is right about General Duthil. He has made it quite public that if Charette is not executed he will do the job himself; and I found out from the officer who came in here for a fitting this morning that he has pressed for him to be returned here on Easter Day. Your ambush will be necessary to save him.'

After arranging for her faithful tailor to collect the necessary letters of credit from Marie-Anne who was in Nantes, Madeleine waited for the wet nurse to arrive. She was a strong, healthy-looking girl who assured Madeleine, vigorously, that her milk was the best in Nantes. So, after explaining to the girl she would be gone from the city for just a few days, she bade her little baby goodbye.

It was a painful parting, reminding her of the young peasant girl, Marguerite, and what agony it must have been for her when she had to throw her baby to Madeleine so that it might live. Not knowing whether she would see her own son again, she left Nantes.

An hour had passed after the appointed time of their meeting, and Madeleine began to worry that Lucas Championnière and his men were not coming. It was windy and cold on top of the Mont des Alouettes and she wondered why she had settled on it for a rendezvous. Besides the climb, it was a sad choice, the blackened remains of four of its seven windmills a grim reminder of the incendiary columns; but she could see from a military point of view the republican need to give a grim warning to the countryside. The spectacular view from the hill took in the whole countryside. It was easy to see how the millers had been able to use the great sails on their windmills to alert the royalists of enemy troop movements. And she remembered from her days with Westermann and Kléber how perplexed they had been that the royalists were always ready for them.

What a beautiful province it was, she thought, looking out over the landscape; yet secretive, like her people. To the west lay the Marais, where the peasants, like mighty grasshoppers, leapt the six-foot canals with their staves; where empty, lowering skies, marsh and forest gave no welcome to the stranger. The Bocage, with its maze of deep broom-covered tracks, condemned the traveller to ramble, lost for days. Yet she had grown to love this province as fiercely as its people.

At the sound of horses, she sighed with relief and saw, included amongst the horsemen, the Chevalier L'Espinay.

'He's to be tried at Nantes,' she cried without wasting words. 'General Duthil wants death. He's being brought back tomorrow.'

'Then it's too late for us to warn him,' said Lucas Championnière, leaping down from his horse.

'Yes, but knowing François, he'll be expecting something to happen.'

'Yes, Madeleine, but don't forget he's badly wounded.'

'No I haven't forgotten, my friend,' she said sadly.

'Well, at least the Republic provided us with powder and shot,' the divisional leader said, with a huge grin. 'So if you'd care to mount, Mademoiselle, we'll pick our spot to blow some Blues sky high!'

The ride across country to the route from Nantes

to Angers was painful for Madeleine. She was still very tender after the recent birth, but her anticipation overrode her physical state and she was in incredibly high spirits. Surrounded as she was by thirty of the fiercest, most seasoned fighters, she felt they could not fail.

With great care they selected the point for the ambush. It was where the road turned like the leg of a dog, with steep wooded slopes on either side. Before and after the actual bend, the road narrowed dramatically.

'It's perfect,' said Madeleine, looking down on it with L'Espinay and Championnière.

'Yes, I do believe there's a chance,' said the young chevalier, turning to her with a smile.

'Timing will be everything,' said Lucas Championnière. 'The moment he's through at the bend those large boulders must be rolled down, cutting off the rear of the column. At that moment every man around him must be marked and brought down. At our first shot two men must separate the vanguard.'

'Gunpowder?' suggested the chevalier.

'Maybe – but I feel it's risky. It might not go off or we might blow everyone up, including Charette.'

'What about a tree?' said Madeleine. 'If we cut almost through and secured it with ropes, on the signal, one blow and it would fall.'

'Yes, that might do it,' agreed Championnière. 'Let's go and talk to Nicholas. He's a woodsman, he ought to know how to direct its fall, and he can let his axe do its proper work for a change,' he grinned.

By ten o'clock the following day they were ready and in position. The Chevalier L'Espinay, having the fastest horse, was stationed a league further up the road so that, upon the first sight of the Blues, he could ride back to give the alert. Beyond the bend, Nicholas and another peasant waited to send the tree

543

crashing down across the road, whilst six others were hidden behind the overhanging boulders at the crook of the road. Madeleine, together with the rest, was positioned to pour down a fusillade at the soldiers around Charette. Like the others, she had barely slept, but a tremendous energy was surging through her body, masking and overriding her physical and mental exhaustion.

One of the men was smoking a pipe and she found the smell of the tobacco comforting. It would be some hours before the convoy arrived so they chatted quietly amongst themselves, talking of old times and lost friends. From time to time they got up and walked about, stretching cramped limbs, ducking behind cover when travellers passed on the road below.

But by four o'clock, and then five, still the Chevalier L'Espinay had not come. Their nerves were stretched to breaking point as they waited for action. As darkness fell the chevalier returned.

'What should we do?' he asked.

'We must stay. Perhaps they will come tomorrow,' said Madeleine firmly.

It was a terrible night. They were all cold and hungry, for they had brought only enough food for one night. But when daylight broke, they took up their positions once more. For an hour the road remained empty. Then suddenly, around the bend, a single horseman galloped into sight, and as his horse slowed because of the incline, Madeleine recognised one of Boëtz's apprentices. All the while he cast anxious glances up into the trees bordering the road.

'He's looking for us – something has gone wrong,' she cried, springing up. 'Claude, wait!'

The young boy looked up, waved and walked his horse into the side of the road.

'What has happened? Have you any news?' she shouted, tearing down the grassy slope to his side.

'Charette has arrived at Nantes, Mademoiselle Madeleine.'

'But that's impossible,' she gasped. 'We watched the road all day!'

'They brought him by river,' said the boy glumly.

. It was as if he had kicked her in the stomach. 'By river,' she said dully.

'Yes, they left the harbour at Ancre with troops of the sixty-second brigade. On board with him was Adjutant-General Travot, and other high-ranking officers. There were batteries every half league along the river. Each one fixed a salute to honour him,' the boy said desperately, as though to comfort her, for the beautiful young woman, her face breaking apart with grief, had sunk to her knees on the road.

'I've lost him,' she wept. 'Oh my love, they have taken you from me.'

The grim prison of La Bouffay was bristling with soldiers. For a long moment the officer studied their papers and checked off their names against a visiting list.

'Marie-Anne Charette, sister of the prisoner?'

'Yes,' replied Marie-Anne.

'Madame Charette de Thiersant, cousin of the prisoner?'

'Correct,' answered Madeleine.

'Proceed.'

With a sigh of relief, Madeleine walked with Marie-Anne down the dismal stone corridor, lifting back the black veiling which she had attached to her bonnet to be inconspicuous. Though the officer had been exact in carrying out his duties, she had felt a warmth, a sympathy towards him which immediately set her at ease in her borrowed role. How different the soldiers were to those under Carrier's direction. Then, thugs had been recruited, besmirching the early days of the revolution. These were proper soldiers who respected valour. Brought into close contact with their old foe, it would not take long before François's charismatic charm won their hearts. She gave a little frown as she thought of him. The meeting which she had so desperately desired now frightened her. What would it be like to see him captured, helpless in others' power? She had made him her hero and could not cope with the thought of seeing him vulnerable. If only they could have foreseen the journey by river. Was it too late for bribery? she wondered, as the guard unlocked the cell door.

He was standing with a glass of wine in his hand when they entered, looking through a window down into a courtyard. Around his temples was a thick bandage and she saw his hand had been bandaged to a block of wood to support his severed fingers.

Turning around, he smiled, raising an eyebrow in mock irony. 'I hope, ladies, that those are not for my benefit,' he said, indicating the black hats and veils.

Feeling awkward, conscious that it would be their last meeting if he were not acquitted in the morning, Madeleine hung back, completely overwhelmed with emotion, not able to speak or move. She watched the tall, elegant figure move forward to embrace his sister. Then he looked towards her where she stood still by the door.

'Come, *chérie*,' he said, stretching out his hand with a sweet smile of understanding.

She hurled herself forward within the safety of his arms. 'We tried, François,' she whispered brokenly. 'We waited on the road.'

'I know, little one,' he said, kissing her cheek. 'I knew you would. Withhold your tears, my love. Do not weaken my courage, of which I have greater need than ever.' Slowly he raised her face and kissed the tears from her eyes. 'I suffer greatly from my wounds, my love. I will not be sad to die. I have faced death many times on the battlefield without fear. I can face it so for the last time.'

Madeleine smiled up at him, trying to be brave. 'You know we have a son? I've named him François.' It was as though she had given him the key to the cell, for the large black eyes widened and the chevalier's whole face blazed with joy. Then sadness clouded his expression and, for the first time, despair filled his eyes.

'I shall never see him,' he whispered.

'Yes you will,' she said fiercely, unable to see him for the tears blurring her vision. 'I shall stand by with him in my arms if needs be, but I know it won't be necessary. Villenave is the best advocate in Nantes. Soon you will teach your son how to use your sword – for it's not lost, I have it.' She wiped her eyes, feeling more composed, willing herself to believe he would be acquitted. 'And you'll see,' she said, placing a finger on the end of his upturned nose, 'your son has inherited this.'

Smiling wistfully, he held her away from him, his black eyes looking over her in the way which always set her blood racing. 'And now we must say goodbye, Madeleine. Marie-Anne will stay for a while longer to discuss final arrangements.'

It was their last parting; she knew it with every fibre of her being. Her tears were gone, for she wished to hold on to this moment for the rest of her life. Silently she gazed at his dear, sweet face – so earnest, so vital. Carefully she memorised every line and feature.

'Thank you, my darling, for teaching me to live!' she whispered. Raising her lips to his, they kissed until their breath expired. Then she turned and left.

* * *

The clock of Bouffay beneath the lead dome was striking the hour. It was four o'clock. Just as the Nantais had packed the streets to see Charette ride to make his submission, now they waited to see him go to his death.

Madeleine stood at the first-floor window overlooking the route Charette would take. Used as she was to the moods of Parisian crowds awaiting the condemned, Madeleine recognised that here there was no hostility, rather a respectful curiosity.

In prison Charette had not wished to see his wife, and it seemed natural, therefore, for Marie-Anne and her parents to invite Madeleine to sit with them. From the first introduction, the elderly chevalier and his wife accepted her as a daughter, but grief-stricken as they all were, there was little conversation in the room.

Since her first and only visit to the prison, Madeleine had moved as if in a trance. Marie-Anne and Boëtz had done everything. They had organised this room on the rue des Gorges, where he would be able to see her and his son. Also, a window further along, where abbé Remaud would be waiting to make the sign of the cross to absolve him; for with great reluctance, Charette had been forced to make his confession to the abbé Guibert, a constitutional priest. It was something which had made him very unhappy and the brave abbé Remaud had immediately volunteered to hide along the route.

At her side, the sound of Marie-Anne's voice broke into Madeleine's thoughts. 'Can I read you something, Madeleine? It's very private, given to me after the verdict, in person, by General Travot. I'll read you the end of the letter: "your brother was a god of war; a worthy and generous adversary. It has been my privilege to know him and all France will honour his deeds!"'

The gentle, dark-haired girl took hold of Madeleine's hand and pressed the letter into it. 'Keep it for little François. One day when he is older he will read it and see the high regard his father's enemies held him in. They did not wish to bring him here,' she added. 'If only Hoche had acted. He had the power to insist on Paris.'

'If,' repeated Madeleine, in a dull voice, her eyes sliding back to the street below.

Suddenly there was a buzz of excitement: heads were straining and men were lifting their small sons on to their shoulders for a better view. The sound of drums became louder and she turned round to the white-haired lady who sat beside her husband and Boëtz.

'François will soon be here,' she said gently.

Madame Charette rose and, together with her husband and the tailor, joined Marie-Anne and Madeleine at the open window.

Below, the first lines of the drummers passed, their drumsticks lost in a blur of motion. There were at least fifty and their sound drowned the salvos of gun salutes along the Loire. One of the drummers looked up and, catching sight of Madeleine, winked. In return, she gave a small smile, for he was but a child. She knew she looked lovely, for she had dressed as if for a wedding. His last sight of her, standing together with his parents and sister, would be one which he would hold before his eyes at the end.

Her gown was of spring green, like the young leaves in the woods of Belleville through which they had ridden and loved. Her hair was arranged in gleaming coils; and she wore a bonnet to match her dress, on which were fastened two ostrich feathers; the green of hope and the black of mourning. Whilst on little François she had pinned his father's Grand Order of Saint-Louis and the little lint badge of the

Sacred Heart. They made a stunning picture and she was proud and glad.

Behind the drummers came the musicians, and then over 200 grenadiers. Every man picked for his height and prowess. It seemed miraculous that they had routed this splendid fighting machine of France so many times when foreign countries had failed. Yet they had.

She felt a hand touch her shoulder. 'Tell me, Mademoiselle,' said the elderly chevalier, leaning forward, his eyes fixed on the troops below. 'How did a bunch of peasants manage to beat troops of the line for over two years? I'm an old campaigner myself and I must confess I can't understand how my son did it.'

'Yes, it is hard to understand,' she murmured. 'I think perhaps he inspired them as much as us – both sides believed he would always succeed. By holding the roads he paralysed their movements ... but I think, Monsieur, he invented a new type of war which the military schools do not teach. That's why so many generals departed confounded. He is fearless – and he made each one of us grow and we loved him for it ... We wanted to protect him.'

'Protect?'

'Yes,' she replied, groping for what she was beginning to understand herself. 'There was no baseness in him, it made him naïve. See, here comes our loyal heart.'

Alone, walking unhindered, was the man who, for three years, had been that inspiration. Today he was without his great plumed hat, for that lay in some grave with the faithful Pheiffer. Instead he had knotted a red handkerchief over his bandage in the usual Creole style. She remembered how glorious he had appeared, riding on his black stallion to make his submission; how the sun had glittered on his

550

golden spurs and banner. Yet, today, without his banners and horse, he was still a king. Nothing could rob him of that inborn presence which magnetised and demanded respect.

He was almost level with her window and he looked up, his proud face bearing an expression of great calm. Madeleine held up the tiny baby who was his son and bent forward out of the window so that he should see the ribbon of Saint-Louis on the little chest. She smiled down at him as his face filled with joy. He inclined his head, returning her smile with one of such love that it tore through her heart like a razor. Then he was gone and the space where he had stood was filled by horses and hussars.

Immediately Madeleine withdrew into the room and handed little François to Marie-Anne.

'Must you go, my child?' asked Madame Charette, watching the young woman throwing a cape about her shoulders.

'Yes, Madame. I must be with him at the end. I know by now that abbé Remaud will have absolved him from all sin, but I must go.'

'Then I will accompany you,' said the old soldier. 'My son would not wish you to be alone.'

'I, too, will come,' said Boëtz.

Taking the back streets, they arrived before the cavalcade had reached the place of execution on the Place des Agriculteurs. The sight which greeted them was unbelievable in its grandeur. From every building there hung a tricolor banner, and ranged around the open sides of the place were soldiers. At least 5,000, making a brilliant blaze of blue, white and red; their bayonets and buttons glittering, rank upon rank drawn up in battle formation.

Despite the agony of the moment, Madeleine could not help but feel proud at the tribute. This was no corner execution like those endured by the other royalist leaders. France, in demanding Charette's life, was giving him a hero's death; a death befitting the Lieutenant-General of Louis XVIII's army.

'Ah, if only he'd been on our side,' said an old soldier standing behind Madeleine. 'We have need of generals like that. See how he is directing them.'

Unable to suppress a painful smile of affection, Madeleine watched Charette moving about, as though reviewing his own troops. 'Even now, my darling, you're giving them orders,' she whispered to herself. She watched him stroll over from the assembled generals to the captain who was with eighteen chasseurs of the Alpine division. The captain lifted up a bandage, but she saw Charette shake his head and, smiling, he pointed to his heart, whereupon the captain nodded and saluted.

The tall, athletic figure moved away, and knelt for a moment before abbé Guibert, who made the sign of the cross over his head. Then her chevalier, the man whom she had loved all her life, took up his position in front of a little door. For one moment he looked up at the sky. Then he removed the sling from his injured arm. The drums ceased their beating. There was silence. He made the sign of the cross and, calmly nodding to the chasseurs, he pointed to his heart. There was a loud report. For a second he stood quite still and then ... Her whole body reached out to him, she looked into his lustrous black eyes, seeing the sweet smile on his lips as he had looked up to her at the window on the rue des Gorges. The guns fired their salute. The 'Marseillaise' began. The King of the Marais was no more.

Blindly she stumbled away – the Republic had killed him, and the Bourbons had betrayed him. She could not stay. She would take their son away from France, to Russia. Far beyond the shadow of the tricolor. A sudden breeze caught at the ostrich feathers on her bonnet and soft wisps of green caressed her cheek; the green he had so often worn, the green of hope. Madeleine reached up and touched them, holding them fast against her face. Through her desolation a tiny spark rekindled; slowly she responded, murmuring his motto: '*Battu: Parfois*'. 'Never despair, *chérie*,' she heard him respond, '*Abattu: Jamais!*'

Afterword

François-Athanase Charette de la Contrie was born on 21 April 1763 at Couffé near Oudon (today situated in Loire-Atlantique).

At the age of sixteen, Charette entered Louis XVI's navy, where during his eleven years' service he saw action in the American War of Independence. After resigning his commission, the chevalier went to live at his small château of Fonteclose.

In 1793, the peasants of Bas-Poitou demanded his leadership in their rebellion against conscription and their fight for religious freedom and the re-establishment of the monarchy.

During the unequal struggle against the Republic's troops of the line, Charette became a superb innovator of guerrilla tactics. The speed and brilliance of his operations were recognised by two military giants of the era, Suvorov and Napoléon Bonaparte.

His dramatic use of clothes and his personal élan soon earned him the title King of the Marais, and his headquarters – the court at Légé – were graced by beautiful amazons such as Céleste de Bulkeley, Madame du Fief and the Comtesse de la Rochefoucauld. These amazons, like the simple peasant girls, fought alongside him on the battlefield, and danced with him under the stars at night. As Charette himself said, '*Je veux que la joie règne où je suis!*' – 'I hope that joy reigns wherever I am!'

François-Athanase Charette de la Contrie was executed in Nantes on 21 March 1796 when, true to character, he himself gave the order to fire.